INDIGO JUSTIVE

Book Three
Of
The Indigo Brothers Trilogy

VICKIE McKEEHAN

Published by Beachdevils Press

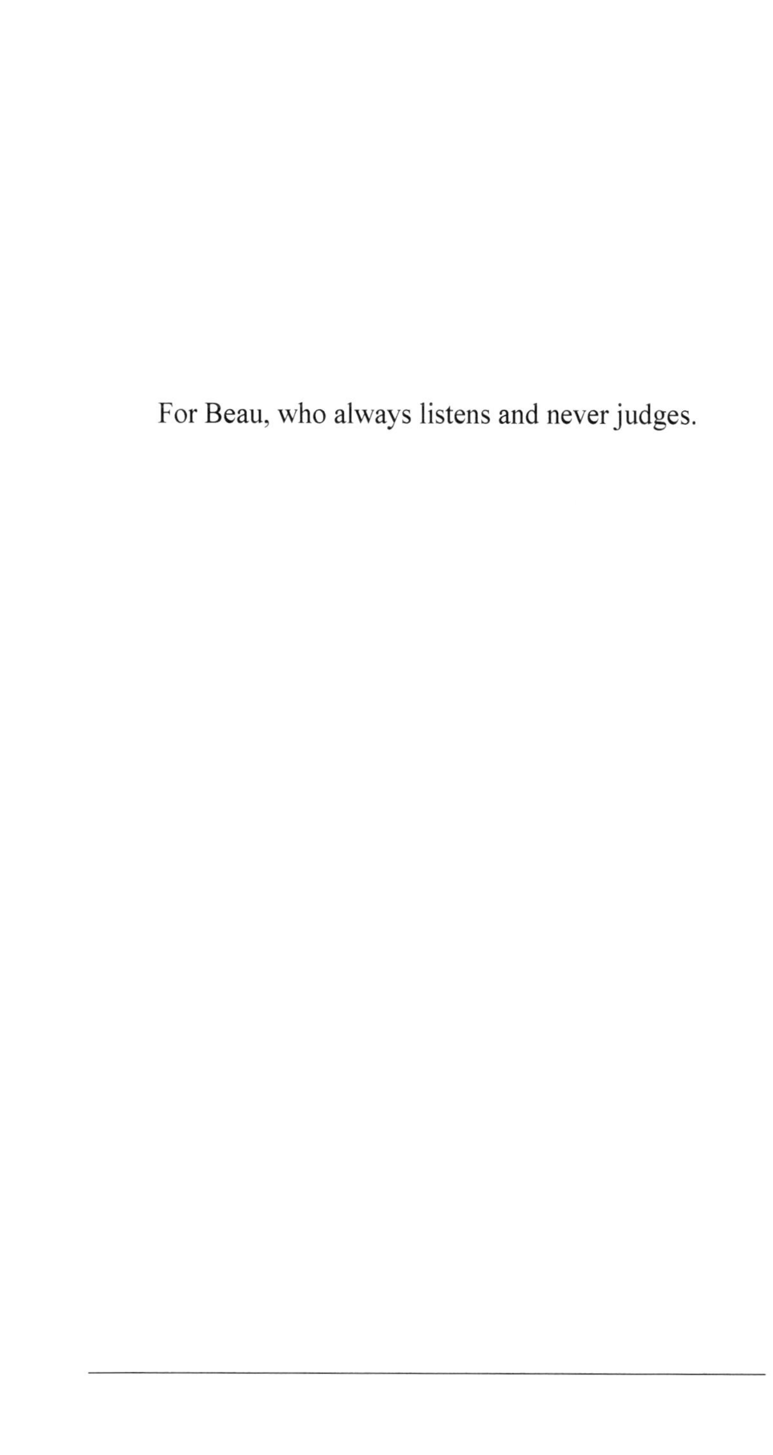

For Beau, who always listens and never judges.

Justice is sweet and musical

~ HENRY DAVID THOREAU

The First Warrior looked out on the land and his Home.
He saw the hills
And the stars
And he was happy.
For giving him his home, the first warrior told the
Great Spirit
That he would fight and win many battles in His honor.
But the Great Spirit said, "No, do not fight for me.
Fight for your tribe,
Fight for the family born to you,
Fight for the brothers you find.
"Fight for them," the Great Spirit said, "for *they* are
your Home."

~ HENRY STANDING BEAR
Longmire TV series

Part Three

Mitch

Prologue

Jackson almost didn't recognize his best friend from high school. The man certainly didn't look like the bank president who'd been so helpful at the bank the day they'd started the search for Livvy and the kids.

Nathan Hollister had dyed his hair an awful shade of platinum blond and let it grow out, but his dark roots were beginning to show. He'd grown facial hair, a little goatee that made him look very much like the cartoon character, Mr. Van Driessen from *Beavis and Butt-Head*. It wasn't a flattering look.

When the hood was yanked off his head, Nathan's eyes darted around the galley. When he tried to move, he found one hand cuffed to the table. He was surrounded by Indigos. Maybe that's why he should've been more prepared for the fist to the face.

Jackson connected to Nathan's nose and flexed his right hand. "I haven't hit anyone since Mitch ran my car into a ditch and broke the axle the night before high school prom. But I swear to God, I'll beat you senseless if you don't tell me what the hell's going on. What are you doing helping Dietrich look for treasure? What the hell did you get Livvy involved in that got her killed? You're nothing but a low-life snake!"

"You broke my nose!" Nathan screamed, the words coming out nasal.

Mitch ignored the blood and stepped in front of Nathan's face. "I'm gonna break more than your nose if you don't start talking. Jackson is the levelheaded PhD, the scholarly one. You know it's true. Me? I'm volatile and unpredictable. And you were never my best friend. So start taking, Hollister."

"Okay. You caught me. I need a doctor first."

"No, first we ask questions and then you answer," Jackson fired back. "What happened to your fear of the water, Nathan?"

"Uh, well, I live on an island. I finally got tired of watching everyone else enjoy what the place has to offer. I did something about it. I took lessons from Dave Oakerson's outfit."

"I bet you took lessons from the esteemed mayor. So now you're good at diving, are you?"

"I'm okay. I know enough to not get the bends on deep dives."

Jackson wanted to smash his lying face again. "Enough to get Dietrich to hire you on the *Pike*? That sounds like you're more than okay. You want to tell me how you and your new pals killed Livvy?"

"What? No. I loved Livvy."

"Then why did you disappear and go to work on Dietrich's boat using a disguise? You colored your hair. You changed your appearance from the dull and stoic banker to make yourself look more like a member of a motorcycle gang wannabe. What are you hiding? What do you know about Livvy's murder? Come on, you snake, spill it."

"Livvy and I've been so secretive over the years, it became second nature to keep quiet."

"We know you're lying through your teeth," Garret said, getting to his feet. He circled the man, then reared back like he intended to throw another punch at Nathan's face.

The banker flinched and put his free hand up in defense. "Okay. Okay. I'll tell you what I know. Livvy and I were planning to take the kids and get out of our lousy marriages. Livvy mentioned Walker's plan to find the gold. He'd been obsessed by it for months. Walker seemed convinced he could find it with Werner Dietrich's help. That's when things started going south. Royce had brought Dietrich in on the resort development—the project that was going to make everyone involved a bundle. That is, if they could squeeze your old man into giving up on the preserve and get him to stop fighting them at every turn."

Mitch exchanged a look with his brothers. "So now you're saying that Dad's environmental stance got an entire family killed? That's not what happened, Nathan. Try a different fairy tale."

"Sure. Okay. The truth then. One-night Walker met up with Hugo Reiner in Mattito's Bar. You remember Hugo, that old sailor who tells all those outlandish stories about knowing how to find Nazi gold. He claims some U-boat went down around here off the coast in '45 carrying gold bullion."

"It seems everyone in town suddenly got interested in it at the same time," Jackson stated.

"Well, Walker certainly did. He swallowed it like a catfish on a grub worm. The two started plotting. But Walker knew they couldn't go looking for gold using his yacht or Hugo's tub of a sailboat. Neither man had the means or the equipment to pull off that kind of operation. And Dietrich? Walker had already met him a couple of times before through his dad. Walker knew Dietrich had a successful salvage operation. According to Livvy, Walker contacted him for help, got turned down a couple of times in the process."

Mitch interrupted him. "How do you know these kinds of details?"

"Livvy. Walker went home at night and told Livvy about all of it. She in turn, told me. During all those nights drinking at the bar, Walker had been listening to Hugo's tall tales about Dietrich's ties to the Nazis. Hugo claimed he had papers to prove it. Livvy told me Walker stole the papers and tried to use them to coerce Dietrich into cutting him in on the gold. But you don't blackmail a man like Dietrich and get away with it."

"So we've heard."

"By that time Dietrich had his own salvage operation heading to the Keys. He must've had his own leads about Hugo. I know for certain the *Patagonia Pike* won't stop until it locates that sub. Dietrich certainly didn't need Walker or Hugo to get that done. But he must've wanted those other documents back, enough to kill them all. Livvy and I thought we could use her share to start a new life together. But then things unraveled. It all went to hell."

"And you knew all this that day I walked into the bank and asked you for help," Jackson charged. "What a nasty piece of work you are."

Jackson reared back and smacked Nathan across the face again. "You lying sack of shit. You got Livvy killed because you stole the papers from Walker. You betrayed Livvy."

"Me? Not me. I wouldn't do that. It had to be Dietrich's henchmen who killed them."

"Oh, we know that, Nathan. But the murders are on you. You got them all killed because you took the papers and when Baskin tried to beat the information out of them, Walker gave up the location to save his family and himself. But when his accomplice, Boone Dandridge, went to retrieve them, the papers were gone. They weren't where Walker said they were. So Baskin turned his wrath on Livvy. Unfortunately, Walker had already given up the information. Livvy had nothing new to offer, nothing to divulge. She trusted you. And she and the kids lost their lives because you'd already stolen the documents out from under her. So their deaths are on you, buddy. It's your fault they all died!" Jackson said, his fists still clenched at his sides.

"No. I loved your sister. For years, I had to watch her live with that lying, cheating Walker. It made me sick. I...I wanted to take her away."

Mitch picked up the narration. "You were so concerned about Livvy that after she went missing, you weren't all that interested to find out what happened to her. Why is that, Nathan? Because you already knew."

"I was afraid I already knew. Yeah. Dietrich had gotten to them all. I was scared, afraid for myself."

"You were afraid for yourself? Poor guy. So what were you planning to do, Nathan? Take off with all that gold without Livvy? You don't look like you've been in mourning all this time. You don't look grief-stricken either." Mitch glanced around the room. "Is it just me, or does he look like he's taking his lover's death really well?"

Garret cocked his head, studied Nathan's face. "To me, it looks like he's gotten over Livvy just fine and moved on to count the gold he hopes to get. Plus, he felt like he was entitled to a bigger share than everyone else. So he took a job on board the *Patagonia Pike* and began to sabotage things for the crew. One by one, his goal was to eliminate anyone who was entitled to their fair share of the loot."

He turned his attention to Nathan. "Duarte apparently caught on to your little scheme, that's why you were locked up. You've been a busy boy since you lied to your wife about going to Denver."

Jackson circled Nathan. "Ah, I'm beginning to get the picture. You never lied to Wendy. That's why Anniston had such a difficult time talking your wife into filing a missing persons report. Wendy dragged her feet because she already knew where you were all along. And my guess is you planned on dropping Livvy at the first opportunity if she'd lived. After Walker had done all the legwork to get the gold, you and Wendy were off to Fiji. How long had you been using Livvy for information, Nathan? Maybe you knew Dietrich planned to kill them all along since you wanted to keep the gold for yourself. And then there's your wife. She wants the gold as badly as you do. And so does her lover, Dave Oakerson."

"No, that's not it," Nathan protested.

Jackson grabbed hold of his shirt. "Bullshit. You're such a lying weasel. The murders didn't have a thing to do with Dad trying to protect the damn preserve. When did you become such a scum sucker? Where are the documents Dietrich killed for? When exactly did you steal them? You already admitted Livvy told you where they were."

Nathan's eyes got bigger. "How do you know the rest of that stuff?"

Jackson leveled a deadly gaze at his former friend and decided it was time to bluff. "What did you take out of the safe deposit box, Nathan? There's surveillance video of you going in there, coming out fifteen minutes later. You might as well tell us."

The banker started twitching in his seat. "You couldn't possibly know that."

"We know more than you think we do. We've been talking to Duarte since Garret took you off that boat. Matter of fact, Duarte wants you back, bad. He wants to cut your throat himself because of all the misery you caused on board his ship. So it sounds to me like you've worn out your welcome there. No gold for you, Nathan."

"Hey, that's not fair."

"Neither is murdering a family of four, add two more to that count—Ryan Connelly and Dack Hawkins didn't deserve bullets to the head. I got news for you. You aren't even welcome on *The Black Rum*. I could send you back to

Duarte and let him take care of you." Mitch turned in his chair. "Bring in Hugo Reiner."

A few minutes later Walsh brought the old sailor into the galley.

Nathan went icy-white. He started to hyperventilate and sputtered out, "What the hell is *he* doing on your boat?"

"Hugo? We agreed to keep him away from Werner Dietrich."

Nathan stared at the old man, his eyes blinking at a rapid rate. The wheels were turning in his head. Beads of sweat popped out on his brow. Tears began to stream down his face until he broke into genuine sobs. His chest rattled out a deep, high keening sound a he continued to weep and moan and twist in his chair trying to get his cuffed hand loose. He tried to catch his breath enough to speak. When he finally took a gulp of air, the sudden crying stopped. He started wheezing again.

As quickly as he'd turned on the waterworks, his mood changed. The wheezing became a hysterical howl that turned into laughter. He laughed so hard that he doubled over. Blood dripped down his face from his busted nose. But the banker ignored it. He looked like a half-crazed man losing the slim tether he'd had on his sanity.

When Nathan did manage to open his mouth, his voice was a high-pitched, unnerving squeal. He screamed, "You fools! Don't you realize, we've all been played!"

Chapter One

Mitchell Taylor Indigo had pirate's blood running through his veins. Thanks to his ancestor Koda Indigo—a swashbuckler who'd lived three hundred years before—the lure of the sea had grabbed him early on and never let go.

At the age of eighteen, Mitch had gotten lucky when he'd hopped on a freighter called *The Outlander* bound for the Indian Ocean. Three years earlier Captain Kidd's shipwreck had been found in that same Madagascar region, exactly where he yearned to be. He'd been a sophomore in high school at the time the discovery made headlines. Even then, he knew in his heart that someday he'd haul up a similar bounty.

To a young kid looking for adventure, a chance to find a shipwreck like that—one that carried a cargo full of treasure—was too great a pull. Mitch left town to make his fortune and never looked back.

Those first years at sea were hard—bad weather coupled with long hours that made for a sometimes tense learning curve.

He might've had trouble at first, but he was a quick study. It took four years working for someone else before the crew he was on hit the mother lode—a Spanish galleon filled with gold and silver coins and precious gems for the taking, scooped up off the ocean floor like candy from a piñata. The haul had totaled close to two hundred and fifty million dollars split among a crew of twenty.

His share had given him the money to start his own salvage business—Seeker Marine Excavation. He poured his money into a modern, state-of-the-art ship and hired the best crew he could afford.

Then three years ago Lady Luck had smiled on him again when his crew had dived on a British frigate off the coast of Duncan's Bay in Jamaica. The ship, *Lord Whitby*, had gone down during gale force winds in the fall of 1814, carrying a full manifest of silver and gold. Most of the crew made it to shore, but the boat sank with all that loot. The find and recovery had made Mitch Indigo a wealthy man.

He'd carried on Koda's tradition the only way he knew how. What had started out as a fanciful tale about a Spanish countess and the fact Koda had fought his crewmates to keep her said it all.

Fighting ran in his bloodline.

It seemed a lifetime ago that he'd left a dive near Little Bahama Bank looking for a Spanish ship that went down in 1658. Instead of searching for gold and gems, he'd tried to find his sister, Livvy, and her children.

It hurt to know Livvy's entire family had been wiped out the night she went missing. He'd promised his parents he'd find the people responsible.

In the vastness of the Atlantic, *The Black Rum* motored full speed ahead. After successfully stealing Nathan Hollister from under the noses of the *Patagonia Pike*, they needed to put as much distance as they could between the two ships.

The boat pushed through a cloud of haze and mist that shrouded it in thick fog. The gloaming gave the rocky surf an excuse to bite back, as the waves roared up, battering the portside in a show of strength. The sea whipped, wild and high, and slammed onto the deck. White caps churned in its wake making the crew and passengers well aware that for the next few hours the boat was at the mercy of Mother Nature.

But weather was the least of Mitch's problems.

Thirty-year-old Mitch had reached his limit for the night. The dark circles under his eyes showed the strain of the past few hours. He and his brothers had been embroiled in a war of words as they set out to get to the truth.

Mitch was convinced that one of the men responsible for his sister's brutal murder was suffering from a mental breakdown right in front of him. Or it might've been a clever acting job.

Had Nathan Hollister's mind really snapped?

Mitch didn't think so. He needed to cut through the guy's act to get answers. He glanced around the galley at the audience of men. Walsh Kingston, his crew chief, had his arms crossed over his chest. Just as defiant and determined, his brothers, Garret and Jackson, were ready to pounce. Their faces were drained of emotions, as lack of sleep became a prime factor for their irritable state of mind.

Mitch stared down at Nathan and watched the hysterical binge continue and take on a life of its own. Done with listening to the tantrum, he shouted, "Stop your ranting, Hollister. Tell me what the hell you're talking about or shut up!"

The laughter died on the banker's face. "You idiots. That man's Werner Dietrich," Nathan fired back. "That's not Hugo Reiner at all."

"He's lying!" the old man screamed, his white hair sticking out wildly on the sides of his head above his ears. In broken English, laden with a thick German accent, the old man yelled across the galley, "He'll say anything to save his sorry hide and keep the suspicion off him. He's the one who killed your sister! Ask him. Go ahead, ask him!"

"I ought to know who he is," Nathan protested. "Dietrich's the man who hired me on the *Patagonia Pike*. He's the one you want! Not me."

But the old man had no intention of taking the accusation without a verbal battle. "Ask him about the murders."

"Shut up! Both of you," Mitch finally called out as he pulled his sidearm out of his holster. "Jackson, I know he's cuffed, but maybe you should take hold of your former buddy there just the same."

Once Jackson moved into position behind Nathan, Mitch whirled on Hugo. "How would you know who killed our sister? Tell me that."

"I...I...heard...people talking."

Mitch moved closer to the old man, glared into his pale blue eyes, clearer than the day they'd brought him on board. "Lately, I've been boning up on my research about Nazis. One thing I learned about the Fascist regime, and it actually surprised me. They had a number of little idiosyncrasies they practiced that began as soon as Hitler came to power. And there's one surefire way of knowing which one of you is lying."

Mitch eyed both men, "It seems if you were high enough in rank, like a colonel, or a member of the Sicherheitsdienst, the intelligence agency, any SS officer including members of his immediate family, including his children, were given a small black tattoo located on the underside of the left arm near the armpit. When the practice began in 1933 it was meant to show the individual's blood type."

Mitch glanced at Garret. "How's the shoulder doing where Duarte's men shot you?"

Garret lifted it without a problem. "Like I said, it's just a flesh wound."

"Good. I want you to yank up this guy's shirt. Check his arm. Let's see if the mysterious stranger we've been hosting has the blood tattoo."

The old man struggled to keep Garret from pushing up the sleeve of the T-shirt he wore, cursing him in German. But he was no match for the athletic Garret, who soon had him subdued enough to reveal the ink mark of an "A" on the man's wrinkled skin. "Well, well, well, what do you know? Look what we have here."

"My name's Reiner," the old man insisted. "I told you my father was a lieutenant. I got that when I was a boy."

Mitch's golden-brown eyes stared at the old man. "You did tell us that. But from what history tells us, the families of most lieutenants were excluded from getting inked, especially in the latter days of the war. You said your father was only twenty-five. I doubt they'd extend the practice to the children of a low-man-on-the-totem-pole lieutenant."

Garret chimed in, "The likes of Josef Mengele and Alois Brunner were smart enough to opt out of getting them altogether. It's one of the reasons that kept them from being captured. Well, that, and the fact that they moved around a lot every time the Mossad came sniffing around."

"Good point. So let's review the options on our side," Mitch stated. "From where I stand, I don't believe I'm looking at the offspring of a lowly lieutenant who just happens to carry the tattoo. Me? I think you're the baby boy of that high-ranking SS officer who made his way down to Argentina and hid out in Bariloche."

Mitch turned to his brothers. "What's the verdict, guys? I'm asking for a vote. All this time, I think we've had us a very important man on board."

"It makes sense that he's Werner Dietrich," Jackson noted. Ever since he's been here he's never acted much like you'd think a man living off the grid would act."

"Same here," Garret said in agreement. "Mr. Dietrich leans more toward demanding a lot better food than what he's been getting, like he's used to talking to servants."

"So you believe me?" Nathan asked.

Mitch nodded. "About this? Sure. I do. About the other BS? Not even a little bit. I want to know where your friends got the barrels they used to put four people in the ocean. In fact, there's a long list of things I want to know. Here. Now. Tonight."

Anniston walked in, followed by her brother, Sebastian. She went over to Garret, unwrapped a Band-Aid and stuck it to the owie on his upper arm. She patted the shoulder where a bullet had grazed it and lightly kissed his cheek. "There, all better. If it's all right with you, I'd like to take a swab of Nathan's mouth for DNA testing."

"Be my guest," Garret said, still holding on to Dietrich's arm. "It has the makings of being a very long night."

Anniston stepped over to Nathan and stood in front of him with a long Q-tip. "Open up like a good boy."

"I don't think so," Nathan said, balking and pulling his head away from the stick.

Growing tired of the whole thing, Jackson put Nathan's head in an arm lock. "Just do it. For once stop your bitching and cooperate."

"What's it for?" Nathan returned.

"Comparison," Anniston hissed as she none-too-gently poked his mouth with the swab. "There. All done. That didn't hurt, did it?"

Nathan was far from satisfied. "You aren't pinning anything on me with some phony DNA results. I want to talk to a real cop. Get me Sinclair. Or better still, a lawyer."

Jackson laughed in his face. "We'll get right on that. In your dreams. We're nowhere near the Key. In case you haven't noticed, banker boy, we're in international waters. Besides, we already know your buddy Sinclair is one of the biggest crooks in town."

Fed up with Nathan's attitude, Jackson smacked him across the face. "What is it with you, when did you get like this? When did you become such a greedy bottom-feeder?"

Across the galley Dietrich sent a lethal glare aimed at Nathan. "If you want to take many more breaths, I suggest you keep your fucking mouth shut, boy."

Garret began to pace in front of Dietrich. "From the moment we stepped on the *Schneewind*, this guy snookered us. Do you think he had anything to do with those two bodies that washed up near Sugarloaf Key?"

Anniston stared at Dietrich. "Chuck's back at work now after taking a few days off since Dack's death. When he pulled the autopsies on those two cases, it turns out, they were both male. One was in his seventies, the other in his forties. They were both shot. The older guy hasn't yet been identified, but the other one was a Swedish national, fingerprints on file with Interpol say he's Leon Sundström, a gun for hire with a long history of violence in Europe. Sundström's been on a terrorist watch list. His last known gig was in Buenos Aires working for, wait for it, Werner Dietrich. The murders in Sugarloaf Key had likely just happened, no more than fifteen minutes or so before you guys stumbled on Dietrich's three-act play ramping up."

"What Anniston and I think happened is this," Sebastian began. "Dietrich likely showed up to confront Hugo about his supposed cache of papers. He wanted whatever Hugo had in his possession. Some type of gun battle ensued where Hugo got the drop on Sundström first, got off a shot, and then in turn, Dietrich killed Hugo. He must've panicked when he spotted you guys headed to the boat and realized he had two dead bodies on his hands. He probably dumped them over the side, threw on some of Hugo's clothes, and went into his Hugo act."

Mitch leveled his pistol at Dietrich. "That means you still don't have what you were looking for, do you? You've killed members of my family. There are consequences to that."

"What I'd like to do is spend some time with him asking about the chat room setup he uses to communicate with Baskin and Dandridge," Sebastian prompted.

Dietrich waved a hand. "Nein, I'm not talking, done talking."

"Fine. Because we're done being nice," Mitch warned. "Let's see what your pals Baskin and Dandridge do after not hearing from you over the next several days. Let's see if they go into panic mode. Bets? Walsh, would you get this piece of shit out of my face?"

"Happy to," the crew chief replied. Walsh took hold of Dietrich's arm as Garret relinquished his grip.

"Keep his cabin locked and guarded at all times," Mitch ordered. "See to it personally."

"Will do. What about the other snake?"

Mitch slapped Nathan on the shoulder. "Good ol' Nathan, here? We aren't quite finished yet interrogating our weakest link," he replied.

"What do you mean by that? I'm no one's weakest anything," Nathan challenged.

As soon as Walsh had taken Dietrich out of the room, Mitch holstered his weapon and angled toward the banker. "Duarte keeps pressuring me to give you back to him. You know what he wants to do with you, right? So far, I've resisted his taunts. I'm not sure you're even worth keeping."

Nathan swallowed hard. "But I've known all of you for most of my life."

"And that didn't stop you from turning on Livvy the minute you thought you could get to a big score. You really picked the wrong family to mess with, Nathan."

Franco Duarte, captain of the *Patagonia Pike*, was pissed. They'd stolen his diver right out from under his nose, the one he'd planned to use as a warning to the others, to use as an example.

He glanced over at the crewman, the man he felt was responsible for letting it all happen. Duarte realized the man wisely stood just out of his reach—his back pressed up against the cabin wall as flat as it could go. The captain narrowed his eyes. "I know you left your post. Where were you? No, don't answer that. I might kill you if you open your mouth to try and defend your actions."

Duarte took five steps toward the shaking crewman, stretched out his arm and leveled his pistol against the man's forehead. Duarte pressed so hard the barrel left a red, round indent in the crewman's skin. "Get out of my sight now before I kill you."

The crewman scurried out the cabin door before the captain's words faded from the air. Duarte placed his gun on the table to pour himself a shot of whiskey. He pounded his fist on the table and turned to Sandoval, his crew chief. "We need a plan to get the diver back."

"Dietrich should be consulted. Don't you think?" Sandoval suggested.

Duarte ran his hands through his thinning, gray-streaked hair. "And provoke his anger? You know Dietrich. He'll be furious. He may own this ship, but he's left it up to me to run things. Don't ever forget that." He sat down at the table, threw back the bourbon. He let his head rest on the back of the chair. "All right. Give me the damn satellite phone and I'll call him. But I don't think we'll be getting his blessing."

After placing the mobile call and letting it ring at least twenty times, Duarte finally hung up, a wave of relief moving through him. "I'm not sure what's going on, but it seems Dietrich has gone back to South America without telling us. Which means I'll handle this on my own," he told Sandoval. "We need to show the people on *The Black Rum* we mean business. If we don't make a statement now, they'll be all over the Florida coastline looking for the gold."

"Then you need to make certain they understand to back off," Sandoval said.

"Don't worry. I'll put a stop to that."

"Dietrich's the one who brought Hollister on board," Sandoval pointed out.

"So what? No one takes a prisoner off this boat without paying a penalty for that kind of arrogance. We have a score to settle."

Duarte's next call went to the mayor back on Indigo Key.

"What the hell are you doing calling me this time of night?" Oakerson grumbled.

"You want a piece of the pie, Mr. Mayor, you'll carry your load."

"Yeah, well, Dietrich's gone MIA. Baskin keeps pestering me, wanting to know if you have any idea where Dietrich is. Apparently he hasn't been at his house for days."

Duarte was no longer interested in Dietrich. "Don't know. Don't care. Dietrich goes off like this sometimes. Just bring me what I need for leverage."

"Yes, well, it's not that easy. Boone is starting to get antsy, mainly because he and Roger have both been under surveillance."

He was in no mood for excuses. "You have your problems, I have mine. I don't care who does the job, but it has to be tonight. Make it happen. I don't care how you do it. Just get me that bargaining chip we talked about earlier and get it fast. But make sure it stays alive and unhurt. It does me no good to strike a deal if it's dead or damaged. Do you understand me? Don't make another stupid mistake like you did with the others."

"Hey, that wasn't me. I had nothing to do with what happened with the Buchanans. But don't worry, if Baskin and Dandridge can't slip out, I'll get Sinclair to do it."

"Try not to get caught. I'm depending on you to do this one thing."

"No problem. I know what I'm doing."

Duarte doubted that. But since he was nowhere near Indigo Key, he had no choice but to rely on Dietrich's inner circle.

"Why are we doing this again?" Oakerson asked.

Duarte rolled his eyes at the bumbling idiots Dietrich had taken into his confidence. "If you want the gold it's time to make a statement. In order to do that we have to let the men on *The Black Rum* know they can't stick their noses into our business. Now get on the phone to your buddies. Tonight. It has to be done tonight."

After hanging up, Duarte sat back, poured himself another drink. He hoped Oakerson wouldn't chicken out and let him down. If the deed was done right, then all he had to do was wait and get ready for a game of brinkmanship with Mitch Indigo.

Chapter Two

Inside The Blue Taco, Raine Manning had spent the past several days trying to stay busy. It wasn't a difficult thing to do at work. Running a restaurant seven days a week came with responsibilities. To say she wore many hats was an understatement. If the cook didn't show up, she manned the grill. If the order taker called in sick, she stepped up to the counter. She bussed tables, morphed into dishwasher, scrubbing pots and pans. It was her job to see to it that customers stayed happy with the food, drink, and atmosphere. It usually kept her hopping from ten in the morning to six at night. If things smoothed out, she took Wednesdays off.

That's why she was so grateful for the newest addition to her staff, the redheaded Tessa Connelly. Tessa worked like a fiend five days a week. For a former blogger who'd created DIY projects and passed them along to her blog followers, Tessa had been a surprise. Raine had been pleased that Tessa put everything she had into learning how to use the cash register, familiarizing herself with the menu, even the specialty items that only the locals were known to order.

Over the past few weeks, the two women had become fast friends, united during a time after Tessa came to town to find out what had happened to her brother, Ryan. They'd become part of that bigger team, that joint effort with the Indigos to find a killer. Six murders in a place this small meant there was a dirty side to Indigo Key that had to be stopped.

For amateurs, it was a daunting task. Even though she hadn't heard from Mitch in almost forty-eight hours, Raine was happy to do her part. The problem was Jackson hadn't called Tessa either. She wasn't sure what that meant. Were the brothers in trouble? Should she start to worry about all of them?

After her shift ended and she made sure her assistant manager, Charlotte, had everything under control, Raine left the restaurant and took the scenic route home. She needed a walk on the beach and access to fresh air.

She breathed in the October breeze, warm and humid, as temperatures still hovered in the seventies. But at least out here the air didn't carry the smell of grease that tended to stick to the four walls, and no deep-fried splatter from the kitchen.

As she strolled along the sand, she watched the sun drop over the water, content to be outside. She took her time perusing the beach for sea glass—those shiny little gems that littered the shoreline like bursts of wildflowers in a meadow.

She carried a small yellow pail with a handle she'd had for as long as she could remember. Left over from childhood, it was scuffed with scratches and dents from years of wear and tear. She remembered how it had started out holding chocolate Easter rabbits, jelly beans, and assorted candy eggs, a present from her older brother,

Danny. She kept the metal bucket at the taco stand as a reminder to end her workday doing something frivolous, something Danny would've encouraged.

These days hunting for sea glass was about as frivolous as Raine got. It amazed her that the beer and wine bottles people dumped into the bay came back to her in glazed petals of green or brown or clear glass. Those colors might've been the most common, but to Raine they held the prettiest angles and curves. Not bad for a piece of glass that took years to weather, for the sea to scar, to beat up with the grit and sand and salt until its surface was frosted and smooth.

If she was lucky she might stumble across rarer colors—red or blue or amber or the antique black from Jamaica—polished and worn from centuries of effort.

She liked to make up stories about where the shard started out. How far had it traveled before ending up a bauble on her beach? Had it been dropped into the sea by a crossing duke or duchess, drunk on making a new life in another part of the world?

Her imagination made the hunt almost like an adventure, something she sorely lacked in real life. Adventures were for other people. She'd learned that a long time ago. Sad to say, Atlanta was the farthest she'd ever traveled. And that hadn't been until two years ago when she'd taken a week off. Instead of going to some tropical destination like any sane person her age would've done, she'd opted to see the energy and vitality of a lively city, a spot where she could tour the botanical gardens and stroll through a real arts district complete with galleries and museums.

She scanned the shore for anything that glistened, stopping to admire a brown starfish with bright orange bumps. She almost danced in place when she picked up a thin, palest of green glass shard the size of a nickel. She held it up to the light, prizing the translucent hue like a diamond. There were other little bits of clear glass that she dropped into her bucket.

Over the years, she'd found scads of the stuff littered along the strand, filled so many jars with the castoff jewels that she'd had to come up with new ways to showcase it all.

Several years back, she'd started making jewelry from her collection, putting together the different shapes in a pattern that made for striking earrings, necklaces, and bracelets. For her, the little jewels came to life in a beachy theme. It was an outlet she'd come to enjoy. She'd even sold a few pieces to friends.

There were always opportunities for the sea to give up its little treasures, she thought now. It occurred to her that while Mitch had sailed the world looking for a fortune in exotic places, she'd settled for bits of glass less than a mile from where she'd grown up.

Raine hadn't quite filled up her little tub when the light started to fade. She hustled toward the houseboat she called home. Its eclectic paint job was done in turquoise and splashed with bright blue trim. She'd packed the sundeck with planters that overflowed in red, white, and blue buds.

Using her key, she unlocked the front door, crossed through the living room to the kitchen. It was small but tidy, the counters filled with state-of-the-art appliances. She set down the bucket in the sink, dumped in dish soap and ran warm water to wash off the dirt and sand.

After rinsing off the beach glass, she got out vegetables—carrots, leeks, potatoes, sprigs of rosemary and thyme, and fresh green beans—to throw together a soup. With the skill of an executive chef, she diced and chopped her way to a stew, tossing it all into a pot of chicken stock to simmer.

Cornbread sounded good, so she mixed up a batch, shoved it in the oven to bake. It took her five minutes to boil water for a pitcher of peach tea, something she craved on a warm evening like tonight. When she was satisfied that supper would be ready within the hour, she wandered off to the bathroom for a hot shower.

She shed her jeans and top that reeked with an all-day flood of grease and overbearing spices that seemed to stick to everything she owned. One-handed, she turned on the water.

Stepping into the spray, Raine scrubbed as she always did with her best fragrant shampoo—a minty apple combination that took the odor out of her hair.

Feeling better and cleaner, she put on a pair of greenish yellow shorts and a midnight-blue button-down blouse and started a load of laundry.

By this time the aroma from the kitchen had her stomach rumbling. The idea of veggie soup and cornbread browned to a golden, crispy top had her rushing to dish up supper.

She still hadn't heard a word from Mitch. As she ate, she thought about calling Lenore for an update. But then what if all she did was launch Lenore into a state of worry? That wouldn't do.

In lieu of that, she sent Tessa—who was on duty at the restaurant through the late shift—a text message. *Any word from Jackson?*

It took ten minutes before she got a reply. *Not yet. I left several messages for him. Something big must be happening. I hope they're all okay. I'm beginning to worry.*

Don't do that. I'm sure they're fine. Maybe the satellite phone went down.

Or maybe something bad happened when they tried to grab Nathan.

Have you talked to Anniston?

Texted her, too. No word.

Then they must all be super busy. Let me know when you hear from Jackson.

Will do.

Raine let out her own worried sound. She no longer felt quite so left out. It was clear Mitch had a lot on his plate and was in the midst of dealing with...something.

She shook off her concern and cleaned up her mess in the kitchen, putting away the leftovers and doing dishes. With time to kill, she decided she was too fidgety to watch TV.

To stay busy, spring cleaning would have to come early. She dug through her bedroom closet, spending hours purging old junk from the bottom. She got rid of old jeans and tops, reducing the number of hangers and creating more room in her cubbyhole of a closet. She tossed out shoes she hadn't worn since tropical storm Isaac pummeled the area with high winds and rain. She even threw out purses she hadn't carried since high school.

On a roll to rid herself of the hoarder she'd become, she organized the stuff she intended to give away to Goodwill into boxes and tossed the rest into plastic trash sacks.

It was well after midnight when she gathered up the bags and headed outside to the nearby dumpster located twenty yards down the wharf.

Stepping out the front door, she was met by a cool, damp fog. The light breeze off the water rushed past her face and lifted her short tufts of blond hair.

After being cooped up inside all evening, the wind felt good as she walked toward the brick enclosure that hid the large metal waste receptacle. The lid was closed to keep the seagulls from foraging for food, so she set down her sacks of junk to open the top.

Standing on tiptoes, she was about to hurl the stuff over the rim and into the trashcan when she got the eerie sense someone was standing behind her. Before she could do anything, a masculine hand clamped over her mouth. She felt a sting on the right side of her neck. As she turned her head, the last thing she remembered was the dumpster lid slamming shut.

And then, nothing.

Less than five hundred yards away from Raine's houseboat, two brothers named Roberto and José were hard at work inside the waterfront warehouse Dietrich had rented for the island's base of operations. The two men had been loading and sorting through supplies all evening, getting the next shipment ready to go out to the *Patagonia Pike* by morning, when the phone rang on the metal desk.

Since Roberto was nearest, he picked up the receiver. On the other end of the line was the mayor, going over a litany of instructions for the next run.

Roberto's face showed an intensity as he listened to the man nitpick his way around the directives. "Yeah. Sure. Yep. I got it. Don't worry, Mr. Mayor," Roberto vowed, nodding at every other word before hanging up. He went over to a cabinet where a whiteboard was enclosed behind the double doors along with a series of maps. He swung open the flaps hiding the contents and studied the chart for several long minutes before waving José over. He pointed to an area on the map, circled it with his finger. "The next run's been moved up to tonight. This is where Duarte will be waiting for us."

"Wait. We have to go out on the water at night? You know I don't like that."

Roberto grimaced. "Doesn't matter what you like. We have some additional cargo that has to go out within the next few hours at all costs. The boss is paying double."

José blew out a sigh. "If jobs were easier to come by, I wouldn't be working for that prick Dietrich in the first place, I can tell you that much."

Roberto leveled a finger at his brother. "Quit your bitching. Listen to yourself. It pays the bills."

"Yeah, but I don't like the guy. I'm not even sure I like the chief of police or the mayor or those other jerkwads. And going out at night...? I guess we're using what worked for us in Tobago, right?"

"Why not? We need to have everything ready to go in twenty minutes. The extra payload is inbound as we speak, and should be here shortly," Roberto claimed. "All we have to do is get it to the ship by morning…intact."

A few minutes later, a police-issued SUV pulled up to the dockside parking lot and honked the horn. The driver waited with the engine still running while José hit the button to raise the massive cargo doors. José watched as a black cruiser rolled into the loading area.

Roberto was surprised to see the chief of police himself crawling out of the vehicle. Jessup Sinclair adjusted his gun holster, the one holding his 9mm, before skirting around to the rear of the car.

The chief opened the door and pointed inside. "Had to wait damn near all night for her to come out of the house. Thought I'd have to go in and drag her out myself until, lucky me, she finally made a midnight run to the trash."

Roberto stared at the cute blonde, stretched out on the width of the carpet in the back. "Did you give her a dose large enough to keep her out until we make it to the ship? Because I don't want to deal with a hysterical female along the way."

"I'm not a fucking amateur," Sinclair barked. "I've done this a few times before tonight. I guarantee I pumped her with enough Ketamine to immobilize her for the next twelve hours or so."

"Oh, man, yeah," José said in agreement. "Is that what Dexter used on TV?"

Sinclair cut him a lethal glare. "Don't be an idiot. Twelve hours should allow plenty of time for you two bozos to get your asses in gear and get the job done. Now do I dare leave her in the capable hands of you two clowns, or what?"

Insulted, Roberto promised, "We'll get her there. You can trust me on that."

Sinclair studied the younger man. "Son, I don't even trust my own deputies. Right now, the only thing you can do for me is to help me get this bitch out of my squad car. See that bench over there? You and your brother park her over there until you get the boat loaded."

"You're leaving?" Roberto asked.

"Damn straight I am. And son? Don't try any funny business with her. Duarte wants her unharmed. Do I make myself clear?"

"Yes, sir."

José stepped forward. "Could you tell Oakerson we want our bonuses?"

"Tell him yourself," Sinclair grumbled as he got behind the wheel of his cruiser and started the engine. He threw the car in gear and thumbed a hand behind him. "Open the bay door and let me out of this joint. It's way past my bedtime."

Once the cop had gone, José turned to his brother. "You know who that is he kidnapped, don't you? It's the woman who owns The Blue Taco."

"Yeah, I know. But what do we do about it now? She's already here."

"We just keep getting into these people deeper and deeper. Anyone finds out what we're doing, we're sure to get jail time for this."

"Shut up!" Roberto sneered, running his jittery hands through his hair. "That's not what I need to hear right now, okay? Let's just bind her hands behind her back and make sure she's secured before transporting her to the supply boat. We still have to get everything else loaded up. Just make sure she's still breathing and hasn't died on us."

"That'd be our luck, wouldn't it?" José groused, leaning over to check for a pulse. "She's got one, but it seems faint to me. We never did anything like this before, Roberto. Not even in the army. You know it's the truth."

"Look, Dietrich pays us a lot of money to do our jobs and keep our mouths closed. This is no different. Just don't let her get a look at your face." He shoved a tubular mask toward José. "Wear this. Now quit your bitching and load up. We're wasting time standing around."

José helped his brother load the woman's limp body onto the supply boat. Within the hour, they'd headed out into Sugar Bay, gunning the twin motors to full throttle and disappearing into the foggy night.

Chapter Three

Mitch slapped his hands down on the table in front of Nathan, made a point to get in the man's face. "You understand why we're having a hard time believing anything you say, right? Your answers about Livvy have been vague at best. What is it you keep hiding? When did you first know Livvy was in danger? Tell us what you know."

He watched the banker's eyes. It even looked as though he might get the guy to open his mouth and say something relevant, truthful, something that made sense. But hope was short-lived when Nathan hesitated and clamped his lips together again, without saying a word.

Even though he was bone-tired, Jackson refused to give up. "What did you hope to accomplish on the *Patagonia Pike*? My guess is you needed to find out where the gold was and then kill everyone on board to get it? That's not even plausible. Or were you there to be Dietrich's personal snitch?"

The questions were met with stony silence and had Mitch glancing at his watch. They'd badgered the guy for forty-five minutes without getting anything more out of him. With each question, Nathan had grown more insolent and stubborn.

Mitch finally decided they weren't getting anything more out of the man tonight. "Get him out of here and put him in with Dietrich."

"No!" Nathan shouted. "I want my own cabin."

Mitch patted the side of the man's sweaty face. "I hate to burst your bubble, but this isn't a Princess Cruise Line. You'll bunk where I put you. You aren't afraid of a seventy-five-year-old man, now are you?"

"Fuck you!" Nathan shouted, along with a string of other toxic suggestions as Garret led him away.

"What do you think?" Mitch asked Jackson.

"It's obvious both men know what happened and have chosen to keep it to themselves."

"Any suggestion how we get it out of them?"

Jackson blew out a fed-up breath. "Men like Dietrich and Nathan are greedy. They think everyone around them has exactly the same mindset. Nathan doesn't give a shit about what happened to Livvy or those kids. All he cares about is getting the payday, the bundle of cash."

Garret came back in, his eyes glassy from exhaustion. "Nathan's locked up for the night. I think I've narrowed down the person who killed Livvy and the kids to three people. My guess is Dietrich ordered either Roger Baskin, Sinclair, or that piece of crap I just tossed into his cabin to do his dirty work."

"My guess is it's all three," Mitch suggested. "Because I'm thinking they all had a hand in it."

"Don't forget Dandridge," Jackson reminded.

Garret rocked back on his heels. "Look, I hate to be a party-pooper, but I have to get some sleep before I drop. That run to get Nathan took everything out of me. And we've been at this for hours. Anniston and Sebastian crashed about an hour ago."

Mitch bobbed his head. "Yeah, I'm beat. We should get some shuteye before we drop. Let's get a few hours and meet back here in the morning, take another whirl at getting Nathan to crack before getting into port."

"Good idea." Jackson took out his cell phone. "Is 2 a.m. too late to text Tessa?"

Garret slapped him on the back. "I'll say, unless you want to get yelled at. It's better to wait until first thing in the morning, then get yelled at."

"Why would she yell at me?"

"Bro, how long has it been since you called her? Who knows why women get upset about anything? But when a man least expects to get into trouble...pow! That's when we land in the middle of it, so deep we don't know what hit us."

Dietrich sat in the locked cabin, his mind searching for ways to bargain with his captors. If he failed in reaching a deal, he would need to come up with a plan to escape.

For the thousandth time he studied every detail of the cabin's enclosure, every crevice in the four walls for a weakness he could exploit.

Weakness. The word reminded him of that spineless piece of shit, Nathan Hollister. No doubt, the man would get them both killed.

Dietrich sneered to himself as he muttered curses under his breath. The Indigos had kept that weasel for a long time, probably had broken him. Which meant all his plans were at risk, all he had worked hard for and built up would disappear in a puff of smoke. He realized now he should've killed that snake the first time Nathan had slithered into his office. He would correct that mistake if he ever got out of here. He had one thing going for him, one card up his sleeve he hadn't yet played. Those stupid Indigos had initially bought his story, the one he'd trotted out back on that leaky excuse for a boat. To his surprise, they hadn't searched him. They'd missed the opportunity to find his six-inch knife he always carried with him. Others had made the same mistake before and it had cost them dearly.

He heard footsteps approaching in the passageway. The sound made him jump. He steeled his spine. He wouldn't go down without a fight. Fingering the knife his father had given him, he unfolded the blade, revealing the motto etched there. "Blut und Ehre," he repeated to himself over and over again.

Blood and Honor.

He would taste the blood of the Indigos, those inferior beings who'd come between him and his plan to get what belonged to him. If the brothers intended to kill him, he'd die with honor. He'd go out with dignity like so many had done during the war. He'd live up to his family's proud name and die fighting, not begging for his life like that gutless wonder Hollister. Right now, the man was probably singing like a bird, spilling everything he knew.

Dietrich saw the key turning the lock and primed himself for what he had to do. Maybe he would take them by surprise, and with a little luck, one or more of them would join him in death.

He ran his finger over the Nazi emblem on the handle, and muttered the motto again. With all the strength he could muster, he readied himself for the attack.

But to his surprise and relief, the Indigos didn't enter. Instead, someone tossed Nathan into the cabin, or to be correct, hurled him into the room. Hollister ended up head first, meeting the floor like a sack of cement.

Dietrich's smile was cold as he watched Nathan bounce off the deck. The door slammed shut and the lock turned again.

It was just him and Nathan now, two men locked up in a hundred and seventy square feet of cabin space. There was a discussion outside about whose turn it was to stand watch. After much debate, the footsteps faded.

Dietrich turned his attention back to the shaking lump of flesh on the floor. He folded his knife up and slipped it back into its hiding place near his bunk.

He went over and kicked Nathan in the side. When the man didn't respond, he kicked him again, harder.

Nathan let out a groan. "Stop that, you old fart, or I'll get up and beat the shit out of you."

Dietrich's eyes narrowed. "What did you tell them?"

Nathan slowly got to his feet and went over to sit down on one of the bunks. He looked at Dietrich. "Wouldn't you like to know?"

Nathan rubbed his throbbing nose. "Do you think I'm crazy? If I tell them anything, anything at all, they'll cut us both up and feed us to the sharks."

Nathan spied the bottle of water next to the bunk and unscrewed the cap. He took a long drink, almost draining the fluid before going on. "As long as I stick to my story that I'm just a dumbass island banker who loved their sister and wanted nothing more than a better life for her, I can play them like the hicks they are."

Nathan guzzled another long drink. "But you, I think your time is about up, old man. I heard them talking earlier about what they want to do with you, and it wasn't pretty."

Dietrich smiled at that. So the little snake was trying to scare him. That's all right, he decided. He could easily play both sides. When the time was right, he'd willingly point the finger at someone else. Any one of those idiots back on the island would do. The Indigos seemed to already hate Baskin and Sinclair the most.

As long as he could make a deal to save himself, all would be right with the world. He certainly wouldn't be like the bottom-feeder, the double-dealing banker he saw before him now. He would strike first, though, before morning. As soon as Hollister fell asleep, he'd make certain the scum didn't live to see another day.

Dietrich smiled to himself and fingered his knife again. Before morning, he thought now, as he watched Nathan curl into his bunk.

Stretched out on top of his own mattress, Dietrich fixated on the only light coming through the porthole—a persistent ray of moonbeam that shoved its way through the low-hanging clouds outside. It bathed one spot on the wall in a shaft of glint and glimmer.

He listened to Nathan's shallow breathing grow deeper and deeper before throwing his legs over the lip of the bed. He stood up and took out his beloved weapon from under the bedding. He flipped back the razor-sharp blade. It gleamed in that one circle of moonlight, flashing as if it had caught on fire, like the flaming swords the Norse gods of old carried into battle.

As he crossed to Nathan's bunk, he picked up a sock off the cabin floor. He would use it to stuff in Nathan's mouth to keep him from calling out for help.

After all, this wasn't his first kill. He always relished that look in the eyes as the life slowly drained out of a person. That was the part of killing he enjoyed the most, that look of terror, or maybe it was the blank dead look in the eyes. He loved that look and the feeling of power it brought with it. It hadn't changed over the years. From his first kill at the age of twelve, when he'd taken the life of a peasant farmer's daughter he'd lured into the woods. After all these years he could still see her face and feel her terror.

That was the day his father had been so proud of him, so proud he'd rewarded him with the knife. Afterward, his father had helped him get rid of the body. All these memories came flooding back as he stood over Nathan and watched him sleep.

Dietrich stood for a minute longer and waited. He was as quick as a cobra when he struck. First, he stuffed the sock deep into Nathan's mouth and then launched himself on top of the younger man's chest so he couldn't move.

The frenzy began as he plunged the blade into Nathan's throat, watching as the man's eyes fluttered open in terror just as he'd hoped they would.

Again and again, the small dagger found its mark. He could see the life fading from Nathan's eyes. The sight thrilled him, giving him a sense of power, the ultimate control over life and death.

When Dietrich was satisfied Nathan was dead, he moved off his chest. Standing beside the bunk, he rolled the body over so that it faced the cabin wall and pulled the blanket over what he thought was a lifeless piece of flesh.

He shuffled back over to his bunk.

But Nathan wasn't quite finished with his struggle. His closed eyes popped open. He realized he was dying because he could feel his life's blood flowing out of his body from the dozens of wounds.

He tried to force out a scream, but something prevented him from getting his lips to work. His mouth was full of…something. It was hard to breathe through his busted nose. It took every ounce of energy he possessed to raise his arm a few inches off the bed. Ever so slowly, he moved his right hand. With his forefinger dripping blood, he began to form the first letter on the wall where Dietrich wouldn't see it. He had to tell Jackson the truth before it was too late. In his sluggish state of mind, he believed in his heart that Jackson would understand the message.

Seconds ticked by.

Nathan could feel the last of the blood draining out of him. As he slipped away, he grew colder and colder until finally he began to shiver. Before he could do anything else, blackness closed in around him. He tried holding it off, but soon he floated into the darkness.

Across the room, in his bunk, Dietrich watched Nathan for any signs of movement. Finally, after twenty minutes or so, he hid his knife in his sock and drifted off to sleep, a warm feeling of superiority coursing through his veins.

Dietrich would tell the Indigos a story about how Nathan had confessed everything to him. The banker had admitted murdering their sister and her family in a fit of rage.

He would pretend that he'd been so outraged by the man's evil nature—the murderer of women and children didn't deserve to take another breath of air—that he'd taken it on himself to avenge their deaths. After all, he'd done them a favor. He was only there for the gold, not to harm women and children.

Yes, he'd be the one making a deal. He'd be the one pointing the finger. He'd be the one getting off this boat...alive.

Chapter Four

The cool October dawn brought chaos.

It was Walsh who let young Prentiss into Dietrich's and Nathan's cabin. The young sailor carried a tray that held breakfast for two.

The first thing Prentiss noticed was the iron smell of blood. He'd been on fishing boats enough to recognize the scent. He spotted the red color dripping from one of the bunks, forming a large pool underneath on the floor. Instinctively, he dropped the tray and reached for his sidearm, yelled for Walsh. The scrambled eggs went flying into the awful red sea.

Prentiss glanced over at the older man, noted his calm, serene demeanor as he sat in his bunk, looking like a choirboy. The twenty-year-old knew then what had happened. "What have you done?" he yelled at Dietrich.

Walsh peeked his head in the doorway and surveyed the room. He zeroed in on the blood-soaked sheets where Nathan lay. Unlike Prentiss who stood like a statue, Walsh went over and tossed back the covers. He sucked in a breath at the sight. Nathan had stab wounds around his chest, but it was the gash puncturing his throat that had caused him to bleed out.

"That took some time," Walsh said, quickly covering the body back up again. He shoved Prentiss out of the room. "Go get Mitch, boy. Now!"

Walsh cut his eyes toward Dietrich. "You really are a stupid man, aren't you? I thought rich people were supposed to be so much smarter than the rest of us. I thought I'd run across a new kind of low when you ordered the deaths of women and children. That alone put you at the top of the monster list in a category all by yourself. But this…you're in international waters. You're an idiot if you think you won't have to pay for this…and quickly."

"I had my reasons. The Indigos will want to hear what I have to say."

"Doesn't matter," Walsh hissed. "You're a dead man either way."

Mitch came running into the room. Behind him trailed Garret, still trying to wake up. The hallway outside started to buzz with everyone else gathering to get a look inside the cabin.

Dietrich went into his spiel, recalled for Mitch how Nathan had confessed his sins about killing Livvy and the kids.

Mitch traded looks with Walsh. "He couldn't possibly think I'm as much of a nitwit as he is. Did you explain to him about international waters?"

"I mentioned it."

Mitch whirled toward Dietrich, his fists clenched at his sides. "Did you really think we'd buy into your crap this time? Just because you pretended to be Reiner for a few days doesn't mean we're idiots. We knew something was off with your performance; we just couldn't peg what it was. In case you haven't noticed, *The Black Rum* flies under the Bahamian flag, and as such, assesses whatever crime occurs on board dependent of that jurisdiction. In other words, Mr. Dietrich, coldblooded murder equals capital punishment. In the Bahamas the penalty for murder is hanging. When it occurs in international waters justice is carried out at the sole discretion of the captain."

Mitch tapped his chest. "That's me."

The old man paled, his face turning white as a ball of cotton. His eyes were red-rimmed from lack of sleep.

Mitch let that warning sink in, unwilling to wait for Dietrich to respond. "Where's Anniston? Get this man in handcuffs and put him in the aft cabin storage. Garret, restrain him until she gets here."

But Anniston hurried into the room and slapped cuffs on the old man's wrists herself. She patted him down just as she'd once done back in South Beach walking a patrol beat. She pulled his pockets inside out, but when she got to his ankle, her hands touched the metal. She brought out the six-inch knife with the Nazi emblem on the handle. "Murder weapon," she muttered. "I need a baggie in here."

Sebastian handed her a brown paper sack he'd taken from the galley. "Use this for now. It's all I can find that's handy."

Anniston traded Dietrich for the sack and slid the knife inside.

While Sebastian led Dietrich out of the cabin into the passageway past the crew, she turned back to where Walsh stood still guarding the body.

"There's something you should see," Walsh said, pulling back the covers.

She saw the lettering, traded looks with Walsh and Mitch. "What does that even mean?"

Through the sea of faces standing at the door, Walsh hunted for Jackson and motioned for him to come into the cabin. "I think Nathan left you a message. Does that word jog anything in your brain?"

For several long seconds, Jackson struggled with the scene and all the blood. He did his best to get past the mess and stench of already decomposing remains to see what Walsh was talking about.

To his surprise, Nathan had written one simple word in his own blood. The letters P-O-T had been written in a shaky scrawl with the T running down the wall to where Nathan's finger had dropped, leaving a trail of red.

"What the hell?"

Walsh put his hands on his hips. "So you don't know what it means?"

Jackson looked puzzled. "Other than the obvious connection to weed? Not a clue."

"He was trying to tell you something."

"We'll have to figure out what," Mitch concluded. "He obviously thought 'pot' would mean something that only you two would know about. Begs the question, was he trying to lead you there? If so, why?"

Jackson scratched his chin. "The only thing that comes to mind is when we were in high school we used to smoke weed inside his family's vault."

"You mean the cemetery?" Garret asked, appalled. "Even I wasn't that warped."

"Part of my misspent youth I'm not proud of," Jackson admitted.

"Was there somewhere special you used to hide your stash? Who did you buy it from?" Mitch wanted to know. "Maybe Nathan was trying to lead you to a name."

Jackson thought back to that time in his life, considered the possibilities. "Back then our supplier was Daniel Savitch."

Garret's mouth dropped open. "The teacher of literature and the classics? That explains a lot. That asshole never did give me anything better than a B plus."

Jackson decided he'd have to sway his brothers to action. "You know what we have to do. As soon as we get back we have to go talk to Daniel Savitch and check out the Hollister family vault."

Garret stuck his hands in his pockets. "I'm not keen on walking through a graveyard. But it would be a kick to mess with Mr. Savitch."

"As long we get some answers," Mitch stated.

For now, Garret threw one arm over Mitch's shoulder. "By the way, nice job scaring the crap out of Dietrich."

Mitch's lips bowed up. "Wasn't it though?"

Walsh stood proud beside the boss. "Yep. Your threat was good enough to almost make me stain my shorts. I'm sure it had the same effect on Dietrich."

Mitch paced away and back again, did so several times. "The thing is what the hell do we do about all this? I can threaten all I want, but I have a dead body on my hands and haven't called the Coast Guard about it yet."

Anniston came back into the little room, crowded now, and put both her hands up for calm. "Just hold on a sec. Let's not panic. We have time. I need to get back in here and document everything with my camera phone, make notes, before we think about doing anything else."

"Then do it," Mitch directed. "If Dietrich was expecting a hero's salute, he won't get it from us."

Raine dreamed of terror, blackish and murky. She tried to crawl out of the bog, but it kept pulling her down. She wanted to surface, to leave it all behind, but couldn't quite make it to the top, out of the gloom. She was drowning, drowning, going under...

She fought to breathe as her eyes fluttered open from the nightmare. She tried to sit straight up. Big mistake. Her skull felt like it would fly off her shoulders if she did. Since she dared not move her head, she cut her eyes around the room. The bed rocked like she was on a boat. Mitch? She didn't remember seeing Mitch. Her stomach churned like she could easily throw up the supper she'd eaten the night before. The right side of her neck ached. She didn't remember getting to this place. Had she been drugged?

The last thing she did recall from…was it last night? She'd made the decision to clean out her closet. How long ago had that been?

When she could manage it, she eased her legs off the bed. Immediate vertigo hit. The room went into a spinning frenzy. She gripped the side of the bunk as if she might just fall off the earth.

Once the dizziness dissipated, she took four steps to get to the cabin door, tried the handle. Of course she found it locked. She yanked and jerked and kicked at the wood. She pounded on the door. "This isn't funny. Let me out of here! You can't keep me like this!"

She thought she heard footsteps outside and beat on the door with her fists until her hands hurt.

A voice in the hallway shouted, "Shut up!"

"Just let me out," she begged.

But nothing she said or did helped to get the door open.

Her eyes landed on the porthole. Even though her legs were still wobbly, she climbed up on the top bunk to get a better idea of where she was. Wishing she had more of a height advantage than her five-three, she had to stand on tiptoes to peer out.

The sun had broken over the water, flaunting a dazzling orange and pink canvas on parade. It made Raine long for home. She felt like a bird with clipped wings that had been relegated to the inside of a cage. She had to find a way out of these confined four walls.

About the time Raine was waking up, Jackson's cell phone buzzed with a series of text messages from Tessa. After reading the first, he pivoted toward his brother. "Mitch, we might have a problem. Tessa says Raine didn't show up at The Blue Taco this morning. No one's heard from her. When Tessa went over to the houseboat, she found the front door unlocked and no Raine. Her cell phone, handbag and other personal stuff were still lying out on the counter."

"Oh God," Mitch said, rubbing his forehead. "Did Tessa check Marla's house? Maybe something happened to her mother or grandmother. You should point her in that direction, ask Tessa to check the hospital."

Before he could go on in more detail, Jenkins walked up, stood in the doorway. "Duarte is on the satellite phone. He says you'll need to take his call."

His stomach twisted into knots as he followed Jenkins into the command center. He picked up the receiver. "What can I do for you, Duarte?"

"You can give me back the lying, cheating snake you took off this boat. Give me back Hollister."

Mitch's brow creased. "Why? Why would you want him back?"

"Other than the fact he's a lying traitor who tried to sabotage my dives? That man could've killed two of my divers, namely Andre Todd, who just happens to be my son-in-law's second cousin. I gave him this job myself, promised his mother I'd take care of him. Now he has something wrong with his brain. I want Hollister to pay for that. I have a score to settle."

Since Nathan had been dead for hours, all Mitch could do was bluff. "Why should I give him back to you? Just because you asked me so nicely? Hollister holds the answers I need to find out what happened to my sister's family. *I* have a score to settle."

"I figured that might be your first response, but I have someone here who wants to talk to you," Duarte said.

Mitch's insides flipped and something dark moved through his brain. He guessed what was coming and when he heard Raine's voice on the other end, he swore under his breath. "Are you okay?"

"Other than the headache banging my skull, I'm fine. Someone gave me a shot of…something. It put me out. I don't remember what happened until I woke up a couple hours ago."

Mitch heard Duarte's voice in the background. "Tell him you're fine for now."

"I told him already," Raine said to Duarte.

"Do it again. Make him believe you're okay."

Raine sighed into the phone. "I'm okay. I'm not hurt or anything."

"I'll get you out of there. You'll be back home by the end of the day. That's a promise. Hang in there, baby. Now put that asshole back on."

"So now that you know I have a bargaining chip, I propose an exchange, the woman for Hollister."

"If you hurt her, I'll hunt you down—"

"I'm not in the habit of abusing women. I have a daughter, grandkids of my own."

"Then you should know if anything happens to Raine and she doesn't come back to me, I'll make it my personal mission to hunt down your entire family myself. Are we clear on that?"

"Yeah, I got it. But it won't be necessary. I just want to trade her for Hollister."

"Okay. I think I can work something out. Give me twenty minutes." Mitch hung up knowing full well all he could give Duarte was Nathan's dead body. It might be enough, Mitch surmised. If not, he'd trade Dietrich for Raine. The old man might have a certain value after all.

Five minutes later, Mitch called a hurried meeting and everyone gathered in the galley. He told them about Raine. "Don't give me a hard time about this because I've already decided to give him Dietrich…and that's it. The floor isn't open for further discussion about it. I don't want to, but I feel I have no choice. I'll try to pacify Duarte first by offering Nathan's body up. It'd be proof I'm not lying about the guy being dead. But if that doesn't work—and it probably won't—I'll have to have a backup, and that's the old man as the bonus. End of story."

"I wouldn't think about giving you a hard time," Garret admitted, sending Anniston a long look from across the room. "If Duarte had her, I'd do exactly the same thing."

"Same here if they had Tessa," Jackson added. "How do we work the exchange though? And if you intend to give Duarte…a…body…then…how do we handle that aspect of it? Because, let's face it, we won't be able to call the Coast Guard after the exchange. They'll want to know why we let Dietrich go. Too many questions to satisfy an official inquiry."

"Most people already believe Nathan took off anyway," Mitch concluded. "Which works in our favor."

"Wendy knows different though," Jackson pointed out. "But if she's as heavily involved in this as I think she is she won't be a factor in raising an alarm."

"That's right, one less person around to divvy up the gold," Garret added. "Besides, I'm looking forward to bringing all those sorry bastards in town to their knees."

Mitch turned to stare at Sebastian. "Who took Raine? Was it Baskin or Dandridge or both?"

Sebastian was already primed for the answer. "I've had access to the surveillance we set up and I've been monitoring them from on board. Neither one was out and about last night. But there are a number of security cameras near Raine's houseboat. Her neighbor has a top of the line, upgraded system she's shared with us already when we were looking to find activity about Ryan's whereabouts over Labor Day. If Raine's abduction happened anywhere near her place, we'll have the CCTV. I'm confident of that."

"I want to know who it is as soon as you hit port. I'm doing the exchange," Mitch said matter-of-factly. "Don't even try to talk me out of it. Anything happens to me—"

"You aren't going alone," Jackson told him. Crossing his arms over his chest in a stubborn bent, he added, "That's nonnegotiable. You'll take me, Garret, and Walsh with you as backup or we'll figure out another way."

Mitch blew out a breath and glanced over at the other members of his crew—Prentiss, Jenkins, and Blaine—and the friends he'd made over the past few weeks, Anniston and Sebastian. "I'm counting on y'all to handle things until we get back. All of you—together as a team." He pointed a finger at Prentiss. "And don't be so hard on yourself because of what happened earlier. It wasn't easy walking into that cabin and seeing all that blood."

"I'll clean it up," Prentiss promised. "By the time you get back the cabin will be…it'll look a lot better…not so bloody."

"That's fine," Mitch told the young man as he glanced at his watch. "Now it's up to me to sell Duarte on the exchange for Raine. Jenkins, get me Duarte on the phone again."

Back in the command center, Mitch was at his best. "Look, I can't give you Hollister alive. The truth is, the man's already dead, an unfortunate accident last night at the end of a knife. Does knowing that satisfy you?"

"I want the body."

"Figured you would."

But Duarte wasn't stupid. "Do you plan to come after the gold? If we're your competition that changes things."

"I just want the people responsible for killing my sister and her family."

"All right. Will you tell me what happened to Werner Dietrich? He hasn't been seen in days. The scuttlebutt is he's on board *The Black Rum*."

"As it happens, I can confirm that rumor. But how did you know?"

"Actually, it was my crew chief, Sandoval, who figured it out. Apparently, Dietrich had tried to persuade him to make a trip out to Sugarloaf Key to find Reiner. In case you haven't heard, they found two bodies there. The thing is, when Dietrich pressed, I refused to allow Sandoval to accompany him, saying I needed him here more. After that, it appears Dietrich improvised."

Mitch couldn't believe what he was hearing. "So you knew Dietrich intended to kill Reiner all along?"

Duarte sighed into the phone. "You can't stop Dietrich from doing anything. You might as well trade the old bastard to me along with Nathan's body for the woman. I'm happy to take Werner off your hands."

Jackson handed his brother a map with an area circled in red and mouthed the word, "here."

Mitch nodded. "Okay, it's a deal, but I pick the meeting place. Write down these coordinates." He rattled off the latitude and longitude.

On the other end, Duarte repeated the GPS numbers to his crew. A few seconds went by before he responded. "That's an uninhabited sandbar. That'll work for me."

"Is Raine okay?"

"She's fine. Just don't go messing with me, Indigo. I don't like to be double-crossed."

"I wouldn't dream of it. All I want is Raine, smooth and easy, and no one else has to suffer. But if you hurt her there's nowhere you'll be able to hide."

Raine had had better mornings. On board the *Patagonia Pike*, her stomach still hadn't settled. She'd thrown up once, which left her with a horrible taste in her mouth that told her she needed a toothbrush and soon. She couldn't shake her headache. It held on like a hungry shark chomping away at its prey. She'd overheard a member of the crew tell the captain she'd been given Ketamine. While she wasn't sure exactly what it was, she did watch CSI shows and knew it was often used as a recreational drug. She could attest to its nasty side effects. That's why she felt lucky to be standing at all.

At least they'd finally let her out of that dreary stateroom and put her on deck.

Even if she was still wearing the same clothes from the night before—that pair of brightly colored yellow shorts and her navy button-down blouse, she felt glad to be alive. Underdressed though, she shivered in the path of the northerly wind that whipped around her bare legs. Her feet were cold—she had no idea what had happened to her sandals, and at this point, didn't care. She wanted off this boat, away from the stares and ogles of the crewmen, who just kept eyeing her like she was the next piece of tasty candy out of their Halloween bag.

Feeling like a disheveled hag, she kept her eyes glued to the water, waiting on deck for any sign of the island or Mitch's boat.

It took ninety long minutes before she saw a speck on the horizon, and even then she could barely make it out as land. Her heart beat faster knowing, hoping, praying, she'd be back home by nightfall.

The Black Rum reached the unpopulated morsel of sand known as Mutiny Bay before the *Pike* did. The strip of land had held that name since the 1700s when it became a notorious spot where pirates often switched sides, marooning captains and crew there, if not downright disposing of them before continuing on to Jamaica and their quest for more loot.

Mitch stood at the rail with a pair of high-powered binoculars scanning the horizon.

"Any sign yet?" Jackson asked.

"There's a dot coming in on the portside. Get Dietrich ready."

Garret came up behind his brothers. "Any idea why that old man doesn't want to leave this boat? Anniston and I can't get him to do anything but scowl at us. He keeps repeating he's not leaving unless he can take his knife with him. And so far, neither one of us has gotten Dietrich to budge."

Mitch squinted as the other ship began to get closer to the island. "My personal opinion is he's losing it. Did you see his face this morning? After killing Nathan, he went off the deep end. He probably didn't sleep more than an hour or so. That's what it looked like to me anyway."

He shifted his focus back to the *Pike*. "They're coming in on the western shore of the beach, dropping anchor across from us. Our two launches will come in from the opposite side. Walsh and Garret in one, holding Dietrich. Jackson and I will be in the other with Hollister's body. Then we meet Duarte in the middle of the island. Walsh will have his weapon drawn and ready while Garret stays back holding on to Dietrich. Anything goes wrong, don't shoot until I get Raine out of there. Are we clear?"

"Yep. We'll have it covered," Garret promised.

Mitch watched through the field glasses as Duarte assembled his men on deck. They scuttled down the ladder with Raine in between. His heart pounded at the sight of her. "Let's load up."

Sebastian appeared with a reluctant Dietrich. "Nathan's corpse is already loaded in the one you and Jackson will take."

Mitch nodded. He'd never been part of anything so morbid before in his life, but to get Raine back, he'd make a deal with the devil if he had to.

Dietrich started to protest. "I want my knife back. It's a valuable keepsake from my father. I'm not moving from this spot unless I get my knife. I'm not going back with Duarte unarmed."

"Why is that?" Mitch wanted to know. He held up his hand. "Never mind. I don't have time to stand here and argue with you. Either get in the damn boat or I'll shoot you where you stand within sight of Duarte."

Dietrich recognized the steely determination in Mitch's eyes and scrambled down the ladder.

The showdown came fifteen minutes later when Mitch met Duarte on the sand.

Duarte's focus ran to Dietrich, who was standing some distance away with Garret. "So this is where he's been keeping himself. I wondered."

"Your men can check out the body, it's wrapped in a sheet," Mitch offered, pointing to the launch they'd left at water's edge. "But I want Raine. Now."

Duarte bobbed his head toward the raft. "As soon as I make sure it's Hollister."

Sandoval went over to inspect the remains. "It's him, captain!"

"You're certain?"

"It's him," Sandoval said again.

The captain motioned for Raine to come closer. "Very pretty woman. Yours?"

Mitch smiled. "Yep, has been for a long time back."

"You should keep a better eye on what's yours then, I think."

"From now on, I intend to."

Duarte eyed Dietrich and leaned closer. "This might turn out to my advantage."

"Maybe so, since he's the one who killed Hollister," Mitch replied, reaching out his hand to Raine and drawing her into his circle before pushing her behind him. "Add Hugo Reiner into that and I don't think Dietrich is opposed to killing anyone. At least you'll get your boss back."

Duarte frowned at that. "Don't worry. I've made plans for him." He tipped his captain's hat toward Raine. "You have a good day now."

She'd never been so glad to see anyone before in her life as she was to see Mitch.

And no one was more surprised than Mitch when she practically jumped on his back, eventually working her way to leaping into his arms.

Mitch lifted her off her feet, swung her in a circle. He pushed her hair out of her face, framed it and kissed her flat on the mouth in front of everyone. "You okay?"

"Better now."

Looking into those sharp green eyes of hers, the golden amber around the edges always made him think of fire. He'd always thought she looked like a young version of Meg Ryan. Today, she looked even better. When he noticed she was shivering, he removed the leather jacket he wore and draped it around her shoulders. He started walking her back toward the raft while his brothers kept a careful eye on Duarte's men to make sure they weren't planning a double-cross.

But just as Duarte had promised, Sandoval took possession of Dietrich and Nathan's body and they all climbed back into their rafts, heading toward the west, and the opposite direction.

Mitch's crew was halfway back to *The Black Rum* when they heard the first shot echoing off the water. Then came another.

Certain they were being fired at, Mitch gunned the boat. "Stay low. Don't give them a good target," he shouted and motioned for everyone to crouch down.

For cover, Mitch went around to the starboard side, out of sight from the shooters, so they could disembark.

Mitch secured the lifeboat and helped Raine climb up the ladder.

Once everyone was on the deck, Anniston came running up. "Did you see that?"

"We were too busy trying not to get shot," Garret told her.

"Duarte wasn't shooting at you guys," she explained. "It seems as soon as he got back to the ship, he and Dietrich got into a very animated shouting match. I saw the whole thing through the binoculars. Dietrich kept pointing in our direction and yelling at Duarte, cursing actually. Then all of a sudden Duarte got fed up, took out a pistol and shot him in the head, point blank. I tried to use my phone to video the whole thing but it's too far. There's no detail." But she handed off her phone to Mitch anyway so he could take a look.

"But there were two gunshots," Mitch pointed out while he watched the scene play out on Anniston's phone.

"Honestly I think Duarte put that second one into Nathan's body. Duarte had his men throw Dietrich overboard first and then the sheet followed." She snapped her fingers. "Just like that, they're both gone."

As if she'd just realized Raine was with them, Anniston grabbed her in a hug. "Are you all right? They didn't hurt you, did they?"

"Other than pumping me with something called Ketamine, I'm fine." She wiggled her toes. "You wouldn't happen to have a pair of shoes I could borrow, would you?"

"We'll see if we can rustle you up a pair," Mitch told her.

Trying to get caught up to speed in a hurry was a problem. "Wait. Just wait." She slid her arm around Mitch's waist if for no other reason than to steady herself. "Are you saying Nathan's dead? How'd that happen? Did he tell you anything about Livvy and the kids? Does he know who killed them?"

"To answer all that could take a few hours. Let me get underway and I'll tell you all about it." Mitch turned to his crew. "Let's see how fast we can make it back to Indigo Key. Flank speed!"

Pulling Raine along behind him, he headed below deck to his cabin. "Let's get you into some clean clothes and a hot shower."

"Really? Hot water? Is that allowed? What if I use it all up?"

He laughed and swung her in for a kiss. "I'm pretty sure you've earned it."

Chapter Five

He wasn't used to sharing his personal space, but he'd make an exception for Raine.

"I should call my mom, let her know I'm okay."

"When you've cleaned up, I'll take you to the bridge. We have a satellite phone that makes it handy to call anywhere in the world."

She twirled into the stateroom like she was on a cruise. "Oh my, this cabin is so roomy, much larger than I ever thought possible," Raine drawled, looking around. "I thought you'd share a bunk or something with four other guys. Is that a king-sized bed?"

"I *am* the captain," Mitch reminded her with a wide grin. "There are benefits to owning my own boat."

"And you do have long legs and big feet," Raine added with a smile.

He couldn't stop his lips from curving up. He could barely believe she was standing in his cabin. She absolutely lit up the room. He was amused by her reaction to the bed, knowing he'd bought the boat—paid a little more than he should have—because of this very large stateroom that included an oversized place to sleep.

In addition to the big bed framed out in golden oak, he had a desk, a nightstand, and an entire wall of bookshelves brimming with hardcover bestsellers and paperback thrillers. The cabin had its own mini galley with a compact fridge. He didn't have to share a bathroom with any of the crew. He had his own personal head with a roomy shower, a huge bonus since it gave him the privacy on board he craved.

"How is this possible?" she asked, running her hand over the soft, downy sheets. "It's like a first-class stateroom on a cruise ship. I've seen the brochures." She plopped down, gave the bed a testing bounce that made him smile again.

"Not quite like that. But the boat builder did promise me a state-of-the-art fiberglass design that offered considerable less weight than older boats. I signed the papers and made sure he kept his word on that score." He went over to a dresser and pulled out a shirt and a pair of sweatpants. "These are way too big for you, but it's all I have."

"That'll work. Anniston's so tall, her stuff will probably be just as baggy as your clothes."

"I'll get out of your way then and let you get settled."

"How long before we pull into port?"

He glanced at his watch. "Three hours, tops."

"Okay. And Mitch?"

"What?"

She slid off the bed and came over to him. "Thank you for getting me off that boat and away from Duarte. I've never been that scared before in my whole life."

His lips curved as he framed her face. "No problem, since we got you into all this. I'm sorry."

"Don't be silly. Livvy was my best friend. And after this, after what they did to me, I'm determined to help you get those bastards."

"We're working on that." He ran a finger down her cheek. "Besides, I couldn't let my best girl sail off into the sunset with the bad guy. That just isn't done."

He pulled her against him and scooped her up off the floor, clamping his lips over her mouth so quickly she had no time to deflect.

She thought of nothing but rapture as she plunged headlong into the kiss. Steam rose up between them and hauled her into the wall of heat. She felt his hands grip her hips. It would be so easy to tumble into that big bed.

Her head was spinning when he finally let her go. "That's just a sample. I have a lot more stored up in me."

She fanned a hand in front of her face. "I've found through the years that no one kisses quite the way you do."

"I'm glad you remember. Now what can I fix you to eat? It's my turn in the galley tonight and you must be starving."

She put a hand over her stomach. "I'm still kinda queasy, but I could use some chicken soup if you have it, maybe with a piece of plain bread."

"I can handle that. There are towels in the bathroom cabinet and my robe is hanging on the back of the door. It's clean. If you need anything else, give a holler."

"Will do." She patted his face. This time she brought his head down, stood on tiptoes to reach his lips. "I won't be long."

Twenty minutes later, she floated out of the steam and back into the bedroom wrapped in a pale blue robe, soft as Egyptian cotton.

Mitch handed her a bottle of water.

She didn't seem surprised to see him sitting on the bed. "My gosh, that bathroom is downright luxurious. And all these years I thought you were roughing it at sea."

He shot out a laugh. "Believe me, I did. For the first four years I shared a cabin with three other guys, one of them was Walsh. I can tell you this much, it was hardly a ride at Disney World. Hard work from six in the morning until I dropped into my bunk around eight at night. But I'm not complaining. It got me here, at this spot, watching you, half naked, standing in my cabin. What more could a man ask for?"

"I'm not naked, half or otherwise."

"You could be."

"Aren't you supposed to be cooking?"

"I got the stew started, Garret offered to watch it simmer."

"Get out of here and let me get dressed," she said, sending him a laugh when he got to his feet. "We can't do this here, Mitch. You have a boatful of crew and…there are friends on board."

"I know that. But I can still kiss you while you're standing in my cabin wearing my robe, a dream of mine on so many long nights at sea."

She let him ravage her mouth again because it felt good. So did the strong arms that wrapped around her body, especially after what she'd been through the last twenty-four hours. But the comfort he gave her was no excuse to toss out the caution she'd practiced.

"I'll take that soup now," she said, taking a deliberate step back.

He simply grinned at her restraint. "You want it delivered?"

"No, I'll come to you."

"I'm counting on it."

Later they bunched around the galley table, taking turns catching Raine up on the past few days. Mitch went over everything, detail by detail.

"Then you didn't recover the documents and neither did Dietrich?" Raine concluded.

"No," Mitch said sadly. "But like I said, we're working on it."

Anniston told her about what Nathan had written in blood.

Skewing her mouth up at the word, Raine mulled it over for a full minute. "Nathan must've thought the word 'pot' was a significant enough clue."

"More like three letters is all the time he had before he bled to death," Mitch pointed out.

"The fact his last word was 'pot' has to be *the* clue," Raine said in disagreement. "He has to be referring to the family tomb where he used to hide out from his dad and smoke weed all the time."

Jackson cocked his head. "How do you know about that?"

She slanted him a long look. "How do you think? Because I went out there with him a time or two." She lifted a shoulder. "Back then everyone did."

"I never did," Garret stated. "Why wasn't I included?"

Raine patted his face. "Because you had your own spot, that place underneath the bridge just this side of town."

Garret grinned. "You knew about that, huh? Why didn't you ever come out there with me then?"

She sighed and sent Mitch a knowing look. "At the time I was madly in love with your brother and wanted to hang out with the older crowd."

Mitch reached across the table, squeezed her fingers. "Hey, madly in love, once upon a time."

"Aww," Anniston said. "You two made up."

Raine tilted her head to look at Mitch. "I wouldn't go that far. But he did save me from ending up in Romania or South America, probably targeted as a sex slave for the rest of my life. You know, that was my first thought when I woke up, locked in that cabin and couldn't get out. At the time, I had no idea why they'd kidnapped me. That's the only reason I could think of."

Mitch tightened his grip on her hand. "I'm sorry. You had to be scared sick."

"Oh, I was. I pounded on the door to the cabin, but no one responded. A man eventually showed up. I know now it was Duarte. He came to settle me down, but he never said a word then about trading me for Nathan. I didn't know about that until he brought me up on deck as we were nearing Mutiny Bay. Then he sent one of his goons to stand next to me so I wouldn't jump off into the ocean. As if."

"What do you remember about being taken, about that night?" Mitch asked. "Were you in the house?"

She shook her head. "I'd done some cleaning to keep my mind off things. I tossed a lot of unwanted stuff in trash sacks. I've made a hundred trips to that dumpster late at night without a problem. Never again though. I raised my arm to open the lid and toss the bag inside and that's when a hand clamped over my mouth." She sat there a minute before going on. "Wait. He wasn't wearing gloves. I remember that now. His skin was a little wrinkled, like an older man had hold of me. He had a ring on his right hand, one of those class rings, but different, not a school or university, but something else with an insignia. I remember fighting for a few seconds and as I did, I touched the ring. I'm sorry. I don't know anything else about what it looked like."

Anniston patted her arm. "Sneaky bastard, picking on women. It sounds like something this bunch has down to a fine art. Women and little kids."

Raine sighed. "It just makes me want to help even more. I have my own score to settle with whoever did this. I can't believe Dietrich is dead."

"I wouldn't have believed it either if I hadn't seen it with my own eyes."

Walsh came in to get coffee. "So what's the plan once we get back to Indigo Key?"

Mitch finished off his plate of stew and stretched out his legs. "We try to get our hands on Hugo's precious documents, line up the translator for the diary, see if it holds any clues about this mythical Nazi bullion, and if it does, we get to it first."

Walsh lifted his brow as he sipped his mug. "Even if that means going up against Duarte's men?"

"What do you think?"

"I think you're serious."

"I am. There'd be a sizeable finder's fee involved from all the countries involved that got ripped off during the war, all the countries that had banks plundered and raided, their gold stolen. Off the top of my head I can think of three, France, Czechoslovakia, and Poland, to name a few."

"I read something about sunken war ships. Many are considered war graves," Garret offered. "War graves would revert back to the original country automatically."

Mitch crossed his ankles, leaned back in his chair. "I can tell you this much. Duarte wouldn't give a rat's ass about returning anything to anyone, including remains. Any U-boat found in these waters would likely fall into that category. Germany would definitely want its missing-in-action soldiers back. But after that, I would say the countries I mentioned would fight to get the gold returned to them."

"It'd be a mess," Walsh decided. "Do you really want to get tangled up in the courts for several years?"

Mitch agreed. "It would indeed be a lengthy process. Plus, it could take years to find the damn thing. Maybe we should take a vote, here and now, about what we do going forward."

Garret held up a hand. "I hope you're talking about getting to the gold *after* we set our sights on taking down that rat nest in town."

"That's a given," Mitch assured him. "The rat nest is our number one priority."

Raine didn't hesitate. "I'm in. Whatever it takes to knock down Baskin's house of cards, I want to be a part of it. If it includes messing with Duarte's plans for the gold,

I'm fine with that, too. I want my payback from them for scaring me half to death."

"As long as we get Baskin, Dandridge, Sinclair, and the rest first, then I'm good with hunting down the gold," Jackson stated. "Maybe if our share of the finder's fee is enough we could start a scholarship fund in Livvy's name."

"That sounds like a fine idea to me." Mitch turned to Anniston and Sebastian. "Your thoughts?"

"I like the scholarship idea," Anniston said. "Is there any way we could include Dack in that?"

Mitch looked around the table. "Sure. If we end up going for the gold, everyone involved would get an equal share, including my crew. What each individual decides to do with their portion is up to them." He turned to Sebastian. "Anything yet on who Dandridge really is?"

Sebastian sent him a wry smile. "I've done some work on that in my spare time over the past forty-eight hours. Thanks to Raine coming up with that blog post Willis Hartman wrote before he died, I set up an appointment with Hartman's daughter. As soon as I learned we were heading into port, I made arrangements to see her. I'm taking off for Port Saint Lucie tomorrow to see if she remembers anything about Dandridge. It's a long shot I know. Could be that Dandridge simply lifted the sermon off an obscure website out of desperation. Maybe that Sunday he ran out of anything to preach about and stumbled on Hartman's post."

"Could be, but something tells me it's more than that," Mitch said. "Maybe because since we came back home to Indigo Key that's all we've been doing is uncovering everyone's darkest kept secrets. These upstanding citizens we've known for years—the pastor, the string of businessmen, the chief of police—have something to hide. They aren't who we thought they were. It disturbs me to know that. A dozen years ago I left a town behind that I don't even recognize today. Knowing how easy it was for these guys to hide in plain sight within the community and no one questioned their backgrounds, it upsets me. The fact that no one truly knows who they are is something we should all take note. I mean, Mom and Dad attended that church for more than twenty years, thought they knew Boone. They didn't. The fact that he was able to fool Dad is huge."

When he stood up to clear his dishes off the table, Garret had something on his mind. "Now would be a good time to mention we need to make absolutely certain that we've pinpointed the right person responsible for killing Livvy and the kids. Dietrich may have ordered it, but someone, likely more than one, within the town, carried it out."

"I thought we agreed that was Baskin," Anniston pointed out.

Garret looked doubtful. "Baskin had a hand in it, as did Dandridge. No doubt about that. We know because Baskin's car was spotted near the Vitamin Hut that night when the burglar alarm went off. We know Dandridge, or someone that looked like him, was pulled over in Livvy's minivan on its way to the Tampa Bay Airport. But neither event equates to murdering a mother and her kids."

"What are you saying?" Mitch asked. "That's good enough for me, obviously it isn't for you."

"No, it isn't. I think someone else got their hands dirty that night and we don't know who that someone is...yet. It's essential to figure out every single person who's involved, narrow down exactly what role they played—that includes Wendy Hollister, by the way—and then identify who actually tortured and beat to death Livvy and the kids."

Mitch stared at his brother. "Do you know something we don't?"

Garret and Anniston traded looks. "We think Livvy might've been raped that night. She'd had sex with someone. The lab put the DNA profile in the system."

"And you're just now sharing this nugget with the rest of us?" Mitch charged. "What else have you two been keeping to yourselves?"

Garret shrugged. "Just that. I got dibs on the bastard who did it."

"And we're sure it wasn't Walker?" Jackson prompted.

Anniston shook her head. "Once the Coast Guard brought in Walker and Blake, the lab was able to rule Walker out as the contributor of the sperm."

"Son of a bitch. Okay, so we'll dig a little deeper and make sure we have the right man," Mitch promised. "We owe it to Mom and Dad to find out the truth."

Garret nodded. "Speaking of Mom, I called her, told her we're headed home, but not to wait supper on us. You should know that after talking to her for fifteen minutes or so, I don't think Dad intends to take Mom and leave town like we'd hoped."

"Tessa's been staying with them while I'm out here dealing with this. She doesn't think they'll leave either," Jackson provided.

"Then I guess we'll have to make certain we cage the rats in record time and keep them away from Mom and Dad."

Chapter Six

They pulled into port a little after eight o'clock that evening.

Mitch followed Raine down the plank to the wharf, intent on seeing her home safely. When she noticed him tagging along, she stopped, pivoted to face him. "What are you doing?"

"I'm going home with you."

"But I didn't ask you to do that. I need to call my mom, tell her I've arrived back home."

"I'll wait while you do. Would you like me to take you over there, to stay with her?"

Raine's eyes got wide. "You're asking me if I want to stay with my mother and grandmother? Are you nuts?"

He chuckled. "I guess I am. Sorry."

"I don't like the idea of having a babysitter."

"Don't be stubborn. After what happened to you, I don't think you should be alone. In fact, I won't let you go into that house and stay there by yourself."

"You won't let me?" She opened her mouth to really put some meat into the argument, but had to admit he had a point. She really didn't want to be alone tonight. She laced her arm through his. "Okay, but you should know I don't plan to sleep with you right off, otherwise, we'll just end up right where we started out and nothing will ever get resolved between us. If you won't agree to that—"

He glanced toward the night sky. "It seems I'm destined to practice the art of abstinence while I'm here. I'm being punished for something. I just can't figure out what it is."

She patted his arm. "Don't be so melodramatic. We spent our teen years sneaking off to have sex every chance we got. Surely you can be patient for…I don't know…a few days until we reconnect."

"Reconnect, huh?" He let out a breathy sigh, on purpose, maybe louder than it needed to be to make his point. "It's a deal. As long as you understand where we'll end up."

"You're that confident, are you?"

"Yeah. I am."

Once they reached the houseboat, the first thing Raine did was change out of his sweatpants and shirt and into a pair of blue shorts and white top.

After that, she set about cleaning up the mess she'd left behind. Mitch helped her by rummaging through her boxes slated for Goodwill drop-off.

When Raine saw what he was doing, she groaned. "The idea is to declutter, not rifle through my stuff."

Among all the items, he eyeballed something familiar. He scooped up a raggedy, stuffed, very pink elephant with huge black bug eyes. "You're giving away Dumbo?"

She snatched it back from him, waved it back and forth. "No doubt Dumbo served his purpose well over the years for a silly teenage girl. But now it's time for him to go make someone else happy." She inched back on her hard line approach. "You won him for me when you were fourteen at the carnival that breezed through here. Remember that?"

"The summer we started dating. Of course I do."

"How much money did that thing end up costing you?"

Mitch laughed at the memory. "Almost my entire earnings that week from mowing lawns. All this time you kept it."

Embarrassed by that, she threw her arms out wide at the stuff still on the floor that hadn't made it into trash sacks. "Like I said, hoarding isn't pretty. It's past time to part with my junk from when I was a girl."

Together, they began to box up the rest of the stuff and cart each bag and container down the street to the donation box until they had it all cleared out.

After tidying up, they rewarded themselves by sitting outside on the deck under the stars, kicking back in the Adirondack chairs and enjoying a beer.

Raine took a slug of beer. "Did you ever think we'd be this close to each other, talking like normal people do who used to be such close friends, instead of yelling and screaming at each other? You know, without ragging on each other about something?"

"I wasn't sure it was possible." He took a pull on the bottle he held. "But after you explained things about Baby Taylor, everything seems so clear to me now. Mistakes made. Miscommunication on both sides. Years lost between us."

"Baby Taylor. I haven't said that name aloud much. I didn't think I was allowed to…feel for him."

Mitch lifted his shoulders. "You can say it as often as you want. Baby Taylor deserves that much."

She turned her head to study him. "At the risk of making you mad now and ending our détente, there's something I need to know. Well, quite a few things."

"Go ahead, now's the time to air it out and ask me."

"What do you do for a sex life?"

Since that was the last thing he expected her to say, he choked on his beer.

"Seriously, going from dive to dive like you do? Do you have a special person in your life? Where do you actually live when you aren't on the boat? I happen to think they're valid questions."

He cut his brown eyes to hers. "I see that. A couple of years back I built a house on the leeward side of Cape Santa Maria, right on the beach. It sits vacant for long periods of time, but I have a caretaker I trust who keeps an eye on the place for me when I'm gone. As to your other question, I'm not a saint or a priest. I've had women come and go over the last twelve years. There's no one special." He paused, looked out over the water. "When you didn't write me back all those years ago, I had to go on with my life, Raine. I told myself you'd moved on and there was a reason you lost interest in me."

"You wrote me letters?"

"Of course I did. I wrote every day and mailed a letter at least once a week, no matter where we were in the world. You didn't answer a single one."

Raine's eyes grew wide. "That's because I didn't get any of them. I got one postcard from you around Thanksgiving and that's it."

They stared at each other. "Raine, I know I had the right address. I practically lived at your house before I shipped out. I sent letters full of stuff that might not have been interesting to you, but they were to me. I described all the places I'd been, the dives I worked, the ports where I ended up pulling in for supplies."

"Hmm, that's interesting. I wonder."

"Wonder what?"

"If my mother intercepted those and got rid of them."

"Marla? Why would she do that?"

Raine swallowed hard. "Because during those summer months she was really upset with you that you left me."

He gaped at her. "You let your mother believe I knew about the baby…and just…took off anyway?"

She took a drink from her bottle of beer, chewed her bottom lip, squirming in the deck chair, stalling for time. "I may not have set the record entirely straight there. That's on me."

He lifted his head to the sky, took in the canopy of stars above, the full moon hidden behind a swath of patchy clouds. "With so much working against us, no wonder we were destined to fail. We didn't stand much of a chance."

"I never considered my mother would do something like that. I'll have to ask her about it."

"Wonder why she didn't mention how angry she was with me to my mother? If Marla was so upset with me, I'm surprised she kept that to herself and didn't run straight to my mom with all that fury, calling me every nasty name in the book."

"I don't know the answer to that. But I intend to find out. After the miscarriage she did make me promise I wouldn't tell anyone about what had happened. I wasn't really allowed to mention the baby at all. That was fine by me. It hurt too much to talk to anyone about it, except maybe Livvy. It was like your sister figured it out on her own, though."

He squeezed her hand. "If it's possible, we need to put all the hurt and anger behind us. Now there's something I have to ask you. It's none of my business, but…did you sleep with doughboy?"

She let out a laugh from deep in the belly. "Carson? Of course not."

Relief moved through him. "That's something, I guess. Are you hungry?"

"As a matter of fact my appetite's slowly coming back. I have leftover vegetable soup in the fridge."

"As tasty as that sounds, I was thinking you need something more substantial than soup. You had that on the boat. How about I order us a pepperoni pizza? You used to love pepperoni."

"Not for me. But I will take a medium veggie."

He looked at her funny. "Since when did you become a vegetarian?"

"Since I work around taco meat all day. You try handling beef, pork, and chicken, cooking and smelling that stuff from ten in the morning to seven at night and see how your taste buds change."

"Wanna know something? My taste for you has never changed. That's the truth of it."

"I truly missed you, Mitch. With all my heart. The day you left it was like part of me wasn't here anymore. I don't think anything has ever been the same for me since."

He stood up, pulled her out of the chair and against him. "I want you, Raine. I've never stopped wanting you."

"Then we should probably make it like old times."

"Trust me, I can do better than a horny eighteen-year-old this time around."

She recognized her own weakness, her own willingness to give in while his hands roamed down to her hips and his mouth took hers.

"Hey guys," Sebastian called out from the pier.

"Go away!" Mitch bellowed. "Now's not a good time."

"Sure. Okay. Sorry. I don't mean to interrupt. But you said you wanted to know who kidnapped Raine."

That got Mitch's full attention. He rested his chin on the top of her head. "I really need to know who abducted you."

She nibbled at his earlobe and came out of her sex-starved daze long enough to send a wave toward Sebastian. "Come on up. Want a beer?"

"I won't take up much of your time. I can see with my own eyes you two have definitely made other plans already. I wanted you to know though that your neighbor Deidra is a go-to wonder in a clutch. I knocked on her door about forty minutes ago and looked at her video from last night. It was Sinclair who took you, Raine. Bold as brass. He's the one who gave you that shot and then dragged you into his police cruiser. Deidra's camera captured it all."

"That son of a bitch!" Raine said. "That's a helluva strange way for my own chief of police to protect and serve. I pay his damn salary."

"We'll get him for that," Mitch charged. "Sinclair just made a huge mistake."

"He did," Sebastian chimed in. "Because I'm taking the tape up to Paul Briggs in Tallahassee myself after I make a stopover in Port Saint Lucie to talk to Hartman's daughter. By tomorrow night, I'll have delivered the video to Briggs personally. There's no way the department will be able to ignore that kind of evidence. If that doesn't shake this case to the core, nothing will."

A skeptical Mitch still wasn't convinced. "What if you're delivering it to the wrong person, though?"

"I'm making copies, leaving one with Anniston and sending one to my dad in Miami. Sinclair won't get out of this, Mitch. He won't. Not this time."

"I hope you're right."

Jackson and Tessa walked up. "We're headed out to Nathan's family crypt. We thought you guys might want to come with us."

"Even though that sounds…uh, fascinating, I'll have to pass," Sebastian said. "I'm headed out of town and need to pack. I'm not sure how long I'll be gone." He slapped Jackson on the back. "I'll let Mitch get you up to speed on the latest."

"Let us know what Briggs says about the evidence," Mitch called out to him as Sebastian took off down the wharf.

"What was that all about? What evidence?" Jackson wanted to know.

"Sinclair's the one who abducted Raine," Mitch recounted. "I knew that old man was dirty, but that's a new low even for him. I want them all to go down, Jackson. Duarte obviously made a call to…somebody here in town and Sinclair showed up as the lackey who carried out the orders."

"Which makes Duarte higher up on the chain than we first thought. That might explain why he killed Dietrich outright. We're getting closer, Mitch. Now we just have to keep at it. Which is one more reason we need to get into that vault as soon as possible before someone else beats us to it."

"You're right." Turning to Raine, Mitch said, "We really should go see if those documents are in Nathan's hiding place. Are you ready to skulk around a graveyard?"

Raine didn't want to admit that's the very last place she wanted to be tonight, but she also didn't want to be left alone. "Sure. I guess."

She looked over at Tessa and Jackson. "You guys aren't wasting any time with all this."

"We can't afford to waste time." Tessa looked at Raine with a certain amount of sympathy. "I wanted to bypass your place and just go, but Jackson had this idea that we should all do this together as a team."

Raine eyed the disappointment on Mitch's face about having to wait, patted his cheek and whispered, "There's always later for us to…get together. You are staying the night, right?"

"Damn straight I am, but I've waited years for later." He sighed. "I guess a couple more hours won't hurt. Come on, we might as well go see what's in the vault and get this done with."

Chapter Seven

Nightfall offered up a crisp, clear moonlit evening for a walk through the town's cemetery. The breezy twilight and its rustling leaves were a reminder they were almost to the end of October, a time of year with its own ghostly right to celebrate.

The eighty or so acres of graveyard had rows of marble mausoleums peppered with tombstones throughout and too many cherub angel statues to count. A lovely pond in the center, complete with trickling waterfall, was a gathering place for gulls and herons and ducks. Several concrete-slab benches provided a place to sit and contemplate, or to rest after saying a final goodbye to friends and family members.

In the daytime, the setting was like a picture postcard, an opportunity for a photo shoot full of nature. At night, it held a different vibe altogether.

There was nothing scenic about it to Raine as she sat in the back seat of the SUV and gripped Mitch's hand before they even reached the iron gates.

"We should've brought more flashlights," he suggested from the crowded back seat, shoving an elbow into Jackson's side to get him to move over.

"There's one in the glove box," Anniston said to Garret, who was riding shotgun in the front. "Don't tell me you're the one tasked to break into a crypt tonight," she groaned as she tapped the brake outside the front entrance.

"He won't need to," Jackson explained. "I remembered where there was a key. Unless Nathan changed the lock, we shouldn't have a problem."

"You're kidding? You have a key? How did that happen?" Mitch asked, clearly surprised as he threw open the car door and stuck a foot onto the pavement, grateful to have more wiggle room. He took hold of Raine's hand and drew her out into the parking lot.

Jackson did the same on the opposite side as he grabbed Tessa's hand to help her out. "I went through boxes of stuff in the carport until I came across my old tin box, the one where I kept what I thought at that time were priceless treasures, at least they were to a little kid."

"More like a stoner, who needed to keep his pot hidden from Mom and Dad," Garret suggested, as he walked up to the gate, shined his flashlight into the first rows of vaults. "And you had the nerve to give me a hard time."

"You don't understand," Jackson went on, "Nathan and I used to hang out here quite a bit when we were kids. It wasn't as morbid as it sounds. It wasn't just a place to smoke pot as teenagers. That came later."

"If you say so," Mitch noted. "But to me, it explains all those crypt-keeper comic books you used to read."

"Like you weren't weird in your own way," Jackson fired back, as he took out the flashlight he'd brought and focused the beam on the walkway so they could see where they were going in the dark.

Laden with the sweet, dewy smell of magnolia, the six of them walked among the headstones, with Jackson leading the way.

"It might sound strange. Sure. But when you're two nine-year-old boys looking for something to do on a Friday night during a sleepover, it's not so weird. Think about it. We'd sit up on the roof of his family's vault because it was the highest one around with a mostly flat surface. We'd take out the telescope we bought—the one we pooled our allowance for and ordered out of a catalog together—to look for comets or meteors or falling stars. We used to keep our gear and accessories inside the vault. We each had a key."

Raine pulled her sweater tighter around her body. "Tell me again why we have to do this at night. It's creepy out here. I'm not sure I want to be a part of opening a crypt."

"Because we have a better chance of doing it out of the prying eyes of you-know-who," Tessa reminded. "At the same time we're keeping an eye on Baskin and Dandridge, they're more than likely returning the favor. But if you want to wait in the car, that's okay with me."

"By myself? No way," Raine tossed back. "I'm not waiting in the car alone. I'll just watch you guys...do...whatever...from afar."

Mitch clutched her hand. "I'm right there with you. I'm not exactly happy about being out here." Looking around, he added, "I still say it's weird that Nathan would choose this place to stick a bunch of documents he stole from Livvy."

"Not so weird really," Jackson insisted. "You had to know Nathan. And I've been going back over things, reading some emails he sent me from a couple years back. Nathan was obviously stone-cold bored with his job at the bank, had been almost from the beginning. I think he knew his marriage was a bust right out of the gate. In one of his longer emails to me, he mentioned Wendy was in love with her job and he wasn't sure what to do about it. I read this stuff and never realized the importance of it all. At least I didn't at the time. I mean, who would? It turns out, the man wasn't any happier with Wendy than Livvy was with Walker."

"No wonder they were drawn to each other," Raine decided as they approached the last row of crypts. "Is it bad of me to hope they both found some measure of happiness before…all this?"

"That's one way of looking at it," Jackson said.

"We're hoping that you're getting to a point somewhere in that story," Garret cracked. "Hopefully it'll be before morning gets here."

"I am," Jackson said as he came to a stop in front of a stone crypt with a plaque that read Hollister above a tarnished, bronze door wide enough for casket entry. He stuck his key into the lock. "There's no bodies inside lying in state."

"None at all? Are you certain of that?" Mitch asked.

Jackson grinned. "Positive. All Nathan's relatives were cremated, all the way back to his great-grandparents. Nathan's great-grandfather, Gordon Hollister, bought this mausoleum to show his status in the community, no other reason. No one's inside because he felt like it was a bad idea to bury above ground. Period. He didn't like the idea of a hurricane rolling through here and uprooting him or his loved ones, centuries later. Gordon felt so strongly against it that he didn't trust the funeral home and its owners to follow his wishes, so he instructed his lawyer to supervise each cremation personally."

"You might've mentioned that chunk right up front instead of scaring Raine half to death with this trek through *American Horror Story*," Mitch grumbled.

Jackson sent Raine a sheepish grin. "Sorry. It'll be okay."

But she still wasn't keen on the idea of standing around in the dark waiting to get into a crypt. "So you're saying it's an empty vault?"

"That's what I'm saying. See for yourself." Jackson opened the metal door, listened to the hinges creak as it swung back and hit the stone wall.

Once inside the chamber, he aimed the beam of his flashlight around so everyone could get a good look at the interior. In the middle of the room stood an ornate slab pedestal that could hold a casket, but of course it held nothing.

The vestibule itself was a ten-by-fourteen-foot space with shelves made of granite and two stained glass windows on opposite side walls. "See, no caskets. It's completely empty as far as bodies resting here."

"The lack of cobwebs suggests someone's been here recently," Garret decided as he wandered around the chamber with his own beam of light. "Where would Nathan have hidden those papers?"

"I have an idea," Jackson assured him. "Hold my flashlight, Tessa, while I get us some more light in here." Once he'd relinquished the penlight to her, he went over to a familiar section of the vault with an arch opening built into the wall and took down an old-fashioned lantern from the shelf. From his pocket he drew out a lighter and lit the wick.

Light danced off the four walls, creating flickering shadows. He handed the lantern off to Mitch before proceeding to another area, deeper into the vault. He went over to a spot in the wall, waist-high, and stood in front of what looked like a solid piece of marble. He began to try to work the stone plaque out of its block. "This is where they would place the urns."

Raine took a few steps into the shadows. "Wait. So there *are* Hollister remains in here? I knew it!"

"Yes. Just not bodies, but not in the one I'm opening up. This one is where Nathan and I used to hide our stash." It took some muscle to get the square plaque to budge where he could get a good grip on it. But once the panel came loose, Jackson stared at the hole. "Shine the light in there for me, Tessa."

Tessa pointed the beam into the black cranny. "There's something back there all right."

Jackson heaved the solid mass of stone toward Garret, dropping it into his hands. "Hold onto this."

"Sure," he groaned, taking the weight and trying to keep from dropping the block of granite on his toes.

Without the stone in the way, it left a cubbyhole that wasn't so empty. There was an old, brown leather attaché case crammed toward the back. The well-worn briefcase showed its age, frayed around the flap, possibly from years of lugging it around from place to place. The flap carried a Nazi emblem, along with the name Klaus Mühlhauser engraved on the clasp.

Mitch breathed out an air of shock. "How did we get here? In a million years I'd've never thought to look in the Hollister crypt for Hugo's papers."

Jackson handed the messenger bag to Mitch. "Open it up."

From her position at the doorway, Raine cleared her throat. "Uh, guys, if I might make a suggestion. Could we maybe do this somewhere else? Let's go back to my place where the lighting's a lot better and I'm not waiting for Sinclair to bust us on some trumped up charge."

Anniston spoke up. "I'm all for that. I'm not spending the night in jail for robbing a grave. My vote is we get the hell out of here before someone finds out we've been inside this place."

Back on the houseboat, Raine put on a pot of coffee while they examined what looked like a lawyer's bag. After they'd spread the contents out on the table, Raine watched Mitch paw through the papers like a cat playing with a mouse.

"A lot of people died for what's in that briefcase," Raine pointed out.

Garret latched onto several pairs of Nazi dog tags. "This is just like what Hugo slash Dietrich described to us, the stuff he was looking for. I've wondered why he was so forthright. He could've easily lied to us about the documents and made something else up. I mean, Dietrich was play-acting the whole time we knew him, pretending to be someone else. And here we are staring at just about everything he mentioned."

Mitch picked up a pay book belonging to the man named Klaus Mühlhauser, flipped through the pages. "This would be pretty damning for anyone. There's proof here that one Mühlhauser named Walter was an SS officer who spent time working at Belzec, Poland. The higher ups put him in charge of exterminations beginning in March 1942."

Garret got out his phone to search the Internet for more information. "The SS killed a half million Jews during the time that camp was open. Only seven laborers walked out of there alive before the Nazis dismantled it in 1943." He looked out at the massive pile on the table. "Why wouldn't you get rid of this stuff? Why keep it around?"

"Who knows? Pride in what he'd done for the Führer," Mitch noted, holding up a photograph of two young boys, arms outstretched in the Hitler salute. "But you've got to hand it to the fascist regime, they were anal retentive about their recordkeeping."

Raine bit her lip. "Just look at this, various ID cards in the same name, Mühlhauser, along with a slew of family pictures showing two young boys who look like twins to me, with a man dressed in his SS uniform."

"Apparently all this belongs to Dietrich's family. There are passports using the Mühlhauser name and logbooks from U-boat 492. But I don't see anything here that mentions the names Dietrich or Reiner."

"Which is why I suggested those names were likely made up and chosen by the two men after the war," Anniston noted. "Mühlhauser was probably Dietrich's family surname back in Germany. Once his father reached

South America he created another ID, started using that. The Mühlhauser son eventually became Werner Dietrich."

"What I'd like to know is how Dietrich and Reiner knew each other. What's their connection?" Jackson pondered.

"The answer's here somewhere," Garret said. "Look around. This pile of stuff alone would certainly be enough to prove beyond a doubt Dietrich's personal link to the Nazis and the role the father played at Belzec. Not a particularly proud moment for someone who had taken great lengths to distance his family's history in order to make millions in business."

Raine picked up the photograph of the two young twins with their soldier father. "This must've been taken during the height of the war." She flipped the picture over and read what was written on the back. "Someplace called Dinkelsbühl in 1944." Raine kept staring at the picture. "Are you sure Reiner and Dietrich weren't related? Could they be the brothers, the boys depicted in this photo?"

Garret used his phone again for a search. "Dinkelsbühl is a town roughly five hundred and thirty kilometers south of Berlin, which equates to three hundred and thirty miles. Maybe that was Dietrich's hometown. Maybe both men came from there."

Mitch exchanged long stares with his brothers then looked over at Anniston. "Is there any way to get your friend in the coroner's office, Chuck, to send you a picture of the body found near Sugarloaf Key? If the man looks similar to Dietrich, then we've just figured out how Hugo Reiner came by all these documents."

He laid a hand on the scattered mess on the table. "This is from his family's history. If the men shared a father, then maybe that's why the mother finally took the trip to South America, in search of him. She wanted to see Werner, a long lost son, one last time before she died."

"But if Hugo and Dietrich had the same father, then why make up a story about U-boat 492?" Jackson pointed out. "Hugo's father couldn't have been both an SS colonel at Belzec, Poland, *and* a young lieutenant on a German sub."

Mitch scratched his chin. "Yeah, I agree that's a problem. And it just means we need to use the diary to solve another level of the puzzle."

Raine brought over more coffee, refilled mugs. "There has to be a reason Walter Mühlhauser was given a ride on that sub. Not just any SS officer could simply take off for Brazil whenever he felt like it."

"Which means the connection had to be solid," Mitch stated. "No one's gonna take a risk like that for anyone who isn't family or—"

"A significant amount of money exchanges hands," Raine finished.

"Exactly. Now we just need the professor to get here and decipher what's in that diary."

Chapter Eight

Once everyone cleared out for the night, Mitch reached over to Raine, captured her hand in his, and brought her onto his lap. "I thought they'd never leave us alone."

She framed his face. "It's been a very long day. We should get some sleep. After that walk through the cemetery, I don't think I want you to leave me alone tonight."

"When will you know for sure?"

For an answer, she touched her lips to his. "I'm sure."

With open mouths, they tasted each other, sampling all that arousal offered while it built to stirring need.

Acting on that alone, he savored the taste of her, juicy like a mango, just peeled.

She welcomed his mouth on hers as he ran his hands up and down her back. She drew him up and out of the chair and through the house to the bedroom. The entire way they were kicking out of their shoes, wrestling for position.

"I want to rip your clothes off, but after what you've been through maybe we should wait. I know what you said earlier. But I won't hold you to it unless you're absolutely sure."

She stopped, held him at arm's length. "Are you trying to back out now? After getting me all worked up you've changed your mind? You don't want to be with me?"

"My God, how could you say that, how could you think it? I want you more than I did when I was sixteen and that was a lot."

"Aww." She shoved him back against the bedroom door. "That's all I needed to know. Go ahead, tear my clothes off because I know exactly what you can do with those hands of yours, and that mouth."

With his teeth nipping at her throat, he echoed his skill set. "I remember all the things you like, detail by little detail." Slipping off her top, he worked on releasing the catch to her bra and filled his hands with small, firm breasts.

She dropped her head back, as his hands found their mark at the curve of her breast. His roaming mouth made her blood ignite. "Ahh. That's a sweet way to a girl's heart. Remembering what she likes from a dozen years ago. Not fair."

Stopping long enough to lay his hand over his chest, he declared, "You rip my heart out, Raine. You always have."

"I don't mean to. On second thought, maybe I do." She latched onto his face, ran her tongue to his throat. "This has to be better than that time we did it on my mom's kitchen floor. Remember that?"

"Hard floor, you on top, every minute. We had the house to ourselves for an entire weekend. As I recall your mother had taken Danny and your grandmother down to Ramrod Key."

"And your parents were out of town for your cousin's wedding."

She established her ground, or tried to. But by the time he reached to peel off her shorts and toss them over his head, heat had taken over. Her eyes danced with need. "I hate to admit it but it's been a long time for me, a really long time."

"Same here."

"You're kidding?"

"You're surprised at that? Why?"

"More like shocked."

He rested his head on hers. "What is it you think I do? Steer my boat into port to get laid every time the urge hits me?"

She rolled out a belly laugh. "You mean you don't? Actually that's exactly what I pictured you'd do."

Her burst of laughter warmed his heart. "You obviously don't know the dedicated treasure hunter I've become."

She heaved off his T-shirt, ran her hands up his toned muscles. "I don't remember these. You have a nice set of abs now."

"A working man puts on more muscle than a scrawny high school kid, which is what I was the last time we did this," he pointed out, his mouth lingering along her curves.

She loosened the button on his jeans, slid her hands inside, watched as he shoved out of the pants.

His hands journeyed down to her hips before he boosted her up off the floor.

She threw her legs around his waist.

"You're still just a little bitty thing, hardly weigh a hundred pounds I bet."

"And you're still six-two." She ran her fingers over every inch of his massive shoulders. "You know I practice yoga these days. I'm a lot more limber than I used to be."

Naked, they sunk into the mattress as he planted little kisses along her throat. He glided his lips to a breast, beaded and budded, perfect for coaxing out to play.

She quivered, little jolts dancing along her nerves, as his mouth tightened around a nipple.

"Let me know if my weight is too heavy."

"Shut up, Mitch. I don't remember you talking this much."

He scooted to the end of the bed, began to track her body beginning with her tiny feet. He trailed little kisses over her toes, up to her ankle, along the calf to the back of her knee. He licked along her thigh, skimming slowly, slowly, toward the center, ripe and pink for the taking.

She rose up, her back in an arch. She threaded fervent fingers through his hair, tumbled into the lazy pleasure, spinning with red-hot heat. He kept building on sensations she'd forgotten existed, battering through to the edge like a hurricane wielding its force.

Blind need had her bursting toward the white hot eye of the storm, under a long stream of swirling heat that spiraled on and on.

Mitch pinned her to the mattress, thrusting through sizzling reds, plunging into aching, throbbing blues. Limbs tangled. Setting a rhythm, fast and hard, he wrapped her up, biting back his own need.

Their slick bodies hammered out a familiar rhythm. Relentless pleasure stoked a fire within her. She called out his name. Like a melody it bounced off the walls and drew him in and up.

Over her head, their fingers curled together, seeking, touching, reaching out for that melodious bond. They hit the first notes, strong and bold, like Beethoven's Ninth, starting out bone-slow before building, igniting into its brilliant tempo.

Need coiled and snapped. It raged along slippery lines that shattered through both of them until the pleasure unfurled like gold-ribbon lace, burnished long and deep, etched in a fanciful scroll.

Mitch raised his head to peer at the rippling moonlight dancing through the window. He noticed she saw it, too. It was the first thing their eyes drifted to when they came up for air.

"So many times I looked up at that moon and wondered where you were, what you were doing," Raine told him.

"I did the same. We let so many years go by," Mitch admitted as he brought her into his arms, placed a kiss on the top of her sunny crop of hair. "Do you remember that time we snuck off and spent the whole day on Ramrod Key? We had the little house there all to ourselves."

"Wait. Wasn't that the very first time we had sex?"

"It was. I think about that little house all the time, the way it was just the two of us, like we were the only two people who existed in the world."

"You never told me that," she said, staring into his soulful eyes.

"I was too young to know my heart, Raine. Back then, I was just too young to appreciate what I had, who you were, what I wanted from you. I'm sorry if I wasn't the man you wanted me to be back then."

She pressed her lips to his. "You were a boy, hardly a man. We were in such a hurry to experience everything about each other, I guess neither one of us took the time to find out what the other one wanted or what we expected from each other."

"I know what I want now. I want you in my life."

"What are you saying? Where are we going with this, Mitch? We're still the same two people at odds over the same thing. You know I can't leave and you can't stay. Maybe we should just enjoy each other while we can."

He cocked a brow, questioning that attitude. "Is that enough for you? To be without me when I'm gone for long periods at a time? It's not enough for me, Raine."

She let out a low sigh. "I'm too tired to process this right now. Nothing will change the fact I have to be here to take care of my mother and you have to leave."

He tightened his hold on her. "So this is all we'll ever have? I'm not ready to accept that."

She patted his chest. "Get some sleep. I'm no longer that silly teenage girl looking for forever after."

He closed his eyes, wishing he still had a chance with that naïve girl he'd left in the dust. As he fell into sleep, he longed for another time and place.

Chapter Nine

The next morning Mitch woke to the smell of bacon. When he stretched out his arm across the bed, he realized he was alone. Reluctantly he swung his legs to the floor, all the while sniffing the air. Even though his stomach rumbled with hunger, he had something else on his mind.

Grabbing his jeans, he shoved into them and went out into the living room with the express intent to coax Raine back into bed.

That idea died on the vine when he spotted Tessa and Anniston already sitting at the kitchen table. He rubbed his hand across his bare chest in a self-conscious gesture. But his eyes landed on Raine. She wore a sundress the color of spring, a hint of soft green peppered with little chocolate flowers.

"Ladies. I didn't know anyone else was here. I didn't hear you get here or come in."

"You were sacked out," Raine explained as she plated a golden waffle for Anniston. "Come, sit down, have breakfast."

Tessa stifled a giggle as Mitch dashed back in the bedroom to retrieve his T-shirt. "I guess we put a crimp in his morning plans."

Raine loaded more batter into the waffle iron. "Probably. But neither one of us got much sleep last night."

Anniston bit into her strip of bacon. "It never occurred to me I'd fall for a guy who lives in Hawaii. We're still trying to work out the logistics of that *and* him getting back on the circuit at some point while still trying to build our relationship. Life is complicated."

Raine gnawed on a piece of toast. "You'd move to Hawaii?"

Anniston raised one shoulder. "Honestly, he's talked about coming back here. I think he plans to rent out his house in Oahu and live in Florida. I could easily live on the Key as long as we clean up the scum here first."

"You mean Indigo Key? Really?" Raine said in surprise. "That's interesting. I thought you were rooted down in Miami with your family."

The private detective sent her a wry smile. "I did, too. But life has a way of throwing up a roadblock when you least expect it. Like I said, complications."

"That's true. I can tell you I never thought I'd live anywhere other than Nags Head," Tessa acknowledged as she forked up a bite of her waffle. "Jackson and I are thinking about settling here for real in his grandmother's little cottage."

"What about his job in New York?"

"I don't think he wants to go back and pick up where he left off. He's talking about trying for a teaching job with one of the local colleges around here or applying to the state to study marine ecosystems on one of the ongoing watershed projects. It's kind of surreal the way our relationship has taken off. It's happening so fast."

Raine patted Tessa on the shoulder and pointed her spatula at the man rounding the corner of the living room for the second time that morning. "Tell me about it. Surreal is a good word that fits. Just look who I spent the night with last night. Who'd've thought we could be in the same bed together without killing each other? Now that's the very definition of surreal."

Mitch stood a few feet away, fully dressed, his lips curved in a wide grin. He went over and planted a kiss on Raine's mouth. He sniffed the air. "I think you've turned into a chef extraordinaire."

"Not really. But I enjoy cooking." Raine poured more orange juice, freshly squeezed, from a pitcher into a glass for him and took a seat. "Anniston's lined up the translator for the diary. He's agreed to meet all of us at your mother's house at two this afternoon. I've arranged for Charlotte to work what amounts to a double shift so I can be there. She isn't happy about it."

"This is hard on you," Mitch said in realization.

"No harder than it is on everyone else."

He stared at her. "If I ask you something, will you tell me the truth."

"Of course," Raine replied, curious as to where he was headed.

"This sounds serious," Anniston noted, getting to her feet. "Maybe Tessa and I should leave you two alone."

Tessa took the hint and stood up with her plate. "Thanks for breakfast, especially after we just dropped in on you this morning. We'll see you at Lenore's later."

Raine waved off any inconvenience. "I enjoyed having you stop by. We should do it again, maybe another girls' night out."

After the two women rinsed off their dishes and took off, Raine stared at Mitch. "You really know how to clear a room. What gives? After last night I thought you'd be in a good mood."

"I am in a good mood. I just wanted to know if you're happy running the restaurant. It's a simple question."

"Why wouldn't I be? Happy is a relative state of mind anyway and doesn't actually exist."

"You're evading."

"Are you trying to pick a fight with me? It's really too early in the morning for that. Eat your breakfast before it gets cold."

He picked up his fork. "I'm not picking a fight. And you're avoiding giving me a straight answer. Are you happy working six days a week there?"

"Who else is going to do it, Mitch? In case you've forgotten, my mother is a—"

"Your mom is a functioning alcoholic," he finished. "I'm aware of that."

"Obviously you haven't been around her lately. She's not that functional. She sits on the couch all day swigging down vodka, watching her TV programs with my seventy-six-year-old grandmother, and basically, acting as if she's waiting around to die. At least that's how it seems to me. By six o'clock every evening she's usually passed out. Since Danny died she's given up on living. She barely leaves the house. That's why I was so shocked she actually went to the memorial service the other day."

"You mean she doesn't even go out to shop?"

"Are you kidding me? I order her groceries once a week, usually the same time I place my order for the restaurant, and have them deliver the order directly to her house. Otherwise, I'm not sure she'd keep any food on hand, certainly nothing that's nutritious. My grandmother once told me she went fourteen hours without eating after Mom locked her in her room. If I don't stay on top of the situation who knows what'll happen."

"That's not good. Your grandmother Mimi was always pretty cool. So you've basically been dealing with this for years now, stuck here taking care of your mom and grandma and working at the restaurant full-time. Is it what you want out of life, Raine?"

She moved her shoulder up and down. "What else do I have to do?"

"What do you want to do?"

She sent him a look, raised her eyebrows up and down. "I'd like to get you in my bed again as soon as possible. Having you here, like this, is a luxury for me."

"Nice segue into changing the subject." He stared at the short dress she wore that showed off her tanned legs. The sight had him revving up, so he ran his hand along her satiny shoulder. "But I'm not complaining."

Raine managed to roll out a giggle when he started pulling her to him. The laugh morphed into a satisfying breath as he slowly slid down the straps on her sundress, exposing bare skin. He kept peeling fabric away until she was naked to the waist. His hungry mouth fed at her breast.

And the room went into a spin for her. She wanted him, every part of him. "Hurry. Hurry. I want your hands on me."

"Whoa. Maybe we should slow this tidal wave down."

"Tidal wave? More like a tsunami," she uttered, spreading little kisses along his throat.

His laughter rang out like a song while his rough hands splayed along her flesh. "We always seemed to be rushing headlong into sex."

She stopped long enough to stare at him. "You're complaining about having sex? That's a new one. What have you done with the real Mitch Indigo?"

"I'm not complaining."

To prove it, his mouth ranged over her breasts again while the heat roared between them hotter than a beach bonfire.

Pleasure gripped her as she let him take, feed, ravage. Her fingers moved into warmth as she directed his mouth down to meet hers.

He leaned her back on the table. Plates rattled as he made room. He took her there on the flat surface while gentle waves rushed headlong against the houseboat and sunlight dappled the walls with a golden spray.

Tessa joined Anniston in the SUV to make the short drive to the cottage she shared with Jackson. "I've never seen anyone do such a one-eighty like Raine. Now those two don't seem to be able to keep their hands off each other."

"I'm not surprised. First love is always the deepest."

"Hmm, I'm not sure I ever had that kind of first love."

"Then my guess is you weren't really in love," Anniston deduced. "I've never felt anything for a man like I feel for Garret."

"That's exactly the right note with Jackson. He's unlike anyone I've ever known. Since my first boyfriend was a bit of an ass, I'd say those two, Raine and Mitch, hit the mother lode with each other as teens."

"They just didn't know it at the time."

Tessa smiled, remembering the serene look she'd seen on Raine's face. The woman had been downright placid. "Well, they're certainly making up for lost time now."

After a round of shower sex, Raine got ready for work by throwing on a pair of jeans and a tank top.

She was dragging a brush through her hair when she picked up her cell phone and heard her mother's meandering voice mail messages. "Oh, God."

"What's wrong?"

"My mother's upset that Maddie and Charlotte had to work double shifts yesterday because I wasn't there."

"You're kidding? But she knows you didn't get back on island until last night. She knows you were abducted."

"I think somehow she missed the importance of that."

"That's nuts."

"Now you're beginning to see my point."

There was some discussion about Mitch tagging along to watch over her at the restaurant during her shift.

"Bodyguard," she spat out, the word bringing full distaste at the notion of having him underfoot all day. "I can take care of myself."

"Be reasonable," he began. "You got kidnapped and used as a bargaining chip. Or have you forgotten already?"

"That's just it. I'm the one who got drugged and woke up woozy, sick at my stomach and terrified. I'm not letting that happen again. Trust me on that."

"Trusting you isn't the problem…"

"You can't babysit me every second of every day. I'm more aware now of how unsafe we all are. Besides, Anniston dropped off a can of pepper spray this morning." She held it up for him to see. "And Tessa gave me a pink keychain shaped like a kitty-cat with really sharp, pointy ears to use as a weapon." She pulled that out of her purse and dangled it in front of his face. "So you see, I'll be fine because I'm just going straight to the restaurant."

"Raine, I'm not letting you out of my sight and that's final."

"Humor me. At least allow me the pretense of doing this without a guard dog at my elbow."

He blew out a long sigh. "You know I'll just hang back and follow you, so there's really not much you can do about it."

He bent down, kissed her forehead. "Then I'll be across the street watching if you need me."

"As funny as that sounds—you waiting by the curb like Magnum PI—you're not babysitting me in broad daylight."

The argument had gone on for another ten minutes before Raine gave in. It wasn't easy giving up control, but it did give her some comfort, knowing her lover was nearby. Her lover. What a concept that was.

"But I'm driving," she insisted. "My car hasn't been started in a couple of days anyway. It needs TLC a little more often than it used to."

"Danny's roadster always was finicky. It's all the humidity on island. It makes the carburetor stick."

But when she went outside to the marina parking lot to crank up the engine, the Fiat refused to turn over. "Come on, I'm only going four blocks, surely you have that much mileage left in you," she mumbled under her breath.

Mitch got out to fiddle under the hood. "You really need a new car."

"Don't start. Just get it started for me, will you?"

It took him less than five minutes to judge the car wasn't going anywhere. "Your spark plugs are shot. When's the last time you had this thing looked at, or at least had the oil changed?"

"Really? You're lecturing me now about auto maintenance? Want me to head over to Baskin's shop, let him fix all that ails it?"

"Baskin's not the only mechanic in town, just the loudest braggart. Take it over to Clay Don Bigelow's. Clay has a repair shop just down the street next to his fueling station. He's cheaper, doesn't bitch about working on foreign cars, and will probably give you a discount. Plus, there's the bonus because you won't have to deal with Baskin."

"Fine. How do I get it there?"

He took out his cell phone. "Hi Clay, it's Mitch Indigo. I need a tow. Can you help me out?" After several minutes, he hung up. "He'll be here in ten minutes."

True to his word, Clay Don's tow truck pulled up, a twenty-year-old, fire-engine red Ford Super Duty with the name Bigelow's printed in gold lettering on the side.

Clay Don bounded out of the cab of the truck, wearing a light blue mechanic's shirt sporting grease stains and a pair of well-worn dark blue pants with more than a few oil spots.

She'd gone to school with him back when he played centerfield for the Indigo Iguanas. He'd been married for the last ten years to Gabby Pittman, a cheerleader from days of old, and had two little boys. Raine usually saw the family once a week, eating out, as they made it a point to come in for tacos on Tuesday nights.

She caught the knowing look Clay Don gave Mitch and turned to see why. Mitch wore a full, satisfied grin on his face. She wasn't sure if it revealed they'd had down and dirty sex less than an hour earlier, or the fact that he'd been right about the stupid state of the car. Before she could react to either notion, Clay Don cleared up the why.

"Well, well, well. I see you two finally patched things up. 'Bout time if you ask me. What's a matter with the old girl today, Raine?"

"You better be talking about this piece of crap car," Raine shot back, lips curving up. "Wherever Hudley Slocum is he must be laughing his ass off at the Mannings."

"Now you know I was referring to your 'snickety wheels here," the mechanic said as he rounded the hood. "Mitch here says she's overdue for spark plugs."

"*She's* overdue for a rest home," Raine snapped, wondering how many minutes it would take for the whole town to realize she was sleeping with Mitch again. If Clay Don caught on in less than five minutes—and he'd never been the brightest bulb on the tree—how long would it take for everyone else to know?

Living in a small town could be a major pain in the butt.

"Might as well change out the carburetor while you're at it," Mitch noted. "And put on new brake pads. Send me the bill."

After realizing that Mitch seemed to be taking over after less than twenty-four hours, it didn't take much to push Raine's temper into lava-mode. It wasn't lost on her that she'd been in such a good mood until she'd picked up the damn phone and heard her mother's messages. So having Mitch offer to pay for her car repairs was the final straw. It sent her over the edge, icing the morning's crappy turn of events. "Oh, no you don't. I'm perfectly capable of paying to fix my own car."

"You guys work this out amongst yourselves," Clay Don declared as he began to hook up the Fiat to the Ford. "But there's no denying she needs some fixin' or you'll get stranded somewhere and be on foot. Might as well do it all while I've got her in the shop."

"Fine," Raine muttered. "Let me pour another six hundred dollars into the care and feeding of Danny's old car."

Some twenty minutes later, still feeling a little loose, a little dirty, she sailed through the doors at The Blue Taco on a fantastic high, a lighter step to her walk. She didn't want to get sappy or anything about what had happened earlier with Mitch. But at the same time, she could appreciate the mind-numbing sex going down on her kitchen table. Which was probably the result of doing without for so long, she mused.

Thankful her drought was over, and with a certain amount of sexy images and thoughts still spinning around in her head, she strolled to the kitchen and took out the ingredients to make today's special—pork tamales.

Before her harrowing ordeal with Duarte, she'd already simmered a pork shoulder with plenty of zesty seasonings until the meat became a mouthwatering treat and fall-apart tender. It was a dish she'd perfected.

Despite her absence, she had her longtime cook, Maddie Denham, to thank for picking up the slack where she'd left off.

But right now there was the masa to throw together. She was in the process of filling up a commercial food processor with the flour and shortening mixture when she heard the back door open behind her. Thinking it must be Mitch, she was surprised to see Maddie standing in the doorway.

"What are you doing here so early?"

Maddie, a longtime single mom who'd raised two kids running her own hamburger dive back in her native Memphis, answered in an overworked, Tennessee drawl, "I wanted to see for myself that you were okay." Maddie rushed around the prep island to wrap her up in a hug.

"I'm fine. Thanks to Mitch."

As if she'd conjured the man up just by saying his name, Raine looked over to see him meander into the room right behind Maddie. "What's going on here?"

Maddie sent her a sheepish look. "I found him sitting in his truck outside. No point in that when there's plenty of comfy chairs in here to plop down in. I offered him a fresh cup of coffee."

"Which I gratefully accepted," Mitch explained. "I'll stay out of the way or pitch in to help." He pointed a finger toward Raine. "Either way, don't make a fuss."

"Isn't he sweet?" Maddie uttered. "Thank goodness you brought our girl back home in one piece." The older woman held Raine at arm's length to study her face. "You look…different…somehow. Are you sure you're okay?"

Raine rolled her eyes toward Mitch and smiled. She knew she felt different. She supposed it was normal to look the part, as well. Changing the subject away from herself, she wiped her hands on her apron. "I'm fine. How'd it go yesterday without me?"

"Worried sick about you, wanted to close down, but your mama wouldn't hear of it. We had a busy night. At some point do you ever intend to hire any help? I'm gettin' old, Raine, old as your mama."

"Fifty-four is not old," Raine insisted. "But I concede the fact we're shorthanded."

On the other side of the counter, Maddie went about grinding beans for the coffee she'd promised Mitch. She raised her voice over the machine's noise so she could be heard. "I can't work these long days like I used to. You need to get someone in here who can."

Raine waited for the earsplitting sound to end. "I'm seriously considering it."

"You always say that. I remember your mama taking over this restaurant from your grandmother. Damn it, if you aren't just like both of them. Stubborn to the end, wanting to do all this by yourself. Must run in the family. Gonna work yourself to death in this place is what you're gonna do."

"That sounds like a bleak future...I hope not." This time it was Raine who paused to search Maddie's face. "Do you plan to tell me what you're doing here so early?"

"Your mama's on the warpath. She sent me over here because she said she left four voice mails for you and you haven't answered a single one." Maddie pointed a finger at Mitch. "I don't think she likes him very much."

Raine snatched up her cell phone off the counter. "I didn't realize I had it turned off. Jeez, look at all these. She called four more times since I got out of the shower, says she wants to talk to me. She also left four text messages."

"Sounds serious," Mitch commented.

"Nothing but serious with Miss Manning," Maddie admitted. "I pulled you out of your truck 'cause I know that woman is bound to give this one a hard time about something. Been doing that too long to count."

Mitch moved toward Raine. "Ah. Let me guess. It's about me. Us. I really need to keep an eye on you no matter where you go. Although I'm not sure I'm ready for the evil eye Marla's sure to give me. Maybe I'll wait out by the curb while you go in and settle this."

"Chicken," Raine charged. "I'll go talk to her later. Right now, I'm in the middle of—"

"You go on," Maddie urged. "I'll finish the masa."

"But the lunch crowd will be here in three hours. We're cutting it close as it is."

"She's making excuses," Maddie told Mitch. "Sooner you get it over with, the better."

"Fine. But I'm not ready for a fight this early in the morning."

"You didn't have a problem fighting with me less than an hour ago," Mitch pointed out.

She shot him a look. "All of a sudden I feel pushed around. Okay, Maddie's right. The sooner I get this over with the sooner I can get things back on track."

Mitch knew better than to tread further into deeper water as he headed over to Marla Manning's place. He veered to the curb in front of a stylish Cape Cod and cut the engine. One glance at Raine told him she didn't want to get out of the truck. Her fidgety hands and body language were dead giveaways to the cold relationship she'd always had with her mother.

He squeezed one of the nervous hands. "I'll be right out here waiting for you when you're ready to leave."

"Thanks. I don't know why I dread this so much. Maybe because I know exactly what she'll say."

"I've got a boat and crew just waiting to whisk you away from all this."

That made her laugh. She took a deep breath and grudgingly opened the door.

He watched her walk up the flagstone pathway to the front porch and mumbled to himself, "Oh baby, for the next thirty minutes, I don't envy you at all."

Raine found her mother sitting on the sun porch at the back of the house. She could remember growing up here, believing her mom looked a little like Carole Lombard, the actress she'd watched so many times gracing the small screen on late-night TV.

Marla Manning had that same blond hair, a petite frame, and haunting, soulful hazel eyes that said deep emotions were just a scratch away from the surface.

Growing up in a household without a father, Raine knew how hard her single mom had worked, sometimes keeping the restaurant going in spite of major staffing problems. There were always folks coming and going, working for short periods of time before moving on for one reason or another, leaving Marla shorthanded and in the lurch. Then there were the battles with unscrupulous wholesalers, who raised prices without warning or unreliable vendors who couldn't meet delivery requirements. Problems came with the job and occurred on a weekly basis.

Raine had always respected that about her mother. But she'd also witnessed Marla's tendency to throw a tantrum when things weren't going well. As manipulative as any diva who'd ever walked across a theater stage, Marla could be one part actress, overly dramatic, and two-thirds controlling. There were times her mother could be unreasonable and overtly cruel.

Her grandmother Mimi had once told her it was for that reason her father had left Marla and never looked back. There was a part of Raine that couldn't blame him too much for seeking his freedom.

Because Marla had taken over the reins at the restaurant from Mimi, Raine had grown up watching both women deal with the headaches of running their own business. Her grandmother had even tried to play referee over the years to settle a dispute between mother and daughter. But Marla usually ended up getting her way because Raine would give in.

By the time Raine and Danny were old enough to carry a plate of food without dropping it, the two had worked there after school, or after whatever extracurricular activities they'd been allowed to join. Rain or shine, the business always came first.

Once school was out for the summer, the kids were expected to do their fair share of work bussing tables, washing dishes, and taking out trash. While other teens were out on the water surfing or lounging at the beach, Raine and Danny had worked side by side ringing up orders or doing prep work in the kitchen.

From that side of things, The Blue Taco was very much a family-oriented business. That is, until Danny decided to buck his mother and join the army.

All hell had broken loose at the news. Marla had not been happy about his decision. In fact, the woman had taken to her bed, devastated but determined one way or another to change his mind. But to Raine's amazement, no amount of drama or guilt or manipulation tactics on Marla's part could alter Danny's mindset.

Raine had always known her mother favored Danny. There was never any doubt about that. It was just the way it was and Raine had long ago accepted her place in the hierarchy, or lack thereof. When Danny played sports, Marla never missed a game. Whether it was baseball or basketball or football, Danny could count on Marla to show up and cheer him on. When Raine competed in the district volleyball championship, Danny had been the only family member who bothered coming to watch. Of course, Mitch had been there, rooting her on from the sidelines. He'd always supported her no matter what.

But to Marla Manning, where Danny was concerned, Raine could never quite measure up. And when he didn't return from Afghanistan, Marla simply decided she didn't want to have anything more to do with the restaurant, any more than she wanted to do with her daughter.

Without warning, Marla had announced her retirement, anointing Raine the new successor to the taco throne.

The day of Danny's funeral, Raine had watched her mother pick up a bottle of vodka and the woman had been drinking strong ever since, waiting, it seemed, for death to find her just like it had found her son.

The solarium, as Marla referred to the sun porch, was awash in light when Raine walked in through the French doors. The room had high ceilings and a concrete floor painted pale blue. Done in white wicker and rattan furniture, the look pulled off a tropical feel with a pop of striped teals and beiges.

"It's about time you got here. What took you so long? I know how you love to ignore my voice mails and text messages."

"That isn't true, even though you did leave several of each," Raine stated bluntly. "For your information my car wouldn't start. I got here as soon as I could."

"Ah, that explains why I didn't hear you drive up. The muffler on that Fiat makes too much racket. You should get it fixed or get rid of the damn thing."

"I thought you'd appreciate my keeping it around."

"Why is that? Because it's a reminder to me that I'll never see my precious boy again? Why not drive it off a cliff or let it float down to Cuba in the tides. What's it to me?"

Raine clenched her jaw. "You said you wanted to talk, so talk."

"Don't use that tone with me, young lady. For your information Marachelle Fordham called me last night to tell me you've taken up with Mitchell Indigo again. She says she saw you two making out on the wharf last night."

"Oh, for God's sakes," Raine began. "I'm a grown woman. If I want to make out on the stage at the amphitheater in front of the entire town, I think I'm entitled to make my own choices."

"Like you did when you were eighteen? Is that right? Did you think I wouldn't find out? I thought you couldn't stand to be around that man. My friends are beginning to talk."

"I didn't know you had friends."

"Don't you get smart with me, Raine Manning."

"How come Marachelle Fordham didn't gossip about me getting kidnapped? Or weren't you going to bring that up?"

"See, that's exactly what I'm talking about. Mitch has been back less than a month and he's already got you deep into some horrible situation. Kidnapped indeed. I'm telling you that man's no good."

"Is that the reason you destroyed all his letters he wrote me? You knew I was waiting to hear from him. You knew how I felt. Did you purposely set out to beat me to the mailbox every day? How could you do that?"

Marla's face, puffy from the vodka she'd binged on the night before, turned pale. But she straightened her shoulders at the accusation. "I did what I thought was best for my willful teenage daughter, who seemed determined to screw up her life. I wasn't going to sit around and watch you throw away your life on the likes of Mitch Indigo, the sailor, or whatever he claims to be, when he left you without a backward glance. Or don't you remember all the pain he caused you?"

"Oh, I remember because you wouldn't let me forget." Those painful months came rushing back to Raine in vivid color. But this time the resentment wasn't aimed at Mitch, but at her mother.

"That's because he left you when you were eighteen and pregnant. I can't believe you act as though it never happened."

"It's hard to forget when you toss it in my face every other month."

"So you don't make the same mistake ever again, that's why. I do it for you."

"Right. Well, I guess it's time I set the record straight. Mitch didn't know about the baby, okay? Mitch didn't know I was pregnant when he boarded the freighter and took off to see the world."

Marla narrowed her eyes that glazed over in fury. "But you said he did. Are you changing your story twelve years after the fact, trying to protect him now?"

"No, I'm not protecting him. I don't even know what I'd be protecting him from exactly. I was eighteen, hurt and furious with him," Raine explained. "I'm pretty sure it's the way immature teenage girls act when they've been dumped."

"He's no good for you, Raine."

"How do you know that?"

"He hurt you once, he'll do it again."

"If he does, that's my business, not yours."

"You always were my difficult child."

Raine huffed out a breath. "I know you think that. But I'm the one still here, trying to do the right thing by you and getting nowhere."

"Surely you wouldn't put me through something like that again, would you? Don't you dare get pregnant again! The gossip I had to endure, the nasty things people said about me behind my back, raising such a promiscuous little girl who didn't have the sense to keep her legs closed."

Raine's eyes tapered to slits as she stared down her mother. "You're such a mean drunk, Mom. I didn't realize you thought so little of me and to what degree you'd been maligned all those years ago. But it seems to me only you and Mrs. Fordham are the ones doing the gossiping. I suddenly realize how little I care that you or anyone else is talking about me. Big deal. What I can't figure out is why you begrudge me a small sliver of normal, a slice of happiness? What is it with you, Mom? What did I ever do to you that made you dislike me so much? I've known for years Danny was your favorite. Why? What did I do? Why was I never good enough for you?"

"Don't you speak to me like that!" Marla screamed.

"Oh wow, enter the drama queen." Raine decisively glanced at her watch. "And it only took fifteen minutes for that side of you to emerge. Look, I run myself ragged keeping the restaurant going. I've been here for you whenever you needed me. Haven't I?"

"That's beside the point. I don't want you falling for that man's lies all over again and him pushing you into running off with him. I mean, if you left, who would run the restaurant? I'd have no one I could trust."

"Ah, I see. In other words, you don't want to lose your able-bodied, reliable manager who shows up on time every day and gets the job done. Unless of course someone abducts me off the street. I got it. I'm well aware you and Mimi need me around, so I'll stay here in Indigo Key and do my duty as your daughter. But don't expect anything more from me, okay? I'm done with you taking me for granted and being your slave. I'm done with you treating me like dirt compared to the way you acted toward Danny when he was alive. So I'll run your restaurant for you and do a good job like I've always done. But don't expect anything more from me. Got it?"

With that, she all but ran out of the house.

As soon as Mitch caught sight of her, one look at her face, her arms tightly wrapped around her body, told him it hadn't gone well. But then it never seemed to go well with Marla.

"Are you okay?"

"Just get me out of here."

Chapter Ten

Mitch helped Raine work through a busy lunch crowd. But he no longer had to ask if she was happy. He already knew the answer.

After spending the night together, they'd started the day on a high, only to have Marla literally suck the air out of the happiness Raine had felt.

It pissed him off. He wasn't sure who he was angrier at, Marla or himself. Why hadn't he been able to pick up on how unhappy she'd acted over the years, the years he'd returned for a simple, quick visit? He'd accepted her antagonism toward him and totally ignored the rest. He'd known the woman for most of his life. He should've been able to use that to understand how deep her bitterness ran and to whom she'd directed it at besides him.

He'd seen the joy on her face when he'd made love to her. It had given him his own sense of well-being to know he'd been responsible for putting it there.

Dealing with Marla's disapproval had to sting. For the past three hours, he'd watched Raine morph back to the irritable, grumpy manager of a taco stand with too many demanding customers to deal with and a fast-paced environment that provided little downtime. Not to mention an angry, alcoholic mother stewing about their relationship.

He'd be damned if he let Marla win the day with that one.

As the clock ticked toward two in the afternoon and their meeting with the professor, Mitch pulled Charlotte aside. "Take over for Raine, will you?"

"Sure. The crowd's dying down anyway."

He found Raine in the kitchen, dishing up rice and beans. "It's time to go, baby."

"I'm ready, just let me finish this order."

Twenty minutes later, Mitch opened the door at his parents' house to a welcoming committee of sorts. His mother greeted Raine by throwing her arms around her shoulders in a big hug.

"Get in here, baby girl. Thank goodness you're back home safe and sound." She held the younger woman's chin, giving her a serious motherly once-over. "Did they hurt you?"

"Just scared me half to death is all."

"Aww, honey, I'm so sorry you had to go through something like that. Jackson said it was Sinclair who did it. The bastard got caught on tape."

"Yes, but he isn't in jail yet. I won't rest until I see him locked up."

"Give Sebastian time and he'll get the state police down here. We're just grateful you're okay. Come on in here and get settled. I'm sending Mitch off to make hors d'oeuvres."

Mitch looked baffled "Me? Why me?"

"Because you've logged some valuable time in the restaurant business lately. That should come in handy for some tasty appetizers." His mother gave him a firm poke in the ribs. "Now show me what you've got."

Raine watched the grown man slink off to the kitchen, grumbling. "I guess you already know your son made a deal to save me. I owe him big time."

"He gave us a heads up once the whole thing was over and he was headed back home with you on board. But we started walking the floor with worry as soon as Tessa said you didn't show up at work. From that point on, my boys kept us in the loop."

Raine laughed and hugged her one more time, deciding this woman was so unlike her own mother. "Lenore, there ought to be more moms like you."

Mitch came in carrying a tray loaded down with cheese and crackers.

Lenore put her hands on her hips and eyed her son. "Really? That's the best you could come up with? I thought we discussed earlier about serving those little parmesan cheese straws with my marinara sauce."

He grinned, leaned over to plant a kiss on his mother's cheek. "The sauce out of a jar I could handle. But I'm no good at making pastry and you know it."

He angled his head toward Raine, pressing his lips to hers. "Everyone's waiting for the professor. He called Anniston to say he's running late. So have a cracker."

Raine patted his cheek. "I could work on rolling out that dough for you."

"Now see what you did?" Mitch charged, sending a playful look toward his mother. "Now she wants to help make cheese straws after getting kidnapped and standing on her feet all morning dishing out tamales."

Lenore shook her head, clucked her tongue. She turned Raine around by her shoulders toward the sofa. "Absolutely none of that for you. Get off your feet, settle in on the couch. We're all so anxious for that professor to get started on the diary we're running around here on pins and needles." The last was said as she took off for the kitchen.

"Your mother's a true wonder," Raine stated.

"She's a bit of a perfectionist, goes well with her bookkeeper mentality, I think. You watch, she'll go in there and whip up some tasty snacks in fifteen minutes or less and serve them up with a southern drawl, probably charming our guest into working round the clock to get his job done."

Their guest turned out to be a squat fellow dressed in a cream-colored golf shirt and navy pants with glasses sitting on the bridge of his nose.

"Hollings Bishop," he announced, hurrying into the living room carrying a leather messenger bag. The man set it down and took off his rounded, John Lennon wire-rims to wipe his face with his handkerchief. "I apologize for my tardiness. I took the wrong turn off the Overseas Highway, went right instead of left. And the AC in my Volvo decided to quit working about halfway here. Humid as all get out the rest of the way here."

"It's a long way from Tallahassee. I'll get you something cold to drink," Lenore offered. "What would you like?"

"I'd love a Diet Coke if you have it, been craving one since West Palm Beach but I was too stubborn to pull over and take the time."

"No problem. Make yourself at home. Tanner will see to it you get settled." Lenore disappeared into the kitchen.

"Have a seat," Tanner said. "We'll crank up the air conditioning and get you cooled off. We thought you'd be a lot older since Anniston mentioned you were retired from teaching history."

"*German* history," Hollings corrected. "And I'm just shy of fifty-two. I gave up my job as professor at Florida State to go on sabbatical. I wanted to do some traveling to South America for research. I've been itching to write a book about what happened to so many former Nazis immediately after the war, after they took up residence in

Argentina, Paraguay, and Brazil, and how they fit into the culture there."

From across the room, Mitch and Jackson traded glances. It was Jackson who took a seat on the sofa and turned to the man they hoped could translate the papers. "In that case, this little junket to the Key might be right up your alley. There's just one thing you need to know, though."

Still wandering around the room, Mitch jangled the change in his pocket and picked up the thread. "You understand discretion is vital in this particular situation. We're paying for your time, putting you up at the hotel, which we don't mind doing. But part of the agreement is that you can't tell anyone why you're in town or what you're working on. No one. Not even if they come calling wearing a police uniform and stick out a badge."

Hollings paled. "Really? Well, okay. The woman I spoke with on the phone already faxed me a confidentiality agreement and had me sign it. I faxed it back to her a few days ago."

"That was me," Anniston chimed in, stepping into the room. "When you hear the backstory and get a look at what we have, you'll understand why we're taking so many precautions."

Lenore brought back a tray filled with food, a glass of ice, and a can of Diet Coke. "Here you go. In case you're hungry, I also brought you a batch of cheese straws still hot out of the oven and a warm red sauce for dipping, along with a piece of my homemade apple pie."

Hollings's eyes bugged out at the amount of food. "Much appreciated. I could eat."

"In this house, going hungry isn't an option," Tanner boasted.

"Where should I put my stuff?" Hollings asked, clutching the backpack he'd brought.

Tanner led him into the other room. "We'll get you settled around the dining table. Think of it as our command center."

Hollings popped the top and poured the liquid over the ice. He chugged half the contents down before setting the glass aside on the buffet. "I promise to treat this whole thing like a top-secret project. But if this diary contains even half of its potential value to history, I'll be able to tell right up front and not waste your time with worthless entries. If it does have value, I'm certainly on board with whatever steps you have in mind to keep the information secure. From this point going forward, my lips are sealed."

"We're counting on your discretion and reputation," Garret stated. "There's always the possibility we're making a fuss over a simple journal from a silly girl and we've been totally misled about the contents."

"Yes, well, we've found some other items that might be of interest…to history," Raine explained from the hallway. "We need someone like you to tell us different, someone who comes highly recommended, someone who knows his stuff."

"I know my stuff," Hollings assured her as his lips curved up. He detailed his background with pride. "I'm fluent in German, read it, as well as write it. You should probably know that my mother escaped Poland in 1939 as a baby. My grandparents went to great lengths to get out of the country by going through Switzerland. They could certainly tell you a thing or two about living under Hitler's rule and the horrors of what he could do. Through unbelievable adversity, my grandparents eventually reached the United States. By that time, the war was almost at an end. But my grandmother never seemed to be able to put the experience behind her. I won't go into the starvation and the cruelty she witnessed firsthand because I'm sure you're already aware of the hardships of that time period. Some of my grandmother's family were lost forever after being sent to death camps. She never saw them again. So I'm well versed in the history and I bring an understanding of the time period that's needed to get this job done."

"Good to know. Because after hearing me out, hearing all of us out, you're about to relive a few of those ugly reminders along the way." Mitch went into a rundown of the past few weeks, their own loss, the murders, and the dangerous situation they were still dealing with. "Having the facts at hand, if you're still interested in tackling the job, then I suggest you get comfortable before we overwhelm you with documents."

Eager to get on with it, the professor sat down at the table and dropped his backpack on the floor. "If you don't mind my saying, what you've described sounds like you're dealing with a bunch of egotistical bullies."

"I don't mind you saying. That pretty much sums up these people. They consider themselves bigwigs, rules don't apply to them, and they're very much used to getting their way." Mitch handed him the well-worn leather attaché case. "This bag contains the papers we're interested in learning more about, we've figured out some of it, but not nearly enough to do any good."

Hollings stared at the bag, itching to see what was inside.

"And this is the diary," Mitch went on. "We think, we hope, it holds a lot of the answers as to why all this happened in the first place."

Hollings turned his attention to the book, larger than a paperback, bound in frayed black leather and looking very similar to an old Bible. The professor's eyes widened at the significance of Mitch's last statement. He put his hand on the journal, left it there. "You think what's in here is the reason your sister's family was murdered?"

"We do."

To everyone's surprise, Hollings removed a pair of thin latex gloves from his satchel and slapped them on. He went after the briefcase first, gently examining the aged leather. He scrutinized it from every angle, sometimes pushing his glasses up on top of his head to get a closer look at a scratch or a dark worm spot.

He didn't even notice when Lenore refilled his Diet Coke or pushed the appetizers and pie closer at hand within his reach.

Hollings stared at the engraved flap and its faded gold lettering. The look on his face was that of pure joy, like an excited six-year-old boy opening the largest gift under the tree on Christmas morning.

He slowly, and with great care, laid the flap back on the table. Suddenly he started digging around in the knapsack he'd left on the floor. After a few seconds, he pulled out a magnifying glass that looked like it came straight out of a Sir Arthur Conan Doyle novel.

For several long minutes Hollings studied the engraving before taking a yellow pad out of his backpack and started jotting down notes. As he took out each item from the attaché case, he carefully assessed the document before making a comment on his legal pad. He did that with each item until he had emptied everything out of the case.

Once the contents were spread out on the table, he turned the bag upside down and gave it a little shake. When nothing dropped out, he gently ran his hand around the inside.

When he realized all eyes were on him, he stopped to explain. "I'm looking for a little secret compartment. These old cases all had them."

"But we've already dumped the contents out before you got here, quite a number of times. We didn't find anything other than the papers," Jackson informed him.

"We'll see," was all Hollings said as he moved his fingers back and forth several times along the lining. He put the case down and poked around in his bag again, pulling out a small, metal LED penlight. Hollings aimed the beam on the odd lump his fingers had found. It was then he showed them the small bulge in the lining. "What do we have here?"

Ever so carefully he worked the object, moving it toward the opening until a key popped out and clinked onto the table.

Hollings proclaimed his victory by holding up the key. "I knew I'd find something. The SS loved keeping their secrets hidden from view. All these cases have little pockets filled with surprises."

Garret took the key from the professor's hand and turned it over several times. "Too new to come out of the World War II era. More like 1990 to 2005, a key issued by a bank, and likely opens a safe deposit box…somewhere. See the markings along the top here. With any luck I should be able to trace it back to the bank it's associated with."

Mitch didn't see it that way. "Come on, that's gotta be to a box right here in town. Why not start down the street with Nathan's own First National Bank?"

"What am I thinking?" Raine said as she dug into her handbag and brought out her own keychain. "I have a safe deposit box at the bank. I mean, who doesn't, right?" Holding up her key, she compared it to the one in Garret's hand. "It's a match to First National."

Lenore ran to her own purse on the counter, pulled out a key that looked similar to the other two. "Here's ours. I'd say there's a good chance that key either belonged to Livvy and Walker or—"

"Our good buddy Nathan," Jackson tossed out.

"Could it be this simple?" Garret noted as he leaned over and kissed his mother's cheek. "We'll need to come up with a plan to get into the right box." He came up short as he looked over at Hollings. Somehow he didn't think the professor would appreciate the value of breaching security within a bank vault. "Later."

For now, Garret dropped the key into his pocket while Hollings went back to work.

It didn't take long before the professor leaned back in his chair. "I'm fascinated by the dog tags, the pay books, the passports, all belonging to a man named Walter

Mühlhauser. But what really impresses me the most is that someone kept all this knowing it proved the existence of an SS officer who actively worked at the extermination site in Belzec, Poland. Most officers distanced themselves from having anything to do with the death camps."

Mitch thought back to Dietrich, remembering how proud the man was of his cherished knife. "Likely a narcissist, proud of his ties to Hitler. Too arrogant to ever destroy something that reminded him of his place in history."

Hollings glanced up at Mitch. "My take exactly. These are historic, a telling piece of the puzzle to a horrific time in Germany. Thank you for letting me be part of it."

"So they are the real deal," Raine decided. "Because they looked genuine to us, but then…we aren't experts."

"Oh, they're the real deal all right," Hollings replied, flipping through each document as if he held precious cargo. "The name on the leather case is Klaus Mühlhauser, however, the information on Walter is abundant in these papers. What I'd like to do is research the Mühlhauser family history, dig deeper into their past." He finally looked around the room. "I know you want answers quickly. But surely you realize this is going to take some time. I could give you broad summations, but to do this right, I need time to read line by line without missing anything."

"We were afraid of that," Mitch grumbled. "But we want it done right. We want the information correct, not hurried. A lot depends on the stuff you find within these documents and that diary."

Hollings picked up the worn leather-bound book, thumbed through its pages. "This little journal could very well be an extraordinary addendum to history. It could even hold the answers to several farfetched theories and unanswered mysteries, like did Hitler really make it to South America or did he die in that bunker in 1945 like the history books tell us? From what I'm able to tell at first glance, much of what it contains is in coded messages."

"Tough to break?" Mitch asked.

Hollings gave him a wry smile. "Not necessarily. This is what I suggest. I've written several software programs with algorithms that have been extremely successful in the past at breaking anything written by the German cryptographers. They arrogantly felt their codes couldn't be broken."

Mitch's skeptical nature wanted to raise its ugly head. "Please tell me you have it covered, is that what I'm hearing?"

"My programs have been successful in the past. But in order to use them to their fullest, you'll have to trust me because I have to use my computer."

As a researcher Jackson knew full well where this conversation was headed. He cut his eyes around the room at the others. "What the professor is saying is that he wants us to allow him to scan the documents into his software program on *his* laptop, keep them filed there when he leaves this house. In order for success, the program needs to be able to search for key words, key phrases, and pick up repetitive patterns."

"Uh, that won't work," Mitch declared. "I'm sorry. We're normally very trusting people, but that'll be a problem, maybe even a deal breaker."

Disappointment spread across the professor's face. "The top secret thing again? But the confidentiality agreement I signed prevents me from sharing the information with anyone."

"People often betray others with good intentions." Mitch paced the room, searching out faces. "What do you think? Do we risk it?"

"Do we have a choice?" Jackson tossed back. "We need his expertise and, it seems, his software programs."

Mitch spun back toward the professor. "I'll tell you what. You make sure you honor the contract and when all this is over, I mean, all of it, you can use the material on this table to write that book you want." He stretched out his hand. "Deal?"

Hollings didn't have to think about it for long. "Absolutely. Deal." He pumped Mitch's hand, the enthusiasm still written on his face, like that captivated six-year-old boy who had just been handed a new plaything.

Mitch watched as the professor took out his laptop. With a few clicks, he opened up a new document. "I won't try to kid you. This process takes patience. I'll have to go line by line to write the translation on my legal pad and then when I'm certain that I have it written out correctly, I'll transfer it into my document on the computer. That way, if I find an anomaly in the code, it'll show up immediately."

Raine leaned over to Mitch, whispered in his ear. "This could take forever."

Hollings overheard the comment and looked up, annoyance written on his face. "There's a method to my madness. If I'm thorough with each written line, I should be able to go back to 1945 Germany and unravel the entire mystery, where it all started, who had the original idea, where the sub was headed, and why, instead of providing you with a piecemeal picture."

"I'd prefer the whole story," Mitch declared. "I think we all would."

The professor spent the next hour going over the pay book. The ledger contained distinctive handwriting, itemized entries that showed care in each detail it revealed. Hollings was a slow reader and took his time studying the records written down more than seventy years before. When he had questions, he quizzed them on each item found in the briefcase.

The brothers did their best to go into the backstory, taking turns laying out what they knew from the story Dietrich had given them.

Hollings took lengthy notes until it was time to open the diary. His eyes grew wide at what he read. "A lot of these summaries are nothing more than nautical notations. But there's no doubt in my mind they came directly from a

German submarine firsthand. U-boat 492 to be specific," Hollings confirmed. "Officials did some dancing to make sure the Allies thought it had been scrubbed. But, of course, it hadn't been. Instead, they created a clever ruse to try and fool all the interested parties involved with phony paperwork."

Mitch gave out a half-laugh. "So we've heard. Who's the author though? Who wrote the thing? We've been told it was a young lieutenant."

Hollings frowned. "Not a lieutenant by the time this was written, more like a seasoned officer, Captain Klaus Mühlhauser. Klaus writes that he had a brother in the SS by the name of Walter. Klaus's account is very proud of that. His records cover the latter days of the war and goes into great detail about which officers were slated to make the trips down to South America. But that's just part of what's in here."

The professor looked up from the book. "There's always been speculation that 492 was earmarked for a special mission, one that was so highly secretive that only a few high-ranking officers knew about its real intent. That's why they claimed it never made it out of the construction phase."

"And what do you think that mission was?" Mitch asked. "Care to speculate?"

"I don't have to. What I've been able to ascertain so far is that Klaus mentions a plot to assassinate President Roosevelt in Warm Springs, Georgia."

The room grew silent. Everyone's mouth dropped open.

It was Garret who found his voice first. "Warm Springs, Georgia, known as Roosevelt's Little White House during his presidency. The natural spring there was good for the President's health problems left over from his polio. But we all know that assassination in Warm Springs never took place. The only one I remember anything about is the one we learned in school, the attempt in 1933 in Miami."

Anniston nodded. "The mayor of Chicago died as a result of getting shot in the hail of bullets. The assassin was an Italian immigrant, a bricklayer, who was tried for murder and put to death in the electric chair some months later."

Jackson rubbed the back of his neck. "There was speculation about one more. The Russians claimed they uncovered a plot to kill FDR during a summit between the big three—Stalin, Churchill, and FDR—held in Tehran, Iran, in 1943. Nothing came of it, though. I've never heard about a third attempt on his life."

"So what happened to this attempt in Georgia?" Mitch asked. "What went wrong? Did the sub fail to launch the assassin? Did the man reach his destination, but couldn't get to the intended target? Or did something else happen to U-boat 492 before this could all take place?"

Raine grabbed Mitch's arm in a death grip. "If it's true that something happened to the sub, then why would Dietrich's men be looking for it so far south? The Keys aren't exactly next door to Warm Springs."

He eyed the look on Raine's face. "Warm Springs is roughly seven hundred miles from here. Which might mean the sub is located off the southern tip of Georgia and the northern corner of Florida rather than anywhere near the Keys."

Jackson let out a laugh. "If the sub went down at all in these parts. Remember, we're speculating about Dietrich's claims this U-boat had gold on board. If it turns out to be true, that means the *Patagonia Pike* is looking in the wrong place, and way, way off course."

Mitch grinned. "Wouldn't that be a kick in the butt?"

"We may never know what went wrong," the professor muttered, deeply engrossed in what he found in the diary. Mired in his own thoughts, he seemed bent on figuring out the rest. "The people who hatched the plot knew they had to get close enough to the coastline to drop off the assassin, the person who would actually carry out the plan.

This is all so very fascinating. There are a number of things that could've gone wrong. Why isn't that in here?"

Mitch watched as Hollings began to flip furiously through the pages for the answer. He put a hand on the man's shoulder in sympathy. "I'm sure you'll stay with it until you find out why. Thanks to you we know now that U-492 wasn't just sailing down to South America to unload a bunch of SS officers intending to start a new life."

"According to the entries that's the way it started out," Hollings reiterated. "Apparently the crew had made several runs already to do that during the fall of 1944. Klaus clearly states the sub specifically carried enough gold on those trips to buy government officials in Argentina, to bribe them in order to set up safe havens in case the war effort turned out badly. Which of course it did. After they'd accomplished their initial goal, however, the crew of 492 set their sights on a different objective entirely. Whether the idea came from the top or someone on board acting out of desperation, Captain Mühlhauser decided on a bolder strategy. It may take breaking these codes to find out the actual story and the author of the plot."

Hollings adjusted his wire rims. "I can tell you this much. The Berlin Document Center or BDC, would loved to have had this account of 492 on file. Officially."

"I thought they moved all that info to the National Archives in D.C.," Garret proffered, surprising the professor with his knowledge on the subject.

"In the '90s, they did put everything they had on microfiche and shipped it off to Washington, but the actual papers were left in Berlin. To this day, the BDC remains an excellent source for tracking down the actions of those in the Nazi party, those who tried to deny their involvement in the war. Curious relatives still go there to scour the records for the truth."

Garret moved around the room, thinking, considering. "But a lot of the information slipped through the cracks.

From last count the archive is still missing about forty percent of the records. That's a lot of documentation, especially when you consider there were officers in the Sicherheitsdienst intelligence agency who burned their files just so they could hide any participation and renounce their association. Only after checking pay books and other types of documents did their roles become very public, and very specific as to what they'd actually done."

"You know your German history," Hollings said with approval.

"More now than before," Garret stated.

With each page of the diary, Hollings became more enamored with its contents. "Apparently there were Nazi sympathizers living in the Florida area during 1945 who promised they would help the crew carry out their cunning plot."

"Another jaw-dropping moment for our side," Garret quipped. "Nothing like finding out your neighbors were old-fashioned traitors to the cause. Does it say in there who these guys were?"

"It uses several code names for the people onshore who were willing to help."

"Code names? Jeez, how will we be able to break a code this long after the fact?"

"Code is something I'm an expert in. This is why I need to use my software programs. Not to brag but I am considered somewhat of an expert by my peers. Now that I know what we're up against, I have some materials back in Tallahassee that contain many of the codes the Germans used from that era."

"The diary and all of the documents have to stay put," Mitch insisted. "We can't allow you to take them back to your house for study. I wish that were possible, but it's not. We're keeping them under lock and key for a reason."

"I understand. How about if I get my wife to send the rest of what I need overnight to the hotel?"

Mitch had a better idea. "Have her overnight them here to this address."

"Okay. In the meantime, if I could use a workstation. I can't continue to take up space in your dining room."

"No, you're fine where you are," Tanner assured him. "Since this thing started we've been eating a lot outside. You can work from right here. Or if there's another spot you prefer, just make yourself at home. You don't even have to go to the hotel if you don't want to."

"I sometimes work straight through the night until the crack of dawn. I have a feeling this will be one of those times."

Tanner slapped the man on the back. "You'll be fine right here then. There's a couch over there that's fairly comfortable. My boys have slept on it a time or two since they've been back. Bathroom's down the hall, kitchen's through there. Anything else you need, just ask. We'll act like the Indigo Hilton if that's what it takes to get some answers."

Chapter Eleven

While the others watched Hollings work, Mitch and Raine snuck out of the house like kids, daring anyone to stop them. He led her to the backyard, to a thicket of lilac trees and magic dogwood. His mother had stuck a bench underneath, the one his dad had built for her out of driftwood.

With its long shadowy Florida afternoons and sea breezes wafting off the ocean, the spot was perfect to sit with a book and read for hours under the fragrant canopy of blossoms.

Mitch plopped Raine down and gathered her close.

After being cooped up inside, with so many people, Raine welcomed the peaceful spot. "So this is where your mother disappears to whenever she picks up one of the classics to reread for the umpteenth time?"

"Mom does love her *Cannery Row* and Steinbeck."

"So I've noticed." She rested her head on his shoulder. "What do you think of the translator?"

"Seems to know his stuff well enough. I'm a little concerned with how long he intends to take. He doesn't strike me as a man who does his work without plodding through it."

"If you put one of those outlandish golf hats on Professor Bishop's head and stick him in a pair of wild Bermuda shorts, a metal detector in one hand, and a glass of vodka in the other, he could pass for my uncle Sid, the noted treasure hunter on *my* side of the family."

Mitch hooted with laughter. "Did Sid ever find anything with his metal detector?"

"As of last Christmas, Sid proudly claims he's uncovered a grand total of ten dollars and fifty-nine cents in change and that's directly from the beach. He's also amassed a collection of dime-store jewelry, mostly one earring, a tray of colorful toe rings, and several bottle caps he's added to his collection. But my aunt says the only reason he really makes the trip to the beach is to ogle the women in bikinis."

He pressed his lips to the top of her blond hair. "I remember Sid, strange getups, strange guy."

She elbowed him in the ribs. "My whole family is strange." She reached up, framed his face. "So much deceit floating around here lately. To think we had Nazi sympathizers living among us."

"*Have*," Mitch amended. "Their relatives are probably still living here...somewhere. Think about it. Not many families have moved off the island over the years."

"That's true. Even more reason we don't trust anyone outside the group. Talking about all that history in there, reminds me I should've found a way to tell you sooner. You know about—"

He put two fingers up to her lips. "Stop beating yourself up about that. I'm sorry your mother gave you a tough time this morning. But I think moving forward we should agree to leave the past in the past where it belongs."

"I know, but after all this time, all that anger. Once I finally let it go, the possibilities were right there in front of me. If I'd held onto the mad, just kept clutching it to my chest like it was worth a fortune, where would that have gotten me? Nowhere. So many years wasted between us, such a mistake. I'm really sorry."

"Stop it. I'm glad we're here now, glad we were both able to let it go. That's what's important."

"How did you—let it go?"

"Garret and Jackson had a big hand in that. They made me realize I needed to make peace with you, somehow, some way. Otherwise we might never have gotten together like we did last night."

"And this morning. Twice. Want to do it again as soon as possible?" she added, poking him in the ribs. "You do, don't you?"

"You know the answer to that already." He slid a finger along her jaw. "I know you're deeply-rooted here, Raine. The thing is I love you. I've always loved you. Surely you knew that even when you were pissed off at me."

"It's hard to think of love when one part of the equation spends all his time on the other side of the globe."

"You've really built a wall around your heart, haven't you? It's strange but even after all the time we've spent apart, I still kept hoping every time I made it back home, that one day I'd walk into the restaurant and you'd talk to me, that we'd get back together. All those visits back home, I just didn't act on how I felt. It's time I did."

She stroked a hand down his cheek. "And you want to know…what exactly? If it's too late? If I'd be okay with sending you off on an adventure, treasure hunting whenever you decide the dive is worth it? Watch you go somewhere else, some place where I'm not, and then leave me back here alone again?"

He chewed his lip. "I guess so."

"Do you have to have an answer right this minute?"

He laughed and tugged her hair. "I'll give you a few hours to think it over. Come on, there's something I want to show you."

Mitch took her hand, led her into the carport where an old arcade game stood next to the wall. Covered in dust, the Alien Storm game, about an extraterrestrial species invading Earth, sat in the corner.

"You bought this thing?"

"Yeah. Wanna play?"

"Does it work?"

"After a little tinkering it does." He went over, dropped several quarters in the slot. "I bought it from Mac Perkell's son when he decided to close the game center four years back."

"A staple of our youth and now it's a relic. Makes me feel old."

"Nah, we're still young kids at heart."

"Then scoot over and watch the master beat the pants off you…again."

Everyone stayed for supper. Even the professor gathered around the picnic table in the backyard with the family. They waited for Tanner to pull the burgers off the grill that sizzled over the open flame.

Raine stayed despite Charlotte's pleas to come save her at the restaurant.

"Want us to help you out?" Mitch offered.

She met his eyes and realized she had only to ask and all of them would get up from the table right there, pile into different cars and head over to The Blue Taco to help with the dinner rush if necessary. That kind of support hadn't been available to her in a long time, if ever.

"That's okay. Charlotte's swamped is all. I've been there plenty of times by myself and had the same panicked feeling. I should probably hire more staff."

"We'll eat supper and head over there," Tessa told her. "I don't know how you do it. This is my first night off in ten days. I was really looking forward to a break."

"And you shall have it," Raine said, patting Tessa's hand. "Don't worry. I'll make it over there after inhaling one of Tanner's infamous burgers."

"You'll eat meat?" Mitch asked with a shake of his head. "I can't keep up."

She gave him a half-smile. "Your father's burgers are too good to pass up. Besides, I'll also scarf down plenty of carbs from Lenore's macaroni salad. Once I get some home-cooking in me, I'll be fine."

Anniston came up to them, handed both women a glass of tea. "Then I guess I'd better bring this to a discussion and go over some business now while I've got all of you here."

She turned to Mitch. "I received a photo from Chuck of the unidentified older man's body found near Sugarloaf Key just as you requested," Anniston began, slapping down the image from the medical examiner's office. She pulled out the one they'd taken of Dietrich on *The Black Rum* for comparison. "Chuck said they cleaned John Doe up in order to do the autopsy. As you can see, eyeballing the two, their eyes are very similar, same nose, a similar mouth. So what do you think? Before you answer, I already put both images through facial recognition software."

Raine examined both faces. "I think they're at least related."

Anniston nodded. "Bingo. The percentage is very high that the two men are brothers."

Mitch took a slug of his beer. "Define very high."

"Eighty-five percent."

"Wouldn't it be more if they were twins?" Raine speculated.

"That remaining fifteen percent discrepancy is explained away by the real fact that one led a life of luxury while the other was a virtual pauper, life of wealth and privilege versus off the grid kind of thing."

"Maybe that accounted for the animosity between the two, obviously it existed. Somewhere along the way one branched off with the money and left the other destitute. But somehow Hugo managed to get the documents away from his brother," Mitch pointed out.

Raine dug into her pasta salad. "Definitely a story there so deep that we may never know the whole truth of it."

Anniston sat down with her own plate. "Garret, do you still have all the images of those contracts you found in Dietrich's safe?"

"They're still on my phone. Why?"

"Because we need to go through all of them to learn as much as we can about Dietrich's shady business dealings with Sinclair, Baskin, Dandridge, etc., and find anything we can to bring them down that way. The more charges we're able to pile on, the greater chance we have of getting something solid to stick. I should start a spreadsheet."

Garret cut her a look. "Don't forget one of those people involved in the shady crap is your buddy Royce Buchanan. Maybe you should warn him we're about to use the contracts to put the squeeze on his pals."

"And maybe you should start thinking about utilizing Royce Buchanan more in all this," Anniston fired back. "That man is hurting every bit as much as anyone else. He's motivated to find who killed Walker. It makes more sense to employ that anger to bring the bad guys down than to ignore it." She pointed her fork at him. "And before you say another word, I realize Royce is shady. I read his background just like you did that tells me his business dealings are less than open and honest."

Tanner brought over a platter piled high with burgers, put it down on the table. "You might be right, Anniston. So far, the only thing I see Royce guilty of is greed and dubious business practices."

"I've said all along Royce is a land grabber, a greedy developer, maybe even considers himself a bit of an elitist, but I don't think he had a hand in killing his own son." Turning to Garret, she let out a huge sigh. "If you could just put aside how you feel about him long enough to look at the situation from my point of view, you'd see I'm knocking heads with you because I truly believe Royce wants the same thing we do. Who knows Baskin and Oakerson and the rest better than Royce does?"

"But once we let him in the door, can we trust him completely?" Garret shot back. He looked around the table. "That's the thing that bothers me the most. If you think your spreadsheet will turn up anything in Royce's favor, you're delusional. But you guys do what you want. I'll sit here on the fence, happy to echo I told you so."

"I tell you what," Tanner began, angling toward Anniston. "You do your database thing about Royce's dealings with Baskin and the like. Then you set up a meeting with him to confront him about all his crap. Then we'll see if you still think he's someone we can bring to the table. How's that sound?"

Anniston's lips curved. "A challenge? I like it. Okay, you're on. Tonight, I'll go back to Royce's early days and get everything on him I can find, business-wise. If he's lying about bringing all these felons to town back in the '90s, then I'll be able to see a pattern."

But Garret persisted. "You're ignoring the fact that Royce routinely hands out cash to them—business loans to Frawley, political donations to Oakerson, a regular paycheck to Baskin as his chauffeur and God knows what else, and then outright cash to Dandridge through the church. The only one who slips through the money machine seems to be Sinclair. Is that because there's something you haven't uncovered about our chief of police yet? Why are all these people on Royce's payroll in one capacity or another, if his hands are so clean?"

Anniston patted his face. "You always were a tougher sell. But I can work with that. I still say if you give me twenty-four hours I'll be able to decide one way or another if Royce is worth trusting."

Garret looked over at Mitch, picked up his beer. "What do you say?"

"Go for it. But know this, if Royce is in any way part of what happened, he's going down just like all the rest."

"Goes without saying," Anniston noted. Switching gears, she drew out her cell phone. "Sebastian texted me about his meeting with Willis Hartman's daughter, Peggy. He spent an hour and a half with her going over what she remembered right before her father was murdered. She verified a couple of things and corrected us on a few more."

"Like what?" Raine asked.

"First, Willis Hartman isn't Boone Dandridge. Two entirely different people. *But* Reverend Hartman did apprentice a man who approached him in the summer of 1991 claiming he wanted to become a pastor. Peggy remembered his name, or rather the name he used at the time. It was Whitley Shepherd. Sebastian ran a background on the name. Turns out, Shepherd has a connection to Roland Wainwright from their days in Vancouver, British Columbia. The two went to school together until they both dropped out and became locally known as common grifters, guys to avoid, scammers. They were together in Oregon and were in trouble for running the same basic cons on the elderly. But then something happened and they split up."

"Does Shepherd more closely resemble Dandridge better than Wainwright," Garret asked.

"Yep. Peggy remembers a tall, gangly guy. And when Sebastian showed her the photo we have of Dandridge, she identified him as Shepherd, older of course, but with the same basic features. So Shepherd is Dandridge."

"Then these two guys obviously intersected again at some point after they left Oregon," Garret surmised.

"Maybe. That's one way to look at it. But there's another possibility. One of the men died, which would be Wainwright, while the survivor, which would be Dandridge, took over the con games of the other, used them for several years after their time in the Pacific Northwest was up. Sebastian discovered that even the authorities got the two men mixed up in their system a time or two. It isn't unheard of. Dack caught the height difference. I didn't. While Wainwright is listed at five-nine, Shepherd/Dandridge is the right height at six feet. It might explain a few things. It bears checking out further."

"And might solve a cold case in Port Saint Lucie," Raine prompted. "Wouldn't it be great if we could bring Shepherd, or rather Dandridge in for that?"

"That's the plan. Anyway, according to Peggy, Reverend Hartman tutored this Whitley Shepherd guy toward the goal of becoming his own pastor at his own church. That was the story and apparently Hartman believed Shepherd was serious about learning the ropes. But after the reverend was found in his parsonage with a bullet through his head on the Friday morning of March 20th, 1992, Shepherd disappeared, vanished without a trace. At the time Reverend Hartman had been working on his Sunday sermon, reportedly with his young apprentice nearby."

Lenore let out a gasp, put a hand over her mouth. "So Shepherd shows up here in our little town less than a month later as Boone Dandridge?"

Tanner pushed his plate away. "To think, all this time…we hired a murderer and a con artist and have dutifully followed him in prayer. I may never trust anyone again."

"Peggy confirmed that her father came up with the saying 'faith is belief that turns into bravery.' I think the reverend, the real one, trusted the wrong guy. Hartman was murdered for his trouble."

"Dandridge shows up here in Indigo Key, probably thinking it's too small for anyone to ask questions," Mitch noted. "That might serve as a nail in Boone's coffin right there."

"Want another nail?" Anniston said, dangling the nugget like bait on a fishing line. "I think Garret discovered a biggie. Go ahead, tell them."

Garret put down his burger so he could talk. "I've had some time on my hands since we got back. Last night Anniston and I went back and forth on it."

"That's code for a big discussion ensued where we exchanged our differences of opinion using our very loud voices," she admitted with a grin. "He won. That's why I was up so early and stopped by your place this morning, Raine. I had to leave him alone to…make the best use of his computer."

Tessa took a long gulp of iced tea. "And she dragged me with her. But since I got breakfast out of the deal, I'm not complaining. You'll have to give me your recipe for waffles, Raine. They were delicious."

The lighthearted banter made Mitch grow impatient. "Could we agree to exchange recipes later, ladies?"

Raine smiled. "Sure. Go on, Garret."

"I won the argument, which is what it was, because I wanted to hack into the phone records for Dandridge." He glanced toward his dad. "And yes, I know it's illegal. And thanks to Mom's excellent memory as to which phone service Dandridge mentioned using, I knew where to start."

"I've got my retirement savings, not much mind you, but it'd be enough to put it toward your legal fees if it comes to that," Tanner offered with a wink.

Garret grinned. "Thanks. I knew I could count on you. The thing is after Dack told us about the traffic stop on the way to the Tampa airport, I needed to know for myself if we could put Boone, not a lookalike, but Boone himself, in that general vicinity. Turns out, we can. On September 24th at 3:30 a.m. Boone's phone hits several towers going up Interstate 75. Remember when Anniston told us a cell phone trail was better than DNA. I wasn't sure I bought it back then, but I'm getting the gist of it now. If you follow the trail that Boone's cell phone made heading north, it goes straight to the airport and back to Indigo Key. That's the 'ah-ha' moment everyone's been waiting for…"

"Otherwise known as the smoking gun," Anniston concluded, beaming. She leaned over and kissed Garret on the mouth. "His hacking skills make me proud. But he isn't finished quite yet."

"Thanks to Anniston getting an up close and personal view of Baskin's phone bill—left out in plain sight on the counter at his repair shop—I also hacked into his cell records for that night. His cell phone never left town, not Wednesday night or Thursday morning. In fact, during both nights, his phone pings off the tower in town closest to the repair center and body shop."

Mitch swung his feet up, propping them on the nearest empty spot on the picnic bench. "So Baskin will probably be the tougher bastard to bring down. He's not as stupid as some of the others. Let's refigure the math. Dietrich and Nathan have been eliminated. We don't have to waste time on them. If Sebastian nails Sinclair with that video of Raine's abduction, we can bring him down for that until we figure out the murder angle. Then there's Dandridge. If using his cell phone records connects him to the murders, that leaves us with Baskin, Oakerson and Frawley to deal with. I'm okay with those odds. Am I leaving anyone out?"

"Wendy," Jackson tossed out from the end of the table. "Don't forget Nathan's wife. Wendy could be our *second* weakest link. The question is, do we make her a deal? I have an idea on that."

"Let's hear it," Mitch prompted.

"Once we nail Oakerson, Wendy will talk if given the right incentive."

"Ah, I see dollar signs."

"So will she. But not the way you think."

Mitch cocked a brow and kicked his feet off the bench. "You're planning on blackmailing Wendy?"

Jackson smiled and shrugged. "Not at all. I'm just eliminating most of her options and taking them off the table."

"I like it. And has Mrs. Hollister inquired about her loving hubby yet?" Garret asked.

"Not so you'd notice. She's too busy spending time with Oakerson to care about what happened to Nathan."

Raine laughed. "It's a shame really. I saw her on Oakerson's yacht after you guys left to go get Nathan. She was laughing it up, drunk, and dancing her way across the deck. I never noticed before how much time Oakerson spends away from his office. Anyone could be mayor." She glanced at Mitch. "Even you."

"Not my style," Mitch muttered.

"The point is, the voting public may not understand how frivolous Oakerson is with the town's time and money. That could be the nail in his coffin."

"Good thinking."

Raine swallowed down her last bite of salad and stood up. "I hate to eat and run like this but I really do need to go relieve Charlotte for a bit. If we're done here, I need to check on things at the restaurant."

Mitch got to his feet, as well. "Okay. Let's do it. I'll help."

"You've been very agreeable all day."

"Turns out, I like serving up tacos and bussing tables. Who knew? I could take a turn cooking in the kitchen just like I do on board the boat. You know Mom taught us all to handle the basics."

"You bet I did," Lenore offered. "That's why I tried my best to push off fixing the appetizers on him this afternoon."

"I'm on to you, Mom," Mitch admitted with a kiss to her cheek.

Raine smiled at the mother and son byplay. There'd been times over the years she'd watched the teen boy use those long lean fingers of his to crack eggs or dice veggies. And right this minute she knew he was trying to show her he cared. "Fine. But I don't want to hear any bitching about it when I put you to work washing dishes or bussing tables at eleven o'clock at night."

"Hey, my mother also raised me to know the importance of keeping the galley tidy."

By the time they reached The Blue Taco, the place was still packed with hungry people. If he'd thought the lunch crowd had been busy, the dinner rush was more like bedlam.

The dining room was bustling to capacity. The throng included several crying babies and little kids under six. The precocious youngsters had finished their meal and used the aisle next to the tables as their own personal football field. They ran back and forth tossing a Nerf ball around.

"Doesn't anybody cook at home anymore?" Mitch asked, glancing around at the pandemonium.

"I'm grateful they don't, although it does get a little hairy when it's like this and parents let their toddlers run wild. Looks like we could have a food fight at any minute."

As soon as Charlotte spotted Raine, she waved her over to the counter. "Thank goodness you showed up. You're both lifesavers," the woman breathed out as she took another order. "We ran out of queso about an hour ago. I haven't had a chance to make more. We ran out of the pork tamales around six, so I substituted the steak carnitas. I hope that's okay?"

"More than. I'll take care of the queso," Raine said as she moved through the swinging door. She pushed it back open again and aimed a wide smile at her assistant manager, thumbed a hand toward Mitch. "He's your slave for the next three hours. He can deliver the food to the tables."

To get him started, Raine handed him a plate of enchiladas. "Table six."

Thrown into the mayhem, but willing to help, he asked, "Which one is that again?"

"Center table next to all the screaming kids."

"Oh jeez, I have to wade into the middle of that?"

"Yep." She slapped him on the back, gave him a little push. "Welcome to the wonderful world of food service."

After that, Raine joined Maddie in the kitchen. "How's it going?"

"Been on my feet too long, girl. You gotta get us some help in here."

"You go on home now. I'll take over from here."

"Really?"

"Yes, really. Now shoo." Raine deftly took over at the grill, searing up an order of shrimp for tacos. Mitch sauntered through the door and headed straight for Raine, placing a kiss on her mouth. "How can I help? Point me in the direction of what you need me to do."

"Grab more sour cream out of the fridge and pick out some ripe avocados. In fact, you could throw together the guacamole."

Maddie yanked off her apron, but stood back curiously watching the two interact. She couldn't believe her eyes when Mitch planted a smooch on the boss again like he'd done it every day for the past year. "Don't think that just because you came in here three hours before closing time you saved the day," Maddie scolded.

"No ma'am. I won't think that," Raine said with a grin. "Tell me again how you managed without me for a day?"

"That new girl you hired, Tessa, she slogged through here just fine. She's got some moves in the kitchen. Maybe you could promote her and hire counter help. Between Tessa, Charlotte and me, we had things covered just fine while you were gone. Worried about you just the same, though."

"Well, I'm back now."

Unwilling to let it go, Maddie kept up her counsel. "But you need to put an ad in the paper, or online, wherever they do that these days and bring in the applicants, as many as you can coax in here, and look for another cook."

"Are you giving me your notice, Maddie?"

"Naw, I didn't say that. I'm just give out working double shifts is all. I want a life outside this place."

"Duly noted. Will you train someone if I hire a novice?" Raine teased.

Maddie smiled and showed a set of perfect teeth. "Damn straight I will. You get me someone eager to learn and I'll show them the ropes."

"It's a deal," Raine said right before Maddie walked out the back door.

"She's a tough one," Mitch noted.

"Maddie? She's been singing that same old song and dance ever since she walked through that door ten years ago. But she's right. It's time I hired another cook. Charlotte is my backup at managing things, but I can't expect everyone to consistently work two shifts like this on a regular basis. I've been putting it off too long now."

She watched as Mitch neatly whipped up a batch of guacamole. "Let me taste that."

He obliged by scooping up a spoonful and holding it up to her lips.

"Not bad, Mr. Indigo. Maybe by the end of the week I'll have you making your infamous macaroni and cheese casserole and put it on the menu."

"Happy to."

They worked like that—Raine cooking and plating while Mitch carried the orders out to the dining room—until the packed house thinned out.

They were wiping down tables together when Jessup Sinclair swaggered in ten minutes before closing, wearing his uniform, complete with gun.

"What can I get you, chief," Charlotte asked him.

"Got any more of those carnitas? I know it's late, but I've been out on patrol. One of my deputies called in sick."

"Sorry. All we have left is pork, ran out of the steak hours ago."

"That shows your owner ought to plan better," Sinclair complained.

Raine went over to where Mitch stood and whispered in his ear. "Do you see Sinclair's right hand? Look at the ring he's wearing. That's the ring I remember the night he grabbed me."

Mitch cut his eyes toward the cop, stared at Sinclair's right hand. There on the ring finger was the black and gold insignia of the Florida Highway Patrol. "Are you certain?"

"Positive."

Mitch left his bussing duties and wandered over to the counter. "How's it going?"

"It'd be going a lot better if I could order steak carnitas instead of pork. Never mind. I had my heart set on those. I'll take four shrimp tacos to go," Jessup barked out. He looked over at Mitch, then at Raine. "You got a new job now? What happened to the big treasure hunter?"

"Haven't you heard? That didn't pan out. No gold anywhere around here anyway," Mitch popped off with a wink.

"You Indigos are just full of sass, aren't you?"

"Be careful, chief. I'm no longer sixteen and afraid of going to jail. Why don't you chill? Have a seat and enjoy those delicious tacos you ordered."

After Sinclair ate his meal and left, Mitch went over to clear the table and wipe it down. He gathered up the trash the cop had left behind. Just before he got ready to toss the garbage into the can, he hesitated. Instead of getting rid of the paper cup, he took one of the plastic bags used for waste and dropped it into the bag.

"Did you just save that paper cup?" Raine asked.

"Yep. I'm covering all my bases. Let's get Anniston to send it to the lab she uses for analysis."

Chapter Twelve

Lenore insisted on keeping Livvy's plants from dying. Tanner indulged his wife's trips to their daughter's home because he didn't want to see her sad. But for him, it was painful to go inside those four walls. The entire house seemed like a macabre memorial to Livvy and the kids.

This day, he used the spare key to let them in, and found Royce Buchanan already there, sitting alone on the couch in the living room.

"We came to water the plants," Lenore explained. "What are you doing here?"

"Missing my son," Royce replied, sadness laced on every word.

"I didn't see Baskin or your Maybach parked at the curb," Tanner noted.

"I took a taxi here."

"Anniston told us you've been helping keep an eye on Baskin by letting us bug your guesthouse. Thank you for that," Tanner managed.

"She says she thinks he's the one who killed Walker, beat him to death."

"Beat them all to death," Tanner amended.

The trio found themselves in an awkward silence.

Royce had muttered something and Tanner had to get him to repeat it. "I said if y'all can't figure out a way to kill Baskin, I will."

"Now, Royce," Lenore began. "You don't want to do anything quite so drastic as that."

"Why not? I'm an old man. What're they going to do to me? Lock me up where I wait for my execution twenty years down the road. I don't have twenty years left in me."

Tanner took a seat on the opposite end of the sofa, something he'd never thought would happen before this moment. "You don't think I've thought of doing that same thing? Believe me, I have."

Lenore's eyes got big. "Tanner Jackson Indigo! You would do that to me?"

"I said I thought about it. Baskin's still alive, isn't he?"

"Not for long," Royce cautioned. "I'm serious. You still have some of your family left, three sons, a wife, potential. I have no one, nothing really left to live for."

Lenore scooted over to sit in the club chair next to him. "I'll tell you what you have to live for. Justice. Seeing those awful men pay for what they've taken, what they've destroyed."

"You know Dietrich is dead, right?" Tanner heard himself saying.

Royce cocked a brow. "When? How?"

"I don't know the particulars," Tanner said, lying through his teeth. "All I know is he wasn't a very good person."

"I knew that already," Royce spat out. "Anyone with half a brain knew Dietrich was as sneaky as a shark." When he realized what he'd said, he hung his head. "Oh

God. Why didn't Walker know that? Why couldn't he see that for himself? You think your children, hope really, that they'll listen to you, heed your cautionary tales." He let out a mournful sigh. "Walker obviously thought he could outsmart the shark. Walker going to Dietrich and Baskin for anything was a mistake. Plain and simple, I think they double-crossed him."

"By any chance did Anniston talk to you…recently?"

"She came to my office this morning. We had a long talk about my political contributions to Oakerson, the loans I made to Carson Frawley for his doughnut shop, and the audacity of me giving Baskin a job. She went on to blast me about the business loans I've dished out over the years. I'll tell you the same thing I told her. It's what I do. Business loans aren't always obtained via the First National Bank. When the bank turned down Baskin, I stepped up. Same with Carson. They both came to me with problems and like any businessman, I saw an opportunity to own half their businesses if they didn't pay me back. I gave them both the loans because I wanted to—"

"See the town grow," Tanner supplied. "Yes, we know. And I'm just the lowly carpenter who wants to see my hometown crash and burn. You couldn't be more wrong about that. My family's been on this island for more than three hundred years. That means something to me. I never wanted to see it turned into a Pottersville by your high-handed, backdoor dealings. I didn't want to see families living in squalor, sleazy bars springing up around town, kids hanging out at dingy pool halls, a line of strip clubs dotting the business district like they have down in Key West. I didn't want to see you beating down hardworking families."

Royce looked appalled. "Is that the way you see me?"

"For good reason," Tanner shot back, leveling a finger at him. "Don't deny it. You've bought almost every other home in Indigo Key and turned it into one of your stinking rental properties. Then you and Baskin jack up the rent. What do you think that does to local families who can't afford a starter home these days? You're like a feudal lord sitting in his castle ruling over the serfs and making them pay double, or pay dearly, time and again."

"That was never my intent."

"Maybe not, but it's sure the way Walker tried to follow in your footsteps. I have nightmares thinking about what might've happened if your son had ever found his way. You could've left a legacy, Royce, a good one. You could've left something behind to be proud of. Instead, you hooked up with men who've tried to swindle and steal their way to this town's ruin. You gave loans to people who took down your own son. That's a fact."

"Tell me how to correct it. Tell me what to do about it," Royce pleaded. "I'll do it. I'll do whatever you want to correct it."

"If you really mean that, then let's get down to a serious discussion."

Mitch kept his eye on Raine while hanging out at the eatery. His duties were simple. He filled salt and pepper shakers, rolled up silverware in paper napkins, made pots of coffee, one after the other, all while forced to breathe the continual odor of fried foods cooking in a vat of trans fats all day. He was beginning to realize Raine had a point about the greasy smell.

But he was bored out of his mind bussing tables and washing dishes. If he had to do this for months or years at a time, he'd go stark raving mad.

After the lunch bunch cleared out, Mitch glanced up from wiping down a table to see Walsh walk in with Prentiss trailing after him.

"How's the Magnum PI slash Wolfgang Puck personalities meshing for you?" Walsh wisecracked.

Mitch cracked a grin. "Raine doesn't trust me much in the kitchen yet. She keeps dangling a turn at the grill, but so far, nada. So the Wolfgang Puck thing is a pipe dream.

And I could seriously use that Ferrari and moustache to pull off the Magnum persona."

"You wish," Walsh said. He leaned in so only Mitch could hear. "As long as it's paying off for you in other ways, and something tells me it is."

"What we do for our women," Mitch lamented. "What's up?"

"Prentiss here has something to tell you. Why don't you both have a seat at his clean table and I'll go put in my order for a couple of those fire-roasted shrimp tacos."

Mitch plopped his butt in a chair and motioned for Prentiss to do the same. "What's on your mind?" He was pretty sure he already knew. The young man hadn't been happy the whole trip here. He supposed it was time for him to go back to his family in San Diego. That's why he was shocked when Prentiss finally sat down and started babbling.

"I think I heard something two nights ago at the bar we were in, Lime in the Coconut, that might be important. The night Walsh gave Jenkins and me shore leave, we hung out there for about three hours. The place had a packed house. But there was this one guy everyone referred to as the mayor, sitting at the bar, who kept throwing back shots of rum until he was plastered."

Mitch sat up straighter. "Oakerson. And?"

"The mayor's already so sloppy drunk he can barely stand up when this other man shows up to help him get home."

"You know who it was?"

"Sure. When I told Walsh about it, he showed me a picture of Baskin. It was him. But Baskin can't seem to keep this Oakerson guy from running his mouth about some car accident that went down last year. The mayor's scared that the same thing will happen to him that happened to some woman named Winnie. He kept talking about what a brilliant idea Baskin had to make it look like a car accident when it really wasn't. But the mayor was also afraid that if he didn't keep cooperating and doing what Baskin wanted, he could end up like the woman."

Mitch's eyes grew wider. "So how does Baskin get Oakerson to shut up?"

"This is where it gets interesting. Baskin hauls off and raps the mayor right across his mouth, hard enough to bust the lip and make it bleed. Baskin grabs up a couple of cotton napkins. The bartender drops in some ice and rolls the cubes up so the mayor can hold it up to his busted lip like it's no big deal, happens all the time in there."

"That's because it probably does. What happened after that?"

"Baskin tells the mayor that he doesn't want blood in his car and drags the guy through the back doorway by his shirt. Meanwhile the mayor's cussing a blue streak. But he's also begging Baskin not to mess up his face any more. People would talk about black eyes and the like."

"Not exactly keeping a down and low profile," Mitch noted.

"But that's not all," Prentiss added. "Right before Baskin hit him in the mouth, the mayor kept talking about a tourist who'd ended up dead, shot and killed...by the very guy who had hold of his shirt."

"Baskin. You don't think the mayor was faking it, do you?"

"Nope. That man was genuinely scared for his life. You could see it in his eyes."

"Jeez, that's the closest thing we've come to hearing any of them mention Ryan. Did Oakerson say why they had to kill him?"

Prentiss lifted a shoulder. "The mayor did a lot of laughing and said they didn't want to cut this stranger in on the gold. Apparently someone else had promised him a share. But these guys—Baskin and Oakerson—weren't about to let that happen. Where I come from it's called pure and simple greed."

Mitch ran his hands through his hair. "So much for my hometown. It's like these guys don't even have the decency to hide anything they've done, not anymore. They're flaunting it publicly, talking about Winnie Buchanan's car accident and Ryan's murder in a bar as if it were common knowledge and no one does a thing about it."

Prentiss apologized. "I'm sorry. What could Jenkins and me do? Oakerson was surrounded by a group of friends."

Mitch shook his head. "I'm not talking about you guys. You two did the right thing. By sitting there and letting Oakerson run his mouth like that, it paid off. What ticks me off is that in a crowded bar, no one picks up the phone to turn them in."

"Who they gonna call? Sinclair?" Walsh pointed out, sliding his basket of shrimp and fries on the table and dropping into a chair across from Mitch. "Maybe they're afraid to speak up. Think about it. Baskin and Sinclair have run this place for twenty years without any opposition. That's a long time to work on keeping the natives in line. These guys are used to having everybody kowtow to them, do what they say without questioning it. The people you grew up with know the consequences of bucking Sinclair's system. Baskin and the like don't have to keep their mouths shut because no one's had the guts to stand up to them."

"Until now," Mitch finished. "Yeah, well, that's about to change. Their dynasty is coming to an end."

Mitch stewed on that the rest of the afternoon until he picked up the phone to call Jackson. He went over the story from Prentiss that night at the bar and then told him the part about Ryan. "You know, the whole time Prentiss is telling me his account of what happened, Tessa's working behind the counter, not thirty feet away. The thing is, I thought you might want to be the one to tell her."

"Thanks for that. She's been so downhearted because nothing we've turned over tells her why they killed Ryan. Up to this point, all we've had is supposition."

"Now we have more. We know for certain our dipshit of a mayor was in on it. We build our case and keep piling on until we bury the bastards."

"I can live with that. Do you ever think about settling here back in Indigo Key once this is over? I mean, you must've thought about it now that you're back with Raine."

Mitch glanced over, caught sight of the pretty blonde taking care of a problem at the register. "Let's just say I'm considering a lot more options than I did when I was eighteen and leave it at that." He paused. "I have a favor to ask."

"No problem. What is it you want me to do?"

Mitch detailed the plan and when the call ended, he went out of his way to finish up his tasks with one purpose in mind.

He noticed Raine was happiest when she distanced herself from her mother. A sad fact, but a clear truth. It was one reason his mind went back to their teen years. He recalled how many times she'd made excuses just to get to hang out at his house, spend time with his folks. It explained a lot.

Even though he would've preferred getting her alone back on the houseboat and keeping her all to himself, he knew she needed that social setting for reassurance. Everyone needed to know they were cared for and loved, even if it didn't come from the one person that she needed to hear it from—her mother. That way, when he left to pick up his life, to go back to the Bahamas—

No, he couldn't bring himself to think like that now. How could he leave Raine behind when he was in love with her? Only a fool would walk away from someone like Raine twice. There was a sacrifice to be made in that line of thinking, somewhere.

Was he ready to make it? Was she? She hadn't actually declared her love for him, not in so many words. But then, she probably didn't want to risk putting it all out there again.

Yet.

So he made a point to plan an evening where the two of them could kick back and relax without the pressures of dealing with murder or the added boilerplate of making decisions about the future.

Maybe they'd do something completely normal, like watch a movie. He just had to phrase the invitation where she'd leave work early and spend the evening in a stress-free environment that wasn't all about sex. Not that he didn't want to get her into bed. But it seemed to him there had to be more to their relationship this time around than hitting the sheets.

He waited for her to take a break on the patio before approaching her with the idea. Under a pergola filled with trailing honeysuckle and budding orange blossoms, he took a seat across from her. "I got a text from Mom. She wants us to stop by the house after you're done here. She says Dad wants to talk to us about something." It wasn't a complete lie, he reminded himself.

"Oh sure. Sounds good. I can break away around six. I'll make sure Tessa is free, too."

"Perfect. It works best if the gang's all present and accounted for when Dad delivers his news, whatever it turns out to be."

"I should start more rice and beans," she said, starting to get to her feet.

Mitch grabbed her around the waist and plopped her in his lap. "I'm crazy about you."

She started to object to the display of public affection and then told herself it didn't matter. She patted his lean face and said, "Hmm, funny how that works. I think you're just plain nuts."

"And aren't you glad I am? Who else could get you kidnapped out of a parking lot in the middle of the night?"

She rewarded him with a slow smile. "That wasn't your fault. Sinclair was doing Duarte's bidding."

"The fact is you got involved in all this craziness because of my family."

"I do like the way you saved me, giving up Dietrich like that."

"Dietrich was nothing to me. You're everything."

"Aww." She put a hand over her heart. "I'd forgotten how sweet you could be."

"I'm a little out of practice."

"It's okay. I love to see you try to get the hang of it again."

Shortly after six, they reached the Indigo house.

Jackson had already given everyone a heads up. With strict instructions to stay away from heavy duty topics like assassination plots and murder schemes, the family sat around the fire pit in the backyard drinking beer and roasting veggie and steak kabobs along with hot dogs. Lenore had made a huge bowl of mustard potato salad and a platter of deviled eggs.

"These are the best," Raine muttered as she finished off half an egg in three bites and then started working her way up the kabob, starting with a tasty zucchini.

"Where's Dominka these days?" Tessa asked Anniston, eyeing the green stubby fruit with a certain amount of suspicion before biting into her hot dog.

Anniston picked at the veggie kabob, looking at it from every angle, before breaking down and stuffing a hot dog in her mouth. "She left with Sebastian. Apparently she and my brother have become inseparable. She goes where he goes, thanks to Garret."

Garret grinned. "I should go into the matchmaking business on the side, start a website pairing up soul mates, and charge a fortune for it."

Anniston rolled her eyes. "Don't flatter yourself. I don't see that Sebastian has anything in common with her except in the…you know…sack. She doesn't even like Italian cooking. She barely eats anything except a salad. What's she supposed to do at a Marcelli family gathering? My mother and grandmother aren't exactly known for cooking light fare. So I give it another six months at most."

Raine snickered. "Have you told Sebastian how you feel?"

"Are you kidding? He's enamored, infatuated, whatever you call it."

"Kind of like the professor with that diary," Raine offered. "Where is Professor Bishop?"

Jackson drained his beer. "He's taken the diary and closed himself off in what used to be my old room for some solitude and quiet deliberation."

"Lots of luck with that with this crowd," Garret sang out. "Most times, we make up a grocery list at the top of our lungs."

By the time the cicadas came out to serenade them, the sun had made its way over the water. A few hungry mosquitos buzzed, then dive-bombed seeking to find a repellant-free patch of skin.

Mitch sat back in his lawn chair and listened to the byplay. He watched the day's stress leave Raine's body, layer by layer.

Surrounded by friends and family, there was something peaceful that settled over him. It was like a soothing song that played in his head, the refrain familiar but always there, never appreciated to the fullest, until right this moment.

He didn't realize how he'd missed this. It was nothing spectacular or brilliant or fancy, but it was everything. Having his family around him now, the woman he loved, good friends, it was all coming together. The only thing missing was Livvy. Livvy wasn't here to share his happiness, see his joy, or help guide him into a deeper understanding of what it all meant.

That, he realized, was the hole in his heart. No doubt, Raine filled a good chunk of that void.

When the pesky insects brought friends, doubling the size of their army, Mitch snatched Raine up out of her chair and pulled her inside to the kitchen.

"Tonight the Indigos proudly offer a series of movie choices from their selected stash. The only thing is they're about a decade old. You get to pick from the kid's menu, *Finding Nemo*, or *Despicable Me*. Then there's a couple of my favorites—the action-packed sci-fi thriller, *Terminator 3* or maybe *The Matrix Reloaded*."

"If we're watching *Terminator 3*, I want popcorn," Raine proposed. "With lots of butter."

"You just scarfed down three kabobs," he pointed out. He looked her up and down. "Where do you put all that? Got a hollow leg I don't know anything about?"

"The thing you have to realize about vegetables is they're not as filling as you might think. Besides, movies, even the ones you load up at home, require popcorn. End of discussion."

Mitch got down the pan and set it on the burner. He grabbed peanut oil from the pantry. "My mom doesn't own one of those popcorn machines so it's the old-fashioned method or not at all."

"Even better. The old-fashioned way is best. I'll do it. This is my favorite part." She let the oil heat before dumping in a layer of corn. As soon as it started to pop, she moved the top over to allow the steam to escape. "It takes the moisture out of the corn making it a little drier and crunchier."

Ten minutes later they took their snack into the living room and stretched out on the sofa to watch a string of their favorite movies just as they'd done in high school.

Jackson and Tessa wandered in during the credits, as did Anniston and Garret. When his mom and dad joined them, the smallish living room got even more crowded.

Everyone wanted their share of the popcorn as greedy hands reached into the bowl. They bunched together just in time to see Schwarzenegger shoot his way out of a cemetery, also known as, how to turn a hearse into a convertible in ten easy shots using a blaster from the future.

For Mitch, sitting here like this with Raine, it was like a scene back in time, a step back to his younger self. He sat there wondering how many movies he'd watched with Raine just like this. He stopped counting when the number reached fifty. That last year of high school they'd been inseparable, doing everything together, going everywhere as a couple. What had he been thinking to take off and leave her, leave her at the whims of her mother, who'd forced her to step in and take the reins of a job she didn't like?

He couldn't keep his mind on the movie. Somewhere before the ending, Mitch drifted off to sleep. He woke to a blank screen on the TV, an empty living room, and a silent house. His mom and dad must've headed off to bed. The others must have gone, too. But where was Raine? Panic began to do a slow roll up his throat. He got to his feet, began a search of the kitchen, the hallway, the bathroom.

He found her on the front porch, legs tucked under her, sitting in the swing looking out into the front yard.

She glanced up at him, breathed in the night air, bursting with fragrant jasmine. "I had a nice time tonight. It took me coming out here for some solitude to clear my head before I figured out what you did in there. You knew exactly what I needed to get my mind off what happened this morning with my mom. Thank you for that."

"What are friends for?"

"I thought you said you loved me?"

"Several times. Funny thing about that. You haven't reciprocated using those same words. You've hinted around it. You've been grateful several times for me getting you off Duarte's ship. It's not the same thing."

She let out a weary sigh. "We've been all through this. We keep circling around to the same issue. You know I can't leave and you can't stay. How many times do I have to say it?"

"I'm not asking for a decision about what'll happen tomorrow. You of all people should know there are no guarantees in life. You lost our baby. You lost Danny. I'm asking you what's in your heart, Raine? Tell me what's in here." He laid his hand over his chest, held his breath.

"I love you. I always have. I always will. I don't see that changing. But—"

"No buts. That's all I needed to know." He held out his hand. "Come sleep with me tonight in my old room. It'll be like a sleepover."

"Won't your parents object to that?"

"I seriously doubt it. If the last few weeks have taught us anything, it's that life's way too short to waste a single minute of it. Besides, I promise I'll keep my hands to myself."

The smile she gave him made his heart flip in his chest.

"Yeah. Right. Where have I heard that before?"

"I keep trying to tell you. I'm no longer that same horny teen you knew in high school."

She stood up, took his hand. "We'll see about that."

Chapter Thirteen

At the bungalow across from the waterfront, Jackson rose early and stumbled into the kitchen to start breakfast. He fiddled with the coffee grinder. From there he was on automatic instinct to produce the strongest cup he could create.

The knock on the front door a few minutes before six had him reaching for the SIG pistol he favored, ever since purchasing the weapon from Michael Tang.

By the time he made his way to the living room, the knocking had turned to all-out pounding.

"Jackson, are you in there?"

He recognized the voice and looked through the peephole to see if she'd come alone. Turning the lock and opening the door, he stared at Wendy Hollister.

"What do you want?"

"To talk."

"At six in the morning? You're nuts."

"Dave didn't come home the other night."

Jackson cocked a brow. "His home or yours?"

"What difference does it make? Okay his. I was at my own house at the time."

"You mean the one you own with Nathan?"

"Do you want to hear me out or not?"

"This should be good. I'm holding my breath for the next installment," Jackson mocked as he motioned for her to take a seat on the sofa.

Wendy took the offer but was so worked up, her legs were fidgeting like a drug addict's might. "I called the bar where he was supposed to be. Darryl said he left with Baskin because he was too drunk to drive. Up to that point, he'd been texting me off and on all evening. After leaving with Baskin, nothing, no phone calls from him or texts. He didn't make it home because I used my key around two-thirty to get into his house and he wasn't there. His car wasn't in the garage. He didn't make it in to work the next day, either. That was two nights ago. I'm worried about him."

Tessa appeared from the hallway still wearing her robe. "What's going on?"

"It seems our distinguished mayor's gone MIA," Jackson explained. "Wendy was just getting to the good part."

"I see," Tessa said, although she really didn't. "Why is she here in our house asking your help to find him? Shouldn't she call our capable chief of police?"

He nodded. "I was just about to suggest that very thing. I'm sure Sinclair will write up the same kind of missing persons report he did for my sister's family, for Nathan, and for Ryan Connelly. In case you haven't heard, Wendy, we've had a rash of people going missing in this town lately. I'm sure Sinclair will be all over Dave's disappearance."

"Don't be ridiculous," Wendy snapped. "You know exactly what's been going on in this town, has been for years."

"What do you want me to do about it?"

"Do something," Wendy shouted. "Find Dave before it's too late."

"Too late for what?"

"You're just going to sit there and play games with me, aren't you?"

"Not really. But it's time you understand the situation completely. This entire house of cards is about to come tumbling down. It's just a matter of time before the state police comes rolling down Main Street. They might show up today, it might be tomorrow, or the end of the week. The fuse has been lit on this powder keg, Wendy, and there's no going back to stop it. What you have to decide now is whether you're going down in the net with the rest of these bastards you've been working with. Or will you cut a deal to save yourself? As I see it, this case is winding down and it has a short shelf life. You're caught in the crosshairs of your own making. Did you really think you could get away with such mass corruption, stealing from the people in this town, not to mention a string of murders as long as your arm?"

Knowing how vain Wendy came across, Tessa went in for the kill. "I understand prison adds ten years to the face, and on average, thirty pounds to the waistline, and that's just in the first two years of incarceration."

"You're on the wrong side of this thing, Wendy. When this scandal rocks the town, it won't be pretty. And it will. The residents here will look at you differently. All that respect and standing in the community you've built up over the years, will be gone."

"So you think Dave is dead?"

"Oh yeah. I think Baskin is tying up all the loose ends. It's time to face it, sweetheart, you're a loose end that will eventually have to be put out of its misery."

Wendy's eyes darted around the room in panic. "I'll take off. I'll leave town. I can be packed and ready to go in thirty minutes. If it all came crumbling down, Dave and I had already talked about a plan. It was always to fly to Guyana anyway."

Tessa stared at the woman, then at Jackson. "Interesting. Guyana has no extradition treaty with the US."

"You could do that," Jackson proffered. "But would you really be happy there alone in a strange place?"

"Not really. I wanted to go to Venezuela, more exotic, more tropical. I told Dave I thought Guyana was a mistake, that we'd have trouble fitting in there."

"What about Nathan? How does Nathan fit in with your plans to go to South America?"

Wendy cut her eyes to look out the window. "I haven't heard from him. He was supposed to call. He never did. Which means Nathan's dead too. I'm sure of it."

"So you're alone without the two partners you'd counted on the most to get you out of this mess you're in? You could head to what sounds like greener pastures, but you'd always wonder if you could've stayed and cut a deal, stayed right here in the good ol' US of A. Not here, of course, not in Indigo Key. That'd be impossible now. But you wouldn't have to seek out asylum on foreign soil if the state police valued what you knew enough to keep you out of jail."

"I can't talk to them or the feds. Baskin would kill me. And if he didn't, Sinclair certainly would, maybe even Dandridge."

"It's certainly a pickle you've found yourself in. But you know I can't let you hop a plane to South America now, Wendy. I can't let you leave here."

Tessa did her part by moving to the phone on the wall in the kitchen, picked up the receiver from its cradle. "So what's it going to be, Wendy? Cooperating with the state police or us?"

Chapter Fourteen

Raine was the first one up. She found the professor stretched out on the sofa, the journal spread open on his chest, his glasses askew on the top of his head.

She went through the living room picking up the numerous empty Diet Coke cans scattered around the room. She'd never seen anyone drink so much soda in one sitting.

Her first instinct was to wake Hollings up and send him packing, back to the room he'd chosen at the rear of the house. But instead of rousting him, she removed the journal and his glasses before covering him with a blanket.

Heading to the kitchen, she went directly to Lenore's fancy coffee machine, the one she knew the guys had given their mom last Christmas. After grinding beans, she decided to make some of her locally famous Blue Taco Chorizo, eggs and cheese breakfast burritos, and serve them up with her special super-secret chipotle sauce.

Just about the time Raine transferred the burritos to a large tray for the oven so they'd keep warm, she glanced up to see a bleary-eyed professor yawning his way into the kitchen.

"Raine, is it? Whatever it is you're making, it smells wonderful."

"Yes, it's Raine, Raine Manning. How come you slept on the couch?"

"That bed in there didn't exactly agree with me, hard as a board. So I thought I'd move out to the living room for a bit to get some work done."

"How late did you stay up, Professor Bishop?"

"Hollings. Call me Hollings. Oh. Well. I get zeroed in on what I'm doing and I lose all track of time, happens all the time when I'm deep into a project. Drives my wife crazy. I think I dozed off around four o'clock."

"That's only three hours sleep. How do you do it?"

"I'm used to long hours of research."

Raine motioned for him to sit down and pushed a plate in front of him with a hot fresh burrito on it. "Want coffee?"

"Never touch the stuff."

"Really? Diet Coke for breakfast?"

"Diet Coke is good any time of the day or night and goes with everything. It's the way I get my caffeine."

She watched with great satisfaction as Hollings wolfed down the burrito in five bites. "You *were* hungry. Want another?"

"I should probably pace myself. There are other people in the house that haven't had breakfast yet. I don't want you to think I'm greedy."

"I think you're famished and running on nothing but Diet Coke. I run a restaurant, which makes me a professional." She dumped another burrito on his plate. "I made plenty for everyone to enjoy."

"But you aren't eating."

"Trust me. I've had my share of them over the years. They're world famous, you know."

Mitch came wandering into the kitchen, trying to wake up. On his way to the coffee pot, he stole a morning kiss from Raine. "Missed you when I woke up."

"You're growing on me."

The doorbell rang.

"Who the heck could that be at this hour?" Mitch said as he headed off to get the door. He looked out the window to see a Fed Ex driver with a dolly loaded to the top with boxes.

"Uh, professor, you might want to check this out. It looks like your stuff has arrived." Mitch opened the door and waved the man into the house.

"Where do you want these?"

"Park them in the hallway for now, I guess."

Hollings rushed into the room, his Diet Coke can in one hand, a half-eaten burrito in the other. He pointed to a spot in the corner of the living room where he'd set up his workstation. "Over there, please. It's more convenient for me."

"I thought you meant your wife was sending you a package," Mitch commented. "A couple of books, a list or two of code words. I wasn't expecting you to send for your entire archive."

"Oh, this isn't all of it. During the latter stages of the war, the Germans were known to change their codes at least once a week, sometimes more frequently. There are thousands of variations. Since I didn't know what I'd be dealing with yet, I needed to cover all my bases. Let's just hope the author of that diary didn't go rogue and develop his own personal code. That would throw a wrench into everything."

The driver finished unloading the cartons as Hollings counted and inspected each one. He refused to sign the slip for the delivery until he'd checked each book one at a time for damage.

When it seemed to take forever to placate Hollings that his stuff had arrived intact, the driver grew impatient.

Hollings noticed Raine and Mitch eyeing the huge stack of books. "Honestly, I didn't know what I'd need, so I had Gracie, that's my wife, send the lot. I hope you don't mind." With that he got busy setting up his research library. And within minutes he was zoned out to everything and anyone around him.

Mitch scrubbed his hands down his face and strolled back into the kitchen, ready for coffee. He spun Raine in for a long kiss. "Get a good night's sleep in my old room?"

"You know I did." She grabbed a fistful of his T-shirt. "But just so you know, I draw the line at making weird noises right down the hall from where your parents are sleeping."

"Trust me, I'm not complaining. Besides, they're very sound sleepers."

She sent him an eye roll. "That sounds just like something you would've pointed out in high school." She poked him in the belly. "What happened to that hands off promise? I knew you wouldn't keep it."

"How am I supposed to keep my hands off a tasty morsel such as yourself?"

"That's what I thought."

Sensing a land mine, he veered off course. "I want one of those burritos. I've been smelling them for almost an hour."

"Nice dodge." She plated a burrito and watched him dig in.

"I love these things."

Tanner stood in the doorway, sniffing the air the same way Hollings had done, and Lenore followed him. "Something smells good."

"I need coffee," Lenore announced.

"Do you see what's happening in my own living room?" Tanner grumbled. "Professor Bishop has taken over an entire corner of my house and stacked enough books in there until it looks like I'm starting my own public library. It's lopped over very near my TV watching recliner. I can't even see the whole flat screen TV. I thought when he said his wife was supposed to send him stuff, he meant a box, a couple of research papers."

"Who do you think let the Fed Ex guy in?" Mitch returned. "At least he seems to take the work seriously. That's a plus these days."

The kitchen began to fill up when Jackson walked in by himself. "You aren't going to believe who showed up at my door this morning before six o'clock." Without waiting for anyone to play a guessing game, he went on, "Wendy Hollister. That scene in the bar Prentiss overheard is turning out to be prophetic. Oakerson's nowhere to be found. Wendy says he hasn't been at home or work the past two days and hasn't called or texted. You know what that means."

Mitch rubbed the stubble on his chin. "So the cannibals are beginning to eat their own. I'd think Wendy would be frantic. Did you put the fear of God in her?"

"No, just the state police. But she refuses to talk to the cops, any cops. That leaves us."

"You didn't leave her alone, did you?" Mitch asked.

"Are you kidding? I left Tessa there guarding Wendy, holding the SIG in one hand and the phone in the other."

Anniston and Garret walked in, overheard the last part. "What's going on?"

Debriefing them didn't take long.

"We need a place to keep her, a place no one knows about," Anniston suggested. Inspiration hit and she turned to stare at Raine.

Raine nodded knowingly. "It'll work, even though the idea of having that bitch in my family's vacation home down in Ramrod Key is totally repulsive to me. But it's a good spot to keep her away from anyone else like Baskin or Sinclair. But who plays guard dog? Not me. I don't trust myself alone with her."

"Walsh," Mitch proposed as he picked up his cell phone.

"Wait," Raine said, latching on to his arm before he could place the call. "He's a guy. What if Wendy bats those long lashes of hers at him and he caves like—"

That's as far as she got. Mitch choked out a laugh. "You don't know Walsh. Long story. He's immune, bad history there with trusting the wrong women. Wendy tries that with him, she'll end up gagged and tied to a chair."

Raine burst out a laugh. "I'm beginning to love that guy already."

"Walsh will need directions to this cabin," Jackson prompted.

"No he won't, not over land anyway," Raine said. "What if he uses *The Black Rum* instead of driving?"

Mitch thought it over. "It might be missed in the harbor."

"So what if it is?" Raine asked. "Greedy Sinclair and Baskin would probably think your crew left to hunt for the gold already."

"That's true. Okay, why not? Ramrod Key isn't all that far away. It should be fine. Maybe my crew won't have to disembark to your family's place after all. The boat and our witness might be easier contained inside a stateroom."

"Oh please, please, instruct Walsh to stick her in that mess where Dietrich and Nathan were. Please," Anniston pleaded, all but shouting it. "Give Wendy the blood room."

Mitch's lips curved up. He pivoted his look toward Garret. "Better watch out, little brother. This one has a wicked payback streak. I like it."

Garret went to the coffee machine, filled his mug almost to the brim. "That's what I love about her. She knows the importance of making a statement."

"Which reminds me that I need to get back to Tessa," Jackson stated with some worry. "I keep glancing at my cell phone to make sure Tessa hasn't unloaded that pistol in Wendy's direction. Tell Walsh he can pick up Wendy from Nana's house whenever he considers it safe. He'll have to do something with her car, though. I suggest parking it back at her house to raise the fewest red flags."

"Believe me, Walsh knows what to do. I trust him with my life because I've had to over the years," Mitch assured them all.

"Our news pales compared to having Wendy secured," Garret noted. "Anniston and I heard from Sebastian. He's already delivered the surveillance tape to the state police, stayed to watch it with Paul Briggs to make sure Briggs takes action."

"I feel in my heart that things are starting to shake and bake," Anniston announced.

"If only," Mitch uttered with skepticism. "I'll believe it when they slap the cuffs on our chief of police. I'm not even sure it's possible. Sinclair's one of them. Cops, all cops, stick up for each other. They get the benefit of the doubt."

Anniston laid a hand on his shoulder. "I know it's tough to believe it, but have a little faith. Cops have a major dislike toward other dirty cops. Sebastian's prodding Briggs to keep the door open there. He's sticking around for a couple days to make sure the charges progress through the system with the state attorney's office."

They had to wait several hours for Jackson and Tessa to unload Wendy on Walsh. When they did finally get back, Mitch wanted to know, "How'd it go with Mrs. Hollister?"

"A lot of kicking and screaming and making a fuss in general," Tessa answered. "That is one foul-mouthed woman. But I have to hand it to Walsh. He told her if she didn't move her bony ass, he'd call Sinclair himself and turn her over to him. The threat worked, which speaks volumes to how scared she is of the local top cop."

"Good to know for down the road," Mitch stated.

"How soon before we start grilling her for details?" Raine asked.

Mitch had already considered which course to take. "We let her stew for the first twenty-four hours with Walsh right outside her door. Whenever she starts to howl, he'll make sure to remind her she's hit a wall, that she's completely out of options."

Jackson pulled out a soft drink from the fridge, popped the top. "Are we ready to sit down with the professor?"

"Just waiting for you guys to join us," Garret said, slapping his brother on the back. "Hollings has been itching to hold court in the dining room for the last hour. Got his stuff all spread out for the lecture."

"Then let's get to it. I need to get my mind on something else other than a devious, calculating female."

Hollings's face lit up when he saw his students filing in. "I've come across new information. It looks like the rendezvous point for the plot to kill FDR was scheduled a mile offshore. The navigational point was in line with Fort Clinch Beach. I'm certain of that, by the way. That's where they were supposed to drop off the man slated to go onshore and make his way to Warm Springs from there."

Jackson found that idea fascinating. "So in 1945 a Nazi sub came calling that close to Florida's shores? Amazing. You know that fort was only designated a public park in 1938. So it was probably not that crowded during the time this took place. It's like the conspirators had firsthand knowledge that the spot would provide a perfect launch point for that kind of subversive act, away from a large city, no one around to detect the sub in the waters. Perfect," he repeated.

Curious, Garret threw out a question. "Was the sub supposed to wait around for the guy to come back? It'd be interesting to learn who that was."

Hollings thumbed back several pages. "That's easy. Mühlhauser mentions the crewman's name was Conrad Eisenbart. Mühlhauser notes that Eisenbart spoke perfect English because he was originally from the Florida area. That's the reason he was handpicked for the job."

Mitch shook his head. "No Eisenbarts are on the island that I know of."

"They wouldn't keep that name," Anniston reminded him. "The family likely changed it after the war ended when it didn't go well for their side."

"Right," Mitch said in agreement. "So would there have been an official name change through the courts? I doubt it. Not back then. So the Nazi sympathizers will likely go undetected during our lifetime."

"There might be a way," Anniston said. "Because we're looking for really old tax records, Garret and I could go sit in the tax office and pore over the archives, see if there were ever any Eisenbarts anywhere around here circa pre-World War II."

Mitch looked at Garret. "That's up to you, but it sounds like it'd be right up your alley."

"Maybe. But I'd rather get into that safe deposit box at the bank. Since that will take precise planning to pull it off, I'll bide my time like a good boy and go to the tax office instead."

Hollings turned in his chair. "Look, guys, I've gone as far as I can with the simple translations. The rest of the diary uses those codes I mentioned. I just received the bulk of what I need this morning. Who knows what else the algorithms might reveal once I crack each section of the journal. It may even tell us the names of those Nazi sympathizers you're looking for. All I can do is punch in the software data and see if I can break the code, see what pops up."

"Then that's what you should do," Mitch advised.

Once Walsh got Wendy secured on board *The Black Rum*, it didn't take long for him and the crew to grow tired of the woman's tirades.

"You can't hold me here like this! I want to get off. I have a plane to catch! Take me back home this very minute!"

It went on like that until Walsh shouted over her outburst, "Sit down, shut up, or I'll call Sinclair myself. If he doesn't want you, I'll turn you over to Baskin, and I'll go right down the list until I find someone interested in taking you off my hands. Got that?"

Fortunately, she shut up. But later, when she complained about the food, Walsh picked up the phone and dialed Mitch.

"This woman is a complete pain in the ass. How long do I have to babysit this fiend?"

"Not long is probably too long for you guys. But we do have another ace in the hole left."

"Come up with it soon because even the threat of prison is wearing off. And I'm not certain how long I can keep her in line by telling her I'm calling Sinclair. I don't think she believes me."

"Tell her the deal includes collecting on Nathan's life insurance. Tell her that we'll swear Nathan's dead so she can collect his hefty two million dollars. That should keep her quiet for the next couple of days."

"And will you?"

"Hell, no. That bitch can languish up in Broward where they keep the death row inmates for the next twenty years for all I care."

"Okay then. As long as we're on the same page."

As soon as Mitch hung up the phone his mother was waiting to talk to him.

In a low voice she said, "Let's step outside in the backyard for a minute, away from the house."

"What's wrong?"

Once they reached the spot where she liked to read, she turned to him and said, "I don't make a habit of interfering in the lives of my children. Not even when I saw how unhappy Livvy was did I make it a point to stick my nose into her business. I'd politely ask how things were and leave it at that. When her answer was almost always the same, I didn't question her about it. I realize now I should have. A mother wants the best for her kids. Always. So I brought you out here to ask about Raine. You two are obviously seeing each other again. Does that mean you've decided to stay on island when this is all over?"

"Mom, it's complicated."

"Does Raine know that?"

"She knows I love her and we're trying to find some kind of common ground to build on. But she keeps insisting she can't leave the island because of her responsibilities to her mother. Even though I know she isn't happy running the restaurant." He shuffled his feet, looked around the yard as if the answer might be in the honeysuckle vines.

"Go ahead, tell me the rest," Lenore prompted. "I know when something's bothering you. I've never seen you so tense. It isn't like you to be anything but direct with us."

"These past few days, I've tried to think of the best possible way to tell you and Dad about it. I guess the direct approach will have to do. Take a seat on your bench there and get comfortable."

Lenore eyed him with open interest. "So that bad, huh? I have to sit down? Okay…might as well tell me straight up what's bothering you."

Once he built up his courage, Mitch told her about Baby Taylor.

"Why didn't she come to me? I didn't hear a rumor or a thing about it back then, not a thing." Her eyes filled with tears. "Is there some kind of higher power at work that keeps me from having my grandchildren around me?"

"Mom…"

Lenore sniffled, drew out a Kleenex she'd stuffed in her pocket and wiped her nose. "I'll be all right. I have to tell your father."

"I know. I'm sorry. How do you think I felt when Raine finally got around to telling me?"

"You must've felt like you'd been hit by a cement truck."

"Something like that. If I'd had a clue…maybe…"

She patted the space on the bench next to her, watched him plop down. "So many secrets floating around this town. I've always heard that everyone has them. But you wake up every day in the same place and somehow fail to see what's right next door or right in front of you. All these years, Mitch, I had no idea. How many times did I run into The Blue Taco after work for a to-go order for supper? Too many. How many times did I see Raine around town while I was running my errands? Hundreds. She never said a word to me. I guess that explains why she's been so angry with you."

"Angry, yes. But how could I have known? Was I supposed to play twenty questions each time I hit town? Even then, I wouldn't have guessed that was the reason. Am I stupid because it never occurred to me?"

Lenore took her son by the hand as if to offer some solace. "She was so young. You mustn't think she purposely went out of her way to deceive you."

"I was angry after she finally told me. I could give her the benefit of the doubt for the first two or three years, but after that...it was difficult. Turns out, Marla kept my letters from getting to her. I don't know how she managed that, but she did. After that, our relationship, such as it was, seemed destined to fail, especially since she harbored such resentment toward me."

Lenore started to speak, then didn't know what to say. After several long seconds, she finally got the words out. "Marla is not well." She tapped the side of her head. "Up here. I've seen it getting worse. Once Danny died, she slipped into some kind of non-functioning role where all she wants to do is sit on the sofa and watch TV. Without Raine to run that eatery, there won't be a restaurant."

"I refuse to believe that. There are any number of solutions. Marla could hire a manager, someone other than Raine. Charlotte could easily step into that job, let Maddie continue to run the kitchen. Raine doesn't have to stay stuck there."

Lenore rubbed his back. "Now you just have to convince Raine there's life out there after The Blue Taco."

Chapter Fifteen

Very early in life, the young man who'd started out his life as Roger Thornton, learned how to survive with his wits and fists. That chimerical world of his started out roaming the streets down in the French Quarter between Simon Bolivar and La Salle. He couldn't have been more than nine when he tried his hand at petty theft. Running with a pack of neighborhood kids like himself, stealing came easy. Having a father in Angola gave the boy a lot of instant street cred.

Young Roger caught on at home how to handle women. Long before his father got shipped off to prison, his parents didn't much care for each other and showed it by creating a tempest of domestic conflict that would follow him around for the rest of his life. His personal relationships were doomed to crumble each time he chose a quick backhand that always ended in that first ugly purple bruise.

Those same fists had him fighting his way into the Biloxi branch of the Dixie mafia. As a mob enforcer he'd done his share of dirty deeds—executed a rival, kidnapped a drug dealer, collected debts. But not since coming to Indigo Key had he really hit his stride in that department.

Establishing himself as a businessman had been easy. He'd talked his way into Royce's favor, then won him over enough to get a string of business loans. These days, he owned the busiest car repair shop in town, a body shop that never had to advertise, and a used car lot where customers had their pick of late-model gems. Money streamed in. He used it to gamble at various casinos, to bed all the hookers he could get, and run a little scheme or two on the side that no one knew about.

Many times since coming to the island and morphing into a respectable fellow, he'd been on the cusp of full-blown success, the success he felt he deserved. But it seemed he always lacked the funds, even if his benefactor, Royce, let him live in his guest cottage rent-free. His lifestyle could be taxing, especially when he lost big at blackjack or craps or blew it on thousand-dollar call girls.

That's why to accomplish what he wanted and ice the cake with a tasty cream topping, he'd had to become what amounted to a flunky to the town's wealthiest resident.

Managing the old guy's properties was okay. He could live with it, knowing there was a certain prestige to the job. But driving the old man around town like a chauffeur was a slap in the face. He knew people laughed at him behind his back for doing it.

Maybe that's why he'd gone out of his way to bed the man's precious daughter, Winnie. He'd given Winnie her first drink—frothy margaritas with plenty of tequila, laced with a little ecstasy. Who knew the girl couldn't hold her alcohol or her drugs? But over time, she'd gotten better at it, too good, turning into a raging, spitting drunk, especially when she was pissed.

Killing Winnie Buchanan hadn't been part of the plan. But when she'd started trying to push him into marriage, that had been her death knell. No one was going to tie down Roger Baskin. Her old man's money had been a huge temptation. He couldn't deny that part. But to hook up with someone like Winnie, with a mean mouth on her, just wasn't going to happen. No one told him what to do or when to do it. Not Winnie Buchanan or some snot-nosed tourist who'd believed Walker's promise to cut him in on a share of the gold. Yeah, like that was ever gonna happen.

And when Oakerson began shooting his mouth off in a public place, the mayor had signed his own execution. Stupid bastard.

No one could ever accuse Roger Thornton Baskin of gladly suffering fools. He didn't like stupid people. And to him, Oakerson headed the class right up there next to Walker. Maybe now the two were somewhere holding hands in the dumbass section.

Tonight inside the guesthouse, he met with his friend, Boone Dandridge, and the chief of police, who hadn't exactly been invited, but had chosen to butt in just the same.

"I knew something was up when Dietrich went MIA," Sinclair told the others. "That's why I went along with Duarte's plan to kidnap the little taco queen. It makes me look like a genius now since Duarte's claiming he offed Dietrich."

"Do you think it's true?"

"Are you willing to call Duarte a liar?" Sinclair asked. "Not me."

"So what do we do without Dietrich running the show?" Boone wanted to know.

"Kiss Duarte's ass," Sinclair recommended. "That's what I intend to do. I want my share of that gold and no one, but no one, is cutting me out. You should adopt that same attitude."

"Those Indigos just keep pushing, nosing around."

"Maybe they'll make a mistake and I'll get to shoot them. I particularly don't like that little bastard, the surfer. Every time I see him I think, 'just give me a reason.'"

"I thought they'd get bored with this whole thing and be gone back to where they came from," Baskin commented. "Who knew they'd stick it out this long."

"I told you those three would be a problem," Boone said.

Sinclair groaned low in his throat. "Yeah, you also thought you had their old fart of a dad figured out. Then four dumbasses show up on their doorstep trying to convince him Livvy took off. That might've been the stupidest part of this whole thing yet."

Sinclair sneered particularly hard at Dandridge. "Your idea went south fast, didn't it? I'm glad I wasn't there to see you guys embarrass yourselves like that. You should've at least presented it better. I would have."

Tired of listening to his bragging, Boone set his jaw. "You weren't around though, were you? My reputation's at stake here. I've already lost a small group of my congregation, half a dozen or so, strongly influenced by Tanner and Lenore. I can't afford to have my good name dragged—"

"Oh, for God's sake, shut your pie hole!" Sinclair bellowed. "Quit blubbering on about yourself. You're not the only one who has a rep to worry about. At least you have a job no matter what. I'm up for re-election next spring. People are beginning to flap their gums about me. I've got deputies who look at me different these days."

Baskin tried to get them to settle down. He had to shout over the din. "That's why we got involved in this. I knew Dietrich would figure out a way to screw this whole thing up. But he just couldn't leave it alone with Hugo."

Sweat beaded on Boone's forehead. "If we can't wangle our way into Duarte's confidence, we have to devise a plan to get on board that ship. I'm not sitting back and watching anyone take my share of the gold after everything I've done to get this far. Although I still don't understand why we had to take such extreme measures with the Buchanans."

Sinclair laughed. "Are you kidding? Baskin had been itching to put that sniveling little coward Walker in his place for years. Am I right?"

Baskin grinned. "His wife put up more a fight than he did."

"Good thing I got me a piece of that before we finished her off," Sinclair boasted.

"*You* finished her off," Baskin corrected. "And left Boone and me to clean up the aftermath."

Sinclair raised his middle finger toward the mechanic. "Hey, I'm the one who woke the mayor up at two in the morning to let us use one of his touring boats. My little fishing craft would never have handled the weight."

"I don't know why we have to rehash this," Boone said. "We should just play cards or something instead of talking about it."

But Sinclair refused to let it go. "You sure you boys cleaned up everything that night like I told you? Exactly like I told you. Nathan wasn't sure you could get the job done."

Baskin clenched his teeth and snarled, "Screw Nathan. Carson and I spent practically all night cleaning up while Boone got rid of the van. No one will ever find anything even if they go to the body shop. And why would they bother to look there now? The damn Indigos may suspect us, but they sure as hell don't have the goods to nail us for anything."

Across town, inside the Indigo house, the entire conversation captured the room in a spellbound state of shock. They listened in stunned silence as each word sent chills through the room. In the humidity, the temperature felt like it dropped a full ten degrees.

Lenore began to cry. Tanner swore, clenching his fists at his side.

Filled with anger, hurt, tension, the rage ran hot as the implication of the confession slammed into each of them.

Anniston's eyes misted over. "When Sebastian bugged the cottage, this is the kind of results we were hoping for. I know it rips your heart out hearing it like this but…"

"We always suspected Dandridge was right there when Sinclair and Baskin murdered them, now we know for certain," Mitch said as his eyes glistened with tears, his outlook full of hate. He looked at Raine. "Carson helped them clean up."

The horror hadn't fully settled over her when Raine repeated what she'd heard out loud. "So Sinclair raped Livvy. I wonder if Nathan knew that part. They confessed right on tape. I've known these men my entire life. They're horrible monsters, all of them."

"We all have," Mitch stated, beginning to go numb. "We have to take these guys down, once and for all, so they'll never be able to do anything like this to anyone else. The state police may drag their feet, but we can't afford to wait. We need to up the pressure. Now. Find a way to lure them into some kind of trap."

Raine gripped his hand. "They all talked about it so casually, as if it were an everyday kind of thing—murder an entire family, little children. Maybe they've killed before that night."

"Absolutely. We suspect Boone's killed before. Willis Hartman," Anniston pointed out, her voice cracking with emotion. "Maybe Royce was right. Maybe Sinclair did do something to Darla Pendleton all those years ago."

"That's what I'm talking about," Raine amended. "Their coldness tells me they've all killed right here before."

"I was hoping they'd mention Ryan. That we'd get them on tape confessing to that," Tessa said, her voice bleak, her tone filled with grief. "I understand their mindset a little more now. But I still wonder why Ryan had to die. Couldn't they have just run him out of town or something?"

"Not these guys," Jackson said, taking her hand. "They weren't about to share the gold."

"I know that part. But I guess I may never know all of it. I mean, how does Ryan lose his life over a treasure they hadn't even found yet? The same goes for Livvy and Walker and those babies. What in the world did they do that they had to kill all these people?"

Jackson stroked her hair. "I promise you we'll find out the reason before this is finished. But you might as well get ready to settle for knowing that it was all about the gold, the power of it, and ego. Look at each man involved in this. Sinclair, Baskin, and Dandridge exhibit your basic narcissistic psychopathic characteristics. Everything is about them. Rules don't apply. They think they're entitled, they're even above the law."

Tessa chewed her lip. "That certainly applies to the three you mentioned. I get the sense Oakerson and Frawley are simply followers."

"Simple maybe, but still dangerous," Jackson said in agreement. "I'm with Mitch on this. We have to do whatever it takes to bring these people down who've operated in this town for way too long. We need to get our hands on their DNA."

Mitch traded looks with Raine. "We already have Sinclair's. That cup we gave Anniston for testing came from him."

"And I sent the cup in the day you gave it to me. Whatever comes back, though, it won't hold up in court because it came from you, and you're not a member of law enforcement. But it will give us the ammunition we need to get the state cops to act."

Anniston went on to volunteer a theory. "I think Baskin and Sinclair have a screw loose. I also think those two in particular have a major grudge against Buchanan. It translates to what Prentiss overheard that night in the bar. Something has always bothered me about Winnie Buchanan's death. I should have dug deeper into that. I knew it was too great a coincidence that she died ten months before Walker did. Now we know for certain Walker died at the hands of Baskin and Sinclair. I'm not sure these murders that night were all about getting the location of those papers out of Walker and Livvy. I think Baskin had been looking for an excuse to get rid of both Winnie and Walker for quite some time. The night Winnie died, I suspect an opportunity arose when she was coming back from Key Largo after dining out with friends. It was too convenient for Baskin to pass it up."

"Cunning *and* sneaky how Baskin managed to somehow pull it off and made it look like an accident," Raine said, chills running down her arms at the notion. "If we could find out where Baskin was that night, it might sink him for good."

"I intend to find that connection," Anniston promised. "If I have to, I'll dig into his credit card statements, illegally, of course."

Garret's brow wrinkled, a look of puzzlement filled his face. "But guys, don't we have enough on our plates without adding Winnie Buchanan into the mix?"

"Maybe so, but the more charges we're able to heap on these guys, the better off we'll be," Anniston reminded him.

"I think Royce should hear that tape."

All eyes turned to stare at Tanner as if they couldn't believe the suggestion came from him.

Anniston choked out a response. "That sounds like a definite change of heart on your part."

"*Slight* change of heart," Tanner corrected and told them about the plan he'd devised on his own. "I'm convinced Royce will do his part. That's why I think Anniston should make a copy of the tape and let him listen to it. Just in case he thought I was full of hot air earlier, he'll know the truth for himself. Don't take it into his house, though. It's too dangerous to meet there with Baskin nearby on the premises. I don't trust that crazy rat bastard. You should make sure it's a neutral spot, somewhere spontaneous out of the public eye."

"I don't like sending Anniston there alone," Garret tossed out. "I'll go with her."

Anniston chewed her bottom lip. "No, it's better if you aren't there. It makes the stronger case if I meet with him like I have in the past—without any Indigos around to butt heads with him."

"Fine, but I won't be far away," Garret vowed.

She put a hand to his face. "That's what I like to hear."

Across the room, Mitch heard what sounded like water rushing through his ears. He saw his father's mouth moving but couldn't quite make out the words. Something about listening to Sinclair's voice. It grated and buzzed through his head like a freight train whizzing by at a high rate of speed. He'd tried to latch on to what it meant but couldn't quite narrow down the distant memory and pull it into full focus. It flared in his brain from when he was a kid. He blinked to clear his head, clear his mind.

Next to him, Raine waved her hand in front of his face. "Mitch, are you okay? What's wrong?"

"I...I don' know. I just...I don't know," he repeated. "I guess...I'm having trouble processing the fact they confessed. It's one thing to suspect those guys. It's quite another to hear them laugh about it with your own ears and know what they did. Listening to them has me seeing red." But that wasn't it, not entirely anyway.

She placed her lips on his. "It'll be okay. I'm here for you. I'll do whatever's necessary to help you get them behind bars."

"Could we get out of here?" Mitch suggested abruptly.

"Sure. Are you certain you're okay?"

Instead of saying anything else, he grabbed her hand. "Come on, I need some air." He led her out of the house into the night, taking several deep breaths along the way.

Once he reached the back patio, he turned to her and simply buckled.

She caught him up in her arms. "I'm so sorry." Holding him, she whispered a few soothing words. "It's okay to cry. Cry it all out."

"I don't think that's possible. I'm…numb." There was something else going on inside him he couldn't identify. But for now, he leaned on Raine. Not knowing what else to do, he wrapped her up.

"Do you think Lenore and Tanner would mind if we went back to my place?" she prompted.

"I was hoping you'd say that."

Chapter Sixteen

For the meeting with Royce, Anniston decided not to go alone. She persuaded Raine and Tessa to participate again. After setting it all up, the night began at the marina. It was like a scavenger hunt.

For starters, Anniston directed Royce to leave his office and use a taxi to arrive at the harbor. She caustioned him to make sure he wasn't followed.

Once he arrived, he hobbled over to her Ford Explorer and got inside. "Is all this subterfuge really necessary?"

"We think so," Anniston stated, as she took off heading to the other side of town. They ended up at one of Royce's rental properties, vacant since summer, and well away from Baskin's car repair shop or city hall. "You brought the key, right?"

"I'm not an idiot," he snarled. "There's a car over there without its headlights on," Royce noted as soon as he lifted himself out of the car.

"Nothing wrong with your vision," Raine muttered as she took hold of his arm. "Someone's keeping an eye out for us."

"Three someones I'm guessing," Royce mumbled. "When do you plan to tell me what this is all about?"

"I don't mean to be so mysterious but there's something you need to listen to. Bugging your guest cottage finally paid off."

Royce's face looked drained as he took out the key and handed it over to Anniston. "Why didn't you say so before now?"

With Raine on one side of him and Tessa on the other, the two women helped him maneuver the dark sidewalk and the steps up to the front porch. They waited while Anniston dealt with the lock.

She hurried in ahead of everyone else, flipping on lights as she went. She checked room by room to make certain the house was indeed empty before ending up back at the living room. Since the rental came furnished, she watched as Raine and Tessa led Royce over to the couch. After plopping him down there, the women settled in around him.

Anniston took out a small recorder, placed it on the coffee table, and slipped in a little micro-sized tape. "I want you to listen all the way through, no interruptions. If you don't think you're up to it, tell me now. I'll warn you right off that it won't be easy to listen to and what you're about to hear will make you angry. But I don't want to cause you to have another episode with your heart."

"Don't worry about me, I'll be fine. Just turn the damn thing on."

Anniston pushed the button, sat back and listened to the replay of the men's voices as the ugly words filled up the air. She watched the old guy's face. She knew hearing them discuss Livvy's death and that of the children wouldn't get much of a reaction, so she waited for Sinclair to mention Walker and for Baskin to respond.

"How dare that son of a bitch call my son a sniveling coward!" Royce thundered, full of rage. His forehead popped out in sweat. His vision blurred as rage blinded him. "I'll kill him! No, I'll kill them all!"

Anniston patted his hand. "I'm afraid there's more."

Raine found her nerve to speak up. "A lot more. Anniston uncovered something we all overlooked. Baskin and Winnie were involved in a hot and heavy affair. Without telling you too much, let's just say there's evidence in Baskin's credit cards that proves it. We think something went south with their relationship. Whatever it was, it was enough to make Baskin stage Winnie's car wreck that night to look like an accident. We don't think it was."

Royce's eyes continued to glaze over with fury along with steely determination. He stared at Anniston. "That explains a great deal."

"Really? Well, Baskin's credit card statements reveal several interesting transactions. Over the course of two years, he regularly ordered Winnie flowers from the florist in town. Sage Lowery remembers each one because the roses went to your daughter with a sweet card attached."

"Roger doesn't strike me as that kind of a romantic," Raine pointed out. "He strikes me as cold and calculating. I don't think he'd go to that trouble unless he had an ulterior motive."

Anniston nodded and went on, "There were lots of credit card transactions showing Roger and Winnie often went out for candlelight suppers at Romano's in Key Largo, never here in town though, always somewhere that the hookup wouldn't get back to you. I'm thinking that was orchestrated for a reason."

Royce clutched his stomach. "Had I known, I would've demanded Winnie stop having any contact with him at all. I'd have gotten rid of the lying scum!"

Anniston cut her eyes toward Raine and Tessa before turning back to Royce. "Naturally, we've put our heads together to try and come up with a reason you'd be so opposed to the match. The logical explanation is that you already knew about Baskin's mob enforcer days, knew he wasn't good enough to go out with your daughter and never would be no matter what he did. You don't strike me as the type of businessman who'd let someone live in your guesthouse without doing a thorough background check on them. How long have you known about Roger's past?"

Royce's eyes drifted to all three women. "I…I…all…right…I knew. So what? I didn't expect him to set his sights on my Winnie, not like that. He told me once he wasn't the type of man to settle down with one woman. That alone made him undesirable. He had a reputation for cavorting with loose women, hookers, and the like. It was one thing to have him as my driver, quite another to let him become a member of the family. Besides, I'd never stand by and let him kill my baby girl or my son." He tapped his cane on the floor for emphasis. "How do you think he could've killed my daughter and made it look like she wrecked the car?"

"Truthfully, no idea. My guess would be that he beat her just as he did Walker, then put her back in the car. He did what he could to stage the scene to look as though she'd had too much to drink and ran off the road. Who investigated this so-called accident?"

Royce's face paled at the memory. "Sinclair. He claimed he'd been up in Key Largo that night fishing with a buddy and just happened by the scene."

"There you go. Very convenient. You'll likely never know the truth unless you have the case reopened. I hate to say it again, but keep in mind you're the one responsible for bringing Baskin into your fold, into your home, into your business. He wouldn't have had access to your children without you letting him in the front door. He's here masquerading as a legitimate businessman on the money you loaned him." Anniston leveled a finger at his nose. "Think about that. Now you have to do your part to rid the town of them all."

"I already told Tanner I'd do whatever he wanted me to do."

Raine discovered it wasn't so hard to stand up to a Buchanan after all. "You keep saying that. Now it's time to prove it."

Sitting across the street in the pickup, the brothers held their vigil in silence as they kept an eye out for Sinclair or Baskin.

As Garret sat there, though, he eyed Mitch's demeanor. He and Jackson had talked about their brother's odd behavior over the past twenty-four hours. Thinking it had to do with Raine, they'd agreed to leave the guy alone in his own deep thoughts. But the more reserved Mitch became, the more it bugged Garret. If it was about Raine, then he should be able to needle out an explanation. But he didn't think this mood was about Raine at all. The more he thought about it, the more it irritated him. He wondered if now might be the perfect time to get at the truth.

After another thirty minutes ticked by and Mitch's sulky mood dragged on, Garret had had enough. He angled in his seat to stare at his brother. "What gives with you? You haven't said two words to anyone since you heard that tape last night. What's going on in that brain of yours?"

Mitch clenched his jaw. "You'll think I'm crazy."

"Probably, because you are crazy. Come on, Sally, man up. Tell us what's bothering you."

"Besides the fact that those assholes killed our sister's family, wiped them out like the monsters they are?"

"Yeah, besides that," Jackson replied, scooting up from the backseat to look over the console. "Something's on your mind. Might as well spit it out."

Mitch sat there a full minute deciding whether or not to unburden what had festered inside him for the past day. Finally, he huffed out a breath and said, "Okay. Here's the deal. I heard Sinclair's voice on that tape and it triggered something inside me, a memory maybe. I don't know."

"You've talked to Sinclair lots of times. Did it ever get to you like that before?" Garret asked.

"No. That's why it's crazy and probably means absolutely nothing."

"You're not this upset over nothing," Jackson stated. "Your surly mood is starting to piss me off."

Mitch struggled for the right tone. "Like I said, Sinclair's voice sparked this snippet from childhood, a memory of him..."

"I have memories of that old coot bullying half a dozen people around town," Garret prompted. "I saw it with my own eyes. So what?"

"It probably means nothing. I was too young—"

"Jeez, what is it with you? A memory of him doing what exactly?" Jackson snapped, his patience waning.

"I was probably around seven or eight. I'd gone off exploring even though Mom had specifically told me not to—dragging Garret along because he vowed to tell Mom if I didn't take him with me."

"I learned early to use that threat. It was great leverage. Worked every time, too," Garret boasted with pride.

Mitch sent him a look of impatience. "Do you want to hear this or not?"

Garret held up a hand. "Touchy, aren't you? Go ahead."

"There's this image I have in my head. Garret and I are standing on the bank near the bridge coming into town hunting for river rocks."

Garret nodded. "We did that a lot back then. Used to pick up the smooth ones. Those were best for skipping on top of the water."

Mitch leveled another annoyed gaze at his brother. "Will you shut up for five seconds? It's tough enough to talk about this as it is without you interrupting every five seconds."

"Then spit it out already," Garret demanded. "Stop acting like a diva who can't talk about it because it's too painful."

"Okay. I'm standing on this little ridge looking down across the water when I hear a car coming up on the blacktop below us at a high rate of speed. I duck down and make Garret do the same because I don't want either one of us to get caught. Pretty soon I watch a squad car screech to a stop underneath the trestle near the shoreline. There's not another soul around when I see a much younger Sinclair get out of his police cruiser like he's pissed off about something. I mean really angry. He skirts the hood real fast and goes around to the back door on the passenger side and yanks this woman out of the car by her hair. Her feet hit the dirt like she's already struggling to stand up. Maybe she's been drugged. I don't know. But he doesn't let her gain her legs before he hauls off and slaps her right across the mouth. It knocks her down to the ground. Now that I think about it, they might've been having sex. He jumps on her, and then wraps his hands around her throat. I see him, clear as day, sitting on top of her. Sinclair wearing his uniform, the woman's got on this dark blue business suit, dark high heels. She's kicking and doing her best to scream, but it's not doing one bit of good because Sinclair is much bigger and he doesn't let up. At some point she must've had her brown hair put up on her head in one of those twist things women like to do. But during the struggle with Sinclair, it all comes loose and hangs down around her shoulders. I see it all through a young kid's eyes like I'm terrified and don't know what to do. I see that he's hurting her but I don't know if I should run to get help or simply run away to protect myself and Garret because I know Sinclair's done something really bad and we need to get out of there to keep him from coming after us."

"Did he see you, Sinclair?" Jackson wanted to know.

"I don't think so. No," he added, thinking back. "But I tell you one thing, I was almost too scared to move. I kept my hand over Garret's mouth the entire time to keep him from talking a-mile-a-minute like Chatty Cathy and blowing our cover. That's how terrified I was."

"You'd know it if Sinclair had spotted the two of you," Jackson declared with a nod of his head. "He'd have gone after you at some point because you and Garret were just two little kids, playing at the wrong spot at the wrong time. Two little kids who witnessed him beating up a woman. It stands to reason you'd be scared watching an adult—someone you'd been told to respect—treat a woman like that."

"I don't think he beat her up, Jackson. I think he killed her right in front of me."

All kidding gone, Garret angled in his seat. "What was the name of that woman Anniston mentioned who'd gone missing back in '92?"

"Darla Pendleton. But why would I remember it now, so vividly? Why not ten years ago, five? Why am I just now seeing it so clearly? I don't remember saying a word about it to Mom or Dad or anyone else for that matter. And now, I can't stop thinking back to that day. I even recall cautioning Garret to keep his mouth shut about it."

"Want my opinion?" Jackson asked.

"Do I have a choice?" Mitch snarked.

"Not really. I think it's because of all the stress you've been under lately. Coming back here dealing with all the sadness over Livvy and the kids, then finding out about Raine's miscarriage, then having to face all those emotions that come with it. I think all of it's caused a flood of feelings you had about your past here in town. All those demons have come rushing to the surface. Part of it includes this memory from childhood."

In a voice barely above a whisper, Garret asked, "Do you think he buried her, right then and there, underneath the bridge?"

"I don't know. But maybe we should go out there and dig at the same spot where I remember the attack taking place, the exact place I saw Sinclair last with the woman," Mitch suggested.

"We could do that," Jackson said.

When Mitch looked up and saw Raine along with the others emerge from the rental, he started the engine. He realized he needed to talk to her as soon as possible. There were things he needed to explain.

After breaking away from everyone else, Mitch was finally able to pull Raine back to the houseboat so they could be alone. But after all his bluster, it took him a good twenty minutes to work up the courage to start talking.

"What's the matter, Mitch? You've been acting weird since last night. I know what you heard on the tape is disturbing but…"

"You have no idea."

"Are you upset that I went to meet with Royce?"

"What? No." He rubbed his forehead, realizing this was harder to get out than he'd first thought because it just sounded flat out crazy. "After years of avoiding it, I think I know why I wanted out of this town so much."

Her stomach dropped. She got a sinking feeling in her heart. "Uh, okay. Are you about to tell me you've discovered it's really me you want to—"

"Of course not," he snapped. "When will you get that out of your head for good? Stop thinking that way. It wasn't you. It's all on me."

"Oh, jeez. Are you breaking up with me again?"

"No. Raine, listen to me. What I'm about to tell you is likely to sound improbable and maybe a little crazy, but it hit me when we sat there and listened to that tape. Hearing Sinclair's voice triggered something in me, a memory from when I was a kid. I can't explain it. For a man who goes off to hunt treasure based on nothing but charts and a gut feeling, I haven't been able to fully wrap my mind around this. So bear with me."

"Okay. Then you'd better just spit it out because you're really freaking me out here."

"Fine." He went through the backstory, the logistics of how he and Garret had ended up underneath the bridge. "We were standing on the embankment, not the lowest part but a little ridge where we'd had some success looking for river rocks before that day. But as we're searching and pawing through the runoff from the marsh, I get distracted once I hear a car coming up fast over the bridge. It's a police car. The driver backs up and I remember hoping that he won't stay for long. But no such luck because he's only backing up to hit the turnoff that leads below the trestle. Garret and I take cover so whoever it is doesn't see us there. Pretty soon I see Sinclair get out of his squad car near the water's edge. Even as young as I am I can tell he's royally upset about something. I mean, I see his eyes and they're stone-cold and bulging with rage. He rounds the hood and goes around to the back, pulls this woman out of the backseat. Her feet hit the dirt like her body won't hold her upright. After thinking about it, I'm pretty sure he'd drugged her. But he doesn't give her any time at all to right herself before he hauls off and starts beating the crap out of her. She finally drops to the ground from the blows. He falls on top of her and I'm pretty sure they start having sex. Next thing I see is that his hands are wrapped around her throat. Tight. And he doesn't let up. I see him kill her, Raine. He's sitting there on top of her stomach, wearing his lousy uniform, while the life drains out of this woman."

"Oh, my God. You saw all that? Oh, my God." She snapped her fingers. "What was the name of that woman Anniston mentioned who went missing? Darla Pendleton. How old did you say you were?"

"Yeah, the time frame fits. I was probably seven and it left an impression on me. Garret remembers that I started having nightmares around that time. Mom had to come in and calm me down almost every night after that. I don't know how Garret remembers something like that from five years old but he swears he does."

"My first memory was at three," Raine offered. "So it's more than likely Garret remembers more than he thinks he does about the incident."

"Not like I do. I still see the woman's blue outfit, her dark shoes, her brown hair sinking into the wet dirt. She's kicking and fighting, trying to scream, but it's not doing one bit of good because no one's around to hear her except two little boys who are too scared to do anything, not just of what happened, but of the man, Sinclair. She doesn't have a chance at winning against him because he's much bigger and stronger and he doesn't let up. I see him take her life and I'm too petrified to move and don't know what to do next. I should've run to get help or told someone."

He saw a tear drop down on his shirt. "Maybe if I'd have said something back then to my mom or dad, Livvy might still be alive today."

"Surely you don't really believe that," Raine murmured, pulling him to her. She caressed his hair, trying to comfort that idea away. "You were a frightened little boy, a child. You probably weren't even sure what you saw exactly."

"I knew enough that something bad had happened."

"And this is why you couldn't wait to leave this place?"

"I think so. Consider it from a kid's point of view, a kid who sees a cop, the top cop, murder a woman forty yards from where he's rock hunting with his kid brother. It stuck with me, must've made such a lasting impression with me and not in a good way. From that point forward, I associated Sinclair with a monster, a very bad guy in a position of authority that I wanted, no, needed, to get away from, even if that meant leaving you behind. I'm sorry," he added quietly. "I'm sorry I wasn't the man you thought I was."

She kissed his mouth and then said, "While I see your point, you shouldn't beat yourself up about it. You and your brothers are doing everything you can now to see that

Sinclair is locked up. I think that has to be enough for that little seven-year-old who couldn't process what he saw. No child should ever witness such a violent crime."

She stood up, took his hand. "I think we should go to bed. Tomorrow will have its own challenges. That's enough for tonight."

Later, their bodies slick, they snuggled together, skin to skin. He brushed a hand down her thigh then up to her belly where she'd carried their son. "Every inch of you is so incredibly beautiful."

"I've put on five pounds since last summer."

"I see. So you could really stand to lose this little roll right here," he teased as he tried to pinch a ball of skin along her waist and got nothing.

She hooted with laughter, but hit him lightly on top of his head on general principle. "I'm short, every extra pound shows."

"No it doesn't." He trailed kisses along her stomach up to her breasts. "It's such a cute belly, but I love these the most," he declared, tempting out a swollen nipple for his benefit.

His mouth tugged her into bliss, pulled her along into a fog of gentle blue. He stoked every inch of her to life as quick as a match ignited a dying ember. He slid his hands beneath her hips, moved within her, filling her hotter, brighter.

With each slow thrust they climbed. Heart thudding as they rose. Soaring through the haze, reaching for that pinnacle, that perfect ripple, they danced on the edge. Circling, spinning, pleasure heaved them skyward and into a tower of glowing white. It glistened brighter than silver, shimmered better than gold.

Their skin tingled, their blood heated as they tried to catch their breath.

"I think we left the earth that time," Raine noted, breathless, her fingers still locked in his hair.

"Feels like it. Feels like I ran a marathon to the sun and back."

"I'm pretty sure you've gotten a whole lot better at this over the years. I don't remember it coming together quite like this."

"Told you I'd gotten a lot better." He nuzzled her neck before rolling to the side.

"Hmm, but I don't remember so much sizzle and pop. It's like electricity when we make love."

"I'm pretty sure the pop and sizzle has always been there for me."

She elbowed him none too gently in the side. "You never said those kinds of things when we were kids."

"I know. That's why I'm saying them now."

Chapter Seventeen

"You can't go digging under the main bridge coming into town where just anyone could likely gawk at the three of you standing there with shovels," Anniston stressed. "Not only would you draw attention to what you're doing, you'd also send up a red flag to Sinclair. For one thing he'd probably ask you to cease and desist at the point of a gun. And then he'd likely go on the run to South America just like Wendy had planned to do."

Sebastian sat off to the side, listening to his sister plead her case. Glad to be back in the fold, he hurled himself headlong into the discussion. "Let's say you went out there with regular shovels and picks and did find bones. Your haphazard way of doing it might accidentally destroy evidence. Think about that. Without an official team out there, you could do more harm than good. We're building a pretty solid case against Sinclair. Let me contact Paul Briggs and get a status update. Give me twenty-four hours before you do anything as bold as digging under that bridge."

"I don't like the idea of waiting for Tallahassee to get here," Mitch pointed out. "They're taking their sweet time to figure it out."

"Going through official channels is better than going off and destroying all the hard work we've put into this," Anniston insisted. "Listen to reason. We have a plan in place, let it play out."

Garret sent Mitch a long look. "I hate to admit it, but she might have a point. Let's see what happens when Royce rattles their cage."

Anniston roamed the room. "Just remember, the goal isn't for Royce to be convincing, but rather to stir the pot." She glanced at Sebastian. "You want to tell them or should I?"

"You have the floor, might as well drop the bomb while the gang's all here."

"You remember when Chuck told me there was male DNA inside Livvy?"

"Hard to forget," Garret snapped.

"He was wrong. When I sent him the cup Mitch retrieved with Sinclair's DNA on it, Chuck redid the test just to make sure, cautious to avoid mistakes. He found there were two male donors, not one. We already heard Sinclair admit in his little convo with his buddies that he raped Livvy. That's a given. But the other contributing male sperm was from Nathan Hollister."

She heard Jackson's intake of breath from across the room.

"So he was there that night? I knew we should have crushed him while we had the chance to get more answers out of that lowlife."

Anniston was more practical. "Keep an open mind. It's possible when Livvy went out to run errands that last day of her life, she could've had consensual sex with Nathan. They were having an affair. I doubt we'll ever really know for certain. What we can say with certainty is that scenario doesn't apply to Sinclair. There's not a shred of evidence that says Livvy was involved in any way with the police chief."

Mitch turned to Sebastian. "That's what you meant when you said we were building a solid case against him?"

"We have solid evidence he abducted Raine. We have him on tape admitting to the rape and murder of Livvy, add to that, the murders of Walker and the kids. Now, we may be able to get him for Darla Pendleton's murder. I'd say, it's looking up for the good guys."

"It's about damn time," Mitch grumbled.

That afternoon, Royce played his part by sending out calls to the partners in the golf course deal. When four of the five showed up in his office midday right on schedule, it was the doughnut shop owner who seemed the most fidgety from the get-go.

Carson Frawley took a seat in one of the club chairs but squirmed like a little kid. "What's this all about? Is it about Dave? Have you seen him lately? It's not like him to take off. He hasn't been in his office. I've checked."

"I heard he and Wendy took off for Cancun for the week, no doubt taking a much-needed break from his burgeoning mayoral responsibilities," Royce responded, repeating the rumor he'd been spoon-fed by the Indigos.

"But to satisfy your curiosity, I have good news," Royce went on with a forced smile, hoping to put the man at ease. "We'll wait for the others to join us before I make the big announcement. Trust me, I think you'll be pleased."

Sinclair strolled in with a swagger. "What's up?"

"Royce says he has good news," Carson tossed out. "Any word out of Dave?"

Sinclair dropped into the other chair, clasped his hands in his lap. "Dave Oakerson is an idiot. Let's get on with this good news. I could use some and I don't have all day," the cop snarled.

Baskin and Dandridge came in together and were greeted by the others.

Royce's spine stiffened at the sight of Baskin, or maybe it was having to be in the same room with all of them and make nice. Either way, he did his best not to focus too long on their lying, cheating, murderous faces, especially Baskin.

Recalling what he'd listened to the night before, his stomach churned. His resolve weakening, Royce considered the semi-automatic he had in the top right-hand drawer of his desk. He could easily grab the weapon, point the barrel toward the men he'd known for more than twenty years and take care of these bastards right where they sat. It didn't matter that they had a long history together.

At this moment, he didn't much give a damn about waiting for law enforcement to get around to issuing warrants or making an arrest or justice to wind its way through the muddled court system.

"Well?" Sinclair prompted, snapping his fingers in rapid fire fashion toward Royce. "I haven't got all day."

The insolence was enough to snap Royce back on track. "I've learned through my lawyers that Tanner Indigo is so distraught over what happened to his daughter and grandchildren that he's dropped all his efforts to stop the golf course from going in. As of this morning, Tanner's agreed that the preserve will become history, which means the development is back on track. The man's throwing in the towel."

"So how long until we pour the dirt, get the cement mixers busy, and cover up that stink hole?" Baskin wanted to know. "How long before we can expect to line up contractors and finally get this ball rolling?"

"I'm taking care of it," Royce assured his investors. "There's just a couple of little hurdles we need to make sure are behind us so that it clears the way to the resort."

"What's that?" Sinclair asked. "We've discussed all this till we're blue in the face."

Royce ignored the charge and looked over at Frawley. "Did you grease the wheels with the county commissioner to get the land rezoned for development?"

"Of course I did. It's been taken care of, cost you in the neighborhood of seventy-five Gs or so, but it's done."

"What about you, Jessup? Did you pay your man off at the capitol, get him to continue faking the environmental studies that favor us and make all the disclaimers vanish?"

"Are you losing it, Royce? You know damn well I took care of it months ago. That's where your fifty grand ended up."

"How about you, Boone? How do we look on the construction permits? Are they in place and ready to go?"

"They're all set after paying off the county architect. He wanted a hundred grand. That guy's an asshole to work with. But in the end all he really wanted was to see the green stuff and he rubber-stamped the permits right through the system, put his signature on every one of the documents, and already filed them with the county."

Royce shuffled some papers around on his desk. "Since Dave's not here to ask, does anyone know if he secured the loans from the pension fund like he promised?"

Baskin spoke up. "I watched Dave sign off on the paperwork myself. We got a hell of a sweetheart deal that will never have to be paid back. We fold a couple of the shell companies we've created offshore and we're free and clear of the debt. No problem."

"But is it foolproof?"

"I worked this scam a dozen times in New Orleans and as long as Oakerson keeps his mouth shut, we're on easy street."

"Yes, but can we really trust that the mayor's discretion will hold up? After all, he blew off this meeting."

Baskin smiled. "I guarantee you don't have to worry about Oakerson running his mouth."

Royce nodded and went on as if he were checking off a list. "And let's not forget Dave's assistant, Wendy Hollister. Dave's very generously taken her under his wing. I believe, for a couple of years now, she's been his trusted confidante. He's no doubt used her to unburden some of our most intimate secrets."

"Then I'll have to put having a little talk with Wendy on my to-do list," Baskin promised. "I'll make sure she sees things our way from here on out."

After the meeting concluded, just as Anniston had showed him, Royce cued up the video that had been running the entire time. He hit the send button to email the encounter to her and Tanner with a note that read:

They admitted to wire fraud, bribing public officials, money laundering and racketeering. If I'm not mistaken most of it falls under the RICO act. Which should make the feds happy after handing it to them on a silver platter. You watch, before we're done we'll have the state police fighting for jurisdiction. The one thing they didn't admit to is the long list of murders. That's the one thing we need. Find a way to make it happen. In the meantime, I'll pour myself a brandy and wait for the feds to show up at my door.

Tech-savvy Anniston opened her email first before Tanner did. After viewing the video, she let out a war whoop of victory and brought everyone over to see. "I love this."

Tanner came up behind her, scratched his head. "I don't believe it. The old fart actually came through on a promise. Never in a million years did I ever think I'd see Royce Buchanan implicate himself in all the seedy corruption he's had a hand in."

"Maybe now you'll believe me," Anniston said. "That's how bad he wants Walker's murderer to pay for what he did. And he knows it's likely the only way to draw these guys out, certainly getting them prison sentences at the federal level."

"Five years isn't much consolation," Garret grumbled.

Mitch pointed to the screen. "I can't wait until we show Wendy proof that Baskin's chomping at the bit to get to her. That ought to put a little more incentive into becoming a federal witness and rolling over on her old friends."

"Let's hope this seals the deal then," Jackson noted with some skepticism.

Jessup Sinclair had sensed something was off at the meeting. Even before his contact at the state police had called him that afternoon, Jessup had been suspicious of Royce's news. Call it a hunch, but that impromptu meeting had thrown up red flags. All those needless questions at the end didn't come off as genuine. At least not to him. Everyone else in the room might've bought it, but he sensed a set up. He should have taken care of that old man a long time ago when he had the chance.

Now he'd learned that the state attorney general claimed he had evidence that showed he'd kidnapped the little taco queen. The asshole was on the verge of issuing a warrant for his arrest. Imagine them thinking they could slap the cuffs on him.

Obviously it was all a ruse to try and get him to admit to some kind of wrongdoing. He'd been down that road plenty of times before back at the highway patrol. The state's attorney was simply trying to box him in, to put the fear of God in him, maybe try to get him to turn on his buds. He didn't intend to give the state anything. They'd never send him to prison. They'd have to work at it. He'd die first before he'd let them lock him up like a dog.

His buddy inside the state police claimed the process was already a done deal. All the state had left to do was get a warrant. Lots of luck there, Jessup decided. Personally, he didn't believe they'd find a judge to issue such a thing. He'd been the chief of police here for more than twenty years. That had to count for something. No way would it happen.

At least that's what he told himself as he fixed himself a sandwich and listened to Jerry Jeff Walker blaring from the stereo. The song made him wonder if he could finagle Desiree, over at Magic Hands, into bed for a little afternoon romp in the sack. She'd be a good distraction and keep his mind off what was happening in Tallahassee. He'd load up on his Viagra and spend the rest of the day "on patrol." At least that's what he always told his wife Brenda.

But something nagged at him. He couldn't shake the feeling. His gut instinct told him he needed to be on guard. It was like he had a giant spider crawling up his back waiting to take a bite out of him at the first opportunity.

On second thought, he wasn't much in the mood for Desiree's company. She'd more than likely blather on about her coworkers until he wanted to shove a fist down her throat. But neither did he want to hang around the house and wait for his wife to get back from her shopping trip. Brenda was just as prone at yammering his head off as Desiree. A man needed his alone time. Maybe he'd go seek out his fishing buddy. God knows going back to talk to Baskin and Dandridge was a waste of time. And Carson Frawley was more of an idiot than Oakerson. Which made him wonder if the mayor had already got wind of his own misfortune and taken off for parts unknown. It wasn't like Dave to miss a meeting. Maybe he'd taken that wild-eyed Wendy and caught a plane to Guyana. Why hadn't he considered that before now?

Losing his appetite, he pushed his sandwich aside. Maybe it was time to put this town in his rearview mirror. But first he had a few cards up his sleeve that needed playing.

Chapter Eighteen

After spending a day and a half looking through piles of tax records, the only Eisenbart that Anniston and Garret were able to locate anywhere in the county was a man who settled into the area before the war began. He kept to himself and was known to live in a shack in the northern part of the county close to a swamp. Those notes came right off the tax card, circa 1933. It seemed the shanty where Eisenbart lived didn't even have running water, electricity, or an official address.

"We have to go check this out," Garret said. "It's our only lead in this stack of otherwise useless documentation."

Anniston's eyes bugged. "You're suggesting we go poke around in…" she snatched the card out of his hand, "some place called Lost Gator Swamp and try to get information out of swamp people. Are you nuts? They live off the grid for a reason. Mainly because they don't especially like to be around our type? You know, the nosey kind who asks intrusive questions. They won't exactly welcome strangers, which we definitely are."

"I know that," Garret acknowledged, losing patience. "But we have to try. What else do we do? Ignore it? Not me."

"What exactly are you hoping to gain by going there? What are you looking for exactly? This part of it just points the way to the gold." She stopped talking and stared at him. "Don't tell me you've caught gold fever."

"No. But I'm curious by nature. I keep asking myself why did these guys—Sinclair, Baskin and Dandridge in particular—end up here? How did they know to set up shop here?"

"Maybe they just thought Indigo Key looked like easy pickings."

He sent her a dubious look. "I still think Royce had a hand in it, recruiting people to aid in his business dealings. He relied on those same people that he could either control outright or blackmail. No way would these men come into any other town and get the kinds of sweetheart business loans they received to start up their companies."

She sighed. "My spreadsheet seems to back up that theory."

He looked surprised. "When were you planning to mention that? So you admit Royce had a long-term plan in mind to put these people in key positions so he could control the town?"

"It hurts to admit it, but yes. There's definitely a pattern. Just because he's helping us now doesn't mean we should forget that."

"Do you intend to tell my dad that? Because he should know."

"Eventually."

"Glad to hear it. I was beginning to think you'd turned a blind eye to all Royce's shady practices."

"I'd never do that. Well, maybe with you."

"What's that supposed to mean?"

"Are you serious? I've fallen in love with a surfer dude who has a penchant for cat burglary. How often does that happen? My cop background is shrieking. Plus, at some point, you still have to meet my dad. That'll be a red-letter day I'm sure."

He draped an arm over her shoulder as they walked out of the stuffy office and toward the SUV. "Relax. Look at this as an adventure, daring escapades on the horizon. It's bound to provide us with countless stories, something exceptional to tell our grandchildren."

"Bedtime stories about your criminal activities hardly seem appropriate to share with little kids."

"Ah, but I've a pirate's blood in me. And so will they. Better get used to it, darlin'. Having me in your life, you're in for a wild ride."

Their journey took them north into a serene setting with towering mangrove trees that grew alongside bald cypress. Vines of Spanish moss dangled from the branches of southern oak like a wooly necklace reaching for the ground.

The dense woodland came alive with egrets and blue heron, ducklings, and colorful peacocks. The wildlife nestled among the roots living happily beside fat-bodied sea bass and stone crab. The scene was a sight to behold.

Anniston took out her camera. "It's beautiful out here if you discount the gators and water moccasins."

Garret heard the plop of a slithering cottonmouth rolling off the bank and into the murky pond that held a slick coating of green on top. "Just watch where you step. I can deal with the snakes and gators, it's the two-legged variety we came out here to find that worries me."

"Then for God's sakes why are we out here? I don't think I'm dressed for a trek through pond scum. I can't even tell what's lurking on the bottom."

"It's okay by me if you want to go back to the car."

"And leave you out here with no backup? Uh-uh. No way."

He smiled and took out the GPS he'd brought, jabbed in a few coordinates. "From here, we want to go due east."

Anniston studied what that meant and saw nothing but tangled vines and underbrush ahead of them. "That's what I was afraid of. Where'd you get the readings for a coordinate anyway?"

"Off the tax card with the description of Eisenbart's property. I improvised some, so we'll see where it takes us. We'll try to avoid as much of the water as possible and stick to the soppy shoreline."

"That makes me feel a lot better. Not."

But she followed him along the bank as he charted a path into what she determined as daunting territory. She snapped a photo of two muskrats fighting over a scrawny cattail. She came across a nest of eggs from an unknown species of waterfowl and captured the moment to send to her mother.

They spent another hour going back further into the woods. To Anniston's surprise they came to a clearing, a glade-like field with a structure built next to a crop of paper birch, nothing more than a lean-to really.

"I thought the shack would be long gone by now."

"Oh, come on, that can't be the same one."

Before Garret could dispute that, a man appeared carrying a twelve-gauge shotgun. He had long, straggly gray hair and a beard, and wore a pair of dirty overalls over a yellowish T-shirt.

"Whaddya doin' out here? Whaddya want? This is my place."

Garret held up his hands. He quickly introduced himself, hoping that would make a difference, and started talking fast. "We're looking for a man who used to live around here a long time ago, a man by the name of Chester Eisenbart."

"He in trouble?"

"No, sir. He's probably been dead for quite some time. We just want to talk to anyone who might have lived in the area and might have known his people."

"Name's Payne Wilkes."

Garret was glad to see Payne lower the shotgun, glad to see a woman emerge from the hut behind him.

"Payne, what you doin' out here? Who you talkin' to? Who are these folks?"

"This is my wife Seely. We've been in these parts some forty years now. Seely's great uncle used to talk about the man named Eisenbart, lived over yonder 'cross the bog, buried there now."

"When did he die?"

Payne deliberated several long seconds before deciding to answer. "We'll tell you what we know for a price."

Garret wasn't sure what he had to offer in trade except the cash he had on him. "What were you thinking?"

"Got twenty bucks on you?"

"I think I can manage that."

"Then come on in. We ain't got much but you're welcome to sit down for a chat."

Three hours later, near dark, they were grateful when Payne led them out of the swamp and back to their car. They'd learned from Seely that Chester Eisenbart had been a rugged pioneer kind of guy, who'd carved out a life in the severe living conditions that made up the everglades.

Battling gators and poisonous snakes, he'd settled here with a heavy German accent for a reason known only to him. For years, he managed to live off whatever the land provided. He ate what he could wrestle from a trap, shot the small game that came and went, or netted shrimp and crayfish for his supper.

The sandy soil gave him a place to grow vegetables that he could trade for commodities like kerosene, sugar cane, tobacco, flour, tools, local moonshine—if he didn't make his own—and clothing or boots.

Seely swore Chester mainly kept to himself with one exception. Late in his life, he'd met up with a woman and brought her back to his land. Seely had no idea where the woman came from. But sometime later, she gave birth to Chester's son before succumbing to the complications she'd suffered from childbirth.

Chester had named the boy Jessup.

Chapter Nineteen

"You should've seen this place, Lenore," Anniston said, standing in the kitchen watching Garret's mother remove a batch of sugar cookies from the oven in various shapes of ghosts and goblins. "It was rugged, rustic, a whole lot unnerving, a bit scary, right in line with a set designed for Halloween, but beautiful. And Payne and Seely were so…helpful, even welcoming. I couldn't believe Garret got them to talk."

Garret rolled his eyes. "Yeah, after I handed over twenty bucks they were a lot friendlier."

She swatted his shoulder. "You got information out of them, didn't you?"

"We got a story, I'm not sure what it means yet."

Mitch eyed the cookies with open interest. He finally walked over and tried to pick up a couple from the hot pan.

Lenore slapped his hands away. "Those are for tomorrow night's trick-or-treaters. The girls said they'd decorate them for me to hand out." Her eyes formed tears. "I'll miss my grandbabies coming over in their costumes this year."

Raine patted her arm. "I know it won't be the same but I think it's time we threw together a party, just for that reason. Livvy would want us to."

"A cookie decorating party," Tessa volunteered.

"I haven't decorated cookies since high school but I'm willing to give it a shot," Anniston echoed.

"I think we can do better than a cookie party," Raine pointed out.

"So let me get this straight. I have to wait until tomorrow night to get a cookie?" Mitch bemoaned. "Why? They're right here now."

"If you're hungry, go for the peach cobbler cooling right there on the counter," Lenore pointed out, wiping her eyes.

Mitch changed direction with a purpose, cut a chunk out of one of the corners, and scooped it into a bowl. He waited for the crust to cool down enough to nibble a bite. "You think it's a coincidence Eisenbart's son was named Jessup?"

"No, I don't," Garret fired back. "I've been trying to come up with a connection to the area. Born out there in Lost Gator Swamp might be it, and one reason he'd come back, looking to settle here, with the purpose of running the town like Wyatt Earp."

Jackson came in, headed straight for the pie. "While you were out combing the swamp, Sinclair beat it out of town. That's the rumor I got straight from Harley Dunlap."

"Not for long," Mitch assured him. "Sinclair won't stray too far from that gold. Trust me. He's put in too much time stewing over it to leave it in the dust. And if Garret's right about the connection to Eisenbart, then he has to believe he's entitled to the treasure through a legacy of some kind. He'll be back as soon as someone else finds it. But it won't be Duarte."

Raine rested her chin on her fist. "They're all such greedy bastards, the lure of the gold is all we need."

"Exactly."

"Has the professor made any headway with his algorithms?" Raine asked.

"Been locked in Jackson's old room all day long," Lenore offered. "Hasn't come out for food or to restock his Diet Coke stash."

Tanner hurried through the back door like he had news. "Saw Boone Dandridge eating his lunch at the sandwich shop. Looked drunker than Cooter Brown. For a guy who always swore up and down he was a teetotaler, he looked more like a lush today to me. I think he's losing it, right along with Carson Frawley. Rumor has it the doughnut shop didn't even bother opening up this morning."

Anniston held up her phone. "Sebastian says the state police will be here tomorrow."

Mitch made a derisive noise in his throat. "A little late, don't you think? Who's left to arrest? Oakerson's body hasn't turned up yet and probably won't. We have Wendy on ice. Sinclair's flown the coop. And for all we know, doughboy went with him. If you think Dandridge and Baskin plan to hang around until Briggs swings through town, you're crazy."

Garret took his turn at the pie. "I'm not upset about that. I always liked the idea of taking down their house of cards on our own, without the benefit of having cops around to mess things up. If Briggs is late to the game, then I guess that means it's still up to us."

Making herself to home, Anniston got a fork out of the drawer, used it to nibble on the cobbler right from the pan. "You'll be glad to know Briggs is bringing a forensic team with him."

That had Mitch's eyebrows arching up with interest. "I wouldn't mind being there for that."

Off to the side of the kitchen the bedroom door swung open. Hollings emerged with a wide smile on his face and excitement in his voice. "Get everyone in the dining room. I've cracked the code. The printer's humming away now. Give me half an hour and I'll be handing out the outline for you to follow."

True to his word, forty-five minutes went by before Hollings appeared at the head of the table, papers stapled together, packets ready to be passed around.

Hollings cleared his throat. "I translated this word for word. If you start with the first page, some of you may find Captain Mühlhauser's very detailed descriptions rambling and boring. But I find them fascinating and can picture it all in my head like a movie. Even if you're tempted to skip that part, I don't recommend it because it makes for an excellent reference point. I think you'll find some surprising information in here about what was going on at the end of the war. Not just greed and self-preservation but a top secret mission that's, so far, been lost to history all these years. This log brings it all out into the light and let's us get a glimpse firsthand into the mindset of those who undertook this assignment."

Mitch read the first few paragraphs of the handout. It read like an annoyed first person narrative from an old sea captain. "So the diary begins with Mühlhauser standing on the dock waiting impatiently for his orders to come down from on high. He writes that it's overcast and bitter cold."

"A typical wintry day with the wind blowing out of the north and snow beginning to fall," Raine provided. "For a U-boat captain he uses a lot of flowery words. Sounds like he might fancy himself a writer."

Hollings bobbed his head. "While deciphering all this, I got the sense, and hopefully you will too, that Klaus leaned toward the dramatic, had a flair for setting the scene, which in a way is good for us. So with that in mind, shall we travel back in time to Flensburg to try and get a better understanding of how this all started."

"And what went wrong," Mitch reminded.

"Maybe discover the identity of those Nazi sympathizers," Raine added. "Did we have Eisenbart spies living in Lost Gator Swamp?"

"And did they have ties to Jessup Sinclair?"

Chapter Twenty

Flensburg, Germany
Second week of December, 1944

Klaus Mühlhauser stood on the deck of U-492, taking in the other boats in the fleet awaiting their orders just as he was. He'd spent the last eight months convinced the war was lost. In his mind any man with common sense who couldn't see the end coming was either in denial or delusional. His beloved Germany was on the brink of crumbling.

Even as he looked out over the harbor, the Red Army was poised to move through a side door operation in Hungary and Yugoslavia, outflanking and crushing the German infantry. It was only a matter of time before the Eastern and Western Fronts buckled. Klaus would rather surrender to the Americans any day than see the Soviets rolling into Berlin. That scene would no doubt become a blood bath.

He was glad he wouldn't be here to see it.

From the beginning U-492 had been his sub. He'd taken command after a handful of top officials decided to list the boat as scrubbed, removing it from the rolls of all active-duty navy ships. It had been a lie. The subterfuge existed for the sole propose of using 492 to run long-range covert missions, earmarked to make secret trips to Penang, Malaysia, or to Mexico's Pacific coast.

Only a handful of the inner circle knew its real purpose—to drop off high-ranking officials escaping the end of the war and the crimes they'd committed. That part had come down straight from the top. The Führer needed backup plans in place and 492 was just one of many.

But for others who wanted out of the country and had the cash reserves to get it done, Klaus had seen an opportunity. So he decided he'd fatten his bank account on the side and began his own smuggling operation. His superiors didn't need to know everything. He'd build up his wealth, add to his retirement for those days when he'd settle down in that small village in Argentina known as Bariloche.

But first he had to get there.

He knew this would be his last mission. He'd devised a plan to get away for good.

Each time Klaus left port, he carried enough gold to pay off governments or anyone else along the way who needed incentive to turn a blind eye.

But on this particular day, he paced back and forth the length of the deck, chain-smoking, waiting nervously for his orders to arrive, wondering what was taking so long.

Even though the temperature hovered around twenty degrees and he wore ample layers under his coat, his forehead beaded with sweat. His hands were clammy. A couple of times he felt like he'd soiled himself. Half-scared the Gestapo had somehow gotten wind of his side business, he was terrified they'd show up before he could make his way out of port. If they did, he'd never see a firing squad. They'd take out their Luger pistols, then and there, and that would be it. Having a brother in the SS wouldn't protect him from the fanatics of Hitler's inner circle. Walter had warned him to be careful. But then Walter and his boys were already tucked away in a little village out of harm's way.

Which is why Klaus remained worried. Until he was away from Germany's coastline, he didn't feel safe.

His eyes darted from one end of the docks to the other, eager to leave. All he wanted now was to get his orders in hand, play out the act for a little while longer, and then get underway, hoping like hell he could disappear. If he could just make it to the middle of the Atlantic he would call in an SOS and then go silent, hopeful the brass would consider it just another U-boat lost at sea to enemy fire, just another unlucky crew going down for the Führer's cause.

He spotted a pair of German soldiers getting out of a black Mercedes Pullman. They carried their gear, a couple of suitcases. One had a messenger bag slung over his shoulder.

On approach, both men stuck out their right arms in a salute.

"Sieg heil."

"Sieg heil," Klaus returned.

The younger soldier dug in the satchel he hefted and pulled out a package, handed it off. "Vom Führer, streng geheim. Öffnen Sie nicht , bis Sie auf das offene Meer zu bekommen."

Klaus frowned. He hadn't counted on any top secret instructions, let alone coming from the Führer himself. If he couldn't open the package until he'd been at sea for several days this could potentially be a disaster. How was he supposed to adjust his plan accordingly with these two outsiders joining his crew at the last minute? He had business to conduct that didn't include having a couple of strangers on board.

"Prepare to get underway," Klaus shouted an order to his second in command, Lieutenant Piers Zander. "All engines ahead."

Plotting his course out of the Flensburg Fjord was usually a piece of cake. He'd made this run enough times he could do so in his sleep. So when his wachoffizier or watch officer told him they had an escort, it got his attention.

Klaus looked over and saw two patrol boats ushering them through the straits between Sweden and Denmark. At the sound of aircraft overhead, he took out his field glasses and spotted two Luftwaffe night fighters. Their presence indicated this mission was a high priority for someone.

As the boat moved through the channel, his mind fretted over the situation he found himself in. He'd arranged a meeting with a Swedish fishing boat fifty miles off the coast of Denmark to take on eight Nazi officers, including several of their wives, or mistresses, and four children under the age of twelve. He'd already collected a portion of his fee. Since it amounted to a pouch of stolen gems and several thousand gold coins, Klaus wasn't about to renege on the deal now.

But he was beginning to sweat again.

Zander explained the escort would turn back as they approached the Island of Anholt. For the first time since leaving port, Klaus breathed a sigh of relief. The pick-up was slated to occur at a rendezvous point close to the Danish island of Læsø. Once the escort turned around, they could continue on to pick up their passengers and then swing out and into the North Sea.

Near midnight the patrol boats and planes turned back. After that, it took almost three hours through icy, choppy water to meet up with the Swedish trawler.

Under cover of darkness, his men helped get the battered group settled on board. With so many crammed into such close quarters, it was chaos and a reminder that Klaus had gotten himself into a tough position.

Refusing to leave his post, Klaus kept to the control station alongside Zander. The two men explored their options and bandied about a solution to the problem.

But two days out of port, Klaus was still stewing over the dilemma when he unsealed his orders. He called for Zander.

Klaus tossed the papers on his desk. "This is Hitler's last ditch effort to save Germany from Russia. The two who carried the orders, the ones we brought on board at the last minute, are assassins."

Zander's face fell. "And who will they be assassinating?"

"President Roosevelt. We're instructed to put the men ashore somewhere near the Florida Georgia border where they are to meet up with a German spy living nearby."

"A supporter of the German cause in America?"

"According to these papers, one of the men grew up somewhere in the Florida south. With the help of this American ally they will make their way to Warm Springs, Georgia, where the president resides when not in Washington. They intend to make it look like the Russians are the culprits."

Zander's eyes grew wide with amusement. "A harebrained scheme."

Klaus picked up the documents again and shook his head at what he read. "Hitler's gone off the deep end. These men are supposed to leave behind clues that point to the Soviets. If the U.S. believes this nonsense—that the Russians took the life of FDR—the German High Command will attempt to broker a peace treaty with America, even offering to join forces with them against Russia, hoping an attack will be imminent."

"Such a black-hearted act committed by Stalin would surely be viewed by the U.S. as utter betrayal."

But to Klaus it was just another example of a deranged demigod living in his fantasy world. "They won't be able to pull it off, Zander, not in a million years. But no matter, we have a bigger problem. These men pose a major stumbling block to what we want. There's no convincing extremists like this to abandon their orders or the plot. They'll refuse to join us in our quest for a new life. You know it's true."

"Then we must deal with the assassins ourselves," Zander suggested.

"It will take some acting on our part. Good thing we've surrounded ourselves with a supportive crew, hand-picked. You have assured me all along that the men have long ago lost faith in the Führer and the Third Reich. Yes?"

Zander nodded. "Most have seen for themselves that all signs point to defeat."

"Good. Now, my friend, we simply want nothing more than to reach South America alive."

"Maybe buy a parcel of land so we become farmers. At the least, blend into the culture and live out our days forgetting the atrocities of war."

Klaus carried that notion back with him into his small, cramped quarters where he took a seat at his desk. For an hour he poured out his frustrations, logging his rambling entries into his journal.

He glanced over at the top secret orders that lay open on his desk and swore under his breath. All his plans of meeting his brother in a new land, all his dreams of a life in the small Alpine-like village, were about to go up in smoke if he didn't choose the wise path. But there was so much more to this mission before they could even think about looking upon Argentina.

He had to come up with an alternate idea and do it quickly. Since Hitler had ordered him to rendezvous with a Wolf Pack at the secret refueling station in the Spanish archipelago, he was running out of time to act. Once they reached the Canary Islands the U-492 would hook up with nine other U-boats carrying more fleeing rats to shelter. Several ships would, no doubt, be carrying gold bullion, diamonds, platinum, U.S. dollars, and British pounds to pay off General Perón and his comrades.

The rest was earmarked for starting a new Germany in the mountainous region between Argentina and Chile. His mind whirled with possibilities. Klaus pounded the desk with his fist. He had to make it work. Somehow he had to pull it off.

Hitler and his inner circle could shove it up their asses as far as he was concerned. He would steal from the rats as they had done to others. The money and jewels would set him and his crew up for life. But first he had to make sure his boat carried the lion's share of the loot. If he offered to carry a few of the rats to safety, that would lend a ring of truth to his pitch. Later, he would toss the rats overboard. After all, people were lost at sea all the time, one big wave in the middle of the ocean and they could all disappear, never to be seen again.

But first he had to unload the passengers he'd picked up earlier from the fishing trawler. The women and kids were getting on his nerves.

He charted a course to follow along the coastline to Spain. He'd dump his paying passengers off in the Port of Vigo. They could wait out the war there on the German merchant vessels trapped by the war. He would, of course, tell them he would be back for them later, much later.

It might work. If he dropped off his paying passengers in Spain. He'd already decided to use the two assassins as an excuse to break from the convoy. Then once he got clear of the other ships, he'd throw the two new men overboard and make for the deserted beach, the one his brother, Walter, had located in Argentina. There, he would unload his fortune, scuttle the sub and head into the mountains to wait out the war.

Zander interrupted the reverie. "How do you intend to get the bulk of the gold on board the 492?"

"I'll simply con the commandants by reminding them that we have superior, long-range capability."

Confident in the plan, Klaus was able to hug thousands of miles of beautiful Moroccan coastline on his way to the Canary Islands.

By day, through his binoculars, he took in the spectacular views and rolling hills of Tangier. Like a tourist, he settled back to bump along and ride out the swells of the sea.

The next three days went by quickly until finally, on a dark and moonless night, U-492 pulled alongside a Spanish freighter.

Klaus stood on the conning tower scanning the horizon for trouble. He watched as his crew unloaded the cargo net. They stowed the watertight, unmarked heavy boxes below in the forward compartments.

He fantasized about the gold in each crate. The urge to pry open the lid and look, to hold the heavy weight of it in his hands was fierce. He shook his head to pull himself out of the daydream. There would be time enough later for enjoying the fruits of his labor.

The U-boat to his left was in the middle of taking on passengers. In the dark it was hard to make out their faces, but he knew some of them from news reports. Big fat rats running for their lives to a hiding place far away from war and death.

The joke would be on them once they reached their destinations and discovered they had no money. Without their fortunes to bribe officials, they might just end up as guests of a South American internment camp where they'd wait out the war or be sent back to Germany to face their war crimes.

Klaus glanced at his watch. At two in the morning the order came down to get underway. U-492 took its position in the middle of the pack under strict radio silence, just flags or signal lights from here on.

The pack was able to run on the surface for most of the voyage. To conserve fuel, they ran on one engine, even though they had a fully-loaded supply boat, otherwise known as a milchkuh at their disposal.

It took eleven days to make the crossing. If the weather held they might make landfall in another three weeks.

Of course, if Hitler and his superiors had their way, U-492 would be leaving the pack at the equator and turning north and heading to the American coast to drop off the assassins.

Once the pack crossed the equator, Klaus decided a celebration was in order. He commanded his Obersteuermann or Chief Quartermaster to issue one bottle of beer to all the crewmen. In triumphant fashion the crew marked the last German ale they would taste for a very long time.

Just as Klaus lifted his beer, a signal came in from the Commander. He headed topside to see what the message was about. While climbing the ladder to the conning tower hatch, his mind raced with doubts, hoping that his orders had not been changed. As he climbed out of the hatch, the watch officer handed him a piece of paper. He quickly read it and let out of string of curses.

Klaus shouted, "Have all the officers meet me in the forward torpedo room in five minutes."

The room was small and crowded and hot. The heat from the engines had them all sweating. With all eyes on him, Klaus considered his words carefully. "We have new orders that affect our plan. I've been put in command of two other U-boats as well as the milchkuh. The orders state that the supply boat will wait for us on the east side of Turks Island. The other two will proceed with us along the route toward the American coast, mining several ports along the way for a diversion while we drop off the two assassins. It seems someone at the top worried that we'd be stupid enough to be discovered by an American air patrol."

The captain took in the disappointed faces around him before going on, "Here's what I propose we do. After we drop off the assassins, we'll head out into the Atlantic, a hundred kilometers or so away from shore, send out a fake distress signal, wait a few days to give the other two subs enough time to rendezvous with the supply ship, and let them continue on to Argentina, thinking we were lost at sea. Then we will head to our deserted beach and from there to Bariloche and start our new lives."

Once Klaus saw relief move through his men, he added, "Pass the word to the crew. Make sure everyone knows except the newbies. They'll find out their fate soon enough."

Chapter Twenty-One

Leaving the supply sub some sixty kilometers off Turks Island where it would wait for their return, Klaus steered U-492 on a north westerly course toward the Atlantic coastline. He was careful to avoid the major shipping lanes to keep from getting spotted. When there were several close calls—a ship on the horizon or a plane in the distance—he ordered immediate dives to stay out of sight.

Klaus breathed a sigh of relief when they left one U-boat near Miami and then another one a hundred and fifteen kilometers north near the shores of West Palm Beach.

From there, U-492 remained underwater the rest of the way until approaching the coast of Georgia. Once they reached that point, the sub rested at the bottom of the ocean at a depth of thirty meters to wait for nightfall.

For thirty-six hours, the air was stale and smelled of sweat, oil—and fear. At the precise time, Klaus surfaced to periscope depth. He did a full three-hundred-and-sixty-degree scan of the area, looking for any ship activity. It was only after his watch officer completed the same search that he directed the sub to proceed closer to shore.

Once they were in position, he ordered a slow surfacing. The moment the boat broke the surface, Klaus ordered the gun crew and watch crew out of the hatches.

The new moon offered scant light and there were no lights coming from shore. The only sound was the lapping of the waves on the bulkhead.

As the captain waited for the signal from the German sympathizer onshore, he ordered the crew to ready the large inflatable raft they'd use to ferry the two assassins and their equipment onto land. The crew quietly and quickly lowered the raft into the water.

After getting the landing craft loaded, everything was in place. But still there was no signal from land. The minutes slowly ticked by. Each one felt like an hour. At any moment they could be spotted by a patrol boat or an airplane.

Klaus felt vulnerable, uncomfortable. The sub was an easy target, like a sitting duck. He was just about to give the order to put the two assassins ashore anyway and leave them to their fate, when he spotted the signal, a rudimentary Morse code using what looked like a flashlight.

He had his signalman verify and then answer it. He ordered the raft to push off. It would take twenty minutes or more for his crew to drop off the men and return. He played with the idea of submerging until his men returned, but decided not to; he would wait out the tense situation, scanning the skies and the horizon for any sign of danger.

It seemed like hours before the crewmen were back on board and the raft had been deflated and stored away.

Klaus ordered the crew below as the U-492 silently disappeared under the waves. When the hatch closed and they got underway, Klaus felt relief emanating off the entire crew.

But the reprieve would be short-lived. He wasted no time plotting a course straight down the coast of Florida. They'd traveled perhaps less than seventy kilometers southward when an explosion rocked the sub.

Glass gauges broke. Pipes began to spew water. U-492 went into a tail dive, heading toward the sandy bottom of the Atlantic Ocean. The hull creaked as it descended fast.

Klaus heard the voice of his chief engineer as he ticked off the list of damages. "Engine room is taking on water. Sea water will reach the batteries soon. Prepare to hit bottom."

At thirty-five meters below the surface, they did. Klaus shouted orders. "All crewmen, don your breathing apparatus! Now! Poisonous chlorine gas is imminent! Abandon ship! Abandon ship!"

He turned to Zander. "Flood all compartments on my command."

There was no time for fear as the cold seawater flooded into U-492. But Klaus had to wait until the compartments were almost fully flooded because it was impossible to open the escape hatch with the sea pressure pushing against the metal. He had to be patient, equalizing the interior and exterior pressure of the boat, before he could open the hatch and escape from a watery grave.

It seemed like it took forever for the seawater to reach the level needed to pop the escape hatch. But it gave him enough time to gather his logbook, his journal, a few maps, and other important papers and shove them into a waterproof bag and then into his attaché case for carrying.

Once the pressure evened out, the hatch opened easily and each crewmember floated out and up almost without effort.

As the captain drifted up to the surface with them he could see his boat on the bottom. He took one last look before getting swept away in the current.

He didn't know how many other men had made their escape to the rough sea surface to join him. But he thought he could see a few other men rising with him, slowly rising to the top. Not as many as he'd hoped, though. The chlorine gas must've claimed a portion of his crew and trapped them in compartments, places where they were unable to open the air-tight doors.

Once on the surface, Klaus gasped for fresh air. He did his best to count the heads of his surviving crewmen as they broke through the choppy waves. The largest raft had failed to deploy, but he saw several smaller ones and two more with men trying to climb into them or hang on the rim for their lives. He spotted a few life jackets, along with several rebreathers, or escape lungs, that the crew could use for floatation devices.

Who knew how long it would take before they were spotted or picked up? If the tides worked in a northerly fashion, they would drift back in the same direction in which they'd come, back toward Georgia. If they were lucky they would end up in a major shipping lane. Funny how he'd done everything up to this point to avoid the more common routes. And now, he needed a large vessel to come along and pick them up.

Klaus looked around at the debris beginning to rise to the surface and the small number of lifeboats. He counted eight. In all his time at sea, he'd seen his share of life rafts floating aimlessly with dead men after a battle. But warfare hadn't been involved in this mess.

He knew the first order of business had to be getting the men working on tying the rafts together and taking stock of what supplies they had.

He spotted the launch holding his badly injured chief engineer and one other crewman. "What the hell happened, Hans?"

Despite his gaping chest wound, Hans raised his head. "Sabotage. Someone on board intentionally used a device to sink us. My guess is it had to be the assassins. But why, captain? Why? We'd almost made it."

Klaus's mind raced for answers. "Perhaps they found out about my plan. Maybe they wanted to kill all of us, witnesses to their mission."

His friend Zander agreed. "The bastards tried to kill us so we wouldn't talk of their deed to kill the American president. Why didn't we see their treachery coming?"

Klaus shook his head. "I know one thing for certain. I'll hunt the men down and kill them like the pigs they are. I won't rest until I put a bullet between their eyes."

"Even the farmer in me wants revenge," Zander uttered.

Just as Klaus had predicted, the wind and tides carried them along in a northerly fashion at about two to three kilometers an hour. Slow going, they were drifting away from the resting place of U-492.

That night, he could see city lights to the south in the distance, bright against the total darkness. He figured it was probably a small coastal community.

Three crewmembers offered to try and swim toward the lights but Klaus persuaded them it wasn't a good idea. Too far away. The second night, Klaus didn't try to stop them. The trio left in the middle of the night and he never saw them again. The following day a few of the more severely injured men died. Hans was one of them.

They were running low on water and even lower on hope as time seemed to stand still. The sun beat down on them during daylight hours, roasting their skin to bright red. But at night the temperature dropped thirty degrees or more and no one seemed to be able to get warm enough. Chills and fever spread through the men causing delirium, especially among the injured.

Klaus dozed off, only to wake to a frenzy of hammerhead sharks circling the launch. In his dazed mind, he could hear them swimming through the water, even bumping up against the raft. Blinking at the sight, he heard another noise coming from his right. The sound was the surf pounding, breaking onto a sandy beach. Was he dreaming? Had he conjured it up in his imagination?

Even though he could barely make out the shoreline in the dark, he started shaking his crew awake.

"Zander, wake up. Land!"

Like lifeless shells, the men tried to see what Klaus saw. Thinking the captain might be delusional, Zander squinted into the blackness. "Is land really nearby?"

"We'll have to paddle hard to outswim the sharks to get there," Klaus pointed out. "There aren't enough oars."

"I'm too weak."

"We have to try anyway. It's our only chance," Klaus returned. "Use your arms and hands if you have to."

The idea of that with sharks in the area was more than a little unnerving. But if land was out there this close, Klaus had to persuade them to try for shore. With all the energy he could muster, he started paddling toward the beach.

His men did as he did.

Once they got within twenty meters—although they could barely walk—they dropped out of the rafts to stumble their way onto solid ground. Somehow they managed to reach the sand before collapsing.

Klaus could make out a light in the distance, maybe a city, at the very least it might be someone's campsite. It occurred to him they would soon be rescued. Knowing he couldn't let anyone find his journal, he'd have to find a place to hide it. Looking around what amounted to nothing more than a deserted island, the prospects were bleak.

But with his last bit of energy, he picked himself up off the sand. Dog-tired, he teetered down the beach clutching his leather case to his chest. He spotted a jagged outcrop of rocks that jutted high enough to stand above the high tide mark. He heaved and poked at the rocks until his fingers bled. But he was able to carve out a small cavern large enough to hold his messenger bag. He jammed the leather attaché into the hole. Since the crevice went further back than he thought, he shoved it as far back under the pile of rocks as it would go. Once the bag was out of sight he began filling the entryway back up with rocks and anything else he could lay his hands on until he was sure no one could find it.

He climbed back down on the sand and dropped on all fours. Using his hands to cover up his footprints and tracks, he made sure there was nothing that led to this spot. Only then did he head back to what remained of his crew.

The men slept there on the beach until mid-morning when a shore patrol stumbled upon them. Out of the forty-five-man crew, only a dozen of his men had made it to this spot. Klaus didn't know how many had died on the sub or how many had died in the water.

He knew one thing for sure. He was alive, and for him, the war was over.

The patrol loaded them all into trucks and drove them to a base near Charleston, South Carolina. It was there Klaus learned they had washed up on land known as Folly Beach.

Klaus cackled with laughter and turned to Zander. "How appropriate. We came all the way from Germany on a mission of folly. It's only right we end up on this Folly Beach."

"They'll interrogate us, Klaus," Zander said, fear in his voice.

"They will. But we will tell them nothing."

For months, the Americans asked questions. Klaus told them the same thing over and over again until he was sick of the story. The ship had experienced a bad battery fire on board. He'd made the decision to scuttle the boat, then and there. He even pinpointed the location of the sub, but he painted a picture that was much farther out to sea and much farther south. He even gave them a longitude and latitude somewhere between Miami and the Florida Keys.

When he stuck to his story and refused to budge on the facts, he was flown back across the water to England where there were more interrogations. But he never altered his tale.

Finally, in October 1946, Klaus was released and sent back to Germany. It took him another two years to track down the survivors of U-492, including Zander.

His final act for his homeland was to eliminate each of them, one by one, so only he knew the details of U-492's final mission, the precise location of where the sub rested. And what she carried.

After that, Klaus worked his way back to America, inventing the story that he just wanted to pay his last respects to his lost comrades. The story worked. In the winter of 1949, Klaus finally made his way back to Folly Beach.

It took him half a day to find the outcrop of rocks where he'd hidden his satchel. Fortunately for him, things had changed very little in the years since he'd left his journal.

He had to dig through the sand and rocks again, his hands bleeding just as they had that day four years earlier when he'd left it among the rocks. To his shock and amazement, the leather briefcase was still there. Like welcoming an old friend, he rubbed a thumb over the insignia and the lettering with his name on it.

During the years he'd been imprisoned, he'd learned that the two saboteurs had never even attempted to complete their mission. Something was very wrong there. He'd had plenty of time to commit their faces to memory and think about what he'd do when he finally caught up with them.

Klaus fully believed that he'd crossed paths with two rats looking to get out of the war. Nothing more. He'd find them one day and settle the score. But first he knew where he could find help and the money for what he wanted to do. He booked passage on a ship to Argentina. It was time to see his brother.

Chapter Twenty-Two

Hollings cleared his throat. "I'm fairly certain that last part, where they were rescued off the beach, was added much later to the journal. If you'll study the handwriting, it changed. The entries of that time period were written in different colored pen than the rest."

Nervously, Hollings drank deep from his can of Diet Coke and glanced around the room, waiting for the group's reaction.

Mitch spoke up first. "To tell you the truth, I'm a little disappointed. I was expecting more. This sounds an awful lot like the stories related to the lost city of El Dorado, the city of gold."

"Edgar Allan Poe said it best," Garret offered with a sigh. "Over the mountains of the moon, down the Valley of the Shadow, ride, boldly ride…if you seek for El Dorado."

"That's just it. How do we know the U-boat captain, who fancied himself a writer, wasn't just bored at sea and made up this entire story as he went along?" Jackson pointed out.

The professor smiled. "I would almost agree with you that the journal might be more fiction than a real representation, except for one simple historical fact. Martin Bormann, secretary to the Deputy Führer, enacted a plan in 1943 called Aktion Adlerflug. In English it translates to Project Eagle Flight. Think about that for a minute. A full year before Klaus begins his own smuggling operation, the deputy secretary is already in the process of moving valuables out of Germany and getting them to South America, ostensibly to set up a New Germany."

Garret nodded. "Ah, the operation to move gold and other assets through Spain and on to safe havens overseas for the sole purpose of starting up German controlled companies there in anticipation for after the war."

"Like with Mercedes Benz," Mitch noted. "I'm aware of that. The automobile manufacturer was specifically meant to begin operation in Buenos Aires. It's still in operation today."

Hollings adjusted his glasses. "That's right. The move there was huge. It was the first plant for Mercedes outside Germany's borders. To make sure his plan succeeded, Bormann went so far as to acquire his own Spanish shipping company and an Italian airline to move the goods. In addition to that, liquid assets were trucked through France to Spain and from Spain to Argentina by none other than…"

"The determined U-boats," Jackson finished. "That gives the story slightly more credibility."

"Exactly. Then after the Allies invaded France and cut off the land route, Bormann used private airplanes to accomplish the same thing until the end of the war. Most of the treasure was never recovered. Some believe General Perón took most of it to finance his rise to power in Argentina as well as his luxurious lifestyle. There's no direct evidence of that, mind you. But I might add that

Bormann continued to live openly in Buenos Aires well after the war was over due to his friendship with the Peróns."

Mitch blew out a breath. "Or maybe there's a simpler explanation. Some of it ended up at the bottom of the ocean like U-492."

"We may never know for sure," Hollings admitted.

Raine chewed her lip. "If Klaus took this book with him to Argentina, and it was written in a code Klaus was used to using, then why didn't he tell his brother Walter and Walter's sons the approximate location of the sub?"

"There's only one explanation for that. Bad blood," Mitch asserted. "If the story's true, and Klaus made it to Argentina, the brothers might no longer have been as close as they were during the war. For Klaus to unload those kinds of details, he may not have trusted Walter completely, certainly not Walter's sons. He most likely would've held back on the finite, specific details."

"So if Klaus never revealed the code, then Dietrich and Hugo wouldn't have been able to learn much from the journal. That's why Duarte's focusing his dives in the wrong spot. If they're looking south in the Keys, which they are, they're way off the mark," Raine reasoned. "Duarte has to know that by now."

"I'm sure he's aware his crew's definitely wasting time diving in all the wrong spots. And it's pissing him off royally," Mitch stated.

Raine studied Mitch's face. "What are you thinking?"

"It amazes me that Hugo had Klaus's journal in the first place and Dietrich didn't. He must've stolen it away from his brother very early on, at a young age, maybe hidden it away somewhere and took off, leaving his family behind in Argentina. I'm just trying to figure out the reason for the break in brother loyalty. Either way, when the brothers did have the book in their possession, neither Dietrich nor Hugo was ever able to crack the code sufficiently to uncover the sub's location, not even approximate. It took

Professor Hollings Bishop from Florida State University to do that."

Hollings beamed. "Well, I had incentive. I do want to write that book now more than ever. What will you do now that you have the approximate longitude and latitude?"

Mitch sent him a smile. "We begin the hunt and lure in the local rats for the kill."

Chapter Twenty-Three

Before they could set out on a treasure hunt, though, there were a few loose ends to tie up. Namely meeting with the state police. They expected to butt heads with the team from Tallahassee. But surprisingly, Paul Briggs, along with the two seasoned detectives he brought with him, was willing to sit down in a conference room at the police station—the same station Sinclair had abandoned a day earlier—and reach out to the family.

"I know you think you've tied up this case for us in a great big bow," Briggs began. "But we still have a lot of work to do."

Mitch's tone sharpened. "Yeah, like make a few arrests."

Neither Alejandro Fargas nor Turner Grey, the two detectives sharing a conference table, cared for the dig. The older guy, Turner, seemed especially insulted. "What would you have us do? Go around arresting people just because you deem them guilty? It doesn't work that way. We need rock-solid evidence."

But Mitch wasn't backing down. "In this case, there's a cop involved. I'm guessing that means you need double the evidence before you take out the handcuffs." When he detected a simmering aggression in the older guy, Mitch altered course. "Okay. Fine. Then tell me, Detective Grey, what took your department so long to get here? After Dack was killed we figured the state police would react for sure and be down here the next day. It never happened."

Briggs looked around the room, picked up on the hostility between the two parties. The captain understood it to a certain extent. But he needed to nip that resentment in the bud on both sides. It wasn't getting them anywhere, so he decided honesty was the better way to handle the situation. "Anniston and Sebastian warned me this wasn't a typical case. I should've listened to them then. You're right. Once I lost Hawkins on the ground here, I should've known something bigger was in play. I'm afraid we had to do some housecleaning of our own through Internal Affairs before we could act. Once we got rid of the baggage dragging us down—"

"You mean Sinclair's buddies," Mitch corrected.

Briggs steepled his fingers, sitting behind the former chief of police's old desk. "And then some. The corruption that's been happening here for decades ran deep, deeper than anyone could've predicted. Under Buchanan's leadership, coupled with Sinclair's complicity, and the mayor's, the collusion complicated matters. Bring in men like Baskin and Dandridge, who have long histories of going out and making things happen for the guys at the top, and suddenly you realize you've built a solid wall of greed, fraud, and bribery that works like a well-oiled machine. That's hard to topple."

"When you put it like that, you make it all sound so impossible to bring down," Garret commented sadly. "Why didn't anyone see what they were doing and try to stop them? The only one who even halfway tried was my dad."

Briggs nodded. "One man wasn't going to do much to stop this organization. Make no mistake, that's what it was. I understand we might even be able to solve a couple of cold cases throughout the state once the dust settles. I'm sorry that Sinclair's taken off, and now I've learned this morning that so have Baskin and Dandridge."

Mitch wanted to pound the table, but didn't. Instead he kept a cooler head. "You waited too late. They've all left town. There's no one around to arrest."

Briggs overlooked the embarrassment of it all and went on, "You're owed an apology. I'm here to—"

"You don't get it," Lenore snapped from the other side of the room. "We don't want your apology. We want the men responsible for killing our family, taking them away from us forever. There's a hole in our family that can never be fixed. No one can apologize for that except the men who took them from us. And I doubt that'll ever happen. I certainly don't intend to sit around and wait to hear it."

"You have a right to be upset. It will take some time to sort this all out. I understand you have much of it on tape and a witness willing to back up certain accounts of unethical behavior."

"Murder is certainly unethical behavior," Mitch fired back. "And we have a lot more than that—DNA, phone records, credit card statements—we tied up a pretty package for you guys. Wendy Hollister's even waiting in the wings, scared to open her mouth. I'm beginning to understand why. She's looking for protection from the authorities. That's you guys. But if you can't find Sinclair, Baskin, or Dandridge, I'm not sure that's something you'd even be able to do. How do you keep Wendy safe? What's the point of her risking her life testifying when it could all come crashing down around her if one of those guys wants her out of the way?"

Lenore was the only one who'd taken a seat at the table. She crossed her arms over her chest. "We aren't stupid, Captain Briggs. We know this isn't the way things are supposed to work. The family of the victims aren't typically the ones who solve the crime. You've messed this thing up from the beginning. We're a small town. If we weren't able to trust our chief of police, your agency was supposed to step up."

"What do you want me to do, Mrs. Indigo?"

"I want you to find Jessup Sinclair and the rest. I want you to make them pay for what they've done."

"That's our goal. But we'll need to know the location of the Hollister woman."

"I'll try to persuade her to turn herself in," Mitch promised.

As they left the meeting Mitch put in a call to Walsh. "Ready to get rid of your charge?"

"Is the sky blue? Please tell me it's okay to dump her in the ocean."

Mitch chuckled. "Bring her on in. This afternoon we'll hand her over to Briggs. Then she becomes his problem. What's the mood of the crew? Are they up for a little party before things get serious?"

"They're always up for that. What they really want is a chance at Duarte."

"Then bring 'em in. We're going after the gold."

After dumping Wendy on Briggs, they all switched gears—closer to home.

Everyone dragged out Halloween costumes as hokey as any middle school kid might throw together. They came up with vampire makeup, painted their faces, put on eerie eyeshadow, and spent the aftrnoon turning the front lawn into a reflecting pool of sparkly orange and black. They hung lights around the porch, carved pumpkins, hung balloons, and finished decorating cookies to hand out. Everyone pitched in.

They did it all for Lenore.

By dark, the house resembled a carnival set up to entertain the neighborhood kids. Children of all ages filled the yard. From a tiny fairy princess barely able to toddle around to a scary-looking teenage nightwalker, trick-or-treaters swarmed the house. They set up games like bean bag toss and gave out prizes—plastic spiders and bugs ruled with the older set, while the younger crowd preferred noisemakers and cute gummy worms, glowing toxic green.

For the adults, it was like a masquerade ball.

Mitch and Raine dressed up like a pair of steampunk characters, complete with white face paint, and stood guard over a huge black cauldron handing out cups of blood-red punch laced with Sprite. They greeted Mitch's crew, who hadn't bothered playing dress-up.

Walsh took one look at the crowd, all the screaming kids, and cracked, "So this is what it's like living in domesticated suburbia, a free-for-all that deteriorates into chaos over a bunch of candy. I'm glad I don't have much of a sweet tooth."

"It's not so bad," Mitch stated. "You guys should've worn a costume."

But Raine had a better notion. "See that woman over there wearing the Dolly Parton get-up." She waved them in the direction of Charlotte. "You guys should get over there and stand in line to have your faces painted."

"Get real," Jenkins stated. "Where's the beer?"

Mitch thumbed a hand toward his dad wearing jeans and a T-shirt. "He brought his grill around from the backyard to dish up homemade chili and hot dogs. He's guarding the cooler though and checking ID. That might mean Prentiss has to settle for a soft drink."

"I turn twenty-one in two weeks," Prentiss said in protest.

Mitch slapped his youngest crewmember on the back. "I'm just kidding. But know in advance my dad believes

Pabst Blue Ribbon is the only beer worth drinking at an outdoor cookout."

Prentiss stared at the zombie-like creatures, also known as Anniston and Garret. "Their makeup looks like the real deal. It's pretty cool."

Raine couldn't help it. She took the young guy by the hand and led him over to Charlotte. "Come on, live a little. Let her paint your face to look like that. Become a zombie for the night and roam the yard looking for flesh to eat. Or in this case gooey globs of devil's food cupcakes topped with pink icing, laced with strawberry jam made to look like brains."

Prentiss laughed. "Okay. I'll give it a try."

Raine made introductions and left the two figuring out the best shade of ghoul for the creepiest flesh.

Tessa and Jackson had donned pirate outfits in black pants, hats with bandanas, and eye patches. They went around challenging all takers to a sword fight.

"Livvy would've loved this," Lenore declared. Garbed in a red and gold queen outfit, she scooped up a handful of mini chocolate bars and added it to a little boy's bag who was decked out like a Lego block. "For the first time since that day in September I feel like she and the kids are right here, looking down on us, enjoying the party."

Sebastian sauntered over with a vampire on his arm. Dominka sizzled in a tight silver and black dress with a red corset lace-up front and six-inch spiked platinum heels. Showing plenty of cleavage and displaying a pair of fangs over her incisors, she was a cross between a vixen and a creature of the night.

"How'd y'all pull this together so fast?" Sebastian asked Mitch.

"Give Raine one little suggestion and she'll take it to the next level. She wanted to make sure my mom didn't sit around tonight and mope."

"I'm pretty sure she nailed it. You know, Paul Briggs is knocking heads together trying to figure out where that group of assholes went." He slapped Mitch on the back. "I noticed this morning you didn't let on you knew."

"Why should I?" Mitch stated. "I'm not obligated to tell him the whole bunch marshaled their forces on board the *Patagonia Pike*."

Raine leaned in, lowered her voice. "We're going after the gold. You know what that means."

Sebastian wasn't sure he did. "Duarte's bound to get wind of where you head and follow."

"We're counting on it. If we aren't ready to take on the *Patagonia Pike* now, we'll never be," Mitch explained.

"When do you plan to leave?" Sebastian wanted to know.

"Day after tomorrow." Mitch wasn't going to ruin the party by advocating Raine and the women stay behind for safety reasons. He knew that would create a different kind of skirmish, one he probably couldn't win.

Intrigued with the idea of an old-fashioned battle at sea, Sebastian said, "I'd like to go with you."

Dominka flexed her arm. "I go with you, too. I always wanted to be a fierce pirate and capture gold."

Sebastian crossed his arms over his chest. "These guys on the *Patagonia Pike* are a little too dangerous to mess with, I'd prefer you stay here."

"But I take care of myself," Dominka insisted.

"No doubt you can. It's nothing personal. I'm not in favor of Anniston going either." Sebastian glanced at Raine. "Or any of the women for that matter."

Mitch wasn't about to step into that quagmire. Diplomatically, he pointed out, "We could use all the firepower available to us. But we still have a few things to take care of first, a good deal of work to do before we launch."

"Like what?"

"Like getting into that safe deposit box."

Raine had spent some time considering that. She was about to announce her grand plan when she looked up and spotted her mother getting out of a ten-year-old Cadillac Sedan Deville.

Freaking out at the sight, she seized Mitch's arm in a death grip. "Oh no. What's she doing here? She's been drinking. She'll ruin the party!"

Mitch felt Raine's nails as he watched Marla march her way up the sidewalk, teetering on the brink of falling. "Try to intercept her. If you can, make a beeline for the backyard and I'll meet you around there. Maybe no one will notice."

"Fat chance of that." Before Raine could divert her mother, Marla started shouting, "You're trying to take Raine off island! It's not going to happen!"

Raine managed to steer her to the side of the house and corner her there. But that's as far as Marla would go. "I won't stand around and let Mitch Indigo take you on one of those crazy jaunts he's known for. I won't stand for it! Do you hear me?" Marla shrieked.

"Hard not to hear you," Raine hissed. "Lower your voice. Look around you. Could you drag yourself out of your own selfishness for once? There are a ton of kids here trying to have a good time. Stop making a scene. Now. You're scaring them."

"I'm trying to scare you," Marla slurred. "I'm trying to keep you from ruining your life. What kind of mother would I be if I didn't try to stop you from running off?"

Raine tightened her grip on Marla's arm. "Listen to me. I'm not that eighteen-year-old girl afraid of you. He's not ruining my life. Now calm down."

Mitch appeared at Raine's elbow. "How can I help?"

"Help me get her back to the car."

"I won't go. I'm staying right here until I talk some sense into your stupid head," Marla vowed.

"Nice, Mom, real nice. You're leaving if I have to drag you to the car kicking and screaming myself. Do you really want to make that kind of scene, here, now, in front of all these people?"

Trying to back up and change direction, Marla almost slipped and fell into the bed of scarlet and burnished marigolds. Instead of realizing her predicament, she pointed a shaky finger toward Mitch. "You almost ruined her life once. I won't let you do it to her again!"

"This isn't the time or the place for that," Mitch chided.

Tanner came over to see what he could do. "We could scoop her up and throw her over a shoulder, carry her that way."

"Sounds like a plan." As Mitch fought Marla's flailing arms, the idea of getting her off her feet didn't seem feasible. "Just get her back to the car any way we can."

"Did she drive over here like this?" Tanner asked.

With Mitch on one side and Tanner trailing, Raine steered her mother all the way down the side of the yard to the curb. "Yep. I don't know how she managed to get that huge boat out of the garage without dinging the fender, but she did."

"She can't drive in this condition," Tanner stated. "I'll take her back."

"No, I'll do it," Mitch offered.

Hearing that, Marla warned, "You keep away from my car!"

Once they finagled Marla's weight into the backseat, Mitch got behind the wheel. "Why won't you ever let Raine be happy," he snarled as he started the engine and pulled away from the curb. "Can't you see that she isn't happy running the restaurant? It's not who she is."

"That isn't for you to say."

"You're right, it's for her to say by standing up to you after all these years. You always did favor Danny. It showed. Raine knew that even in school. And the teachers, the teachers were so enamored with Danny, too. She always heard about how Danny aced the algebra test or blew through basketball tryouts to make the team. Even back then, Raine pushed herself, hard, just like she does now to try to get your attention. But you never gave her the time of day no matter what she did."

"Bullshit. You're full of it, always have been. You don't care about her, never have," Marla charged.

"And you do? Think long and hard about what you want for her. As long as she shows up every day to work, you don't much care about Raine. You want her to drop dead of a heart attack like her grandfather did? Don't do that to her, Marla. Don't."

"You don't tell me what to do or say, 'Mr. I don't stick around Indigo Key.' My daughter is rooted here and no matter what you say or do, she's obligated to stay and help me and her grandmother. That's the way it works in our family. So just get that in your head, buddy boy. She's not going anywhere."

"We'll see about that," Mitch muttered as he pulled in front of the Cape Cod. After dragging her out of the car, he left the woman standing next to her front door, while costumed trick-or-treaters bypassed the hysterical Marla, who just wouldn't shut up.

After walking back to Quay Avenue, Mitch stood on the sidewalk taking in the chaos on the front lawn. This had to be the very definition of suburbia, maybe even domesticity—decorating your house for a crazy holiday like Halloween, opening it up to neighbor kids, and then letting them run wild.

It was madness like this he'd avoided for the last dozen years or so.

Panic wanted to lodge in his windpipe so he couldn't breathe. But then he caught sight of Raine in the middle of entertaining two little boys, brothers dressed up like Minions.

His heart felt like it fluttered out of his chest. He walked up behind her, wrapped his arms around her waist. "You're the prettiest zombie here."

"I'm sorry my mother ruined the party."

"She didn't ruin anything," Mitch insisted. "She probably thinks she did, but she'd be wrong."

The claim didn't make Raine any less upset. But since there were so many people around she tried not to let it show on her face. "Not for lack of trying."

"Does she do this kind of stuff often?"

Raine thought back to other times when she'd had to rescue Marla from an embarrassing tirade at the restaurant. "She's always been high-strung. Danny was usually the only one who could talk her off the ledge."

Mitch frowned. "That sounds a little psychotic."

"More than," Raine noted.

"Let's go find a dark corner and make out," Mitch suggested, nibbling a line down her jaw, trying to get her mind off her mother.

She bumped his shoulder. "In front of all these kids? Look at your mom. She's having a blast, as much fun as they are."

He glanced over to see his mother twirling in a circle with a cluster of girls decked out in blue and green mermaid outfits. "She needed this."

"Yeah, she did."

"Thanks for coming up with the idea."

"I was happy to do it. Lenore is so different from my mother. Yours always manages to stay so grounded while mine exhibits a regular flair for drama. And that was long before Danny ever died. You shouldn't take what happened tonight personally."

"I don't."

"Good to know. Because if my mom can't latch on to making some type of melodramatic statement about something, she'll create it out of thin air. That's what she did tonight. She was probably sitting at home feeling sorry for herself, scared I'd take off and leave her in the lurch."

"We must've gone through twenty packages of hot dogs," Tanner said, wandering over to where the couple stood. Knowing Raine was still embarrassed over her mother showing up, Tanner gave her a hug. "Don't spend too much time fretting about tonight. By tomorrow no one will remember it."

"It could've ruined the party."

"But it didn't. Just a little blimp on the radar screen. Life's full of them. I want to thank you for helping put all this together. Lenore really had a blast. First time since Livvy and the kids died that she got her mind off everything and was able to have a little fun. You did that."

Mitch looked around at all the trash. "It was fun until cleanup time rolled around."

"Piece of cake," Tanner boasted. "Toss it all in huge garbage bags and be done with it. We'll have this wrapped up in no time."

Prentiss and Blaine came over to show off their zombie faces.

"Thanks for having us over," Prentiss said. "I had a nice time."

"Did you have a beer?" Mitch asked.

"Your dad's a stickler for dates."

Mitch hooted with laughter. "Yeah, he is."

Chapter Twenty-Four

November began with a rare storm that shoved through the Key, battering the skiffs and catamarans in the marina like they were no bigger than matchboxes. The wind and rain rocked the houseboat, but it was the roar of thunder that woke Raine.

She sat up, blinked, tried to get her eyes to adjust to the light. The Halloween party had gone on well after midnight. The decision to sleep late had seemed logical. But Mother Nature had other ideas.

Groggy-eyed, Mitch heard a phone ding somewhere in the room but ignored it.

Not Raine. She picked up the device and waved it around. "Anniston and Garret are watching a forensic team dig near the bridge."

That had him rolling out of bed. "I'd like to go out there."

"Feel free to see what it's all about. But I think I'll pass."

"Come on, go with me, a few hours at least before you have to head to work. They won't be pulling a body up during that time. It'll take at least a day or two to locate any remains, *if* there are any out there at all."

"Just what a girl wants to hear before breakfast." But she saw this meant something to him. "Okay. Give me time to get dressed. But you're buying me breakfast."

"Will a bagel and coffee do?"

"Cheapskate," she mumbled, dashing into the bathroom and closing the door.

"What, no coaxing you back to bed?"

Silence from the other side of the door.

Finally, after several long minutes, he heard her say, "It's hard to feel sexy when my mother made an ass out of herself last night in front of a lot of people."

Since they'd discussed Marla's public intoxication until almost two, he decided to let the mood pass before addressing it again. With no other choice, he pulled on his jeans and T-shirt.

In the kitchen he put on coffee, toasted the bagels himself and without cream cheese anywhere in sight, opted to spread butter on the bread instead. Raine finally appeared but headed straight out to the deck without a word to him.

After finishing with the bagels, he dug out a jar of peppered pear jam from the fridge, grabbed two mugs of coffee, and piled everything on a wide turquoise tray. He carried it outside where Raine sat, staring out at the spatter of drizzle as it plopped on the water.

They sat in silence and watched the sun rise out of a bank of dark blue clouds, spreading its sunny beam across the harbor. Thunder rumbled again and shook the house, but the rain was already moving further east.

Raine sipped her coffee and spread jam on her crusty sesame seed breakfast bun. "Storm didn't last."

"Still spectacular though," he noted over the rim of his cup. He could tell something whirred around in her head.

But what came out of her mouth next caught him off guard.

"What's it like being at sea during a storm? Is it scary?"

He studied her face before taking a sip of his coffee. It stirred him up that she would even bother to ask. And he wanted more than anything to be completely honest with her. "Sometimes. You've ridden out countless tropical depressions and hurricanes here. Storms are as much a part of island life as a seafaring sailor's. You get used to the tantrums of Mother Nature and do your best to prepare for anything she throws your way. You follow your instrumentation, the best satellite weather radar available, and do the same thing a commercial jetliner does. You avoid towering walls of water, hurricane force winds, or sudden squalls that pop up from time to time."

"Does all that precaution work?"

"Sure it works. I'm here, aren't I?"

"I've never been to sea for long periods of time, just those day fishing trips we used to go on. Do you think I'd get seasick on a longer cruise?"

"Did the surf bother you back then?"

"No. Not really. It never has. I always considered myself a good sailor. And I live on the houseboat which rocks all the time. I don't even think about the motion anymore."

"Then you'd probably be fine. You were okay on the *Patagonia Pike*, right?"

She made a face. "That nausea was from the drug Sinclair gave me. I was fine by the time you took me aboard *The Black Rum*."

"Then there's your answer. When's the last time you dived?"

She blew out a breath, nibbled on her bagel, thinking. "That would be last summer with Livvy."

"Livvy?" That surprised him. "I didn't even know she could dive at all, never bothered to learn when we were kids because she didn't care that much for boats. She'd surf or snorkel in the bay all day long, but put her on a boat and she got seasick every time."

"She did that day, too. It was my day off and Ally and Blake were with your mother. It was just the two of us. Apparently she'd taken lessons from Dave Oakerson's bunch. Someone there taught her how to dive. She'd bought the gear and everything. That day she wanted to practice. So we loaded up everything in Walker's boat and took it out for a short distance in Sugar Bay. Livvy upchucked almost immediately."

"That sounds like her. Was she a good diver?"

The memory brought a smile to Raine's lips. "Not really. For a woman who loved the water, going below a certain depth scared her. And she wasn't too good yet at going through her pre-dive checks. I told her I thought they missed a few steps with her training. After only about three hours of short dives, she was ready to come back home."

The recollection faded as she suddenly blurted out, "My God! She planned to dive for that gold even back then. That's how seriously she took Walker's gold fever."

Mitch frowned, not willing to consider it. But the longer he sat there, the more convinced he became. "It definitely shows she wanted the gold as much as Walker did. And was ill-prepared to help him find it. Maybe that's one reason she brought Nathan into the mix."

Raine took his hand. "I think you just have to accept she brought Nathan in because she trusted him."

"Trusted the wrong damn person," Mitch muttered. "I'm glad Dietrich killed him. Although I would like to have gotten more information out of him at the time."

Feeling better about heading off to a potential crime scene, she stood up. "Come on. Let's go see what's happening at the bridge."

By the time they reached the trestle, Garret and Anniston had been joined by Jackson and Tessa. It was a surreal sight to say the least. Crime scene technicians mulled about the area, spreading out with shovels and pickaxes to flay along the boggy shore. They'd already taken readings from ground-penetrating radar and mapped out coordinates for their grid.

Mitch stared at Anniston as she peered through a pair of binoculars. "It's a shame we can't get closer. If we could, we might be able to make out the radargram."

"Good thing I brought these with me then," Anniston remarked, gripping the field glasses. "Those soil layerings come off as dash lines, right?" She glanced at Jackson for confirmation.

"Yep. Anything else and it falls into either man-made or natural. When man-made doesn't fit in the surroundings you change the equation, then they have to consider the alternative." Jackson continued to study the reactions on the faces of the techs. "Let me see those binoculars."

Anniston reluctantly handed them over.

"Based on what I see it looks like they're using an advanced system with high resolution. They've already picked up on a couple of anomalies in the ground."

"You can see all that from here?" Mitch queried.

"Oh yeah. But don't get your hopes up quite yet. The soil conditions here are far from ideal, too much clay and salt. Unless that state-of-the-art system they're using is able to take that into consideration, they'll likely get false readings."

"All they have to do is start digging," Anniston grumbled, taking back her binoculars. "If they catch sight of us, they'll probably ask us to skedaddle soon anyway. But until they do, I'm planted here for the duration."

Getting caught up in the scene, Raine focused on the techs plotting the gridlines. "If I'm not mistaken, that's the spot where you said you saw Sinclair with the woman. They're already starting to dig there in a twelve-foot perimeter. That's encouraging."

It was, but Mitch decided the grueling part tended to be reliving the scene that day so many years ago as a child. He could still see Sinclair's big hands wrap and tighten around the woman's throat. He remembered how she fought, her eyes filled with fear, her fingers trying to clutch at Sinclair's to stop him. No matter how she'd fought, she'd lost the battle for her life.

They watched together until time for Raine to leave for work. When he started to head to his truck, Raine protested. "You can stay here. You don't have to come with me."

"Nope. It's okay. You're right. This likely will take all day. Maybe a couple. But now, the bagels are wearing off. I'm hungry for a taco."

Chapter Twenty-Five

Raine couldn't believe how well the two of them worked together over an eight-hour period. And not just once or twice, but consistently. She might not be able to picture Mitch doing restaurant work for the rest of his life, but she'd always remember the week he pitched in and slogged through the chores like a fiend to help her out.

It made her smile now and always would.

While she changed out one of the soda canisters at the self-serve beverage station, she thought of waking up that morning to find his hard body next to hers. His arm around her. His breathing shallow, his sleep deep and tranquil. She could get used to starting her day like that.

He must've read her thoughts because he came up behind her. "Need some help?"

She chuckled. "If you knew how many times I've done this per week, you'd know I could change out the drink canisters in my sleep. It's a sad fact."

"Not sad exactly. You'll always have a fallback skillset," he teased, then stared at what looked like a complicated weave of hoses underneath the cabinet that resembled a set of wires to an explosive device. "On second thought I'm not sure I could handle connecting the right barrel of soda to the appropriate tube."

"It takes a couple of training sessions. Which reminds me. I put an ad in the *Indigo Dispatch* for counter help, second shift. I'm hoping I get at least ten applicants."

"Is that possible in a town this size?"

She cracked a grin. "Probably not. But hey, a girl can hope there's someone out there who wants a job in food service *and* who knows what a cash register looks like."

"Maddie's been in a mood ever since the lunch rush. What's her problem?"

"Her daughter, Gabby, recently went through a bad breakup. Since Gabby still lives in Memphis, Maddie worries. It's hard for her knowing her daughter's going through something so emotionally shattering and living so far away..." Her voice trailed off. She suddenly snapped her fingers. "Why didn't I see this before now? Gabby could relocate down here. It would solve two problems. Gabby would get away from the ex who keeps bugging her *and* she'd get to spend some quality time with her mother."

"How old is she?"

"Hmm, Gabby's around my age."

"This is a tourist town, a vacation spot with plenty to keep you busy if you like to live around the water. You think this Gabby would be interested in working here?"

"It's worth a shot. She worked at the same hamburger dive as Maddie, so she knows a thing or two about the restaurant biz."

"You could build the place up, the town, I mean, make it sound like it's a smaller version of Key West."

Raine laughed. "You mean lie?"

"We're just as laidback," Mitch pointed out.

"Yeah, but I hate to exaggerate we're the smaller quirky version when all these murders have happened here."

"I read somewhere the murder rate in Memphis is pretty high."

"And what do you think our murder rate is now?"

"Okay, you have a point. Then stick to the facts and let Gabby decide for herself." Mitch picked Raine up and whirled her around before setting her feet back down on the concrete floor. "Maybe she could work a full forty hours. That way, it would give you more downtime."

"Wouldn't that be terrific? I'm marching in there right now and suggesting it to Maddie."

"Go for it." He gave her butt a little pat before she disappeared into the kitchen.

Glowing with a happiness she hadn't felt in some time, she darted through the swinging door and into the prep area.

A hand came from out of nowhere to clamp around her mouth.

Alarm zipped along her spine.

She felt his breath—heavy on her ear first—before seeing the ring on his hand. That black and gold insignia again. She glanced over to where Maddie lay unconscious on the floor.

The sight of her cook crumpled in a heap had Raine's survival instincts kicking in, a newfound strength surging through her veins. This time she didn't intend to go quietly. She stomped on Sinclair's foot right before ramming her elbow in his ribcage as hard as she could.

While he struggled to tighten his hold, she spotted a fork someone had left out on the counter. Grabbing the utensil, she jabbed it into his forearm. "Not so tough without your Ketamine to knock me out this time, huh, asshole!"

He yanked the fork out of his flesh. "That's like a mosquito bite to me. You'll have to do better than that, missy!" He took out a short-barrel .357 from his waistband, pointed the stainless steel pistol at her chest.

"What, you're going to shoot me now, right here? Why not strangle me like you did Darla Pendleton?" Raine realized she might've pushed the wrong button when she watched Sinclair's eyes glaze over in a crazed, sick look.

"What do you know about it?"

"Haven't you heard? They're digging under the bridge even as we speak." She could tell that one statement got into the man's head.

The wheels began to turn inside as he began to think about what that meant. "Since when? What are you talking about?"

"Since this morning. Once they find what's out there, you're done in this town, history."

Mitch came through the swinging door like a battering ram, head down, diving headlong into Sinclair's body, knocking him off his feet.

The gun went off, sending a bullet into the ceiling.

Mitch grabbed Sinclair's arm, trying to make him drop his hold on the weapon. He was able to bend it back so that the chief lost his grip. The gun skidded across the floor, landing under the prep table.

"Do you ever pick on anyone else besides women?" Mitch yelled as he pounded his fists into the man's face. "Come on, old man. Give it your best shot."

Mitch dodged the chief's attempt at a right cross, and landed another punch, then another. After three blows, one after the other, Sinclair lay sprawled on the floor, his lip busted and bleeding, his nose trickling red.

Mitch stood up, walked over and picked up the .357, pointed it at Sinclair. "I should kill you for what you did to my sister and her kids." He saw the fear in the cop's face. "But I won't. I want you to suffer the humiliation of losing your precious badge and everything you hold dear. I want all your dirty secrets laid bare for everyone to see. I want you disgraced, dishonored, because I know that means more to you than anything else, except for the gold, of course."

Mitch went over, snatched up a kitchen rag to bind Sinclair's hands behind his back and saw Raine holding an iron skillet.

"Just in case you lost the skirmish," she uttered.

He grinned. "But I didn't. Call Briggs."

Raine's hands were still shaking when she went to the wall phone and dialed 911. "See to Maddie. I'll have them send an ambulance."

Mitch went over to the cook and felt for a pulse. He ran his fingers around her head and found a bump and a gash matted with blood. "Tell the EMTs she's unconscious from a bad rap on the skull. But she's breathing. How long before Briggs gets here?"

"Dispatch says he's on his way."

"Good. I want to watch him drag this piece of shit off to jail."

By the time Briggs rushed into the eatery with Vargas and Grey, Jackson and Garret were waiting alongside Mitch outside the kitchen. The trio stood guard next to Jessup Sinclair.

The paramedics had taken Maddie to the hospital and Raine had gone with her.

Mitch shoved Sinclair toward the captain and watched as Vargas replaced the dishrag binding with metal handcuffs. "He came in here armed and tried to kidnap Raine again. I'm getting tired of doing your job for you."

"That's patently false," Sinclair stated. "I came in here to arrest that scumbag and he resisted, broke my nose in the process, and then overpowered me. Get these cuffs off me. Now! You should be slapping them on him, not me."

"Nice try," Briggs fired back with a finger pointed toward Sinclair. "I've got you on CCTV, kidnapping Raine Manning and loading her in the back of your police cruiser. And that's just for starters. I have DNA that matches yours from Livvy Buchanan's body. Because of that I'm charging you with first degree murder under special circumstances, including the kidnapping and murder of Ally and Blake Buchanan."

He angled toward Turner Grey. "Read this asshole his rights and get him out of here."

That proved more difficult as the state cop moved to take Sinclair into custody. The chief of police refused to budge. "You aren't taking me anywhere."

Like a surly teen, Jessup Sinclair began to protest by kicking and elbowing Turner and Vargas. A string of curse words sailed through the air until two uniformed state patrol officers stepped forward and muscled Sinclair to the floor. They got a better grip on his head, locking his neck in a tight chokehold before taking hold of his feet. It took all of the men to lift Sinclair toward the door, all the while battling the chief's fit of temper as he wriggled and twisted his body like a toddler who didn't want to leave the playground.

The men carted him out the door feet first. But midway to the car, Sinclair changed tactics and started the bawling act. His obscenities changed to wailing like a sick beagle. Once they reached the cruiser, they dragged him into the backseat. Changing his method yet again, Sinclair took to kicking the inside of the vehicle.

Mitch glared at Briggs. "This time you'd better keep him locked up. If I go near him again, I'll rip him apart and you won't have to worry about search warrants or gathering any more evidence."

"I'll pretend I didn't hear that," Briggs grunted, assessing the fight scene through the open door in the kitchen.

"I'm just telling you flat out," Mitch warned. "If you don't find a way to keep him in jail for good—"

Jackson stepped in the captain's path. "You owe us, Briggs. If you'd arrested him a week ago, even yesterday, or this morning—take your pick—he wouldn't have been able to come in here today in broad daylight and pull a gun and threaten Raine again. What do we have to do to make you understand Sinclair's a danger to the community?"

Briggs held up his hand. "Okay. Okay. I get it. You're pissed off. But things don't sail through the justice system that fast. We went to Sinclair's house around noon. His wife said he'd packed up and left. We were able to execute a search warrant, though, found a few items that might interest you."

"Like what?"

"Normally my response would be the usual canned PR stuff, but Jackson has a point. I do owe your family a measure of honesty when it comes to the investigation." Briggs shifted his feet. "Sinclair has a shed at the back of his property. My men are still going through it now. But so far, we've found a cell phone belonging to Dack Hawkins, some papers he apparently had in his possession at the time of his death, along with a flash drive. The fact that these items are in Sinclair's possession now points to him as Dack's killer."

"The flash drive should have Walker's emails on it," Garret added. "It's one of the things Dack had agreed to share with Anniston. That's why we were out there that night."

"Ah, I see. Well, Sinclair found out about the exchange somehow and made sure you didn't get your hands on the information. Now I just have to prove it."

"Which means something in the emails must've implicated him and his buddies in a big way. Why would he still keep that stuff around?" Garret wondered.

Briggs tugged on his ear. "These men may have gotten away with a lot of criminal activity over the years, but they don't fall in the genius category, not by any standards. They've simply been lucky. Eventually, luck runs out. I figure the remaining guys—Baskin, Dandridge and Frawley—are somewhere in hiding."

"What about Royce Buchanan? Do you intend to go after him?"

"If the case takes me his way, of course I will. But the feds will be here tomorrow to begin their investigation into bribery charges. I think they're serious about prosecuting him for a string of racketeering."

"What did you do with Wendy?"

"She's on her way to Tallahassee and to an undisclosed location for her protection. Why?"

Mitch narrowed his eyes. "Because if that man you just dragged out of here finds out she's cooperating, she'll never last until you get anyone to trial."

Chapter Twenty-Six

Raine sat by herself near the emergency room entrance, waiting to learn news about Maddie's condition. When she looked up and saw Anniston and Tessa walking through the double doors of the hospital, she sighed with relief.

"You okay?" Tessa asked, squeezing Raine's shoulder. "We got here as soon as we heard."

"I'm fine. Sinclair didn't hit me over the head with a meat mallet."

Anniston made a face. "Ouch! Is that what he used on Maddie?"

"Yep. Picked it up right off the counter where she was standing and walked up behind her, used it to smash her over the head. Bastard knocked her out cold. Have people in this town gone completely mad? Did they at least arrest him this time? I mean, Mitch overpowered him and tied him up, but the way our luck's been running, Sinclair will figure out some way to beat the charges and get out on bail."

"Not this time," Anniston vowed. "Briggs requested a special prosecutor to come down here to oversee all the indictments. The list is long. They said Sinclair cried like a toddler all the way to jail. Want to see his mug shot?" She took out her phone, flipped to the camera logo, held out the series of bursts showing Sinclair's face, so Raine could get a good look, maybe even a good laugh.

"Oh, my God, look at him, he's bawling like a big ol' baby."

Tessa peered over her shoulder. "How the mighty have fallen. I wish I could storm in there and ask him why he and those assholes had to kill Ryan."

"Maybe we'll get some answers," Raine prompted. "Although looking at his eyes and that faraway distant look, I'd say he's already lost it. I hope they put him on suicide watch."

"Hmm, maybe I should suggest that," Anniston noted. "I'll send Sebastian a text. He's there at the station now waiting around for any news of the others. He's the one who sent me the mug shot."

"Personally, I don't care if he does take his own life," Tessa muttered. "I know that sounds cruel, but I can't forget the day I went in there to report my brother missing. Sinclair sat behind his desk, smug and complacent, looking at me like I'd grown horns that made me the enemy. All the while he knew exactly what had happened to Ryan. So I'm not exactly concerned about his welfare now."

Anniston threw an arm around Tessa's shoulder. "How about we get together tonight for a spaghetti dinner, Marcelli-style. Lenore gave me the run of her kitchen so Sebastian and I plan to whip up dinner. It'd be like celebrating Sinclair's incarceration while we prepare to go look for that gold."

"Sure," Tessa said after letting out a loud sigh. "Has Mitch or Garret spoken to you about going after the gold?"

"Dozens of times," Raine replied. "Why?"

"No, I mean have they actually invited us along when they sail out of port? Jackson hasn't said anything to me about it. In fact, whenever I bring it up, he changes the subject." Tessa sent Raine a wry look. "You know I stayed behind with Lenore and Tanner during that whole time Jackson was on board *The Black Rum* dealing with getting you back."

Raine picked up Tessa's hand, squeezed her fingers. "I know you did."

"Running the restaurant wasn't easy while you were gone, especially not knowing what happened to you," Tessa admitted. "Maddie and Charlotte and I were all distraught. Then Jackson texted me they were working out a deal with Duarte for your return. It was all very tense during that time until we got word that you were safe and headed back to the boat."

Raine remembered the exact moment she'd spotted Mitch waiting for her to get to shore. Her heart had flooded with emotion. Thinking about Tessa's question, Raine chewed her lip, remembering how he'd dodged Sebastian's attitude toward Dominka going.

She cut her eyes between the two women. "Now that I think about it, Mitch hasn't said anything about me making the trip with him, not in so many words, but surely he doesn't plan to leave me here when he lures in Baskin and Dandridge, and that asshole Frawley. I've told him repeatedly I want to be there for that."

"Garret wouldn't dare try that kind of crap with me again," Anniston assured them. But there was doubt in her voice. "I didn't like the way Duarte used you as a pawn to get Nathan back. I'm wondering if Garret would try to keep us from going because he and his brothers see us as a liability. We could be used as pawns."

Raine thought that over. "A liability? A pawn? Well, that's not fair. I couldn't help getting captured like a pawn. Okay. So which one of us brings this up to them?"

Tessa didn't hesitate. "I don't mind doing it. I'm mostly concerned they'll sneak off in the middle of the night and then send us a text message."

Anniston's eyes grew wide. "If Garret did that, I'd—"

Raine's jaw dropped just thinking about Mitch slipping off before daybreak like that. "He does that, and Mitch had better make it for good."

Tessa grinned. "It was just a worry of mine. Do you ever think about having kids with the guy who makes you that angry on the one hand, but tries to protect you by not taking you with him during a dangerous mission? Do you ever think of going the whole nine yards and settling down…here…on island?"

Raine chewed her lip. "I've been settling down here my whole life. Sometimes I think Mitch had the right idea to get away and see the world while he could."

Anniston decided this was worth more mileage. "That sounds promising for you and Mitch."

"I wouldn't go quite that far. It's just that, for years, I held his not hanging around here against him. Mitch is the one who got to take off, see places I've only dreamed about, do what he wanted to do. Now, I think I understand things better. He had the courage to leave. I don't fault him for that. I stayed behind because…I had zero ambition inside me to do anything else. There was a fear in me that kept me from ever leaving. I realize that now. It's my failing, not Mitch's. Look, the two of us have always been great in the sack. No question about that area of our relationship. But a blind man could see we're not meant to be together. He does his thing thousands of miles away from here. I do mine in this little town. That's just the way it is."

Before Anniston could point out that Raine had the ability to change her own future, the doctor walked out to the waiting room. "Are you here with Maddie Denham?"

Raine stood up. "I am. How is she?"

"She has a concussion. But with rest, she should be fine. The MRI shows some light bruising but no swelling on the brain or bleeding. She does have a gash on the top of her scalp that took eight stitches to close. I'd like to keep her here twenty-four hours just to make sure her condition stays on an even keel, less likely for inflammation to set in if she remains in a calm and monitored environment. She took a pretty nasty hit."

"I know she did. I've put in a call to her daughter. She'll be here tomorrow. I should go sit with Maddie, let her know Gabby's on her way."

The doctor shook his head. "Actually, you shouldn't. Mrs. Denham needs rest and quiet right now. The less interaction and conversation with anyone, the faster she'll recuperate."

"Okay. Could I at least see her, let her know her daughter is flying in from Memphis?"

"Sure. But you should do it now. It'll take us at least thirty minutes to get her admitted to her own room. After that, I want her resting without any undue stress."

That evening, Raine closed The Blue Taco and watched Anniston and Sebastian make spaghetti Bolognese. Tired of the stress and strain of the last few weeks, she curled up on a side bench in the kitchen to veg. She heard the banter about Sinclair but tried to push the image of him holding a gun pointed at her heart to the back of her brain.

But when the talk turned to what they needed to do to before going after the gold, her ears perked up. She listened as Mitch laid out his plans.

"Klaus's diary may have given us a general location of where the U-boat went down. But it'll still take several underwater sonar scans to narrow down the exact spot."

"Why is that?" Garret wanted to know. "We have the longitude and latitude of where the boat sank."

"Approximate, big difference. Due to the strong underwater currents in that area, the tides would've shifted and carried the wreckage five, ten, maybe even fifteen miles or more from its original sinking. That's a lot of ocean. Remember, this is the same strong current the Spanish used to their advantage in the eighteenth century. The tides helped the galleons make better time as they headed back to Spain. The fleet would catch it in the Gulf of Mexico and then follow the same current around to the Keys, and up the coast before letting their sails catch the prevailing winds."

Garret stared at his brother. "You really are good at this."

Mitch grinned. "Yeah, I really am."

True to her word, Tessa turned to Jackson, hands on her hips, defiant. Out of the blue, she stated, "Don't think you're going to hunt for that gold without us along. It sounds as if you three are planning this trip without us. Here, now, you need to know, we're going with you."

Jackson had a look on his face like he'd been caught with his hand in the cookie jar. "Be reasonable," he said. "This could get very ugly. We're dealing with hardened criminals, desperate men who have nothing to lose. They want this gold at all costs."

But Tessa just bulldozed past his defense. "You seem to forget that I'm the one who got this whole thing rolling by being at Buchanan's house that night. You guys wouldn't even know about Sinclair's involvement, let alone Baskin's or Boone's, if not for me. You'd probably still be scratching your heads over that. I'm the one who brought that piece of the puzzle to the table. You're not keeping me here on land while you guys go off to play cat and mouse with the *Patagonia Pike*."

"Didn't you just hear what I said? It could get very dangerous out there."

"It could get dangerous right here if I stayed," Tessa pointed out, spreading her arms out wide. "Like this entire thing hasn't been risky from start to finish? I lost my brother to these men. I buried him too early in life. When I reported him missing, that lying excuse for a police chief stood two feet away and stonewalled me, made me believe he'd do whatever he could to help, and then did nothing. I know now he didn't do anything but try to make himself look good by hiding behind his authority. So don't even think about leaving me behind. I want to know for certain which one of those assholes put the bullet in Ryan's head. Because I'd like to return the favor. I suspect Sinclair, but I don't know that for sure. And until I know something concrete, I'll wonder if it could've been Baskin or Dandridge. I have to be there with you to make that determination for myself."

"I'm with Tessa on this," Anniston stated emphatically. "I've had my share of tough cases, but this one's topped them all. I've done a lot of hard work here, good work, work I'm proud of. Because of it I'm not sitting here on island waiting for you three to bring in the bad guys."

"You don't understand how risky…" Garret began.

Anniston whirled on him. "Don't you dare tell me I don't understand. I've been in this long enough to know all the risks. I'm going and that's final."

Hands on her hips, Raine's eyes flashed with temper, directed at Mitch. "So you thought I'd stay behind…again?" She shook her head. "I'm coming with you whether you approve of it or not. I don't need your permission. Even if Maddie can't work, I'll offer Charlotte a huge bonus to run things while I'm gone. Give me two days to hire kids to help after school. If that isn't possible, I'll shut the doors until we get back. But I'm not staying behind."

Lenore spoke up. "With Maddie out, no need to close the doors. Tanner and I will work the counter and the kitchen. You go with the others. We can handle things just fine."

Raine's mouth fell open at the offer. "Are you sure?"

"Positive."

"I don't know what to say except thank you. And relieved."

Tanner put an arm around his wife. "Just give us a few pointers before you go, like how you do things, a few tips on how to work your magic in the kitchen, and we'll take care of everything."

When Mitch started to protest, Raine's hand flew out in response to grab his arm. "You don't want them helping me? Unbelievable."

"No, it isn't that," Mitch said. "I just don't think it's a good idea to have you involved in this."

"Involved? I got kidnapped, for God's sake. You seem to forget that I'm the one who discovered Boone's connection to Willis Hartman, which eventually led Sebastian to the man's murder. I deserve, no, *we* deserve to be included in whatever your plans are to bring down those assholes. This is my town, too, just as much as it is yours."

She paused in mid-rant. "Now that I think about it, it's more mine than yours. You live off in the Bahamas somewhere while I still live here every single day. And it's where I'll have to live no matter what the outcome is. Whatever this brings to my door, I'll still be here."

"That's hardly relevant."

She ignored his comment and went on, "You really don't understand how much I want these men off the street, locked up, and gone for good. So I'm going even if I have to somehow get my own boat to do it."

Tessa's eyes lit up. "That's a great idea. We'll get our own boat."

Anniston high-fived the other two women. "What a turn of events. Maybe we'll rent a boat from Oakerson, although he'll never know anything about it. On second thought, maybe we should just take it, right out of the bay."

"Where do you suppose Oakerson's body ended up?" Raine asked. "I guess it doesn't really matter. Surely the mayor would want to help us out by loaning us a boat. We should definitely take one of his. Problem solved."

Mitch shook his head, rolled his eyes. He glanced over at Jackson, who in turn, gave Garret a pitiful stare. All three men's resolute demeanor buckled like a casino imploding under several tons of dynamite.

"As you can see, we're united in this, Mitch," Raine declared. "You won't shut us out and that's final."

Mitch lifted a shoulder, accepting Raine's thundering stand in the name of righteous indignation. "Fine. There's no need to get testy." He pivoted toward his brothers. "I never really thought there was much chance they'd stay behind."

Raine punched his arm. "But you made a fuss any way. Is that it?" She glared at the brothers. "Shame on you. We're equals in all this and deserve to be treated as such. We've all worked so hard to get to this point, it's wrong to keep us out of anything else you have going on."

"Yeah, yeah, we get it," Mitch grunted. "But there's a lot to do in preparation. It'll take planning and timing if we want to get the *Patagonia Pike* to follow us."

Across the kitchen, Garret helped Anniston with her sauce, dicing onion and mincing cloves of garlic. "The plan is simple enough. If we're able to make the rat bastards think we know the location of the gold, things will likely start popping."

"Luring them in has always been on the table," Raine said. "Luring's one thing. Being prepared to ram it down their throats is another matter entirely."

"That's just it," Mitch explained. "We don't have anyway of knowing how this will go down once we bring the leeches out in the open. Duarte's crew is lean and mean and prepared for battle."

"Then we'll be prepared, too," Raine offered. "I had an idea to get into the safe deposit box. I wanted to tell you about it during the party, but we got sidetracked. I think I know a way into the vault where the boxes are located. Every time I go in the bank to make a deposit, one of the vice presidents is always flirting with me."

Mitch glowered. "Which one?"

"Remember Derrick West from high school?"

"That prick? I whipped his ass in tenth grade because he wouldn't leave you alone during biology class."

She poked Tessa in the ribs. "Isn't it cute the way he remembers Derrick bugging me in class?"

"Every woman's heart does a somersault when a man defends her by whipping ass. So what's your plan with Derrick?" Tessa wanted to know.

"I'll sashay in there wearing my halter top and short shorts. It's a sure fire way to get his attention. But I'll need a partner, a volunteer to act at the appropriate time."

Before Mitch could offer, she pointed a finger at him. "Not you. It can't be you. Derrick will never flirt with me if you're standing there shooting daggers at him."

"So once you parade through the lobby with Derrick fawning all over you, what's next?"

"I'll get him to walk into the vault with me to open my box, like he always does. Before he leaves me alone, I'll distract him by bending over or dropping something so his eyes are directed down to my butt. Once I know his eyes land hard on my ass, that's when my partner has to step up and pull Derrick's key out of the lock, make an impression of it, then put the key back in the lock and get out of there."

"How did you come up with that?" Mitch asked.

"I watch a lot of late-night TV reruns." When he just kept staring at her, she added, "Okay. I saw it done on an episode of *MacGyver*, never thought I'd ever get to try it out in real life, though."

"I'm pretty sure it's been done in about two dozen movies, maybe more," Garret pointed out. "And that's probably the only times it's ever worked."

Raine put her hands on her hips. "You don't know Derrick these days. He isn't the brightest. Plus, lately he's all testosterone, never misses a day working out at the gym. He's got this steroid thing going on, has for about six years now. Besides, do you have a better idea?"

Garret twisted up his mouth. "Actually I do."

Anniston elbowed him in the ribs. "Breaking into a bank is a federal crime. If you think the feds wouldn't send you straight to Leavenworth, think again. It won't be that cushy minimum security camp outside Miami, either. I'm sure of that."

"*If* I get caught. Besides, I was thinking of getting it done tonight after we eat."

Anniston gave him a lethal stare. "You're planning to eat my spaghetti and then traipse over to the bank and do a little B&E? You've gone completely off your rocker."

"Maybe you and Raine want to act as my partners? I'll handle all the technical aspects. All the two of you have to do is play lookout at the front and back."

"If you want lookouts," Mitch prompted. "Jackson and I will go with you." He held up a hand before any of the women could stutter out a protest. "We'll take care of this part. Besides, I'd like to go by the police station and see Sinclair sitting in a jail cell. I'll bring my phone with me and grab a photo. I could always use it as a Christmas card."

Raine snickered. "Or a Facebook post."

For once, they used the dining room table for something other than a meeting place. Raine and Mitch set out Lenore's best tableware while Tessa and Jackson made sure there were enough chairs for everyone.

The professor had hung around and was eagerly awaiting a sit-down meal with all the fancy trimmings, a huge bowl of greens, a platter of hot dinner rolls, and the tasty promise of Marcelli spaghetti.

"Are you really making a stop at the jail?" Raine asked between bites.

"You bet. I already cleared it with Briggs."

"Not me," Raine tossed out. "If I never set eyes on that man again, I'd be fine with it."

Garret piled on more sauce over his spaghetti. "It'd be a perfect time to ask him a couple of questions. Not that he'd answer any of them, but we could stand there and throw the monkey a few peanuts through the bars and see if he'll give anything up. It's worth a try. Plus, maybe we should go check and make sure he hasn't done anything stupid, like taking his own life."

Jackson's eyes got big. "Then what are we waiting for? Let's eat this delicious meal and go pay him a visit."

The police station was a two-story brick building that shared space with city hall. They walked through the double doors into a long hallway that divided the mayor's office and town council from the other side used by the police department.

Another set of double doors led to a small lobby where the desk sergeant, Brill Gaffigan, usually parked himself this time of night working a crossword puzzle when he wasn't manning dispatch.

They'd known Brill most of their lives. He'd started out as a carpenter like their dad. But while Tanner had stuck with his skillset doing renovations, when the economy tanked in the 90s, Brill had opted for a second-shift job as a patrol officer. The steady income meant Brill started out mostly running radar on Main Street and handing out tickets to tourists who didn't have the sense to read a speed zone sign and slow down going through town.

These days, Brill had moved up the ranks to sergeant and was content to sit on his butt behind a desk from three-thirty in the afternoon to midnight, heading up his domain and keeping the peace.

But tonight Brill's chair sat empty.

"Is it just me or is it eerily quiet in here tonight," Jackson commented as he stood there looking around.

"Hello? Anyone here?" Mitch called out to an echo that reverberated off the walls. "Brill? You here?"

"Maybe he took a pee break," Jackson suggested, glancing to his left and right, cautious of how dead the place seemed. "I'll go check the bathroom."

Garret watched Jackson disappear down the hallway and considered the situation. "I'll go check the break room. Brill might be eating his supper about now."

That left Mitch to wander around the perimeter. He stuck his head around the corner where Sinclair's office used to be, but found the room unoccupied and locked. He switched directions and started down a short hallway that led to the lockup area. He spotted Brill's big feet sticking out from under a workstation.

"Get back here!" Mitch shouted to his brothers. "I found him!"

Mitch leaned over Brill's prone body, relief swelling through him when he realized the man was still alive. He patted Brill's face. "Come around now, Brill! Come on. Tell me what happened."

Brill tried to sit up. "I heard something back here coming from Jessup's cell. He's the only one we got back here tonight. Someone hit me from behind. Hard. Knocked me out cold, I guess."

"Seems like there's a lot of that going around," Garret muttered from the doorway.

Brill pointed to Sinclair's empty jail cell. "I'm sorry, guys. I guess whoever hit me, let him loose."

"Son of a bitch," Jackson said, as he walked further into the area where Sinclair had been held for a mere two hours.

"I'm sorry, guys," Brill repeated.

"No, it's my fault for leaving Jessup alive this afternoon," Mitch admitted. The words burned in his throat like cheap whiskey. "I should've killed him when I had the chance. Believe me, I won't make the same mistake twice."

"Don't beat yourself up," Jackson said. "You tried doing the right thing, turning him in, letting the system play itself out."

"Yeah. And didn't that work out grand?" A sick feeling washed over Mitch. "Do you think Jessup would go after Raine again?"

Garret scratched the side of his jaw. "No. I think this time he's long gone. He's met up with his buddies by now."

"I'm not taking any chances." Mitch took out his cell phone and sent a text to Raine. *Don't panic but Sinclair escaped. Stay with Mom and Dad till I get back.*

While he waited for Raine's reply, Mitch gave Brill the once-over, beginning to wonder if he'd been hit at all. He ran his fingers over Brill's head to verify he'd actually taken a blow to the head. After feeling the bump, Mitch studied Brill's eyes. They were glazed over like Maddie's had been earlier that afternoon.

Mitch's phone dinged with Raine's response. *Be careful. Anniston wants to know if you need her.*

He keyed in his message. *Stay put. All of you, until we get some answers.*

After responding to Raine, Mitch took hold of Brill's chin. "You need a doctor?"

"Nah. I'll be okay. I got a hard noggin."

"You feel like standing up?" Mitch wanted to know.

"Sure. It'd be better than the floor."

Mitch helped the older man get to his feet. "Did the chief have any visitors tonight, Brill?"

"Just one of Briggs's men."

"Not Baskin or Dandridge?" Garret asked, surprised.

"Nope. Roger never come in here. Boone didn't either. You can check the surveillance camera if you want. It's right up there in the corner and you can access the feed through this workstation." Brill tapped the table. "Nowadays, this whole place is on CCTV, that's what they call it, so it'd be mighty hard for me to lie to you."

"Which one of Brigg's men?" Jackson asked.

"The older guy. The one with two last names."

"Turner Grey? I knew something was off with that guy," Mitch stated. "What did he do, walk in here and hit you over the head?"

"It wasn't like that," Brill protested. "Grey came in here about six-thirty. Said Briggs sent him over to make sure Sinclair was okay. I let him in the back, right where we're standing now, but never opened Sinclair's cell door. I came back here with him, stayed for a few minutes and then left to go back to the front desk. After that, I kept an eye on them through the monitor."

"So Sinclair and Grey were left alone for a few minutes while you made your way back to the lobby, is that it?"

"I guess so. The two of them had a brief conversation. No idea what they talked about. And then Grey left about fifteen minutes later. Sinclair was still in his cell. I swear it."

"Mind if I take a look at the feed?" Garret asked. But he was already tapping the keys to access the computer's hard drive and view the video from an hour earlier.

"What happened next?" Mitch asked, just to keep Brill occupied so he wouldn't notice Garret's activities.

"I heard a noise coming from back here about an hour after Grey left. I came to check it out before I took my supper break. And whack, somebody hit me over the head. I need to call Briggs."

"That ought to be a great convo," Mitch muttered. "Is he staying at the Mainsail Lodge?"

"Nope. The state rented the old Dalfourth place so that all three of them could be at the same location."

"Dalfourth House is a little on the pricey side, don't you think?" Mitch pointed out.

Brill held his aching head in his hands. Despite the pain, the man could still get chatty. "That's what I thought. But hey, it must run up a bill to bunk at the hotel and use up three rooms, right? They'd save a bundle if all three could stay at the same place, less likely to run into the locals, right? They wouldn't have to interact with too many people. And it's only two blocks from here. So…you know…convenient."

"Is that right? For whom I wonder? Doesn't Buchanan still own that place?"

Jackson shook his head. "No, not him. But I'm fairly certain one of the city councilmen does."

"Can you say conflict of interest?"

Brill picked up the phone on the desk to call Briggs. "That's weird. He's not answering his cell."

Mitch traded looks with Jackson. "I don't like what I'm thinking. We'll head over there, Brill. You stay put. We'll call you when we get there." Mitch cut his eyes toward Garret. "You ready to go check out the Dalfourth place?"

Garret nodded as he finished perusing the video and closed out of the file. "Sure. Let's get out of here."

Once outside, Garret made it known what he'd seen on the surveillance. "I don't know how Grey did it, but he managed to come in through a side door to get back inside using a card key. Turner Grey is definitely the one who conked Brill over the head with a flashlight, probably the reason it didn't do as much damage to his skull. I downloaded the file that shows the whole thing, copied it just in case it suddenly went missing and emailed it to myself."

"Good call."

They piled into Mitch's truck, drove the two blocks to a grand old Victorian that sat at the corner of Main and Cobblestone. The original owners had been the Dalfourth family, a wealthy industrialist who lived in upstate New York and used the home as a vacation place once a year. It was more than a century old and had gone through several attempts at renovation. All had failed to bring it back to its glory days. But it wasn't for lack of trying. Outside, it sported a roof less than twenty years old, a new paved driveway that led around back to a carriage house, and newish windows, a result of one of the more severe tropical storms that blew through town. A well-maintained landscape kept the shrubs and ancient trees trimmed, nice and tidy.

Inside, the oak floors had been redone, walls painted in a palette that seemed to appeal to the tourists who fought to rent it out each summer.

Mitch stepped along the sidewalk, up past a trellis of deep blue petunias, climbing to reach the roof, and onto the long planked veranda. He rapped his knuckles against the door. Minutes ticked by and no one answered. "I'm beginning to get a sick feeling about this," he told his brothers.

Garret put his hands up to the front window, tried to see inside. When he caught a glimpse of light pouring from one of the rooms at the back of the house, he offered to go in.

"Not alone you won't," Jackson stated emphatically. "This whole thing is starting to creep me out."

"Do you smell gas?" Mitch wondered aloud, sniffing the air. "I think it's coming from inside."

Before he could say or do anything else, a blast of rolling fire hurled the trio off the porch, through the air, past the railing, leaving splinters behind, small as toothpicks. Panes of glass sent a burst of shards airborne, scattering the debris across the yard.

The fire ravaged the wooden structure even as they sat on the ground and watched.

"Something tells me Sinclair beat us here," Mitch shouted over the sound of crackling and popping lumber. He picked himself up off the bed of broken flowers, dialed 911. "You think the fire department will be able to save it?"

Jackson looked at the destruction. "Not a chance. Whatever's in there is toast." He glanced over at Garret. "Still want to break into the bank vault?"

"Not after that. I need to calm down first. I'm so friggin' rattled I'd most likely set off the alarm." He held out his hands, still shaking from the ordeal. "See?"

Mitch held up his own unsteady hand. "I hear ya. But who's left to respond if you get caught? Brill? I'd think tonight, of all nights, might be the perfect opportunity."

"Okay. You have a point. After we talk to the fire chief, I guess I'll see if I can work my magic. After all, I've never broken into a bank before. Should be interesting."

Blown back a good fifteen feet from the doorway, Jackson rested his hands on his knees and sent them both a knowing look. "I just realized you don't have to break in. I know where we can get the key."

"You're kidding? And you're just now bringing that up?" Mitch grunted.

"It just occurred to me while I'm sitting here staring at that wall of fire. Wendy's off in protective custody somewhere, right? There has to be a key to the bank somewhere inside Nathan's house along with the security codes."

"Likely in his home office. He might've even kept the information on his laptop," Garret decided, wiping the sweat from his face. Giving it serious consideration, he looked at the time on his watch. "Okay. I'm in. When should we do the deed?"

Jackson heard the roar of sirens coming from the fire trucks already en route. The engines wailed as they rounded the corner. He watched as firemen jumped out of the side doors to begin hooking up the water hoses at the hydrant. "We'll head over there as soon as we explain all this to them."

The scene looked like a roaring fire pit, something dreamed up by a Hollywood screenwriter and carried out by actors.

But this was real.

"We think the makeshift bomb was placed at the back," Mitch determined, bending the ear of Tag Linderman, the fire chief. He'd gone to school with Tag—from kindergarten on, right up to graduation. The little boy Mitch had known all those years ago claimed from the very beginning he'd end up a fireman one day.

And tonight Tag showed he was up to the task. "I thought this house was vacant," Tag bellowed over the tube of fire, watching the breeze whip the orange flames skyward.

"It was until two days ago," Mitch explained, going over the story for Tag's benefit. "I'd just knocked on the door hoping to talk to Paul Briggs when the blast blew us clear off the porch."

Tag squinted up at the inferno, saw his men fight to get the blaze under control. "Why do you think the fire started in the back?"

"Bomb," Mitch corrected. "This was some kind of improvised explosive device that set the fire. If it had been placed anywhere near the front of the house, my brothers and I wouldn't be standing here talking to you now. We'd be blown to bits."

"And you're saying you think Jessup did this after escaping from jail?"

"That's right. Turner Grey helped him. I think you'll find at least two bodies in there, Briggs and detective Vargas."

"What a nightmare," Tag stated. "What's gotten into this town? I've lived here all my life and never seen so much crime happening in such a short amount of time. My wife's already looking at putting our house up for sale. She wants to take the kids and move up to Key Largo. Trouble is, I can't think of a reason not to go."

"I wish I could tell you it'd get better, but only if we're somehow able to put Sinclair back in jail and catch Baskin and Dandridge."

"That's another thing. My wife and I go to church at Life Stone. I take my car over to Baskin's place when it acts up. I buy my kids a dozen doughnuts at Carson's bakery. I voted for Dave Oakerson every time he ran for mayor and now he's nowhere around when all this shit hits the fan. If you can't trust the people you've been around for most of your life, then who can you trust? What do we do without the state police intervening, Mitch?"

Mitch raked a hand through his hair. "I'm working on it. For starters persuade your wife to hold off on heading up to Key Largo. Okay?"

"Sure. But from here on out I'm sleeping with a Beretta under my pillow."

Shortly before midnight, Garret picked the lock on the back door of Hollister's stately Southern style home. Standing on the back terrace, he could hear the water from the marina lap at the shoreline. "Nice place. Nathan's come up in the world."

"Yeah. And to think I thought this was all Wendy's doing," Jackson admitted once they stood inside the king-sized kitchen. "Now I know better. Look at this place. I think Mom and Dad's whole house would fit into this one room."

"Did Wendy even cook?" Mitch asked, glancing around at the pristine appliances. He walked over and opened the refrigerator door. "I just answered my own question. There's no food in here, just a bag of coffee beans and a wilted bag of lettuce."

"Wendy did spend a lot of time at Oakerson's," Jackson quipped. "Imagine his refrigerator right about now. Imagine them never finding his body."

"That's what they said about Darla Pendleton. And now, they're trying to find her remains."

Garret wandered off down a hallway to look for the study. Spotting a set of double French doors that led into a nice library, he shoved them open and saw a mess. "Hey guys, you need to see this."

Mitch and Jackson lumbered past the den and into what had been Nathan's office. They stared at the state of the room.

"Sinclair and his bunch have been busy," Mitch noted. "They had the same idea."

Jackson picked up a mess of papers off the floor. "Yeah, but it doesn't look like they found what they came for."

"Don't panic," Garret said by way of assuring them. "All I need is to get into Nathan's laptop or find—"

"We're looking at this all wrong," Jackson told them, pacing in front of a wall of bookshelves. "We have to think like Nathan and Wendy. They wouldn't have left the key in such an obvious place like the office. No, they'd need to think they were outsmarting their so-called allies. They'd store it away somewhere other valuables were kept. And since Wendy has been here alone for several weeks, I'd say she put the key where she liked to have it handy."

"You think it's at Oakerson's place?" Mitch wisecracked.

Jackson grinned. "No. Wendy wouldn't have trusted Dave that much." Jackson took off for the master bedroom with Mitch trailing behind.

He went straight to the walk-in closet, settled on Wendy's side where a layer of fashionable dresses and women's business suits hung neatly on hangers. He pulled back the clothes and pointed to a wall safe. "We need Garret."

Chapter Twenty-Seven

On Quay Avenue, Raine slept fitfully on the couch. She'd convinced Anniston and Tessa to take Livvy's old room and get some sleep. So when Mitch and his brothers tiptoed through the front door, she heard the hardwood floor creak with three pairs of footsteps.

"Where have you guys been?" Raine whispered. "It's almost four in the morning."

Mitch went over to her, kissed her deep on the mouth.

She tasted whiskey. Taking his chin in her hand, she gazed into his brown eyes. "Have you been drinking?"

"Just a little celebratory nip of bourbon Nathan and Wendy had on hand."

"Two-hundred-dollar bottle of scotch," Garret murmured as he dropped into his mother's side chair. "Why don't you tell her what happened?"

"I know what happened," Raine said stubbornly. "Sinclair's on the loose and no one knows where he is."

"It's a lot more than that," Mitch said, relating each detail, starting with the explosion at the Dalfourth House.

Raine's mouth fell open. "I thought that was thunder. It rattled the window panes."

"Not weather related. Once Tag and his guys got there it didn't take them long to put out the blaze. The fire's still smoldering, a total loss, completely destroyed both floors. And afterward, when we were standing on the lawn, you could smell burning flesh emanating from the ashes. We hung around long enough to see the firemen dig out three charred bodies. Most likely, Briggs is dead, so is Vargas, and the guy who helped Sinclair get out of jail, Turner Grey."

"We're thinking Turner must've been the mole inside the state police headquarters back in Tallahassee," Jackson added. "Sinclair knew him from his days as a trooper. His position there made sure Grey could keep the heat off Sinclair by intervening whenever necessary and still be able to take his cut from all the corruption in town. As a silent partner he'd be able to keep his hands in everything from the capitol."

Raine wanted to make sure she was hearing it all correctly. "So Jessup killed Grey even though the guy broke him out of jail? Talk about ruthless."

"Sinclair is ruthless and he's still out there. It wasn't his body they pulled out of Dalfourth House. He was never going to share the gold with Turner Grey," Garret explained. "Turner was doomed the moment he set foot in Indigo Key with Briggs and Vargas, especially after the two were forced to subdue Sinclair, creating that very public spectacle at The Blue Taco when they helped the troopers drag him out of there."

Tanner appeared in the doorway, yawning. "Did you find Sinclair?"

"We were just talking about that," Jackson answered, catching his dad up on the story. "After we left Dalfourth House we went to Nathan's to look for the key to get into the bank."

"He had a safe," Garret began. "One of those wall unit outfits with a code number. Piece of cake."

"Okay, so what was in the safe deposit box?" Tanner wanted to know.

Mitch took out a document, stretched his long legs out on the sofa, bone-tired. "A variety of things. First, and the most interesting, is this old Spanish land grant made out to Koda Indigo, dated 1716, and signed by Philip V, King of Spain."

"Let me see that," Tanner said. "This belongs to me. What the hell is Nathan Hollister doing with it?"

"In order to answer that completely, you have to go back to Koda's day when Spain owned the land we now live on and all of Florida. Then in 1819 the United States acquired this area through a treaty for zero money. In order to cut the deal, the U.S. had to assume a five-million-dollar debt that citizens, like Koda, claimed Spain owed them. It took Congress three years to ratify the treaty. That's when our great-great-great, you get the picture, our ancestor— probably Koda's boy—got his land claim approved. That was in 1822. That document you're holding and the one from the federal government signed by President James Monroe, recognize that the island belongs to the Indigos outright."

"It's no myth. We flat out own it," Garret declared.

"The major point is why Nathan stole it from you in the first place," Mitch revealed.

Raine frowned. "How did Nathan get his hands on that if it belongs to Tanner?"

Tanner rubbed his jaw. "I'll tell you how. Your mother and I stored the land grant in our safe deposit box for security reasons. Worst thing I could've done. Ten years ago there was a fire at the bank. Nathan went out of his way to stop by and tell us everything in our box had been destroyed. Everything."

Jackson let out a low moan. "Wait a minute, ten years ago Nathan had just gotten his job there. He wasn't even an officer yet. He must've set fire to the bank just to get the land grant."

"That sounds about right. Your mother and I used to talk about how Nathan always seemed jealous of you. Maybe this is the way he decided was best to get back at you."

"Me? Really? Nathan certainly had me fooled all these years. That explains what else we found in the box."

"Nathan's lawsuit," Mitch offered.

Tanner looked dumbfounded. "His what?"

"A lawsuit, the brief had already been written, outlining how he planned to wait until the resort was built before taking everyone involved to court, using the land grant to claim that he owned the property, meaning the island, all of it, outright."

Tanner put his hands on his hips and stared at his middle son. "How did he plan to get away with that when there are Indigos right here still on the island? Me. I'm still standing here in this house. And you three boys come home at least once a year."

Mitch winced at that, but went on, "That's just it, Dad. Our coming back so infrequently actually played right into Nathan's hands. And the fact as a family we never talked much about estate planning."

"What was there to talk about?" Tanner argued. "The document was reportedly lost in the bank fire. I never questioned Nathan's honesty."

"None of us did. The thing is, to make this work, Nathan would've had to get rid of you, especially you, first. Nathan was getting very close to acting on that devious plot because his legal brief had been prepared by an attorney in Miami last spring, March to be exact. It claimed there were no surviving Indigos left, which speaks to Nathan's mindset and what he intended to do."

Mitch stared at his dad. "I think maybe you should sit down for this last part."

Tanner opened his mouth to protest, but realized the betrayal must run deeper. He plopped down into his easy chair.

"The final stab in the heart is this. Nathan had another signed document in the safe deposit box, signed by Livvy, notarized by Derrick West that said she was transferring ownership of the island to Nathan."

Raine let out a gasp. "Wait a minute, Livvy signed away her birthright?"

"I doubt she knew how devious Nathan was. Apparently this was his plan all along, long before last summer when Livvy brought up the subject of Nazi gold. Once Nathan latched onto the idea of the bullion, he put this scheme—the one about stealing ownership of the island—on the backburner, at least until he knew for certain the gold story was for real. But make no mistake, Nathan planned to kill us all eventually. That's why I'm pretty certain the night Livvy died, Nathan had a hand in the plot. Once he made the rounds killing off you and Mom, he'd take the island for himself."

"It meant that much to him," Jackson finished, rubbing his aching temple. "There's no telling how long he'd been putting this together. Years. That's probably why he made a play for Livvy in the first place."

"You sure it was her signature on the document?" Tanner asked. "You're certain she signed it?"

Mitch exchanged long looks with his brothers before answering. He pulled out another piece of paper from an envelope. "Unfortunately, we're sure. But you can see for yourself that it's her signature."

"I'm sorry, Dad," Garret said. "She was caught up in leaving Walker. Maybe she was that desperate to get away."

"Don't make excuses for her," Lenore said from the doorway. "I'm done with that. So Nathan was in league with all of them—Boone, Roger, Jessup, Dave, Carson—from the beginning?"

"It seems so, yes." Mitch swung his legs over and made room for his mother, patted the seat so she'd sit down.

"So Sinclair is gone. They're all gone. And Briggs isn't here to catch any of them either?" Lenore said sadly. "What do we do now? Who do we turn to now?"

Mitch took her hand in his. "It's not a big deal, Mom. We know they'll come after the gold. That's a given. They won't give up now after coming this far, not without getting their hands on the treasure, if there is any. We just have to dangle the right bait to get these guys to play the game and get them to fall for the trap we set."

"That sounds serious," Raine admitted.

"And one reason we wanted to leave you out of it," Mitch claimed.

"It just makes us more determined," Anniston said as she came into the room, followed by Tessa.

"No point in backing down now," Tessa added.

"Then we won't," Raine vowed. "When do we leave?"

"First, we get some sleep and then we narrow down the coordinates within a five-mile radius."

On board the *Patagonia Pike*, Jessup Sinclair sat in one of the staterooms Duarte had provided for him, drinking his morning cup of coffee. He looked across his mug at the men, who'd picked him up the night before near the harbor.

"By this time, the Indigos know I took care of Briggs and Vargas. They're wondering who they turn to now, wondering who they should trust."

"You shouldn't have done that to Turner," Carson Frawley said. "Eliminating him is one of the reasons I want out. This whole thing started falling apart with Dietrich's death. Now Oakerson's gone. It's rumored the state police have Wendy in protective custody. Who knows what kind of deal she'll cut to save her sorry ass. And to top it off, now you've screwed us all by killing cops. I'm not waiting around for the FBI to show up. Not me. I'm smarter than this. I'm getting the hell away from this crap. The gold's not worth my hide."

Sinclair didn't like quitters. He'd never been that fond of the former athlete who seemed to think he was better than everyone else because he could toss a baseball around. "We all know you don't like to get your hands dirty, don't we?"

"Carson's too good for that," Baskin chided, pouring a generous amount of whiskey into his coffee before cutting his eyes toward the baker. "You think you can just walk away from all this now. You know too much. Who says you won't hunt up the number for the FBI yourself?"

"I won't."

"We'll hunt you down if you even try it," Baskin forewarned him. "Do I have to remind you that I have associates all over the world? There's nowhere you can go that I won't be able to find out about it."

Carson swallowed hard and glanced over at Dandridge. "You're just sitting there. Tell them you feel the same way."

But Boone shook his head. "Not me. I've waited a long time for that sub full of gold to pay off. If you don't think it's worth sticking around for, then go. One less man to take a cut."

Baskin turned in his chair toward Dandridge. "Do you believe this whiner?"

The former preacher man lifted a shoulder. "To each his own. I'm a little nervous myself about Wendy Hollister telling them everything." He looked over at Sinclair. "If you were planning to do anyone in, why not make it Wendy? That would've alleviated a lot of stress for all of us."

"Because the opportunity to off Wendy didn't present itself," Jessup said quietly. "We're close to getting everything we want. Once we have the gold we'll leave this area for good, make a new start with new names. It won't matter then what Wendy tells the feds or anyone else."

Carson fidgeted. "If only I could count on that, count on everything going down just like you laid it out."

Tired of listening to the man's prattling like a child, Sinclair finally huffed out a worn-out breath. "I say if Carson wants to leave, let him go. It's one less share to divvy up. We'll need to do something about Duarte's entire crew when the time comes anyway."

Carson threw up a hand. "That's exactly what I'm talking about. The *Patagonia Pike* has a crew of at least twenty men. Nathan was supposed to get rid of some of those while he was working on board. Maybe if he'd done his job and hadn't let us down we might've had a chance at pulling this off. Nothing's gone like we planned. Nothing."

Repulsed by Carson's whining, Baskin sent him a disgusted look. "Your unwillingness to stick it out is starting to really bug me."

But no matter the dirty looks he got, Carson was adamant. "I want off the boat. Let me go my own way."

Baskin exchanged glances with Dandridge and Sinclair. "Then go. Get out of our sight. I'm not sure Duarte will allow you to take one of his rafts. But before you take off, understand this. If you tell anyone about us or mention anything about what's happened in Indigo Key over the years, I'll find you wherever you go. I have a very far-reaching network of friends that stretches from one end of the country to the other. No matter where you end up, know that I'm capable of grabbing my enemies by the throat. So keep your mouth shut or you'll wish you had. Are we clear?"

Carson nervously strummed his fingers on the table, but stood up. "Thanks. I won't tell anyone anything. I swear it."

After Carson left the cabin, Sinclair stared at Baskin. "You're just letting him leave like that?"

Baskin's lips curved up over the rim of his coffee mug. "Of course not. Boone, go get Duarte. He needs to know we have a situation."

Chapter Twenty-Eight

On six hours sleep, Mitch had a lot to do. And he needed help doing some of the chores. He sent Prentiss and Blaine on a shopping spree to buy groceries. They needed enough food for at least four weeks at sea. He doubted they'd be gone that long, but on a dive such as this, you never knew what you'd run into or who you'd meet carrying a grudge.

While part of his crew bought groceries, Walsh and Jenkins made sure the boat was in tip-top shape. They had to be combat ready. Mitch refused to go into battle unprepared.

He enlisted Jackson and Garret to obtain additional fuel, ammo, and extra weapons, specifically a shoulder-carried rocket launcher he'd ordered a week ago from Michael Tang.

While Raine gave Lenore and Tanner a quick rundown on restaurant management, Mitch's first stop was to go back to Dalfourth House and walk through the charred stubs with Tag.

What had once been a showplace in its heyday was now rubble.

"Helluva note," Tag lamented. "Happened two blocks from the fire station and we couldn't get here fast enough to save it."

"Do you know yet what he used for an explosive device?"

"The reason you smelled gas is because he turned on all four burners of the stove, took out a box of matches, set the cardboard on fire, and then while the fumes circulated he headed outside. That's when you guys showed up. It went boom and the whole place went up. The county coroner stayed here until nine-thirty this morning. He's sure those three bodies had gunshots to the head. They were dead before the fire."

"Sinclair didn't intend to leave witnesses behind…or evidence."

"Is it true you and Raine are back together?"

Mitch smiled. "I'm hoping for good this time."

"Really? So you're giving up the treasure hunting business?"

He was trying not to think of that. Before he could come up with an answer, Mitch caught sight of an SUV pulling up at the curb.

"Looks like ATF to me, or maybe FBI," Mitch remarked as he slapped Tag on the shoulder and started for his truck. "I gotta go."

"I hope they'll be able to turn the tide," Tag said.

"Don't bet on it. Good luck with your investigation though."

Mitch's second stop was a return trip to the bridge to see if the forensic team was still there. Sure enough, they'd made progress. He got out of the car and was met by a field supervisor, a balding thirty-something who wore an official-looking dark blue uniform.

"You can't come down here. See the crime scene tape. It's off limits to non-personnel."

Mitch held up his hands, unable to take his eyes off the others in the distance, bent over a large hole in the ground and chipping away at the dirt. They wore white uniforms, latex gloves, with rubber boots on their feet and masks hiding faces. "No problem. I see your forensic team's dug a lot further down."

"I can't discuss that. You'll have to move along."

Mitch was about to get back in his truck when Brill pulled up in his cruiser.

"How's it going? How's the head?"

"Better. Did you hear about what they found?"

"No. I asked that guy over there but he wouldn't tell me."

Brill shifted his feet and angled closer. "After two days of digging, they found remains. There was female clothing next to the bones, looked like one of those pantsuits women used to wear in the '90s."

"That fits with what I remember."

"Yeah? Well, before Briggs died he mentioned a woman named Darla Pendleton who went missing from here. But that's not the big news."

"What do you mean?"

"They didn't find one set of remains, they found three, spread out in the general vicinity. They have no idea who the other two are."

By the time Mitch reached the houseboat, Raine's bedroom looked like a disaster area.

"What's all this?"

"Packing."

"Raine, all you have to do is throw some jeans and shirts into a suitcase along with your wetsuit and dive gear." He spotted a black teddy on the bedspread and held it up. "On second thought, correction. Lingerie is not only recommended but highly appreciated." He sidled up behind her, put his arms around her waist, nipping his way down her throat. "Remember that time we made love on that little ketch?"

"The one belonging to Keaton Payne? It was practically moored in the harbor within view of the marina."

Mitch laughed. "It was not. But it'll be a lot different on board *The Rum*."

"I'll say. We'll have a packed house."

"That's not what I mean. The whole time we made out on Keaton's sloop, it bobbed all over the place. *The Black Rum's* a lot more stable."

"And you're telling me this because…"

He ran a hand to her breast and caressed the plump little curve. "Because I'm looking forward to showing you the difference."

Chapter Twenty-Nine

The Black Rum motored across Sugar Bay before six a.m. with a dozen people on board. She was loaded down with supplies along with hope and plenty of expectations.

Armed with a general location of where the U-boat had gone down, they knew they had at least a few days of underwater sonar searching ahead of them before things would start to pop. They'd dropped enough hints around town about their intentions. The information couldn't help but make its way back to Sinclair and Baskin and the rest.

They watched the sunrise together with Raine standing next to Mitch on the bridge, the water glimmering around them like a sea of sapphire jewels. He could tell she was excited.

"You're fidgeting like a nervous cat," he noted. "And it's too early for you to have swigged down that much caffeine."

She grinned ear to ear. "I'm anxious to get out there and dive. How long will it take us to reach the general vicinity of where you think the sub went down?"

"If we sustain top speed at fourteen knots, we should be there by tomorrow midday. ETA around noon, in time to have a nice swim in the ocean and then a tasty supper on deck before the assholes come along and ruin it."

Panic crept up her spine. "You don't think they'll show up that soon, do you?"

"Nah, they'll let us do all the dirty work first before they sneak up on us. We'll have to post guards and keep vigilant, though, just in case."

"Jackson says he expects to take days to study the sonar images and magnetic readings before he has an optimal dive location pinpointed. And that's including going over vast amounts of storm data from decades back."

"That sounds like Jackson, and probably accurate," Mitch muttered as he charted the course out of the mouth of the marina and steered the boat northward toward Georgia.

"I wonder if we're prepared for just how different our lives will be after this hunt," Raine pondered.

"You mean because of the gold?"

"Not that. Because we're attempting to put a group of ruthless men behind bars who've run roughshod over the town for more than twenty years. Sometimes I wonder if we can pull it off."

"Hey, no negative vibes allowed. We have to, otherwise who knows who they'll go after next. It could be Mom or Dad. We have to plan on this being a success and that's all there is to it."

By nine a.m. Key Largo came into view, its pearly sand glistening in the early morning sun.

"God, I see why you love this so much," Raine said, breathing in the sea air. "It's magnificent out here. I feel like I'm on vacation and I've left all my worries in the dust. You're so lucky to get to do this all the time."

Mitch stared at her crop of golden hair fluttering in the wind. Emotions had his heart flipping in his chest. "You should see your face. It's absolutely glowing." He'd love to be able to keep her this happy.

Interrupting those thoughts, Garret stepped on deck. "Jackson's driving me nuts poring over his maps and charts. Like it'll make a difference. If we're lucky enough to pinpoint the right area, it's still a crapshoot whether or not we'll be able to stumble on a sub from seventy years ago."

"What is it with all these bad vibes all of a sudden?" Mitch snarled. "True, we have a vast ocean and a needle in a haystack to find, but with Klaus's diary and Jackson's obsessive calculations, have a little faith."

"I guess we're all a little on edge," Garret admitted. "Knowing what we're about to face is beginning to sink in."

Walsh joined them, slapped Garret on the back. "If you're nervous, I'm planning a little poker game later. Get your money ready and kiss it goodbye. I feel lucky."

Garret elbowed him in the ribs. "Five-card draw? You're on."

Mitch recognized the tactic and had to give it to his crew chief for creativity. "Thanks for coming up with a way to break the tension. We're used to dive spots getting dicey. They aren't."

"Not to this level, anyway. I thought it'd be better than sitting around staring at each other, keep their mind off the strain of the situation about to build up."

It was several hours later when Raine pointed to the horizon and practically danced on deck as the skyline of Miami appeared in the distance. "We're making good time," she decided.

"Let's celebrate. We should go below and fool around."

"With all these people on the boat? No way." Despite her protest, she suddenly turned to him and wadded up his T-shirt in her fists, yanked him to her. "Although the sea air does have a certain aphrodisiac quality about it."

"Good to know. Does that translate to you and me—?"

Tessa wandered in with lunch, thick grilled ham slices topped with melted, gooey cheese on huge brioche buns. That's when it hit Mitch. How could he expect any alone time with Raine when the boat was jam-packed stem to stern with people? He'd have to remember that for later.

Chatting away, Tessa turned in a circle to take in the view. "Sorry I didn't cook, but the time got away from me. I spent the morning helping Jackson organize his storm charts and enter the data into a spreadsheet for analysis. Funny how tracking old storms leads to figuring out how the bottom of the ocean floor shifted and slid the sunken ship into its resting place."

"Usually we'd be able to dig into a set of manifests or archives for optimum position, but in this case, all we have is one man's journal." Mitch picked up one of the warm hoagies and dug in. "Thanks for the food."

"No problem. I'm happy to kick off this expedition taking my turn in the galley, even if it's just sandwiches. It's handy how you've already listed whose responsibility it is."

"Learned that the hard way," Mitch said in between bites.

Raine noticed Tessa gnawing on her lip, obviously hanging around with something else on her mind. She poked Mitch in the belly and said, "I think someone is staring at your digital screens for a reason."

Tessa's lips bowed up. "She's right. Would it be possible to take a turn at the helm? I've always wanted to man the controls."

"Sure. Put your hand on the wheel and I'll give you a tour of how everything works. This is the digital chart display, the GDPS..." He proudly ticked off the features, explaining to her how each contributed to the overall safety of the boat—the Doppler satellite, the echo sounder, and the depth finder.

"Cool. I've always wanted to take one of those trips on a cruise ship."

Mitch laughed but something else occurred to him. "You know we should get everyone else up here for a quick how-to guide. You never know when that info might come in handy."

"I'll go round everyone up," Tessa offered.

Fifteen minutes later, Tessa had dragged Sebastian and Dominka, Anniston and Garret, up to the bridge for a tutorial.

While Anniston stood at the helm, they cruised past the West Palm Beach coastline and waved merrily at beachgoers from the railing.

At mid-afternoon, Walsh took over at the bridge, offering a breather for Mitch. Raine had already disappeared into the galley to start her shift at preparing supper.

Mitch stepped in to get coffee and was blown away at the sight. She stood at the counter putting on a pot roast, piled high with potatoes and carrots. "I'm not sure our oven is big enough for that," he pointed out.

"Sure it is. I already measured. I'm just hoping I didn't wait too long to get it going. How is it you have such a state-of-the-art kitchen?"

"Two things a crew truly appreciates—good pay with benefits and the ability to fix a great meal. If you don't believe me just sit back and watch how they devour that meal."

Mitch was right about his crew. At mealtime, Raine was delighted when the pot roast disappeared.

"I didn't think anyone could cook better than my mom," Prentiss declared as he chowed down.

Blaine agreed. "Best pot roast I ever ate. I don't even mind cleaning up. It's my turn on the roster."

"Save room for dessert," Raine prompted.

Jenkins blinked in surprise. "Dessert? You're kidding? We usually just have store-bought cookies or ice cream."

Raine smiled at their enthusiasm. "Not tonight. I made chocolate mousse tarts with whipped cream."

Anniston glanced around the table. "How am I supposed to follow this in the morning? I'd planned on making oatmeal."

Walsh made a face. "We're not big on cereal around here," he pointed out, wiping his plate clean. "Although truth be told, on my last checkup the doctor suggested I eat more oatmeal to bring down my cholesterol."

Raine brought out the tray of chocolate pastries and watched Mitch's eyes bug out.

"These have fresh strawberry slices on top."

"Garnish," she stated.

"I don't remember buying berries at the store," Prentiss said.

"I brought my own," Raine explained, sporting a smug grin. "I made Mitch lug it down the pier and up the ramp."

Mitch ate the mini pie in four bites, wiping his hands with a napkin. "I'm not complaining now."

After supper was done with, since she wasn't on the roster slated for cleanup, Raine decided to take a stroll around the deck. It was a beautiful evening as she stared up at the cascade of stars spread out overhead.

"Enjoy them now because there's a marine layer moving in before morning," Mitch said as he slid an arm around her waist.

"You'd be able to tell that for sure with all that fancy equipment."

"There's a benefit to having you on board."

"I like the idea of bunking with you tonight. I've been looking forward to it."

Not as much I have, he thought. "I was actually referring to your culinary skills. Told you that meal would be a big hit."

She batted his roaming hands away as they tried to slip under her little cropped blouse. "Come on, Mitch, someone could walk around that corner and see us making out."

"So what if they did? Besides, everyone's back inside anteing up for five-card draw except for Sebastian and Prentiss who are pulling guard duty in the tower."

Embarrassment rolled through her. She cut her eyes toward the signal mast, then over to the wheelhouse. "They could be staring at us right now."

Mitch let out a laugh. "Relax. Sebastian doesn't strike me as a voyeur and Prentiss might have a little crush on you since supper, but I don't think it's serious. Besides, I'm sure they have more important things to do than watch us do a little stargazing."

"I suppose. If there's a game, then why aren't you there? You love playing cards."

"Not tonight I don't. For me, we're the only two people in the world tonight. Those stars you see above are glittering just for us."

He took out his iPod from his pocket, found his playlist and queued the music. The song leaned to soulful, the singer's lilting voice smooth as honeyed cognac. "Dance with me, Raine?"

She sent him a bemused smile. "I'd forgotten this side of you, a definite romantic bent when you're on the water." The tune, soft and dreamy, spoke of light and love. "How could I not dance with you when you've come prepared like this?"

Their fingers touched, linked. His arms went around her, drawing her close. He held her lush little body tight against his, so the moonlit shadows on the deck had them merging as one. His chin rested on the top of her head as they circled and swayed. Dipping her the way he used to, he let the lyrics lead them into time-honored mood and magic.

His hands roamed up her back and under her shirt until he felt skin, dewy soft and smooth. He captured her mouth, and relished her sweet taste until he drew out a low moan from her.

Intent on giving her the tenderness she deserved, he led her down the passageway to his cabin. When he flipped on the light and held the door open for her, she let out a surprised intake of breath.

Somehow he'd managed to buy every pink and red flower in town before the trip, or so it seemed. Every kind of blossom—from rose to dogwood and daisy—covered every inch of wall space like he'd papered the room in spring just for her. The long stems of tulips shared space in clear vases, jars, or whatever container or canister could hold dozens of blooming irises and fragrant lilies—as long as they were red or pink.

"So this is why you made me stow my gear in the galley?"

"Temporarily." He angled his head and pressed his lips to hers. "I wanted to surprise you. Not long ago I read this blog that said pink means affection and caring. Red stands for true love. I feel all those things for you…and more. You're my true love, Raine."

"Oh Mitch. You are such a romantic. They're beautiful."

"So are you." His hand reached to touch her hair. He wanted more, so he pulled her to him, lifting her off her feet. Their willing mouths came together in a torrent of heat.

Within those four walls, at that moment in time, it was just the two of them. The world, uncertain and dangerous, was somewhere else.

Awash in soft fluttering candlelight, they tore at each other's clothes, shedding jeans and shorts, T-shirts and buttoned tops. Getting rid of any barrier, and down to skin, they both stood naked. He sunk his teeth, nipping into silky flesh. As he moved down her body, she smelled of moonlight and magnolia and tasted like sweet orange blossoms.

Diving at each other, they rolled on the sheets, going after what they wanted, what they needed.

Arousal battered her senses. He smelled of musk and man. His hard body moved over hers. Wherever his sailor's hands touched and lingered, she burst to life in pockets of pleasure.

When his mouth latched onto a breast, she hovered at the brink. But when his fingers dipped into the center, slick and hot, it was like dropping into a fountain of molten lava. It erupted in waves of fiery reds.

The buildup came again as he plunged, this time with her matching him rhythm and beat. Deeper and deeper they went toward the edge. The fall from the cliff was like catching a soaring tsunami as it barreled its way to shore. There was lightning, quick and blinding. And then the sea, all blue, exploding and spilling over into a tempest of light and love.

As he caught his breath, he dipped his head and kissed her mouth, a brief show of warmth, a touch of lips to seal the intimate moment.

Rolling to his back, he captured her hand, brought it to his lips. "We have a lot of time to make up for, that should give you some idea of what we missed."

It gave her a lot of ideas. And for the rest of the night, they just kept coming.

Chapter Thirty

At dawn Mitch crawled out of bed and took over the wheel from Garret, grateful when his brother handed him a steaming cup of coffee, strong and black.

"Marine layer's so thick I turned to instrumentation around three. The fog forced me to reduce speed down to twelve knots."

"Good call. You could've woken me up sooner."

Garret smiled that wry grin of his. "I figured you needed the…uh…sleep."

"Thanks. It was our first night together on the boat. I wanted to make it special."

"And did you?"

He grinned back and decided to change the topic. "How much did you lose last night?"

"Ten bucks. Walsh went on a winning streak and I never caught up. Neither did anyone else."

"You played cards till midnight and still took your turn at the helm? Get out of here. Go get some sleep. At least try. You have until noon."

"Such a taskmaster." Suddenly he turned serious. "Are we prepared for this, Mitch? I mean for real? Can we handle Duarte and the other snakes? We brought Anniston, Raine, and Tessa into this. Hell, even Sebastian couldn't talk Dominka out of staying put at the hotel. This is unlike anything we've ever faced before. I'm not so much worried about myself as Anniston. It's certainly not about the gold."

"I know. What if we lose? They'll kill us all and then go back to what they were doing beforehand somewhere else. And that's if they don't head back to town at the first opportunity and go after Mom and Dad before they leave for another part of the world. We can't let that happen."

"They have more personnel than we do. We're outmanned," Garret pointed out.

Mitch shook his head. "Doesn't matter if Duarte has fifty. It doesn't change our game plan."

Garret slapped him on the back. "I'm proud as hell to be your brother."

"You say that now, but if things go south..."

"No, we can't think like that. Won't."

"That's right. Now get out of here. Get some shuteye."

Even at the slower pace, Mitch managed to bring them to their target within an hour of their timeframe.

By the time the haze wore off and the sun broke through the clouds, he could make out Fort Clinch State Park and the beach to the west.

Mitch shut the engines, dropped anchor. "This is the longitude and latitude Klaus wrote down. In my calculations to get us here, I've allowed for the strong currents, the decades of storms, and a shift in the sea bottom. Now it's up to sheer luck."

Jackson wasted no time getting the sonar equipment in the water along with the magnetometer sensors.

"Using the magnetometer like a giant metal detector is the most efficient way to pick up man-made anomalies like the metals from a sub. But feel free to dive to get an eye for the surrounding area."

That sounded like a good idea to Raine. "I figure while we're waiting for your scans and readings, I'd better practice my diving."

Walsh reached over and patted her head. "Not a bad idea, Blondie. Since we've been sitting for weeks in port, the crew could use a string of 'em, call it refresher courses."

"We should pair up and dive with partners," Mitch suggested. "But we'll need to maintain a certain force on board at all times to keep a watchful eye on the horizon."

They paired up in teams, and took turns diving for two hours at a time, at depths of thirty-five meters, which was the depth Klaus had written down in his journal.

Over the course of two days, they gradually increased their length of time on each dive by fifteen minutes. Each time learning to better coordinate with their respective partners as a team.

By the third day, the divers were in sync enough to make it all look routine. And during that time they all became a unit. Playing cards in the evening, listening to music at dinner, building on friendships with idle chatter.

A week flew by before Jackson announced he'd found the most likely spot. The crew gathered around a digital screen in the command center while he pinpointed the area on his chart. "I'm going to suggest we alter course and turn three degrees eastward. Here."

"That's minor, but could be critical to homing in on the exact spot," Mitch said, punching in the change to coordinates. "No problem."

"This has to be it," Jackson went on. "You guys have been diving all around it, maybe even got within forty yards a couple of times. But because visibility is so poor, you didn't see this man-made variance sitting at a forty-five-degree angle. This is where we should explore first."

"I'll take your word for it," Mitch stated. "Raine and I will go in for the first three hours. Anniston and Garret after that, Prentiss and Blaine next when they come off watch. Walsh and Jackson will remain on board at all times, unless we encounter a problem in the water, and then they're our backups."

Mitch grabbed Raine around the waist. "Ready to dive where it counts?"

"You bet. That's what I came for."

After making the course adjustment, Mitch and Raine donned wetsuits and stood on the dive platform shouldering their tanks.

Mitch eased off the side first, dropping into the cold ocean waters before Raine plunged after him.

They began their descent into the dark depths of the sea as several curious fish swam by.

Raine tapped his arm, pointed to a small blue shark that took a couple of laps around them, not quite sure what they were. But after its third lap it spotted a squid and took off after its lunch.

Raine watched the scene play out and thought how calm and lovely the sea could be one minute and exceedingly dangerous the next.

This past week had been sheer bliss. In her heart she knew she'd found what she was meant to do. Nothing before this had ever called to her quite as strong as being on the open sea.

Without thinking, she reached out and touched Mitch's arm just for the contact. This wasn't a dream world, but rather one where she might actually experience adventure for the first time in her life. The icing on the cake was the person swimming next to her. The one person in her life she'd truly loved. Since that first day she'd spotted him standing in the hallway in kindergarten, practically sucking his thumb, he'd been her best friend.

Beside her, Mitch noticed the joy on her face even with the mask. He'd never seen her look as beautiful as she did now, so at peace with her surroundings.

It struck him that he could never leave her again.

When he glanced up he couldn't believe his eyes. Ten yards ahead was U-492, listing at a forty-five-degree angle on her side, partly covered in several layers of sand. Mitch took out his underwater camera, snapping pictures while Raine swam around the hull, filming the damage and looking for a safe way to enter.

After getting enough footage, they headed back to the top, completing their dive stops along the way to decompress.

Back on the boat, Mitch had everyone gather in the command center to pour over the stills, one by one, and then watch the video from start to finish.

"It's obvious the sub suffered from an internal explosion. See the damage toward the rear. The impact was in the engine room. It goes outward, not inward," Mitch noted. "And all the hatches, except for two, were open. We could see inside one of the forward torpedo tube doors. We found two floating Torpedo mines known as TM mines, entangled outside on the bow. I'm sure someone pushed the TMs out of the tube so the crew could escape that way before the boat went down. At least that's my take. We'll have to give these mines a wide berth for now until we figure out how to either disarm them or somehow safely detonate them."

Jackson studied the photos and the layout of a similar class U-boat he'd found online. "I'd say the safest entry point is through the conning tower hatch. It looks to be clear of any obstructions."

Mitch agreed. "Then I think the next step is to do a test run dive with the ROV to ensure that we're safely able to enter the sub."

"One of the dive teams will have to get close enough to launch the smaller ROV through the conning tower hatch," Jackson suggested.

Mitch glanced at Raine, who lifted a shoulder. "It's okay with me if you volunteer us for the job. I can handle it."

"There you go," Mitch told the crew. "We'll take it down and scout the interior of the sub for any hidden dangers. Plus, once it's inside, it'll provide you guys with a live feed, so you'll know what's happening down there every step of the way."

That afternoon Garret and Walsh lowered two underwater scooters, harnessed together and equipped with an emergency drive switch in case anything went wrong with the remote drive.

They also dropped in a sled that could be attached to the scooters. It would act as a trailer, which would allow hauling anything back they found useful on their first trip, or subsequent trips.

The scooters had a range of six miles on cruise speed and could run more than three hours before shutting down. They added reserve air tanks on the sled as a precaution in case they needed extra.

After going through their dive preparations, everyone stood on deck and watched as Mitch and Raine disappeared below the waves.

They reached the sandy bottom without any problems and carefully made their way around the wreck until they were in a position to launch the remote into the sub.

Back on board the boat, the live feed kicked in. Jackson watched as the ROV slowly made its way through the hatch and down into the conning tower. He recognized the control room with its wall of gauges and valves. The little remote operating vehicle cruised past the navigator's table and the periscope.

All of a sudden a small tiger shark swam by and bumped the ROV, causing it to hit the controls belonging to the electrical engines.

Mitch pressed his com button. "Don't worry, I'll put it back on course to head into the main walkway toward the officers' quarters."

"Roger that," Jackson said from above.

Swimming behind him, Raine watched as her dive partner used the controller to steer the remote back on track. Through her com she reported back to the ship. "The ROV easily made it through the watertight hatch into the main walkway. It's passing into the small radio room. Very cramped space in here. I don't know how those guys did this. Garret, you definitely wouldn't like these close quarters."

"I'm getting claustrophobic just thinking about it," he joked.

She watched as small fish darted in and out of the dark corners. The light and movement from the ROV sent small sea creatures diving for cover.

The ROV sent back feed from the sonar room and beyond, passing through the officers' mess. Raine saw broken cups and dishes still lying in a heap on the floor. Of course it was all covered in a fine layer of seaweed and silt.

She kicked past a gallery of pictures on the wall. Watery blurred images of 492's crew and its officers, even one of Hitler.

From the officers' mess she followed Mitch and the ROV into the junior officers' quarters with bunks on both sides of a wall where a small two door closet still contained personal items.

Mitch had to stop the ROV as its light revealed a watertight compartment door locked shut and still sealed that led to the crew's quarters and the forward torpedo room.

Mitch pressed his com button. "Did anyone spot anything we need to take a closer look at because we've hit a dead end?"

"We'll review the tape," Jackson said. "But I didn't catch anything that looked like what we're looking for."

Mitch worked the controls to turn the remote device around and head back the other way. "Okay, we're going back to the control room to explore the rear part of the boat."

The ROV retraced its path back through the control room, stopping twice to explore the dark compartments it hadn't captured on the way in.

"Are we clear to enter?" Mitch asked.

Jackson studied the images. "I don't see a problem. You're all clear."

Mitch and Raine moved through the opening and into the cramped control room.

"I wouldn't have lasted a day in here without going crazy," Raine stated. Everywhere she looked there were gauges with broken glass and damaged panels.

She hoped they didn't come across any bodies. She already knew from the log there had been men who hadn't made it out.

Mitch checked the ROV before sending it through the aft watertight hatch and toward the engine room. The ROV passed a small one-man galley with what look like a Coleman stove you would use for a camping trip. It had a compact refrigerator crammed into the small space.

He spotted a large overhead valve for the air supply that ran on a line to the diesel room. Curious, he checked the gauges and found them turned to the off position. Had there been a fire in the engine room?

The ROV moved on to where more bunks hung on the walls. She spotted the first remains of a crewman. All that was left of the unlucky man was a skeleton with a few tattered shreds of clothing clinging to the bones along with his uninflated escape vest.

Raine had a hard time getting the skull—with its haunting eye sockets—out of her head. She wondered how old he'd been. What had been his last thoughts as he died in the dark depths of the ocean so far away from home?

"There's still no sign of anything that looks like it could hold boxes of gold coins or bars," Mitch reported.

Raine pointed to the aft torpedo room.

He shook his head and thumbed a sign they needed to start back up. "We've been down a long time. We still need to decompress before returning to the surface."

He turned the remote and sent it back through to the conning tower.

They took their time surfacing.

Once they were back on the boat again, Anniston handed them cups of freshly brewed hot coffee.

Raine sipped the hot liquid, hoping she could get warm again. "We'll need to see what's inside those sealed sections fore and aft. Anyone have any ideas?"

Garret spoke up. "We could use an underwater cutting torch to punch a small hole in the bulkhead and slide a rope with a camera into the hole, maybe put some clay or some kind of filler around it to keep it watertight."

Mitch held his cup of coffee in both hands as he studied the layout again. "That should work, we brought several torches with us. We might be able to improvise something to work underwater."

He set his cup down and ran his finger along the diagram of the U-boat, stopping at the engine compartment. "We know for sure the engine room is flooded because of the hull damage here. But these two aft compartments and the forward torpedo room are big question marks. We can't enter the engine room through the blown out hole in the bulkhead because it's too small and there are several jagged pieces of metal around the edges. So we'll either have to make the hole bigger or force it open to get at the aft compartments."

Jackson's jaw tightened. "Either way we have a lot of work to do before we can see what's behind door number one or door number two."

"Bingo." Mitch went back to studying the forward part of the diagram. "I think we should look here first in the forward compartment. It looks to have additional room for storage here under the bunks where the crew slept."

Raine chimed in, "I noticed it looked exceptionally messy, almost like someone had rummaged through the cabin looking for…something."

"And that's why we're starting there."

At dawn the next day, Mitch and Raine were getting ready to dive again when Garret and Anniston joined them on deck already wearing their dive suits.

"What are you guys doing?"

"I'm a fairly good hand with a hot torch and I thought I could widen the hole in the engine room while Anniston gets a closer look at those TM mines."

Anniston spoke up. "I'm pretty sure I'll be able to tell if the mines are live or not, by checking the arming device on them."

Mitch looked over at Raine.

She cut her eyes toward Garret. "I'm just worried those cramped quarters will get to you."

"I'll be fine."

Raine glanced back at Mitch. "Then it's really up to them. Even if you did try to put up an argument, I don't think you'd win. Besides, we could use the help and another pair of eyes."

Mitch angled his gaze toward Anniston. "Are you sure you want to take this kind of risk? Those mines could blow at the least little touch."

"I'm in. I promise I won't fiddle with anything, just look. I'll give you a thumbs up sign, if, and only if, I'm a hundred percent certain the devices haven't been armed."

Mitch turned to his brother. "You'll stay back until Anniston gives us a thumbs up then, right?"

"Absolutely."

"Then let's go."

Once they were on the sandy bottom it was just as Mitch feared. Garret stayed right at Anniston's side as she picked her way to where each mine was located. At each stop, she took a picture of the arming device, then inspected each mine on its own merit, being extra careful not to touch or move anything around the device.

After a tense thirty minutes, she gave the thumbs up sign to Mitch and Raine.

From there, Garret and Anniston disappeared toward the rear of the sub where the engine room was located and to start work on the jagged hole. Before long Garret's torch turned the sharp irregular pieces of damaged hull white hot, enlarging the hole so they could get to the torpedo room.

On the opposite end of the sub, Mitch and Raine slowly lowered the torch through the forward escape hatch to use to punch the hole through the bulkhead wall, big enough to insert a rope camera. Once they got the equipment in place, they'd get a good idea of what was inside the forward crew quarters and the forward torpedo room.

After getting the camera in place, they pulled the watertight plug and widened the hole to let the seawater seep into the room.

Mitch hit his com button. "At this rate it'll take several hours for the pressure to even out."

Raine tilted her head, pressed the com link. "Let the flooding go overnight then?"

He nodded. "In order to pop that door safely, it's the only way. What do you say we get out of here? Go take a look at the engine room hole, inspect Garret's work."

"You just want to bug your brother."

"There is that."

Later that day, everyone crowded into the galley to review the day's work.

Anniston laid out the photos she'd enlarged and printed that showed the arming devices up close. She pointed to what looked like a round knob on the first mine. "I did a little research on this type of torpedo mine after we got back. If I've ID'd them correctly, these are known as floating mines and they were not armed. If they had been, an additional mark would be located on the knob. I inspected them as best I could for any sign of weakness in the outer casing and for anything that looked like it was leaking. In my opinion they look sound enough for the amount of time they've been underwater. Just keep in mind when working around them they could still be very unstable. For now, I'd strongly suggest that no one touch them or try to move them. In other words, when you're near them, keep your hands off."

"I think I've got the hole in the engine room hull large enough to enter," Garret added. "But it'll be a tight fit."

Raine attached the projector to her laptop and opened the video file she'd taken earlier from the rope camera, showing the inside of the forward compartments.

Mitch stood by the wall to point things out as the video played. "Here you can see the boxes under the bunks on both sides. As we continued down the passageway, Raine and I counted close to fifty boxes. The boxes appear to be the watertight kind used for storing ammo, radio equipment, that sort of thing. They look to be in good shape. They should hold up once we start letting the water in to flood the compartments. Once the pressure is equalized, we should be able to open the hatch and enter the forward crew quarters and get the boxes out of there. We'll bring them up through the forward escape hatch located directly above to the surface. It should make transporting them a lot easier than dragging them to the conning tower."

He paused, looking around the room. What he had to say next might not go over too well. "According to Maritime Law we are what is known as a salvor, and the law of salvage says we're entitled to anywhere from ten to twenty-five percent of the value of the find. However, since we know this is looted property, legally, I'm not sure where we stand. That's the truth of it."

Again, he hesitated before going on. "I'm for doing this by the book. I told you that going in. If there's anything of value in those boxes, here's what I propose we do. We turn what we find over to the United States Marshal's office out of Miami, specifically to a man there I think Anniston knows well, and trusts."

Anniston picked it up from there. "My dad has a personal friend named Rick Johansen. He's a very 'by the book guy' and I have no problem involving him in this. He'll make sure everything's done legally and correctly.

Once we see what we've got, I'll make contact and begin the process of setting up a meeting. You're all welcome to show up."

Mitch nodded. "We'll need to retain the best Maritime lawyer in Florida. Then we file a lien for our finder's fee, making sure they know we haven't disturbed any human remains. Because U-492 is considered a wartime tomb. Of that I'm certain. From there, we let the courts decide. Are we in agreement then?"

Raine checked the faces around the table. "Speak now or forever hold your peace, guys, otherwise this marriage between the marshal's office and us moves forward." When there were no objections, she tossed Mitch a beaming smile. "You have your answer."

Chapter Thirty-One

That night, as they waited for the forward compartments to flood, they planned their next dive. It was all they could talk about. Anticipation ran hot about bringing up the first box. What would they find inside?

Over a supper of beef stew and biscuits, which Tessa made from scratch, the crew started a betting pool. The leading wager: gold bars, followed by diamonds and other precious gems. In third place, coins were popular, and bringing up the rear, great works of art.

No one voiced what they all feared. The boxes might hold nothing of value at all. They might be stuffed with boring files or ordinary supplies or even worse, moldy clothing.

As the night went on, the brothers argued about who would get the honor of bringing up the first box.

"It's my boat," Mitch pointed out.

"But I'm the oldest. And so far all I've done is sit behind a bank of computer screens and get us to this spot," Jackson stated. "I want to see the sub for myself."

"So who's stopping you? And you didn't exactly get us here. Klaus did. It should be me bringing that box up," Garret argued. "I'm the best diver here and I'm in better shape than you two guys."

"You really need to do something about that ego of yours," Mitch fired back.

Sebastian butted in with his two cents. "Why not let me go? I'm perfectly willing to trade guard duty to get a look inside that sub."

"Not me," Dominka tossed out. "You should stay put. It might explode with all those bombs on it."

"Your English has gotten a lot better," Sebastian noted proudly. "I've been working with her."

Raine rolled her eyes and cleared her throat. "As I remember back to your childhood, which coincided with mine, your mother used a tried and true method of handling disputes between the Indigo brood."

Mitch leaned back in his chair. "What method was that? Beat each other to a bloody stump out in the backyard?"

"Livvy hit harder than you did back then," Jackson prodded, hoping to get a rise out of him. "She gave me a bloody lip every time I turned around, more often than you did."

"That's because you were always picking on her," Mitch explained.

Raine refused to give up. "Guys, could we focus for a minute? I'm not suggesting anyone gets a bloody nose. Lenore's method back then always seemed to work. If I'm not mistaken she always dragged out Monopoly, had you guys play a game. Winner got the award—whatever it happened to be that you were all fighting about."

Jackson twisted up his mouth. "Ah, I seem to recall that." He cocked a brow toward Mitch. "Got Monopoly?"

"You know I do. I'm the reigning champ."

As Mitch stood up to take down the game from the overhead, Jackson rubbed his hands together. "Okay, so we break this down into diving teams. I'm Team Jackson paired with Tessa. If I win, *we* dive tomorrow at first light and bring up the box. Once we get it to the surface, *we* get to pop it open and see what's inside. If Garret wins, it'll be him and Anniston. And if Mitch wins, he dives with Raine."

But before they could roll the first pair of dice, they had to argue over who got to be the race car.

"This part I remember," Garret declared. "Rock-paper-scissors."

Team Jackson won the car, but was the first to go bust, followed by Team Garret, who landed on Boardwalk, owned by a prosperous Mitch, sitting pretty with three hotels.

Team Mitch did the in-your-face victory dance around the galley to hoots, hollers, and laughter, along with a couple of embarrassing snapshots taken explicitly for posting on social media after all this had come to an end.

Later in their stateroom, Mitch and Raine were tucked into bed, trying to settle in for the night. But both were too electrified with excitement to do anything but think about tomorrow's upcoming dive.

"What'd you bet on?" Mitch asked.

"Well, even though Klaus gave us every indication his sub carried substantial amounts of gold, it's difficult for me to visualize that. Plus, let's face it, I'm not that lucky. So I went with artwork. How about you?"

"Precious gems. Mainly because I have a hard time believing some of the things in that diary."

"But he was right about the location."

"Every boat captain I know would never lie about his location. He'd know where he was at all times and note it down in the logbook, using nautical coordinates or at least describing landmarks along the way. He did both of those things, which helped us get here."

"Let's not forget Professor Bishop's contribution."

"No question we never could've gotten this far without his translation." Mitch wrapped her up in his arms, brushed his lips to her forehead. "We need to get some sleep."

"I'm too churned up."

"There's only one cure for churned up," Mitch said, reaching under the covers. "I'll just have to settle you down the old-fashioned way."

The next morning when they dropped into the water off the dive platform, they had to force themselves to descend at a slow rate even though their adrenaline was jacked up. They stuck to the timetable on their dive watches and made sure to stop at the designated spots along the way, waiting the correct amount of time at each depth.

They'd brought a tool bag this trip and hoped they could finally get into the sealed compartments.

It took patience before they reached the sub. They started in the aft section. After careful inspection, Mitch decided to try to squeeze through the hole Garret had provided and make his way to the engine room where decades ago the bomb had done the most damage.

At six-two it was a tight fit, but he managed to wriggle his way through without ripping his wetsuit or damaging his tank.

Raine followed him in, carefully, but her slim body had no problem swimming through the opening.

Once inside the engine room, she wondered how the crew was ever able to move around to get much done. Everywhere she looked there were wheels, gauges, valves, and the two large diesel engines taking up most of the space.

The flow of the water had deposited sand, and lots of it. Small marine life—starfish, urchins, and crabs—had set up housekeeping here. She spotted several crabs scurrying off when she darted over in their direction.

Mitch pointed to an oversized Atlantic lobster, old and hiding under one of the valves.

Raine returned the favor when sudden movement revealed a yellowish oyster toadfish nestled in the sand next to one of the diesel engines. It moved quickly to devour a small blue fish before disappearing into the cavernous darkness.

Mitch grabbed her arm, aiming a finger toward an eel that looked like a gray piece of ribbon blowing in the wind.

For all the playful activity around them, one thing was still for certain—the watertight hatch to the aft crew quarters and the torpedo room remained tightly sealed.

Mitch motioned to head the other way to the forward compartments. Raine trailed behind him as they made their way through the sub to the other end until they were in front of the bulkhead hatch that led into the forward crew quarters and torpedo compartment.

He studied the crank used to unlock the hatch. Trying to turn the rusted metal got him nowhere. The locking ring wouldn't budge.

Digging in the tool bag, he brought out a long pipe wrench and used it as a lever. Using every ounce of his weight, he pushed down on the pipe until the crank rotated slightly.

Raine added her weight to the wheel crank. With a loud grunt and groan, they noticed tiny bubbles of air escaping as the wheel continued to give. They reset their pipe wrench and pushed down again. They had to repeat the process several more times until the hatch door gave and swung open.

A huge gas bubble spewed its way out into the room as more seawater rushed in to replace it. The force of the seawater was so fierce they had to grab hold of the nearest metal to keep from getting sucked into the compartment.

Back on *The Black Rum*, the crew watched from the railing as a large pool of gas bubbles broke through the surface of the water. The smell was like someone had opened a hundred bottles of bleach at the same time.

Garret waved everyone back from the railing. "Chlorine gas from the U-boat batteries. The odor will dissipate in a few minutes."

In the command center, Jackson picked up the com link. "Are you guys okay?"

On the sub, Mitch looked at Raine before answering. "Thanks for worrying, big brother, but we're fine. About to enter the crew's quarters." He adjusted the camera attached to his headgear. "Are you getting our feed? Is it coming through clear enough?"

"You're looking good from up here. Just be careful."

Mitch stepped inside the compartment and panned his camera around the room.

Raine shadowed Mitch toward the row of boxes.

"Take your pick," Mitch offered with a wink. "Which one's the lucky case?"

She scanned the line of metal chests. "Why me? Pressure's on. Tough decision."

"You pick the lucky box and I'll go see if I can get the escape hatch open directly over our heads."

Mitch retrieved his pipe wrench and went to work on the trapdoor.

Raine slowly moved down the hallway studying each box; they all looked exactly alike to her. Nothing made any box stand out from the others. She tried to move one of the boxes, thinking that if it outweighed another, she'd use that as her selection process, thinking more would be in there. Maybe they could stack several together, like a shopping cart, and she wouldn't be limited to picking just one.

While she grappled with her decision, Mitch struggled to get the hatch door open. He picked up the cutting torch and went to work on the hinges.

Topside, the crew's attention was riveted on what was happening with the divers below. They were so focused on the monitors, no one picked up the military-style inflatable launch, carrying several armed men, as it came up on the port side of the boat.

One by one, the men climbed aboard and headed for the bridge where a lone crewman stood guard.

Prentiss was supposed to keep watch for any ships or planes that got too close and let Garret or Jackson know. But he'd gotten so engrossed on watching the feed and what was happening below the surface he never saw the boat. He certainly didn't expect the blow to the head that knocked him out.

Having taken care of Prentiss, Baskin and Dandridge appeared in the doorway of the command center.

"Well, well, well," Baskin began. "Everyone just step back away from the computers and relax. We're here to take whatever it is you assholes found on that sub off your hands."

Jackson and Garret exchanged looks, noting the AK-47 rifles each man held in his hand. "What took you so long to get here?" Jackson goaded, coolly leaning back in his chair.

Dandridge wasn't buying the unruffled demeanor. "Come on, you didn't know about us. We've been following you at a distance since you hit the Atlantic."

"No kidding," Garret snarled. "Who would've thought murderers and thieves such as yourselves would think to steal from someone else? Certainly not us."

"Just shut up," Baskin ordered. He pointed to one of his men. "Start tying these bastards up and stuff a rag in their mouths, so I don't have to listen to them talk."

Not happy at the prospect of having his hands tied, Garret slipped his toolkit out of his pocket and into the back pocket of his jeans. He leaned over to Anniston, murmured in her ear, "Don't count out Mitch and Raine. Not yet. They'll do whatever they have to do to get us out of this situation."

"It'll take a miracle," she whispered back. "What I want to know is how they got the drop on Sebastian and Walsh. I didn't hear any gunfire."

As the crewman tried to tie up Tessa, Tessa kicked him in the leg. "Don't touch me! Which one of you assholes killed my brother?"

"Sit down and shut up," the man uttered before slapping her in the face.

Jackson got to his feet. "You want to hit someone, try me. Or do you just like slapping women around? Leave her the hell alone."

But Tessa wouldn't be silenced. "Are you too chicken to tell me?" she hollered across the room toward Baskin. "Why can't you admit to killing a defenseless man who had epilepsy and wouldn't have hurt a fly? Which one of you killed my brother in cold blood? I deserve to know the truth."

Baskin strolled over to where Tessa sat in one of the command chairs, got in her face. "You want to know who put the bullet in his head? I did. But you should blame Walker. Your brother's blood is on his hands. Walker just couldn't keep his mouth shut and had to keep blathering on about the gold to any idiot who happened by. Walker thought he could bring Connelly in on the deal and we'd hand over a share to a perfect stranger. Your brother had to be eliminated once he learned about the gold. We couldn't let him go back to bumfuck Carolina and spread rumors about it all over the Internet."

Suddenly Baskin pointed his weapon at Jackson's head. "Any more questions, Miss Connelly?"

Tessa shook her head and grabbed hold of Jackson's hand. "Sit down now. I won't say another word, I promise. Just leave Jackson alone."

"That's right. You won't say another word because I want all of you to shut the fuck up," Baskin barked. "I hate to be the one to break it to you, but your two divers are about to suffer a very nasty accident below the surface. As soon as we make sure the sub is secure, we'll make every one of you disappear and scuttle this piece of shit." He turned to Dandridge. "Get that knucklehead Gaspar over the side and have him take Braxton with him. You go, too."

"Me?" Dandridge questioned. "Why me? Braxton and Gaspar are fully capable of taking care of everything below."

"That's right. They are. And you're going to make sure they do it. Duarte won't be here for another hour and a half. That leaves me here and two other crewmen to hold guns at the heads of everyone on *The Rum* and make sure they don't cause any problems. Now go on, go with Gaspar and Braxton. Make yourself useful."

Before relinquishing command, Jackson had left the com link open so that Mitch and Raine could hear the entire conversation below the surface.

Underneath the water, Raine tried not to panic. She looked over at Mitch and put a finger to her lips.

He nodded in agreement, knowing they needed to shut off their communication device and use hand signals or their divers' boards from here on out.

Mitch snatched up his slate, scrawled the number three, showed it to Raine.

She moved her head up and down in understanding. Three guys were on their way down to kill them. Check.

They quickly took stock of what they could use for weapons. They had the cutting torch and the two heavy pipe wrenches. They'd brought along four shark sticks, also known as bangsticks. Divers used them to defend themselves against large predators. The sticks were mounted to twenty-six-inch poles and loaded with a single .44 magnum shell. All these things were close range weapons that could be used to their advantage in a surprise attack.

While Mitch and Raine waited for the divers who would come for them, they planned their ambush.

Since the hole was only wide enough for one man to enter at a time, they decided on divide and conquer as their strategy.

They would set out one of the reserve air tanks in the engine room with the valve open to create air bubbles and give the intruders the impression they were inside hard at work.

The plan was to lure the first diver into the engine room, wait for the second diver to start in, and then they would emerge from the other side of the sub and take out the lone remaining diver. From there, they'd attack the second diver. After getting rid of him, the odds would be in their favor. They'd go after the diver in the engine room, teaming up against him.

Edgy, Mitch and Raine waited for the three men to come into view. It wasn't long before Mitch spotted three figures swimming toward the sub.

The divers pulled up a short distance from the U-boat, and pointed to the trail of air bubbles escaping from the area. A heated discussion ensued, as if the men couldn't quite make up their minds on how to proceed.

Gaspar wanted to wait and take Mitch and Raine as they eventually emerged from the sub.

But the argument was settled when they heard Baskin over the com link order his men to throw caution to the wind and charge in, making sure they finished the job quickly. Baskin's rash nature and blood lust took over. "Take them out. Now!"

Mitch went into action, arming the four bangsticks and handing one off to Raine, taking the time to press his dive mask against hers, and mouthing the words, "I love you."

She mouthed the words back to him. "I love you, too."

They waited, nervous and anxious.

Gaspar and Braxton reluctantly watched as Dandridge took the lead and went through the door first. Gaspar counted off a few seconds before he too, entered. That left Braxton standing alone.

With his bangstick, Mitch jabbed the end as hard as he could into the man's side.

Raine watched a large bubble of air form around the spot of contact, followed by blood trailing out of the diver's body. The man jerked several times before going limp.

Mitch shoved the body out of his way so he could get to the next diver. Gaspar turned to face Mitch and raised his spear gun to fire. Before Gaspar could pull the trigger, Raine rammed the bangstick into his chest. Another air bubble enveloped his torso, followed by a cloud of red water. He let go of the spear gun as he clutched his chest. His eyes went dead and then he stopped moving.

Raine pushed the body away from Mitch. But before they could head through the hole to go after the third diver, a spear clanked off Mitch's air tank. Dandridge appeared in the opening. He fired off another round, missing Mitch by inches. Dandridge rushed past them on his way out of the sub and headed back the way he'd come in.

Raine spotted the first diver's spear gun lying on the sea bed. She snatched it up and fired. The spear shot forward ripping through the preacher's dive suit, splitting flesh and opening a gash along his thigh.

Dandridge writhed in pain, but kept moving through the water.

Without hesitating, Mitch grabbed up another bangstick and went after him.

Raine located the second diver's spear gun and followed.

Try as they might, Mitch and Raine didn't seem to be gaining any ground on Dandridge. But with his leg bleeding badly, coupled with the blood from the other two divers, it wasn't difficult to follow his blood trail.

But they weren't the only ones interested in the injured man. Raine tugged on Mitch's leg, impeding his progress. She motioned to the left and pointed at the large, dark shadow overtaking them. They stopped swimming and hung back, watching as the hungry great white opened its mouth for the attack. With lightning speed, the shark tore Dandridge in half as it chomped down on its prey.

Mitch grabbed Raine and held her close, trying not to make any sudden moves as the predator circled within feet of them, an arm still dangling from its jaws.

Rattled, Mitch and Raine waited to make sure the shark had moved off before heading back to the dive spot.

Once they arrived back inside the sub, they noticed the strong current had already carried the divers' bodies several yards away from the wreck. But with sharks in the area, there were no guarantees the great white wouldn't be back looking for another meal. Whatever plan they came up with, it needed to be quick.

Mitch used his dive board and grease pen to write the words, "I love you. Are you okay?"

For an answer, Raine nodded and wrapped her arms around his waist.

Next, Mitch wrote the words "Patagonia Pike" followed by a question mark.

Raine took the board from him, writing only one word. "Mines."

Mitch bobbed his head in agreement.

Back on board the *The Black Rum* Baskin and Sandoval were getting a little nervous.

Sandoval paced the length of the command center, unable to stay still. Waving his automatic weapon around at the hostages, ranting to himself in Spanish, he finally blurted out, "Why don't we just go ahead and kill them all now?"

Baskin gave him a hard look. "Sinclair wants them alive for now."

Sandoval sneered back, "But I follow Duarte's orders, not your man Sinclair."

Baskin got to his feet. "You'll follow who I tell you to follow. I'm in charge here. Got that?"

Sandoval narrowed his eyes. "In case it's slipped your mind, the *Patagonia Pike* belongs to Duarte. *He's* the man in charge. He's also my captain, not you." He checked the time on his watch. "And he should be rolling in at any moment now. Perhaps you'd like to tell him to his face how you won't take orders from him." With that statement, Sandoval sent Baskin a disgusted look and strode to the opposite side of the room. But all the while his finger remained on the trigger of his rifle.

Walsh had gone below deck to the engine room to check on a generator that had been acting up. Since dropping anchor, it was the perfect time to fix what ailed it. He'd been tinkering with one of the circuit boards when he'd heard voices coming from the command center, voices he didn't recognize.

He'd come up on deck in time to catch the boarding party taking over the ship. With recon in mind and carrying his sidearm, a silver-polished Beretta, he'd snuck around to the aft position and bumped headlong into Sebastian, who was doing the same.

"What the hell's going on?" Sebastian asked. "I go to the head and all hell breaks loose."

"Yeah, well, I was in the engine room bent over a faulty motherboard. Where's Prentiss? He was supposed to be standing guard."

"They knocked him out, tied him up."

"Damn it. I don't like getting caught with my pants down."

"That would be me," Sebastian corrected. "I'm pissed off about it, too."

"Serves me right for not putting more men on watch."

"We were running on a high. Besides, what's done is done. So far I've counted six. Baskin's in charge. He's taken over the control room. And he just sent Dandridge and two other men I didn't recognize down to the dive site."

"So Mitch and Raine are in trouble, too? Do you have your sidearm with you?"

"Yeah. With three gone, we should be able to overpower the other three. But what do we do about Mitch and Raine?"

"I have faith in Mitch. I've seen him get out of tighter spots than this. Right now the priority is freeing up the ones trapped in the command center with that psychopath. That means we need to get our hands on the rocket launcher before they do."

"There's a rocket launcher?"

Walsh winked. "You should know by now, Mitch plays to win."

Chapter Thirty-Two

Over the dive com Mitch and Raine heard Sandoval announce the *Patagonia Pike* was approaching from the south on the starboard side of *The Rum*. ETA thirty minutes.

Mitch swam over to the bow where the torpedo mines were entangled to get a better look. He needed to determine how best to utilize the devices to their advantage. He'd have to figure out a way to cut at least one loose from the anchor chains.

He headed back to where Raine waited, pointed to his dive watch and then to his air tank, indicating it was time to switch out to a reserve.

After getting that done, they began to unload the sled, stacking the extra air tanks they'd brought and all the supplies next to the conning tower.

Grabbing the cutting torch and tool bag, Mitch dumped both onto the sled before moving it along in a straight shot forward along with the scooters. The idea was to use the torch to cut through the anchor chains and then slide the mine onto the sled for mobility.

The torch made fast work of the corroded metal. Raine tried to keep the torpedo mine steady as Mitch worked to get it free. Once he'd cut through the last link of the chain, he and Raine held their breath hoping the damn thing wouldn't explode. They were stunned to see the mine start to float upward, surprised it still had that kind of buoyancy left in it after all these years.

When it didn't sink like a rock and it didn't blow them out of the water, they bumped happy fists together like they'd just won the lottery.

Gingerly they wrapped nylon rope around the torpedo-shaped mine to secure it to the sled. Mitch hoped the scooters could handle the weight. He slowly worked the throttle to determine the slowest speed, because moving too fast might create a strong vibration that could set the mine off without warning.

Thanks to Sandoval they kept getting updates through the dive com and soon learned the approximate position of the *Pike*.

Raine pointed the scooters on the straightest course she could toward Duarte's ship while Mitch kept a watchful eye on the sled. Foot by slow foot they eventually maneuvered the mine in position as close as they could get under the ship.

Mitch picked up his board, wrote the words, "Swim toward *The Black Rum* as fast as you can. I'll stay put and arm the mine."

Raine ripped the board out of his hand, taking the pen and scrawling her own message. "I'm not going anywhere without you!!! Period!!!"

He shook his head and motioned for her to get moving.

"No time to argue," she wrote, shaking her head. To prove her point, she started untying the rope herself from around the mine.

Mitch finally gave in, and turned his attention back to arming the device.

Raine took hold of his hand. Together they watched the mine start to float toward the surface and the hull of the *Patagonia Pike*.

At that moment, they were prepared to die together. But instead of exploding when it made contact, the mine simply bounced off the hull of the ship like an inflatable toy, continuing to drift along the side and occasionally bump up against the target.

Mitch and Raine traded disbelieving looks. Without another word they grabbed up the spear guns and took off for *The Black Rum*.

On board, Walsh and Sebastian had worked their way to where the AT4 launcher had been stored in a locker in the supply room.

Walsh pulled out the key from his pocket as Sebastian kept watch in the hallway. He reached in, grabbed the weapon, making sure it had a live anti-armor round in it. Handing it off to Sebastian, he picked up the Thumper grenade launcher and an ammo pouch and slung both over his shoulder. On instinct, he snatched up his baby, an MK 12 SPR rifle and an extra twenty rounds.

Sebastian took one look at Walsh's personal arsenal and uttered, "Seals or Rangers?"

"Seals." Walsh led the way down the hall and then up toward the bridge, hoping to surprise whoever was there, dispose of them, and gain the high ground. As soon as they reached their objective, he pivoted toward Sebastian. "Have you ever fired an AT4?"

Sebastian shook his head.

"Rest it on your right shoulder, aim it at the middle of that ship and pull the trigger." But as Walsh pointed to where he wanted Sebastian to place the rocket, he noticed a black object floating next to the *Patagonia Pike*. He spotted two heads pop up out of the water for a few seconds before disappearing under the waves. He pointed to the trail of air bubbles. "I knew Mitch and Raine could take care of themselves."

Walsh used the scope of his rifle to zero in on the black object floating next to the hull. "Mine. We have to wait until Mitch and Raine are out of the water because the underwater shockwave from the mine explosion could kill them."

Both men retraced their steps, trying to come out where they thought Mitch and Raine might try to board the boat.

Sebastian scanned the water, looking for air bubbles while Walsh took off to do a second recon to see where Baskin was holding the others. They also needed to locate Sandoval and the other guard.

Just below *The Black Rum* Mitch and Raine treaded water near the surface, hoping no one had spotted them yet.

Mitch knew they'd been under water too long and that if they made it out alive both of them would have to spend a considerable amount of time in the decompression chamber. But he'd would worry about that later. For now, they first had to take back his ship—with two spear guns and a knife.

He took a deep breath before dropping his air tank and surfaced next to the boarding ladder. Raine followed his lead and did the same.

Mitch latched on to the first rung of the ladder, pulled himself out of the water, trying not to make too much noise. Gripping the ladder, he reached back for Raine's hand to help her up.

When he looked up again, he almost slipped and fell. He spotted someone looking down at them. Recognizing Sebastian's face, Mitch croaked out in a whisper, "You scared the crap out of me."

Sebastian flashed a grin and reached a hand out to pull him up and over the railing. He did the same with Raine. "Walsh is doing a little recon. He should be back soon."

Mitch's face was full of questions. "I thought you guys were taken hostage."

"Not yet. I was in the can and Walsh was in the engine room when they boarded us. We were about to blow the *Patagonia Pike* out of the water when Walsh spotted you guys and the little gift you left for Duarte."

Mitch jumped when Walsh appeared out of nowhere and laid a hand on his shoulder. Walsh gave him a once-over like a mother hen. "You look a little ragged, but the question is, are you ready to kick some ass?"

For the first time in hours, Mitch felt like the odds were shifting in their favor. "What's the plan?"

"In exactly ten minutes Sebastian is gonna fire that AT4 directly at that mine you left and blow Duarte and his ship out of the water."

"Major distraction," Mitch muttered. "Good call."

"When that happens, you and Raine take out the guard who's stationed near the command center. Get everyone free and then arm them with these." Walsh dropped a duffle bag full of guns at Mitch's feet. "I'll take out Sandoval on the starboard side."

"What about Baskin?" Raine asked. "He's in the command center."

Walsh shook his head. "Negative on that. Been all over this boat twice and couldn't find that piece of shit anywhere. He's not with Sandoval or the hostages, so keep your guard up. Who knows where he'll pop up once the *Patagonia Pike* goes up like a rocket on the Fourth of July."

The four moved into position.

Crouched behind a row of supply barrels, Mitch and Raine were counting down the minutes. They heard the swoosh of the rocket race toward its target. But it hadn't been ten minutes yet. Something had gone wrong.

Mitch stood up, still a little woozy from being in the water so long, and came almost face to face with the guard. Without thinking, he used the spear gun to launch the arrow straight into the man's heart before the guard had time to call out in warning.

The man's gun hit the deck with a thud followed by his body. The swoosh had barely faded from the air when Mitch and Raine were knocked off their feet by the jolt from the explosion. The first detonation was followed by several smaller ones that finished ripping the *Patagonia Pike* in half.

Mitch's ears were still ringing as he slowly got to his feet. He bent down to help Raine up just before he was bowled over by Baskin. The force sent him into Raine. They skidded across the deck.

Mitch tried to clear his vision. He saw Baskin standing over him, wearing a smug grin on his face. From there, things seemed to play out in slow motion as Baskin raised his rifle to fire.

But Mitch felt something tug at his leg where he kept his knife. Out of the corner of his eye, he caught sight of Raine's arm going back and then moving forward as she released the dive knife toward Baskin's chest. It sailed through the air, end over end, until it found flesh.

Baskin staggered backward, the bullets from his automatic weapon racing toward the sky.

Despite the knife protruding from his chest, Baskin was still on his feet, trying desperately to reach it and pull it out.

With all the force he could muster, Mitch launched himself at Baskin, knocking him to the deck. He drove the knife deeper into the wound until he could feel the man go limp. Only then did he let go and try to stand up.

Raine bowled him over with a hard embrace. "Are you okay? Are you hurt?"

Mitch shook his head as his arms went around Raine. He looked over to see Walsh opening the door to the command center and everyone in there rushing out on deck.

Walsh sidled up to Raine and put a hand on her shoulder. "You got some great knife skills there, Blondie." He turned to Mitch. "Your little lady here just saved your ass. Big time."

Mitch glanced down at Raine and then back at Walsh. "That's because she's some woman. Where'd you learn to do that?"

"You don't want to know."

"I really do."

Blushing a little, Raine hesitated. "Well, I'm a little embarrassed. But if you really want to know, I practiced a lot in the kitchen at The Blue Taco."

She framed his face in her hands before going on, "After you left I put your picture up on the wall like a dart board. Whenever business was slow, I'd throw sharp knives at your face. I got so good at it, the skill came in handy when I entered dart tournaments at the local bars. Several even barred me from entering because I'd win all the time. But hey, before I got banned, you won me a lot of free drinks, if that makes you feel any better."

Walsh hooted with laughter and slapped Mitch on the back. "This one's a keeper, a woman after my own heart. You better treat her right."

Mitch gave her a kiss on the forehead. "Hopefully you used the picture of me after my face cleared up."

She patted his chest. "Trust me, with all the holes in it, you couldn't really tell."

By this time Garret and Jackson were surveying the debris field from the *Patagonia Pike*. Out of the cloud of smoke, Jackson spotted a large rubber raft headed their way. He estimated the boat carried maybe eight to ten armed men. Sinclair sat up front, firing an M16 at them.

"We have trouble heading our way," Jackson shouted.

Walsh calmly walked to the railing. He slung his Thumper around to firing position, cracked it open like a shotgun, and reached into his ammo pouch. He loaded the shell and put the weapon up to his shoulder, pulled the trigger.

Swoosh! The shell left the Thumper arching toward its target. A few seconds later they heard an explosion. Water shot up like a volcanic eruption, knocking Sinclair off his feet.

Unfazed, Walsh reached for another shell, just like he might reach for another beer at the end of a long day. "You know this was my dad's gun in Viet Nam. He liked it so much he smuggled it home when he mustered out." As if having a conversation with his buddies in a bar, he chatted in a casual tone that left the others staring in awe.

He fired another shot, that veered to the left as the boat made a turn at the last minute. "My dad tried hunting ducks with it, but all he ever killed was a lot of frogs and fish."

Jackson walked over to where Walsh was reloading again. "Mind if I take a turn? The Indigos have a score to settle with Sinclair."

Walsh handed him the Thumper. "In case you haven't noticed, the sights are a little off."

Jackson locked the Thumper into his shoulder, sighted it in, and pulled the trigger. The recoil caused him to take a small step back. The projectile whistled toward its target.

Jackson watched as his shot landed squarely in the middle of the boat, dead center. The impact lifted Sinclair and his men upward, throwing them outward, hitting the water.

Everyone stood at the railing scanning for any signs of movement from the bodies in the waves. For several long minutes, Walsh scoped each body but saw nothing move.

Finally, Walsh slapped Jackson on the back. "Nice shot, but it was pure luck."

Garret turned to Walsh. "What about Sandoval? Where is he?"

Walsh made a motion across his own throat.

It was Garret's turn to high five the crew chief. He stared over at Mitch and Raine. "Time to get you guys into the decompression chamber before you get the bends."

"At least let us change out of these wetsuits," Raine said. "How long will we be in there?"

"Eighteen should do it," Mitch noted.

Raine headed for the stateroom. "Eighteen minutes, is that all? Piece of cake."

Mitch laughed. "More like hours and a chemical toilet."

"Ewww."

Later, Garret marched them both into the boxy chamber and slammed the door shut. He programmed the software for decompression for an eighteen-hour stint. "That ought to give them plenty of time to talk things out."

On deck, they had a mess to clean up on *The Black Rum*. They began the distasteful task of disposing of the bodies, three in total—Baskin, Sandoval, and the unidentified guard.

Anniston and Sebastian watched through binoculars as sharks and other marine life were already at work taking care of the debris field from the *Patagonia Pike*.

"Sinclair and Duarte are fish food," Garret noted. "We may never know what happened to Carson Frawley."

"I still say burial at sea is too good for Baskin," Jackson grumbled.

Tessa rubbed his back as they finished mopping up the last of the blood. "It's over now. Behind us."

Jackson put his arm around Tessa. "Now the fight begins as to who goes down first to retrieve those boxes."

"Anniston and I came in second in Monopoly," Garret pointed out. "As soon as the sharks move on, we're going down to haul up the first box."

"Fine," Jackson muttered. "But after that everyone takes a turn bringing up boxes. Everyone."

"That's fair," Anniston said. "There's more than enough to go around. But I'm not going anywhere in the water till those sharks clear out."

Inside the decompression chamber, Raine sat next to Mitch. "Talk about claustrophobic," she moaned. "This is small. What are we going to do in here for a whole day? I think Garret locked us up for longer than necessary."

The same thing had already occurred to Mitch. "Does pure oxygen always make you this chatty?"

She punched him in the arm. "I can't believe you expected me to just swim off to the boat and leave you behind to arm the mine. What kind of person do you think I am?"

"I was trying to keep you alive. I can't believe you opted to stay put. If that mine had exploded on impact the way it was supposed to, we wouldn't be sitting here now bitching about the fact we're contained in a space the size of an egg."

"A sobering thought. That kind of situation makes you stop and think about the important things in life."

"And?"

She clasped his hand. "You're the most important thing in my life."

"That's all I need to know. We'll make it work somehow. I promise."

"I don't like the idea that our relationship should take 'work.' Your parents don't seem to 'work' at their relationship. They get along without it seeming like a chore."

"Maybe 'work' is too strong a word. If you stay on the Key and I take off on a dive, what are the chances of making long distance work on both sides?"

"See, there's that word again. Could you at least agree to spend six months in town?"

"And you spend six months at sea with me? Fine."

"Hmm. If I spend six months away from the business, I might as well make it a year. Besides, I feel really good about the last week. I like diving with you, being on the water, being on the boat."

"It could get old and tedious. Sometimes it does. It's also dangerous."

She frowned. "I don't understand you. Are you trying to talk me out of the idea?"

He chuckled. "No. I'm trying to paint you a realistic picture that it isn't all roses, twenty-four-seven. Nothing is. Even if you and I stay on island, there will likely be times we disagree about a lot of things. Nothing's perfect, Raine. No situation is perfect."

As she saw it, they had sixteen more hours to figure it out.

When they did emerge from the hyperbaric chamber, they walked out holding hands. The first thing they saw on deck was Garret and Anniston pulling on wetsuits, getting ready to dive on the sub.

"I've had some time to think about this," Mitch told Garret. "I've figured out if you use the cargo net, it'll hold five boxes at a time. Less trips, less time spent in the water."

Prentiss stepped forward. Still sporting a bandage around his head with strands of hair poking out, he was in no shape to take a turn at diving. But he stood ready to do his part. "I'd like to be the one to man the winch. I'm sorry I wasn't paying attention on guard duty. I'm sorry I let those men board the ship. They could've killed us all."

Mitch threw an arm around the young man's shoulder. "Lesson learned then. Next time you'll be more aware of how dangerous men like that can be."

"So you aren't firing me?"

"Do you still want to go back to San Diego to be with your family?"

"Sure. On leave, maybe when vacation time comes around."

"There you go. I'd have to train someone else to take your place, waste of money, if you ask me. No sense in doing that."

Mitch saw the relief pour out of Prentiss. "Are you up to running that winch? It's up to you to let Garret know how much weight she can handle. You're in charge of that."

"I'm up to it."

After reaching the sub, it took Garret and Anniston an hour to load the first five boxes into the cargo net. The metal containers hit the surface around midday as everyone crowded around to see what was inside.

Walsh carefully handled the cutting torch to shear off the wing nuts used to lockdown each box.

"Be careful," Sebastian cautioned. "You don't want to damage what's inside."

"Not after all we've been through to get this far," Garret said, looking on.

As each wing nut hit the deck, the gold fever went up a notch. When the last wing nut dropped, Walsh stepped back. "Who gets the honor of opening it up?"

Garret looked at Mitch, who motioned to Jackson. "You do it, you're the oldest and the one who took out Sinclair."

Everyone jammed in closer to get a better look.

Jackson slapped on a pair of latex gloves before raising up the lid. He lifted out a roll of what looked like canvas material. Placing it on a nearby table, he began to carefully peel back the canvas, unrolling it to reveal a painting.

"This is a Gierymski," Garret announced. "See the signature in the corner. Aleksander Gierymski, a Polish painter." Delicately, he held the corners without picking it up. "This is one of his landscapes. I've only seen his work in a museum in Warsaw. This is big."

Behind the Gierymski they found three other paintings done in oil, created by various French, Italian, and Belgian artists.

All five boxes were opened and found to contain artwork, masterpieces gone missing or thought destroyed.

"Whoever had looted art in the pool won big," Anniston reminded them. "At ten bucks a pop, they won a grand total of hundred and twenty dollars."

"That's me," Prentiss shouted. "I had works of art."

Mitch cleared his throat to correct that, but Raine pulled him back. "Don't say anything. I don't care about the pool."

"Are you sure? He's bound to find out eventually that there were two winners, not one."

"Nah, it's okay. I think most people went for the gold," Raine whispered. "Except for us. Let's just leave it at that.

This is exciting enough, at least it is for me. I'm basking in the moment. Imagine, witnessing the recovery of work from the likes of Tiepolo and Caravaggio, paintings thought lost forever. Who knows? The next set of boxes could hold a Klimt or a Poussin."

"I'm pretty jazzed about it myself. Being a part of seeing these hanging in a museum somewhere is pretty significant."

"Yes, but you've been through this a couple of times before with a lot better loot. As much as I love art, I guess it's okay to admit now that I was secretly hoping we'd find a cargo full of gold."

Mitch laughed. "I think we all were. But hey, there are still forty-five more boxes to bring up. Maybe we'll get lucky."

That afternoon when it came Tessa's and Jackson's turn to don their diving suits, the two followed protocol and checked each other's gear. As they stood on the dive platform, Jackson turned to her and stared. "You look like the Greek goddess Aphrodite."

The declaration caught her off guard. "I do?"

"Yeah. I'm a lucky man."

Amused at his mood, she returned the favor. "And you look like a kid on Christmas morning about to take off running down the hallway to see what's under the tree."

"I kinda feel like that. Do you suppose this is the kind of adrenaline Garret feels every time he rides through a wave? Or what Mitch experiences whenever he dives on a sunken ship?"

"What are you thinking?"

"Maybe for the first time I understand why they do what they do for a living."

"It's your turn to explore," Tessa told him.

"Our turn," he corrected, before stepping off into the ocean's depths. She followed him down into the cold Atlantic.

Once the U-boat came into view, the sight blew him away. Here in front of him was a piece of history, a slice of another era, chock full of treasures. The treasures didn't have to be museum pieces or prized artifacts. That didn't matter. Everything the sub had to offer hadn't seen the light of day since Hitler had been alive.

Jackson persuaded Tessa to indulge him in a tour around and through the boat, poking into all those dark corners they'd only seen on video. Up close was much better than viewing it from in front of a laptop screen.

After forty-five minutes of exploring they started hefting and loading up another five boxes. But as they made their way to the top, Jackson made a decision about his future.

Livvy's death had changed them all in one way or another. Going after her killers had been surreal. But the dive itself had given him an entirely different perspective. He hoped his brothers would agree.

Above them, Prentiss noticed the winch straining more with this haul, more than it had before. "Pass the word that we have a much heavier load this time around than the last one."

That revved everyone's gold fever back up again.

Soon Jackson and Tessa surfaced and stood on the deck with everyone else gathered around, hoping for better treasure this time.

They had to wait for Walsh to burn off the wing nuts. It was Anniston who lifted out something wrapped in cloth. There were ten bundles. She unwrapped the first and uncovered a set of printing plates for twenty-dollar bills. In fact, everything in the box was either plates for United States currency or British pounds. The next boxes were just as disappointing, full of stacks of counterfeit hundred dollar bills.

But they didn't give up. When Jackson wanted to go down again, Tessa gave her spot to Walsh. Since this was Walsh's first look at the sub in person, he had to inspect the boat from stem to stern just as Jackson had done on his earlier trip. The two men journeyed through the wreck like kids exploring a cave. Time got away from them until the alert sounded on Jackson's wrist that they'd been down almost two hours. They quickly loaded up the cargo net with five boxes picked at random and headed topside.

Three of these crates held German firearms, mostly Luger pistols. The other two contained books, old ones.

Garret and Anniston took another turn before supper, but the results of their boxes were the same, a few sculptures that would no doubt be given back to France.

The letdown among the crew was evident as they gathered in the galley to eat a batch of Blaine's chili. That disappointment stayed with everyone until bedtime.

So far, they'd opened a total of twenty boxes. And all they had to show for their effort was priceless artwork that would end up returned to renowned museums or earmarked for displays on the walls of fancy galleries.

That was all fine and dandy, but gold would've been a whole lot better.

Dawn brought a new attitude. The crew bustled around like a swarm of bees attacking a budding honeysuckle vine. The prospect of more boxes renewed their spirits and made them ready to tackle the sub all day long if necessary.

Mitch posted the dive schedule in the galley. And at breakfast everyone found out they'd work in pairs for two hours and then switch out to another pair of divers. That way it would make everyone feel like they were part of the hunt and no one was overextended or pushed to the limit.

"I see you put yourself and Raine on the dive schedule," Garret noted. "I don't think you two are ready."

"Why's that?" Mitch asked.

"Because I saw you at the computer in the command center making out the roster and your hands were still shaking. And last night at supper, Raine dropped her spoon, twice."

Mitch blew out a breath, raked his fingers through his hair. "Okay, we might be pushing it a tad to go back down today, but this is an opportunity of a lifetime. Raine suggested last night we should at least be getting this down on video. We're making history here, even if the crew is somewhat frustrated."

"She has a point. And this is already historic no matter what we find. Everyone on this boat knows that. I listened to them over breakfast this morning and they're revved up. My take is they're having the time of their lives. Which makes my point. You're surrounded by an entire crew willing to do anything for you. Let them. I'm happy to film the dives. Or Jackson could do it. He'd stay down there for hours if you'd let him. I hate to mess up your dive schedule, but consider this. We could make it three divers, one with a camera."

Mitch smiled. "Go for it. Maybe Raine and I should stay on the sidelines at least another day. Fix the roster for me, will you?"

"Sure." Garret took the time to glance over at the stockpile of artwork and other items already tucked away in fresh watertight storage crates. "I know part of what's bothering you."

"I'm sure you do," Mitch said sadly.

"It's hard to come to terms with the fact that all this stuff is the reason Livvy, Ally, and Blake lost their lives."

"Between you and me, I'm fine with doing my part as a salvor, but that's as far as it goes. The truth is I'll be happy to unload what we've pulled up so far. Because the cost was just way too high."

After Garret reshuffled the schedule, Sebastian and Jenkins led off the day with Jackson doing the filming.

Dominka had opted out entirely, explaining that diving wasn't her thing.

This time, when they brought up their five boxes and cracked them open, inside was a cache of antiquities, gold and bronze statues, silver crosses, and one sculpture, wrapped in old German newsprint.

"Will we ever find anything that doesn't go to a museum?" Jenkins moaned. "I'm all for preserving art and all that, but I'd like to see a few gold coins taking up space in one of these crates."

Jenkins got his wish with the next batch of boxes. Prentiss felt well enough to dive and did so with his buddy, Blaine. They brought up gold and silver coins, stashed away in cloth sacks and bundled with rope. Sebastian captured it all on film.

"Now we're talking," Jenkins said.

They'd barely unloaded the chests when another three divers dropped into the water. This time Walsh was paired with Garret while Anniston did the camerawork.

The dives now were mostly routine. Other than spotting several small tiger sharks lurking around the bow, the only other sea life that came calling were squid or the occasional loggerhead or a school of clownfish that brightened up the shadowy sea.

Anniston had never experienced this kind of pure joy from the ocean. She'd been diving for years. But this, the adrenaline rush of holding a piece of history in your hands, was too powerful to pass up. Even if it all got shipped off to a warehouse wherever it had started out, it was a mighty strong pull.

When they reached the top and unsealed these newest boxes, Mitch found a row of tube-like containers. He dumped the first canister out and stared at fat diamonds, sparkling in the sun. There were other canisters filled with rubies and sapphires just as glitzy as the diamonds. Another canister held nothing but pearls.

The next chest was loaded with rows of gold bars stamped with the Nazi emblem. Applause broke out behind him.

But for Mitch the buzz sounded far away.

Standing there on the bridge, Mitch picked up a single bar, held it in his hand as the sunlight danced along the edges giving it almost a halo effect.

His fingers tightened around the bullion. Clutched in his hand, history came rushing back to him. How many people had died for this six-inch piece of precious metal? How had it been formed and from what? How many gold wedding bands and fillings had it taken to create this one piece? Hitler's regime had stolen from so many people, the Jews, stolen their lives, their culture, their possessions, taken anything of value. And for what?

Seventy years later, through a series of bizarre events, an evil greed had swept in and taken a part of his own family. And why? For the lust of this yellow metal.

Raine slipped her arm into his, laid her head on his shoulder. "I know what you're thinking. So much blood spilled to make that stupid little gold bar."

He turned to her. "Some women would beg me to see the light and keep this, all of it."

"I'm not one of them."

"I know. And that's why I fell in love with you so early in my life. Even then, I knew what was in your heart."

Chapter Thirty-Three

Before they could head home, before Mitch could leave the sub in its resting place, he needed more closure. He needed to do one more thing. He decided it was time to dive on the *Patagonia Pike*. Enough days had passed that he deemed the area safe. Fortunately for him, Garret and Jackson agreed.

Raine, however, did not.

"Why go poke around over there? It's over. The sub gave up a chest of gold. The crew's elated. We know for a fact Dandridge is dead. Same goes for Baskin and Sinclair. Duarte didn't survive the blast. Why isn't that enough for you?"

"Because it's not. I need to recon what's there. I won't feel right leaving the area until I do."

"Fine. But you'll have to go without me. I'm still a little drained from all the other stuff."

"Guilt? Over taking out Baskin?"

"Don't be ridiculous. He was about to shoot you. I'd do it again if the same situation presented itself."

"Good to know." His snatched her up, covered her mouth. "I'm grateful you saved my life."

"You told me that already when we were locked up in decompression. If I'd known you'd go diving on the *Pike*, I might not have been so quick to do it, though."

"Ouch. You're making this difficult."

"Me? No. I guess this will have to be one of those times we disagree. It can't be perfect. Isn't that what you said?"

"No couple agrees a hundred percent of the time, Raine."

He was getting his gear ready, which for some reason just infuriated her more. "Where'd you get that advice from anyway? Reading a page or two out of *Cosmo*? You never did say."

"My dad."

Crossing her arms over her chest, she stared him down. "Well, I'm not going. I think it's stupid to even mess with it. We should be on our way home by now."

"I'm sorry you feel that way," he said, picking up his bag. "So are we good?"

Since huffing and puffing got her nowhere, she muttered, "Fine. We're just peachy."

On deck, she still wasn't happy as she watched him pull on his wetsuit. But she stood at the railing as the trio of brothers slipped off the dive platform and into the water, heading for what was left of Duarte's ship.

They found the *Patagonia Pike* resting on the bottom of the seabed in two halves separated by twenty feet. The mine had blown the middle of the ship inward, collapsing it into several compartments.

The engine was blown almost through the far bulkhead. Cables dangled, pipes and equipment hung everywhere, stretched out between the two halves. Debris littered the sea floor as schools of fish swam into and out of the wrecked sections.

Garret had volunteered to act as cameraman, taking colored stills of the wreck from every angle.

Something drew Mitch's eye, something in an odd-shaped pile of sand. It reflected back each time Garret took a picture and the camera flashed.

Jackson saw it, too.

Mitch had seen this before. He moved toward the object, barely peeking out of the silt and sand. It looked as though it had been freshly uncovered by the force of the *Patagonia Pike* meeting the ocean floor.

Mitch swam over, and very carefully started brushing the sand away. He exposed a ball of encrusted metal.

"Cannonball maybe?" Jackson said over his dive com.

"I don't think so."

When his brother kept poking at the thing, Garret touched Mitch's arm. "It won't explode, will it? Because if there's a possibility, I think I'll go take pictures of that starfish over there."

Mitch grinned. "Some treasure hunter you turned out to be. Where's that Garret curiosity?"

"Trying to protect the family jewels at all cost. Someday I might want my own little surfer dudes or dudettes."

Mitch got back to work, doing his best to get the ball to move. "I'm not sure what it is, but I'm not leaving it."

It was covered in coral and barnacles, blackened and discolored with age. With Jackson's help, he began trying to break it free. He took out a rock hammer from his tool bag and chipped away at the crust while Jackson kept using leverage to pull it out from underneath its burial place.

"Whatever it is didn't come from Duarte's modern ship," Mitch declared.

This was old and weighed about twenty pounds. It had obviously been buried there for perhaps centuries. For now, he tucked it away in his mesh collection bag and put it to the side.

He started to move on, but something else caught his eye. Mitch aimed his dive light at the same area where the ball of metal had rested. This sliver of metal glistened in the dark. Mitch motioned for Jackson to take a look.

Painstakingly, they began to remove more sand from around the shiny object. As they uncovered more, it was long, maybe thirty-six to forty inches. From its shape and length, Mitch determined it had once been a sword.

He held it in his hands while Garret took several pictures. Jackson tapped his brother's arm and pointed at his watch, indicating it was time to surface.

"**E**xplain something to me," Raine said to Tessa and Anniston as the women sat in the command center in front of the bank of computers, checking emails.

"Sure, if I can."

"How come you aren't upset that Jackson took off for the *Pike*?" she asked Tessa before turning to Anniston. "Doesn't it bother you Garret went over there with Mitch?"

Anniston let out a half-laugh. "Raine, you're asking me about a guy who spends most of his time in the water with absolutely no fear of sharks or breaking his neck on a surfboard. This is the same guy who cracked into the town's local bank vault at three in the morning. He's scaled walls, stood on roofs like a mountain climber. He's the next best thing I know to a cat burglar. I love Garret's sense of adventure. I'm drawn to it. I don't want to change who he is. Have we butted heads over it? Oh yeah, more than a couple of times. And we'll continue to do so. But I know I have to let the guy be who he is in order for him to stay happy."

Raine crooked her neck toward Tessa. "And you?"

"In the two months I've known Jackson, I've never seen him this happy. I'm afraid he's already been bitten by the treasure hunting bug."

Anniston leaned over. "I'll tell you a huge secret. So have I. It never occurred to me I'd feel this way. But there's something about knowing we found what no one else could find that gives me such a rush. This entire trip has made me feel pride in a way I've never felt before, pride in myself. I'll never look at another case the way I do this one."

Tessa flexed her arm. "We took down what no one else was able to stop. There's power in that. Sinclair and Baskin, Dandridge and Oakerson had people cowering to them for years. We didn't cower. We didn't run. Whatever happens after this, I feel like I could tackle anything or anyone. No one's messing with what's mine ever again."

Raine sat back, letting the words sink in. She stared at Tessa. "Do you think you can pick up and go back to work at the taco shop?" She placed a hand on Tessa's. "The reason I ask is because I'm not sure I can."

Tessa's mouth dropped open to respond, but she didn't quite know what to say.

But the private investigator did. "Are you saying what I think you're saying?"

"I'm not happy running the restaurant. Yes, I know how to cook. I'm good at it. I function as well as anyone else does in a job they don't particularly like, but do it because they have to. Being out here on the water is…blissful. I haven't known this kind of joy in so long it seems foreign to me."

"If you don't go back to the shop, what will you do?" Tessa finally asked.

Raine dipped her head. "Do what other couples do. Work on a relationship. See how it goes."

When the satellite phone began ringing, Raine looked at her friends. "Should I go get Walsh?"

"Nah, just pick it up," Anniston said. "I think Walsh is still tinkering with that circuit board in the engine room."

Raine leaned over the other side of the counter, grabbed the receiver. "Hello?"

"Is that you, Raine?"

"Professor Bishop? What are you doing calling?"

"Hollings. Call me Hollings."

"Right. Sorry."

"I hope I'm not interrupting your treasure hunt. But I've come across some information I thought the Indigos might find valuable."

"Really? Okay. They've gone on a dive. Do you want me to have them call you back?"

"That's not necessary. You can pass the word along for me. I told them I might be able to trace the Nazi sympathizers based on the name Eisenbart."

Hearing that, Raine waved off the professor's call. They already knew about Eisenbart. But manners kept her from correcting Hollings on that score. "Right, the German sympathizer living in the area who was supposed to help the two men after they pulled off the assassination plot. I've always wondered if Eisenbart knew about the sub blowing up."

"You *were* paying attention."

She laughed. "It was an interesting subject and you were a good teacher."

"Thanks for that. I'm not sure we'll ever know how much Eisenbart knew ahead of time. But the thing is, the Eisenbart family—"

"Had a son named Jessup," she finished. "Yes, we know. Garret and Anniston discovered that when they took a trip out to Lost Gator Swamp."

"I'm aware of their excursion there. But I discovered something quite remarkable. Chester Eisenbart had four sons. I've heard you guys bandy the names back and forth a dozen times or more. I thought you'd all like to know."

Raine looked back at her friends. "Wait. You're saying Chester had four kids, not just one? What were their names? Do you know?"

"The oldest son was named Royce. Jessup was his second. Roger was the name of his third child, and Boone was the youngest. My research tells me the brothers had at least three different mothers over the years. For some reason, social services got involved with the family around 1951 and began making regular visits out to the land

Chester owned. That was after someone in town felt the Eisenbart boys were suffering from neglect and turned Chester in to the authorities. The children were eventually removed sometime around 1955 from the only home they'd ever known and farmed out to various families, whoever would take them. The boys were scattered to the four winds. The older ones, Royce and Jessup, were the only two who stayed in Florida, while Roger went to a family in New Orleans and Boone, who was just an infant at the time, ended up with a couple in Vancouver. They changed his name to Whitley by the way, and he became Whitley Shepherd."

"How did you find all this out?" Raine asked. "Aren't adoption records sealed?"

"That's just it. I never used the word adoption because none of the families who took them in ever made it permanent. As far as I can tell, Eisenbart was always sympathetic to his native Germany up until the time he died. He spent some time there during Hitler's reign but left for whatever reason and settled in the Keys. I also found records that showed he went back to Germany a time or two before December 1941, before the U.S. entered the war. But after that date, Chester remained stateside. By the end of the war, he already had a wife and son. That boy was Royce, who by this time was at least five or six years old. But I must add, that's as precise as I can be. I found no formal birth records for any of the boys. Living off the grid like Chester did had its drawbacks when it comes to documentation."

Raine let Mitch and the others get settled around the table in the galley for the noon meal before she dropped the bombshell. She detailed the professor's call, laying out his research, his investigative skills.

"Brothers?" Mitch said, his eyes showing his disbelief.

"Brothers who were basically fostered out to whomever or wherever social services could find anyone to take them," Raine added.

"So not even the wealthy Buchanan family made it legal?" Mitch asked.

Raine shook her head. "Apparently not. Hollings said he did his homework and I believe him. He learned that Jessup was eventually sent to a couple up in Baker County, Florida, who wanted a farmhand, not a son. Jessup didn't like it there and ran away at sixteen. I guess he never looked back."

Mitch went over the things in his head that he already knew. "And Roger ended up with a violent felon for a role model in Louisiana. As the baby, Whitley didn't seem to have any better luck than the others, getting shipped off to Canada. Royce seems to have been the winner in all this. Even then, his good fortune seemed to be better than all the rest. That explains a lot of resentment. There had to be quite a bit between the men."

Anniston had been chewing her lip on the other side of the table. "I'm beginning to question my talents as a detective. Guys, none of this turned up in the background checks I ran."

Garret lifted a shoulder. "Who knows what last names the kids were using at that point? Back then it wasn't like it is today. Back then you could pretty much take in a kid and give them a new name. Keep in mind where these boys came from. Their parents were very reclusive for a reason. They chose to live in the swamp for a reason." He shifted in his chair to look at Anniston. "Royce may have landed in a wealthy environment, had all the trappings money could buy. While he may have helped us out, in my opinion, he's as rotten as the rest of his brothers."

"Wonder who turned them in?" Jackson asked. When they all turned to stare, he went on, "Hollings said someone in town suspected the boys were being neglected. I wonder if the Eisenbart kids ever went out of their way to find out who that was."

"Interesting. And if they ever decided to retaliate in some way? Or, were the kids simply grateful to leave the swamp?" Mitch scratched his chin. "I doubt that last part. Kids wouldn't like leaving the only mother and father they'd ever known. They'd still resent being plucked out of their home."

"And put in an unfamiliar world and possibly a hostile atmosphere," Raine concluded.

"We aren't making excuses for these guys, are we?" Tessa said from the end of the table.

Mitch picked up his glass of tea. "Hell no. You had one guy who had everything and he still turned out like the others. And in the end, their predatory nature rose up, and they started eating their own."

"Not only that," Raine began. "But if Roger Baskin had an affair with Winnie, then Roger knew all along he was sleeping with his own niece on the sly, behind Royce's back."

"No wonder Royce looked devastated when we told him the news," Anniston provided. "He must've felt completely betrayed."

Garret looked at Anniston. "That goes a long way to explain why Royce cooperated with us."

"By that time, Royce wanted Roger dead," Mitch finished. "Can't say I blame him for that."

After lunch, Mitch gravitated to his workroom below deck for some alone time to think. He took out the two items he'd found underneath the *Pike* and stared at the pieces. The twenty-pound ball of metal would have to be soaked in fresh water and then scrubbed before he could even guess what it had been.

He set up a tank of fresh water and dropped the round crusty ball into it. After letting it soak for a couple of hours without too much success, he couldn't wait any longer. He decided he had to know what it was.

He donned goggles and went over the surface again. Spotting a crack in the top layer, he plied a wooden pick into the opening and turned to his trusty rock hammer. Gingerly he began to chip away at the outer crust. Piece by piece he was able to chisel off large chunks that had built up over the years. After an hour of tedious labor, the ball began to take on a different shape, a shape he recognized right away—a brass ship's bell about ten inches tall with an opening of ten inches wide at the bottom.

The clapper was long gone as was the hand-knotted clapper rope. But the bell was in better condition than he could have hoped for. He couldn't make out the inscription yet, but he would take care of that after running it through an electrolysis bath.

He donned his rubber apron, pulled on rubber gloves and adjusted his goggles. Picking up the bell, he placed it in a metal tub with water and dumped lye into the bath.

He cranked up the small generator to three amps and waited for the electric current and chemicals to do their work, separating the nonmetal from the metal, cleaning off centuries-old grime and grunge.

It took almost three hours to scrape off the first couple of layers. But when he lifted the bell out of the solution, he couldn't believe his eyes.

On deck, Mitch held the bell up for all to see. "It's from the *Red Rose*."

Raine had a puzzled look on her face. "So?"

"The *Red Rose*," Mitch repeated.

Jackson saw the confusion. "The family legend. Koda Indigo, the pirate captain, and his ship."

Raine's eyes widened. "Ah, but I thought he lost it in a munity over a countess."

"Exactly. That's probably why it was in that spot. The mutineers must've sailed north after stranding Koda and his woman on the Key."

Tessa sent Jackson an amused look. "You really didn't make up that story. This treasure thing goes a long way back."

"The inscription on the bell reads *Red Rose*, 1702. We have go back down, guys. We need to grid search every inch of that pile of sand. We need to find whatever's left of Koda's ship, and whatever it contains."

It dawned on Raine then. "And I didn't want you going over there at all. We argued about it. If you hadn't gone you never would've found this, your family's legacy. I'm so sorry."

"It's hard to explain. I had a gut instinct."

"Don't ever stop trusting your instincts." She'd take a lesson from that.

Raine learned this wasn't just a pirate ship, but a piece of Indigo history.

Over the next several days they removed the top layer of sand so they could get a clearer picture of where the *Red Rose* lay buried. All the wooden parts of the ship were long gone. What remained had been made of metal or stone.

They documented everything about the dive before they started removing anything from the wreck. They started by moving the ballast stones several yards out of the way.

Right away, Mitch noticed something odd about the wreck. There were no cannons.

After discussing it over dinner one night with Walsh, the two decided that the *Red Rose* had likely gone to her grave during a storm and the crew had jettisoned the cannons in hopes of keeping her afloat. Which meant that if the crew dumped them overboard during the storm, the cannons would be scattered over several miles from the actual resting place.

That night, they put their heads together and marked off a grid so that they could thoroughly excavate the wreck site. Once they laid the grid, next came the tedious task of mining every inch of it.

Mitch decided to start with the air lift excavation tool. It was like a vacuum cleaner, used to suck up the top layer of loose sand and grit to expose whatever was buried underneath. The divers were then assigned a grid square. They used fans that looked like ping pong paddles to further clear their grid section. Each diver carried a mesh bag that they loaded up with whatever they found in their square.

Two weeks later, after all the hard work, they took stock of what they'd brought up. The *Red Rose* had provided them with two hundred gold coins, thirty bars of gold, three hundred silver coins, twenty silver bars, ten gold necklaces, fifteen gold spoons, two gold and silver bowls, five unbroken rum bottles, three gold crosses with gems embedded in them, twelve rings, and one gold chamber pot filled with emeralds.

But the biggest find of all was that solid gold sword, which when cleaned up revealed a jewel-encrusted hilt, laden with emeralds and rubies. The fabled lost sword of Cortés, that according to family lore Captain Koda Indigo had looted from a Spanish galleon the same day he'd made off with the countess.

All in all, a tidy sum when it was sold and the proceeds divided equally among all the crew, everything except the Cortés sword, which would be kept in the Indigo family.

After all, it was their very own legend.

Chapter Thirty-Four

By the time they got back to the Key, Raine had decided she wanted to be a part of that family legend once and for all.

But that meant having a come-to-Jesus showdown with her mother.

If she didn't do it now, she knew she'd be tied to that taco stand until the day she keeled over, just like her grandfather had done. Mitch was right about that.

If running the restaurant wasn't what she wanted to do, she needed to make the change now while she was still young enough to start over.

That morning, Mitch had already begun making plans to head back down to Little Bahama Bank that very night. There was an urgency in her heart and mind because she wanted to be on that boat more than anything else.

Her first stop had to be The Blue Taco. She had to promote Charlotte to manager and give her the go-ahead to hire whoever she deemed fit. Maddie's daughter Gabby could join the staff if she wanted.

Heck, for all she cared, Charlotte could put Marachelle Fordham in charge of scrubbing down the toilets every night. See how the old bat liked being tied down to the taco shop, twenty-four hours a day, seven days a week.

Her second stop was at her mother's Cape Cod. Unlike before, Raine walked up to the door with a renewed confidence, determined that Marla Manning would never lay another guilt trip on her ever again.

When she got to the living room, she spotted the vodka bottle almost immediately. It was turned over at the edge of the couch, next to an empty glass.

Marla took one look at Raine and the verbal barbs poured out. "Where the hell have you been? You have some nerve leaving everyone in the lurch."

"Nice to see you, too. I'm just here to tell you that I'm leaving with Mitch."

"The hell you are."

"Look, Mom, I didn't come here to fight with you. I do love you, but I can't live my life stuck at the taco shop forever. I just can't. It isn't the life I want. I have to make changes, big ones."

"I knew this would happen. I knew Mitch would talk you into leaving me like this."

"That's just it, he didn't talk me into anything. I came to this decision all on my own. And I'm not leaving *you*, I've finally decided to start living my life, something I should've done a long time ago. And thank God I finally came to my senses. I feel like this huge weight has been lifted off my shoulders."

"Of course you do. You're acting irresponsibly just like you always do."

"I'm genuinely sorry you feel that way. But it's taken me four years to realize I'll never be able to replace Danny, not in your eyes, not ever, no matter how hard I try, no matter what I do, I'll never earn the same kind of love from you that you showed Danny. And I've made my peace with that. It was hard at first, but I'm okay now. Mitch loves me and I'm not letting that kind of thing go for any taco stand, certainly not for a mother who sees me as nothing more than a reliable employee. I can't change the fact that you're convinced you lost the wrong child. Having lost my own child, I'm sorry for that."

Mimi heard the argument and came into the room carrying a photo of Raine and Mitch, taken when they'd been teenagers. Mimi tossed it toward Marla. The Kodak moment landed on the couch. "If you weren't so blind drunk all the time, you'd be able to see that those two were deeply in love, have been for years. Anybody with a lick of sense can see that. Let her go, Marla. Raine deserves her chance at happiness. I had mine. You had yours. For God's sakes, let go of all that anger and let the girl live."

Marla tried to stand up, but staggered back on the sofa. She continued to wring her hands. "What about the taco stand? Do you want to go on food stamps? Who'll run that place?"

"We won't go on welfare. If you'd give up the booze, you could easily go back to managing the place. You have a capable staff, more than most. Maddie and Charlotte will see to it that the place goes on. Besides, it's a damn taco stand, Marla, not a shrine to Danny. You keep avoiding it like you think it's haunted with his ghost."

Mimi turned to Raine. "If you love him, like I think you do, don't let anything or anyone stand in your way. Don't let anyone stop you from latching on, grabbing hold of that happiness he offers and giving it everything you've got."

Raine went over to Mimi and put her in a bear hug and kissed her cheek. "Thank you. I knew you of all people would understand. I love you."

"I know you do. And I love you right back. Now get out of here and go find that boy before it's too late."

Raine took off down the dock to the slip where *The Black Rum* had been moored hours earlier. She stared at the slip, blinked and realized the boat was gone. In its place was a ritzy catamaran, probably owned by some wealthy putz from Key West.

Her shoulders slumped. Why was she so surprised he'd left her already without a backward glance? He'd done it to her again. She headed back home, head down, each step a chore.

But when she reached her houseboat, she glanced up and saw him standing on her deck, gear beside him.

"What are you doing here? I just checked the marina and *The Black Rum* is gone."

Mitch nodded. "Yep. She went ahead and took off tonight for Little Bahama Bank, going back to the dive spot there. It's probably overrun by other treasure hunters by now, but hey, the crew wanted to give it a shot."

"But that's your dive site!"

"It is. But Walsh can handle whatever comes up."

"Why aren't you with your crew?"

"Because my heart is here with you."

"Mitch, you can't—"

"Don't try to tell me what I can or can't do. My life is with you and that's all there is to it."

"But I was coming to tell you to wait for me, that I've decided to come with you. I just quit my family's business, no notice, no nothing. I could be your onboard full-time cook."

"You were coming to tell me that? Really? That's a hell of an offer. I really love your breakfast burritos."

"I'm all packed. I didn't want to lug my suitcase all the way down the dock. I thought you'd do that for me."

"Are you sure you want to leave here, that this is what you want? What does your mother say about your decision?"

"She was angry. Very. And gave me a hard time, but my grandmother pointed out a few things. Mimi was a lot more direct. Mimi said I should do what's right for me. If I wanted to go with you, I should go, if it's what I wanted, I shouldn't let anything stop me. You're what I want."

She tilted her head up to his. "So what do we do now? I'm ready to start full-time."

"That's good. Great, actually. We may have to get a bigger boat. Jackson and Garret have decided they want to join the business. But I had something else in mind for you and me. How do you feel about marrying me and taking a two-week-long honeymoon before you join a bunch of guys on a boat? You'd be my wife then and *part-time* cook. As you already know, the crew divvies up galley chores. But I make out the roster."

"You're talking about galley chores and rosters when you've just asked me to marry you? Where's that romantic guy I saw on the boat?"

He yanked her around the waist and off her feet. "I hear Life Stone Church is looking for a new preacher. Funny thing is, Walsh is an ordained minister. He can marry us."

"Walsh? An ordained minister? But he just took off for the Bahamas."

"Depending on your answer, he can always turn around and come back. So what's it gonna be?"

She ran her fingers through his hair. "Yes. If that's what it takes to settle you down, the answer's yes."

Dear Reader:

If you enjoyed *Indigo Justice,* please take the time to leave
a review.
A review shows others how you feel about my work.
By recommending it to your friends and family it helps
spread the word.

For a complete list of my other books visit my website.
www.vickiemckeehan.com

Want to connect with me to leave a comment?
Go to Facebook
www.facebook.com/VickieMcKeehan
I'd love to hear from you!

Go to the next page for a sneak preview
of the first book in the
Pelican Pointe Series

Promise Cove

Promise Cove

The combat post was rural, more like a farming community stuck out in the boonies. The roads were primarily unpaved, dusty twenty-four-seven, and at the moment littered with burned-out equipment. The convoy they were riding in was going a sluggish twenty-five miles an hour in hundred-twenty-degree heat. There was no AC, no hope of grabbing an artery-clogging, delicious-tasting, fast food burger with a pile of over-salty fries, or even indulging in an after-duty dip in a cool, sparkling blue swimming pool.

Because this particular stretch of road had seen its fair share of hostile action the past couple of days, the entire unit had to be extra vigilant.

As they made their way up a rise, a grove of palm trees came into view. The wind picked up causing the fronds of the trees to bend and sway. The hot, arid breeze kicked up the loose grit, causing the tiny grains of sand to become airborne and burrow in and under any exposed pore and crevice of skin it could find. A thick layer of sand stuck to their faces, to their uniforms, and to their weapons. Homemade masks made from scarves and bandanas hid their sweaty faces and did little to protect them from the elements.

Dressed in full combat gear, the stifling heat inside the Hummer caused perspiration to pool down their backs. The prospect of a hot shower, a mere dream in the back of everyone's mind, was as far off at the moment as the idea of ever getting to go home.

But even in a war zone, confined in the cramped space of the Humvee, the soldiers did their best to make light of their predicament by laughing and cracking jokes. Sitting in the back seat, two officers kept up a steady stream of chatter. At least one did. Glancing up briefly when another new barrage of sand hit the windshield, Captain Scott Phillips barely noticed as he yanked the bandana from around his mouth so he could talk. And the Captain loved to talk, especially any bit of conversation that crept into his head that had anything to do with his wife, Jordan, and their baby daughter, Hutton, a daughter he had yet to lay eyes on or hold.

As had become his habit, 1st Lt. Nick Harris listened as patiently as he could. What else was he going to do in such close quarters but listen to the Captain's long-winded stories about home? Nick indulged him, not only because he was a captive audience but because, like most everyone in the unit, he genuinely liked Scott. The men who served under Phillips liked the no-nonsense way he ran his unit, liked the man who could routinely go from all-business to light-hearted in the blink of an eye.

And light-hearted usually meant Scott kept up a non-stop monologue about his family back home. After spending a year of active duty with the guy, Nick felt certain he knew every nuance about the man's personal life. There wasn't much info Scott held back or didn't share. When it came to his wife and newborn daughter, the man simply refused to shut up.

On the surface the two men had little in common. Scott was blissfully married while Nick, unattached, single, and happy about it, had a bevy of women waiting for him back in Los Angeles. But despite their differences, Nick's affection for the guy overrode any annoyance over knowing every detail Scott chose to share. It seemed to Nick, Scott's family life back home in California was an open book, which made him long ago accept the fact that Scott just liked to talk. Period.

Nick watched as Scott tapped his flak jacket and reminded, "I promised Jordan I'd wear this thing 24/7 as long as I'm over here. I didn't have the heart to tell her it won't do a damn thing to stop an IED."

"There's no stopping an IED," Nick agreed amicably.

"When we get out of this mess promise me you'll come to Pelican Pointe for a visit, meet Jordan and the baby."

Here it comes, thought Nick as he shook his head, Scott crowing once again about his hometown and the people in it. Nick responded the way he always did whenever Scott mentioned Pelican Pointe—he made some smart-ass comment—making sure to insult the Captain's small town in a good-natured, guy kind of way. "Now why would I want to spend time in a Podunk town that sounds like a bird sanctuary? I'm a big city kind of guy, Captain. I'd go nuts in a small town. Besides, small towns are cliquish."

"Pelican Pointe's different."

"I doubt that. Everybody knows your business in a small town."

"When we get out of this mess, you come for a visit. I guarantee you'll see for yourself what a great place it is, how great the people are. They'd do anything for you, Nick." Without taking a breath, Scott went on, "God, I sure miss Jordan. And I haven't even laid eyes on Hutton. I wish I'd been there the day she was born. I hate it Jordan had to go through childbirth without me. She's almost five months old, can you believe it?"

"How does it feel to be a dad?" Nick didn't have a clue about being a father, but it seemed the right thing to say at times like this when Scott got that distant look on his face, that wistful gaze in his eye, the look that said he was homesick and wanted nothing more than to get back home to his family.

"Being a father is great, I think. I'd like to be able to hold her though, you know. Pictures aren't the same thing. You ever thought of having kids, Nick?"

A panicked look crossed his face. "Hell no. I can't even sec myself married."

"Marriage is exactly what you need. Might settle you down."

Nick couldn't imagine it. "Marriage would be like a rock around my neck. Too many sweet things out there in the proverbial sea I haven't sampled yet." He wiggled his eyebrows up and down.

"Get yourself in trouble is what you're gonna do. You need to think about finding that special someone. If you ever found a woman like Jordan, you'd change your mind in a heartbeat."

Before Nick could argue, he heard the sound of a rocket blast pierce the air.

Someone yelled, "Look out, incoming!"

Nick heard an explosion, saw a blast of fire, and then a wave of smoke surrounded the vehicle so thick, he could barely see or breathe anything but fire and heat. Soldiers started running toward the lead Hummer. He heard more yelling. His lungs burned.

"Go. Go. Go!" someone shouted.

Chaos reigned as Nick watched the Humvee just ahead of theirs disintegrate into pieces. He saw burned metal fly through the air before he realized it wasn't the lead Hummer at all. He turned to where Scott had sat beside him and saw his buddy's face twisted in pain. Nick heard screaming.

"Promise me, Nick…"

Don't miss these other exciting titles by bestselling author

Vickie McKeehan

The Pelican Pointe Series
PROMISE COVE
HIDDEN MOON BAY
DANCING TIDES
LIGHTHOUSE REEF
STARLIGHT DUNES
LAST CHANCE HARBOR
SEA GLASS COTTAGE
LAVENDER BEACH

The Evil Secrets Trilogy
JUST EVIL Book One
DEEPER EVIL Book Two
ENDING EVIL Book Three

The Skye Cree Novels
THE BONES OF OTHERS
THE BONES WILL TELL
THE BOX OF BONES
HIS GARDEN OF BONES

The Indigo Brothers Trilogy
INDIGO FIRE
INDIGO HEAT
INDIGO JUSTICE

ABOUT THE AUTHOR

Indigo Justice is Vickie McKeehan's eighteenth novel. She writes romantic suspense and makes her home in Southern California.

Find Vickie online at
https://www.facebook.com/VickieMcKeehan
http://www.vickiemckeehan.com/
https://vickiemckeehan.wordpress.com

Printed in Great Britain
by Amazon